P9-DBM-674

CRIMSON PHOENIX

Also by John Gilstrap

Hellfire

Total Mayhem

Scorpion Strike

Final Target

Nick of Time

Friendly Fire

Against All Enemies

End Game

Soft Targets

High Treason

Damage Control

Threat Warning

Hostage Zero

No Mercy

Six Minutes to Freedom (with Kurt Muse)

Scott Free

Even Steven

At All Costs

Nathan's Run

CRIMSON PHOENIX

JOHN GILSTRAP

www.kensingtonbooks.com

This book is a work of fiction. Names, characters, businesses, organizations, places, events, and incidents either are the product of the author's imagination or are used fictitiously. Any resemblance to actual persons, living or dead, events, or locales is entirely coincidental.

To the extent that the image or images on the cover of this book depict a person or persons, such person or persons are merely models, and are not intended to portray any character or characters featured in the book.

KENSINGTON BOOKS are published by

Kensington Publishing Corp.
119 West 40th Street
New York, NY 10018

All Kensington titles, imprints, and distributed lines are available at special quantity discounts for bulk purchases for sales promotion, premiums, fund-raising, educational, or institutional use.

Special book excerpts or customized printings can also be created to fit specific needs. For details, write or phone the office of the Kensington Special Sales Manager: Attn. Special Sales Department. Kensington Publishing Corp., 119 West 40th Street, New York, NY 10018. Phone: 1-800-221-2647.

Library of Congress Card Catalogue Number: 2020945349

ISBN-13: 978-1-4967-2855-5
ISBN-10: 1-4967-2855-6
First Kensington Hardcover Edition: March 2021

ISBN-13: 978-1-4967-2856-2 (ebook)
ISBN-10: 1-4967-2856-4 (ebook)

10 9 8 7 6 5 4 3 2 1

Printed in the United States of America

To Joy

PART I

CHAPTER ONE

McCrea checked his watch as he pressed the smartphone against his ear. Ten-fifteen. He knew she was home, and he'd give her three more rings before he kicked in the door. Finally the connection clicked. He started talking before the other side had a chance to speak. "Is this Victoria Emerson, U.S. representative for West Virginia's Third Congressional District?"

"Who is this?"

He recognized her voice and heard the annoyance. "Please respond to my question," he said. His tone sounded as urgent as he intended.

"Yes, it is," she said. "Now, who is this?"

"Major Joseph McCrea," he replied. "Crimson Phoenix is active. This is not a drill."

A moment of silence on the other end. "Crimson Phoenix?" Her voice trembled. "Not Crimson *Shield*. Crimson Phoenix?" The difference meant everything.

"Yes, ma'am, Crimson Phoenix. I am here to escort you to safety."

"You're *here*?"

"I'm standing on your front stoop. Please open the door for me so I don't have to open it for you. My way will be too loud for the neighborhood at this time of night." He heard footsteps from the inside. A chain slid, and the door opened a crack. Even though he could see only an eye and a cheek, he recognized the face that had been made famous on so many talking-head shows.

Victoria Emerson first focused on him, but then her eyes widened as she saw the soldiers he'd brought with him. Her blank expression showed the enormity of it all. "Is this really real?" she asked.

"Yes, ma'am, it is. You've got five minutes to get your stuff together."

The United States was at *war.* DEFCON 1. Release of nuclear weapons imminent.

"I–I don't know that I can be ready that quickly."

McCrea had expected that. And he had an answer. "Ma'am, I have orders. I'm taking you to safety. You do not have a vote in this." He splayed his fingers. "Five minutes."

The congresswoman spun on her heel and made a beeline to the split-level staircase of their modest Arlington, Virginia, home. McCrea figured it had to be a rental.

"Luke!" she yelled. "Caleb! Out here, right now." She disappeared upstairs. "Luke and Caleb, now!"

Doors opened and adolescents protested in unison: "Mom!"

"How about a knock?" one of them said. His voice had changed. McCrea heard the teenage self-righteousness loud and clear.

"Both of you," Mrs. Emerson said. "Grab your go bags and be ready in three minutes."

"I've got a math test tomorrow. Can't I skip this one?"

"No," she said. Her tone left no room for discussion. "We do these things for a reason. And I wager that math had nothing to do with the way you snapped that computer shut so quickly."

"You heard me, Luke?"

"I'm doing it now," a younger voice said. "Where are we going this time?"

"Three minutes," she repeated.

He heard the sounds of hangers scraping on closet rods and of thumping against the walls. The go-bag reference had not been lost on him. It's as if she'd been preparing for the moment.

"I hate bug-out drills!" the older boy yelled.

His mother yelled back, "I don't care!"

A good-looking blond-haired kid of about thirteen materialized at the top of the stairs. He wore a long-sleeve shirt, jeans and hiking boots. He'd shrugged a good-size jungle camouflaged rucksack onto his back. Maybe a little too heavy for him, but he seemed to be handling it okay. "I'm ready!" he announced.

The boy trotted down the stairs, then stopped short when he noticed McCrea in the foyer. He slung the ruck off his back and started reaching for what McCrea now recognized to be a taken-down Ruger 10/22 rifle. "Mom!" he yelled.

McCrea backpedaled a couple of steps and held out his hands, fingers splayed. "Whoa, whoa," he said. "Easy there, cowboy. I'm the good guy. Which one are you? Caleb or Luke?"

"Mom!"

McCrea became self-consciously aware of his own M4 rifle, which was slung across the front of his body. He slid it around his back. "I know this is startling," he said. "But you're really not in danger." *You're also not coming along.* He considered that last part to be news that was better broken by the mother.

"Mom!"

Victoria Emerson appeared at the top of the stairs dressed identically to her son, complete with rucksack and weapon. "Relax, Luke," she said. "That's Major . . ."

"McCrea, ma'am."

"That's Major McCrea. He's coming with us." As she walked down the stairs, she called over her shoulder, "Caleb! Now!"

A gangly sixteen-year-old appeared at the top of the stairs wearing a T-shirt, shorts and flip-flops. He'd be handsome one day, McCrea thought, once he grew into his hands and feet. McCrea figured the outfit to be a silent thumb in his mom's eye.

"Caleb Morris Emerson," she said in the tone that still inspired fear. "Put the correct clothes on and be ready to go."

"Why? All we do is drive around and—"

She sharpened her look and he backed away.

"Okay, *fine.*" Caleb stormed back into his room. Coat hangers clattered against the walls again, boots thumped against the floor.

"Are you okay, Mom?" Luke asked. "You seem . . . nervous. And why is he here?"

Mrs. Emerson ignored the question, and it wasn't McCrea's to answer. "Is this really real?" she asked him.

"Ma'am, given your position, I imagine that you know more than I do. I have my orders, and you are them."

Caleb arrived at the top of the stairs. This time, his clothes matched those of his mother and little brother. "Who the hell is this?"

"My name is Major McCrea. Pleased to meet you, Caleb. Ma'am, we have to leave right now." He reached out to grab her arm and she pulled away.

"How dare you touch me," she said.

Caleb rushed forward. "Hey, asshole, what are you—"

"Quiet, son," McCrea said. "Ma'am, I already told you. You don't have a say in what follows. I would love for you to follow me, but if I have to carry you, that's what I will do."

"You can't talk to my mom like that," Caleb said. "She's a member of Congress."

"Caleb, hush," Victoria snapped.

"But you're his boss!"

Mrs. Emerson held up a hand to calm her son. "Caleb, we're going with the major."

Luke looked as frightened as Caleb looked angry. "Mom?"

Apparently, she was really going to make McCrea do this. "Just you, ma'am. Not the boys."

"Bullshit," she said. "I'm not leaving them."

"Ma'am, you know the rules. I am authorized only—"

"Major McCrea," she said. "I understand that you have your orders, but if you try to separate me from my kids, one of us—you or me—is going to wake up dead in the morning. Do not try me on this point, sir."

McCrea saw fire in her eyes. His instincts told him she was speaking the truth. His orders were clear. He was to deliver Representative Victoria Emerson to the U.S. Government Relocation Center—the Annex. The rules said no family, but the facility's

the men who surrounded her, then dropped her voice even lower. "The reason this is different is because this time it's not a drill."

He stiffened. "W-what are you telling me?"

"I'm telling you to get in the car," she said. "We can talk all you want in there. But not out here."

To her left, Luke stood very still. A shadow engulfed his face, but glistening eyes shined through. "Mom, I'm scared," he said.

"We're all scared," she said, cupping the back of his head, too, and urging him toward the Suburban.

Mrs. Emerson looked to McCrea, but he kept his expression blank. Next to him, a young soldier looked close to tears. "You should get home to your family," Mrs. Emerson said to him.

The soldier stiffened and shifted his eyes to the ground.

McCrea added more pressure to her back. "Inside, ma'am," he said. "It's not a short drive."

McCrea helped them doff their rucks and handed them to the E-8, who would be slumming as their driver. "First Sergeant, put these in the back, please." Once the family was inside, McCrea closed the door behind them, then climbed into the shotgun seat. The driver closed up the cargo bed, slid behind the wheel and they were on their way.

"Mom, you said we'd talk about what's happening once we were in the car," Caleb reminded. "We're there now."

Mrs. Emerson ignored her son. "Major McCrea?"

He turned in his seat to look at her.

"Why are the roads clear? Why haven't our phones squealed with an emergency alert? Why don't things seem more urgent?"

"I'm not the policy person, Congresswoman. Congressperson?"

"Victoria is fine in private," she said. If this were a different day, she'd have asked to be called *ma'am,* but not tonight. While she was senior to every military officer in the country, and they needed to know that, this was going to be stressful enough without adding unnecessary formality to the mix.

She was tempted to press for an answer when a piece fell into place for her. The NCA—National Command Authority, collectively the president and secretary of defense—wanted the elements of the federal government ensconced in safety before the possible retaliatory strike could be launched. They couldn't alert the media or the general public without alerting the enemy.

"Oh, my God," she said. "We're launching the first strike, aren't we?" She directed her words to the back of McCrea's head, but she was surprised to hear them spoken out loud.

She'd almost nailed it. Actually, Israel was going to launch a strike on Iran, but McCrea hadn't been briefed on what she was cleared to know. He stayed silent.

"Mom?" Luke said through a choked voice. "What are you talking about?"

"Are we going to war?" Caleb asked. He sounded even more frightened than his brother, but a kid couldn't possibly understand the ramifications of war.

"I think we might, sweetie," she said.

"You're a congresswoman," Caleb protested. "Don't they have to get your permission first? We studied that."

"Only for a declared war," she answered. "The president has wide discretion short of that."

And we gave her that power, McCrea thought. The United States had not fired a bullet in a declared war since Japan's surrender in 1945, but it had nonetheless sent thousands of its sons and daughters to die in conflicts all around the world.

Victoria was only in her third two-year term in the House of Representatives, having won each time by huge margins in her district, and while she was as aware as any news junkie of the growing troubles between the U.S. and Iran and Russia, with Israel being the focus of all, she was nowhere near the top secret inside scoop on impending war.

"What about Adam?" Luke asked.

Victoria gasped. "Major, I need to contact my son," she said.

McCrea cast a look to the driver, but said nothing.

"Major McCrea, did you hear me?"

"I heard you," he said. He felt a flare of anger in his gut.

"I need to call him."

"That can't happen," McCrea said. "Operational security is paramount."

"But my *son* is in jeopardy."

Again, McCrea said nothing. He knew that if he spoke, it might get ugly.

"Major, I need your phone."

"Ma'am, I can't allow you to use the phone. I can't allow you to use flares, smoke signals or loud screams. The rules for CRIMSON PHOENIX are very clear on this."

Victoria leaned forward in her seat, grabbed a handful of McCrea's uniform shirt. "I'm not asking, Major, I'm telling you—"

That was it. McCrea whirled in his seat, taking her on, face-to-face. "You're telling me that your son is in danger!" he growled. "Yeah, I get that. So are my daughters. And my wife. And you know what? They're entirely unaware that they're likely to die tonight. Three hundred fifty *million* American sons and daughters are in danger of dying, *Representative* Emerson. You, of course, have a free pass to a safe bunker, because you're more important than the rest of us. You'd be wise to remember, though, that you and your colleagues define the lucky eleven hundred. Countless sons and daughters are about to die. I pray to God that yours and mine are not among them."

Victoria started to say something, but McCrea wasn't done.

"I think there's a very good chance that I won't see tomorrow, ma'am, and I don't think there's a chance in hell that I'll see next weekend. But I have orders to deliver you to safety, and that is what I am going to do. I have orders to maintain strict electronic silence on this, and I'm going to do that, too. If I'm remembered by anyone for anything I've done, it will be that my last act on earth was to obey my orders. Are we clear on this?"

Victoria felt stunned. The heat in McCrea's eyes was blistering. His words infuriated her, but less for the delivery than for the reality of their meaning. America was going to war.

And millions were likely to die.

CHAPTER TWO

THE HILLTOP MANOR RESORT HAD BEEN A PART OF THE WEST Virginia landscape for nearly a century. Located on fifteen hundred acres atop a mountain that afforded unparalleled views of the Catoctin River Valley, the Hilltop boasted two world-class golf courses, miles of riding and hiking trails, its own bowling alley and concert venues, and even skeet and trapshooting ranges. Having recently hired an executive chef who had her own Food Channel television show, it was even more famous now than ever before. Wedding parties commonly spent $400 per head for receptions, and guests were lucky to get away for less than $500 per night to stay.

As House Speaker Penn Glendale sped past the massive white marble structure in the company of his security team, the center of a three-vehicle motorcade, he remembered the weeks he had spent here as a child with his parents as they escaped from New York City to enjoy the quiet, fresh air. He had no idea then—as few had any idea now—what secrets were protected inside the sprawling complex. Colloquially known as the Annex, top secret, sensitive compartmented information (SCI) documents referred to the resort as the United States Government Relocation Facility, its construction necessitated by a reporter's decision in 1994 to reveal the location of the previous GRF that had been built in the 1950s about a hundred miles south of here. That one decision by a journalist, with the support of his newspaper, to release the information to the world threatened the continuity of the U.S. government for nearly twelve years as a new location was found and construction completed.

Strapped in the seat next to him in the back of the Suburban, Arlen Strasky, Speaker Glendale's chief of staff, pleaded with his wife on his cell phone. "Greta, my God, why aren't you on the road yet? Never mind. It doesn't matter. You've got to leave now. I'm sorry, I know I'm being cryptic, and I don't mean to scare you. I mean to impress upon you the importance of getting on the road. What? No, toward West Virginia. I can't answer that question, honey. Soon, I hope. The destination doesn't matter. Just get on the road . . . Hello?" Strasky brought the phone away from his face and looked at the screen, then shot a glance to his boss. "I've got no signal."

"It's part of the plan," Penn explained. "A lot of traffic is going to be filing in here over the next few hours. That'll attract people's attention, and we don't need loose lips sinking our ship." No matter how many times he re-read the laminated red card that he'd been carrying in his wallet for the past eighteen years, he couldn't drive it all into his memory. The government relocation protocol was a complex one.

"When do we let the world know what we're about to do?" Strasky asked.

"When the Homeland Security secretary gives the order," Penn replied. "And I presume he will get the order from the president."

"Don't you think they should have done that already?"

"To what end?" the Speaker asked. "If this goes well, the whole thing will be over before there's anything to report. The Israelis launch, Iran ceases to exist and the war is over."

"Mr. Speaker, you can't possibly believe that it will be that simple. If you did, we wouldn't be about to climb into a bunker."

"Protocols exist for a reason, Arlen. This is a formality. When nuclear forces are in play, the government relocation protocol goes into effect."

"And the retaliation?" Strasky asked.

"NCA doesn't expect one," Penn said.

"And if they're wrong?"

"Don't even think it," Penn said. "That would spell the end of everything, and then an alert wouldn't make much of a difference, anyway."

"With all due respect, Mr. Speaker, I think this is a bad idea."

"A lot of people who're on their way here think this is a bad idea. But Helen Blanton is president of the United States, and this is her call. She fully supports Israel's right to defend itself."

"A preemptive strike." Strasky said the phrase as if it were poison. "You know we'll get blamed for this. Our weapons, our strategy. Israel is merely a vector. History is going to tear us a new one."

"Not all decisions are purely political, Arlen."

"If you ask me, there's no decision that could be more political than declaring war."

"We're not declaring war," Penn corrected, stating the obvious. "Israel is. If Her Majesty, Madam President Blanton, had alerted the House, we would have said no."

"Then why don't we take it public? Leak it?"

"You know the answer to that."

"Yeah, we'd lose the element of surprise," Strasky said.

"Exactly."

"And if we did, then we could pump the brakes on killing a couple million people. How is that a bad thing?"

Penn felt his face redden. "Are you hearing yourself, Arlen? There comes a point when the train is too far out of the station. Our only response at this point is to say *yes, ma'am,* and then get with the program. It's time to start praying for startling success and utter destruction of Iran's ability to make war on its neighbors."

"And the Russians—"

"Won't do anything," Penn snapped. "Look, it's not like this is unearned. Iran is a terror state that has promised to destroy Israel. Now that they've got their nukes, their rhetoric is only getting hotter. Israel has no choice but to react, and we're going to support them."

"What about the Pakis?"

"India would love the opportunity to barbecue their neighbor," Penn said. "I don't worry about that at all."

"I just think this is wrong," Strasky said.

"Duly noted."

"Zero notice!" Strasky raised his voice. "Jesus, sir, we deserve more than a couple of minutes to get on the road."

"That's all security," Penn explained. He wasn't thrilled about springing this on members and their staffs—for heaven's sake, as Speaker, he was brought into the loop only an hour before the others—but he understood the president's concerns. Washington leaked information like the *Titanic* leaked water. For CRIMSON PHOENIX to succeed, surprise was the single-most critical component.

In the front seat, the Army colonel in the shotgun seat turned to face his VIP passengers. The Velcro patch over his pocket read: MILLER. "Mr. Speaker, we're nearly there. Remember to leave everything in the vehicle. No electronics, no paper. Nothing enters into the bunker, sir."

Penn leaned to his left to get a better view through the windshield. A hundred yards ahead, he could see a stone archway illuminated by the Suburban's headlights. An enormous blast door, easily fifteen feet across, had been pulled open to reveal a tunnel, the inside of which was lit rather dimly, but which illuminated a flurry of activity as people in military uniforms swarmed around doing whatever they had been trained to do.

The Suburban pulled up short of the mouth of the tunnel. "This is it, sir," the colonel said. "We need to leave the vehicle here, but we'll escort you to the door."

"And then what?"

"And then I hand you off to the people in charge," Miller said.

"But what happens to you?" Penn asked.

Colonel Miller took a long, noisy breath and scowled. "Mr. Speaker, I have no idea if you're cleared to hear the answer to that question, but I am one hundred percent certain that I am not cleared to share it with you." He sold it with just the right amount of smile as he climbed out of the vehicle.

Out of habit, Penn waited a few seconds for his door to be opened for him, and when he realized that this was not his normal security team—they were military officers, not officers of the Capitol Police Force—he pulled the handle and opened it himself.

The late-summer mountain air felt crisp against his skin as he stepped away from his vehicle toward Miller. His peripheral vision caught Strasky approaching them as he asked the colonel, "What now?"

"Follow me."

As Speaker of the House of Representatives—second in line to the presidency—Penn was used to a degree of deference from his security team, and from military officers, for that matter. No such deference existed in Miller's demeanor. This man was 100 percent business.

And he walked half a step faster than Penn could follow. The Speaker had passed his sixty-fourth birthday just a month before, and his love for rich food, good wine and even better scotch had erased all but the last traces of his youthful athleticism. Arlen Strasky, on the other hand, still competed in two Ironman races a year, and likely hadn't gained an ounce in the thirty years since he'd turned twenty.

As they neared the gaping maw in the mountainside that was the entrance to the Annex, Penn noted that the opening was smaller than it had looked from afar, and that the blast door looked twice as thick. He thought it looked like the most massive bank vault door in the universe.

They were still thirty feet away when a man of military bearing and hairstyle approached them from the entrance. Penn doubted that the man could be forty years old. His neck seemed to slope directly from his ears to his shoulders, and the front of the baseball cap he'd pulled low over his eyes displayed a green-and-black American flag.

"Speaker Glendale!" the man called as he approached. He offered his hand. "Welcome to the United States Government Relocation Center. We call it the Annex, and this will be our home for the next little while. I'm Scott Johnson."

Penn shook the man's hand. "This is my chief of staff, Arlen Strasky. What branch of the military are you with, Mr. Johnson?"

"I used to be Army, sir, but I was seven and done. I work for Solara."

Penn looked to Strasky and got a shrug. "What is Solara?"

"We're the contractor in charge of the Annex, sir. Please follow me." He spun on his heel and headed back toward the blast door.

Penn turned to thank Colonel Miller for his efforts, but the man and his crew had already wandered off to join a clutch of other military folks.

"Speaker Glendale?" Johnson called. He'd pulled up twenty feet ahead and beckoned for them. "We really don't have a lot of time, sir."

Penn and Arlen caught up. "You were saying—"

"Yes, sir, I was explaining about Solara. In peacetime, we're the folks who make sure that all the provisions are in, and that all the comms work properly. Our cover is that we take care of the internet and electronics stuff for the Hilltop Resort. Which we do. In wartime, though, when the balloon goes up, we're in charge of the entire facility."

As they crossed the threshold into the opening of the bunker, the atmosphere of the place changed. The smell of oil and fuel had pushed away the aromas of summer.

Johnson continued to talk. Penn got the sense that he'd rehearsed this more than once. "It's no accident that you're among the first to arrive, Mr. Speaker. There's gonna be a culture shock on the other side of the decon area, and I'll be happy to have your support keeping your people under control."

Something tingled in Penn's spine. "My people?"

"Yes, sir. The elected folks. The people you'll be moving in with. There's gonna be a learning curve with the rules, and—"

Penn held up a hand for silence. "You're speaking in riddles, Scott."

"I prefer *Mr. Johnson,* sir." His face had hardened.

Penn opted not to rise to the bait. This was a stressful evening for everyone. "Mr. Johnson, then. I don't understand what you're trying to tell me."

Johnson seemed amused by that. "Very well, sir, I understand. But you know what? I think it'll all become clear when you come inside. This way, sir."

Penn followed the young man deeper into the tunnel. On closer inspection, the whole area bore a resemblance to naval vessels that Penn had visited. The walls in here were lined with heavy steel. Every surface sported an organized rat's nest of pipes and conduit. Heavy explosion-proof enclosures surrounded all the electrical fixtures. Even the doors in the walls—the access points to whatever lay beyond—looked like hatchways on a ship, including the three-foot spinning wheel that would secure them closed.

Johnson led his charges about thirty yards into the tunnel before stopping at an open hatchway on the right.

"You'll be going in there, sir," Johnson explained. "Everybody will be going in there."

The area inside the hatch appeared to be nothing but a big room, measuring maybe twenty feet square. No chairs or tables, just a black-and-white tile floor surrounded by four gleaming white walls. Another soldierly young man stood on the far side of the room with an automatic rifle—Penn recognized it to be a military M4—slung across his chest and belly.

"Bugsy, they're all yours now," Johnson said. "Gentlemen, this is Garand Bug-something. The name is, like, fifteen letters long and it only has one vowel."

The man with the rifle pronounced his name for them, and Penn agreed that Bugsy would have to do. He had the same military bearing as Johnson, but was easily six inches taller. The massive shoulder-width to waist-circumference ratio would pose a challenge to even the most talented tailor.

"Bugsy, this is House Speaker Glendale and his chief of staff, Mr. Strasky. Please show them the ropes."

"I'll do my best," Bugsy said. He pivoted on his own axis and opened the door he'd been guarding. "This way, sirs."

"Where are we going?" Strasky asked.

"To your new home for a while, sir," Bugsy replied. Every line these guys spoke felt rehearsed and was delivered with a humorless smile. "Just follow me." As he stepped across the raised threshold, he ducked his head to clear the top of the opening, and at the same time pressed a finger against the curly-corded piece in his ear. He waved Penn and Strasky in behind him, and then pressed a button on his ballistic vest. "Decon copies," he said.

"Something wrong?" Penn asked.

Bugsy smiled. "Oh, no, sir. It's just that this is really happening. A bunch of your comrades are on their way in. It's about to get real crazy, real soon."

"Are we the first to arrive?" Strasky asked.

"No, sir, but you're in the first ten. You won't be lonely for long." Bugsy settled his shoulders and sort of winced as he said, "This is the awkward part." He opened a heavy steel bin with a door not unlike that on a blue public mailbox, but many times thicker. "I need you to put everything in here."

Penn took a step back. "What is that?"

"It's an incinerator, sir. Or it will be when we fire it up. Nothing from the outside is allowed in, now that the Annex has been sealed. We have to prevent contamination."

"Contamination from what?"

Bugsy's demeanor changed ever so slightly, and he stood even taller. Penn thought of it as puffing up for a fight. "Sir, in the next hour or so, I have to process five hundred thirty-five members of Congress and a like number of staffers through decon. Since you're among the first, I can tell you that you're about to enter a sterile environment, but as we get busy, I'm going to need people to simply do what they're told. I'll leave it to you to explain the rationale to them on the other side. If it helps, me and my people will have to do the same thing before we button everything up."

"I'm sorry, Bugsy, but I just don't—"

"It's not complicated, Mr. Speaker. Everything goes into the bin. Everything. Jewelry, clothes, eyeglasses, everything. We have duplicates of all prescriptions on the other side of decon."

"You mean *naked*?" Strasky seemed more horrified by that than he did by the prospect of going to war.

"As the day you were born, sir. That happens here in this room and the female facility next door, with everything getting incinerated. You were told to leave valuables at home, were you not?"

"I was told very little of anything," Strasky said.

"Well, I know it's in the written literature you received," Bugsy said. "With your stuff disposed of, your next step is to go through those doors. You'll stop at two different showers. We'll have someone in there to show you the ropes. The idea is to get rid of as much outside dirt and bacteria as we can. When that's done, you go through another set of doors, where we have clothes and shoes and gear for you on the other side. Once you're physically inside the Annex, that's where you stay until you're cleared to leave. Any questions?"

Penn cocked his head. "Seriously?"

"The sooner you get started, the sooner you'll be on the other side," Bugsy said.

CHAPTER THREE

SALLY LAMBERT ANSWERED THE APARTMENT DOOR EVEN AS TODD McElroy was reaching for the knocker. Her intent was to startle him, and judging from the way he jumped, her effort had succeeded. "This had really better be very goddamn important. I don't do three a.m. anymore." As the editor in chief of the *Washington Underground,* she understood that news broke at all hours, but this was ridiculous. And the fact that Todd had refused even to give her a hint over the phone pissed her off.

Todd breezed past, into her living room, without acknowledging her words. "I've never encountered anything like this before," he said. "Do you have any tequila?"

Sally glared at him from the tiny step-up foyer, the doorknob still wrapped in her hand. Tall and gaunt on any day, Todd looked especially bony in his Sheldon Cooper T-shirt, cargo shorts and Birkenstocks. With his unkempt hair and wispy three-day beard, it was impossible to look at him and not recall Scooby-Doo's best friend, Shaggy.

"No, I don't have tequila. Why are you here?"

He plopped himself into her secondhand scratchy beige sofa. "You *always* have tequila, Sals. If not, I'll take whatever you've got. I think we're in deep shit."

What had started in her gut as anger was morphing into concern. In the five years she'd known Todd, she'd never seen him like this. She pushed the door closed, stepped down into the dining room and padded across to the kitchen. He was right, she always had tequila. She grabbed the bottle out of the fridge and a slightly used juice glass off the drain board. She handed both to Todd and watched as he pulled from the bottle.

Helping herself to the threadbare chair she'd purchased at the same yard sale as the sofa, she put a hand on his knee. "Talk to me, Todd."

He poked the nose bridge of his glasses with his forefinger. "A friend of mine called me from West Virginia," he said, following a shiver from the booze. "He works in a place called the Hilltop Manor Resort. It's one of those fancy, high-dollar hotels where mobsters used to stay. Anyway, my buddy—his name is Rick Kauflin—told me there's been a constant stream of traffic into the hotel tonight, and that it's all been way after hours."

He took another pull on the bottle.

"Don't get shit-faced before you can finish your story," Sally said.

"Oh, you have no idea how much I want to."

"You know you're not making any sense yet, right?"

Todd took a huge breath and let it go through his nose. He put the tequila bottle on the coffee table, then thought better and picked it up again. "The thing is, why are a bunch of people flooding into the hotel at this hour, and why have they shut down a big part of the place to any of the employees?"

"Wait," Sally said. "Did they do that? Shut down a big part of the hotel?"

"Yes, Sals. Jeez, pay attention. They won't allow any employees into, like, a whole section of the place, and they even kicked people out of occupied rooms in that section. Why would they do that?"

"Why would I know the answer?" Sally said.

"And why would the people who are arriving all be people from Capitol Hill? Speaker Glendale one of them?"

Sally felt a chill. "You mean Penn Glendale? Speaker of the House of Representatives?"

"Yeah, that one. Do you know another Speaker Glendale? And others, too."

Sally was leaning into the conversation now. "Who else?"

"I don't know. We got cut off before he could tell me. Just *click* and he was gone. I tried calling him back and couldn't get through. I tried calling the front desk of the hotel and just got an error code. Then I called my cell carrier and they told me that the cell towers out there are all down, and they don't know why."

Sally's news sense was piqued, but she knew she was still missing a huge piece of the puzzle. "It's late, Todd. Connect the dots for me, will you?"

"Not yet." Another pull. "Five or ten years ago, another friend of mine—a guy I knew in college before he flunked out and went into the Army—told me that he worked on a supersecret project out in West Virginia. I bought him a couple of drinks, and he told me on deep background that if there was a war, official Washington would be evacuated to a bunker out in the middle of the mountains."

"Was the bunker at this Hillcrest place?"

"Hilltop," Todd corrected. "And he wouldn't say. He didn't give me the specific name, but he told me that the place existed."

"And that's what you think is happening."

"Yes."

"You think we're going to war."

"Yes."

"You're insane. Who's going to attack us?"

Todd reared back in the sofa cushion. "I have no idea. Doesn't everybody hate us?"

"What kind of war are you talking about?" Sally pressed. "I mean, if Washington is heading to bunkers, then it must be nuclear war."

"I assume so."

"Well, that's kind of a big step, don't you think? It's exactly the kind of thing that we have entire alert systems designed for. Did I miss an air raid siren?"

"Do you want to hear the rest of what I've got or don't you?" Todd was losing patience.

Sally gestured for the tequila and took a swig herself. When you're up at this hour, you might as well pretend that it's a party, right? A quick flip of her hand told him to move on.

"First of all, my buddy told me—the guy who first shared the secret—that the civil defense warning system is just there for show. People don't have shelters in their backyards anymore, the way they did in the fifties and sixties. And with submarines parked off the coast, loaded with shit-tons of missiles, we wouldn't get more than a couple of minutes of advance warning in the first place. You sound a bunch of sirens and people just panic."

Sally heard the distant peal of a bullshit bell. "This friend of yours—the traitorous one with all the secret information to share—was he a general or something? A colonel, at least?"

"He was a grunt," Todd said. "A specialist."

"Uh-huh. And of all the people in the world to share this with, he chose a reporter for the *Washington Underground.*" Saying the words aloud made them sound even more ridiculous than they had in her head.

"He's an inside source," Todd said. His tone was both defensive and indignant. "You didn't mind when I used him before to torpedo the last guy in the White House. He was one of the main unnamed leakers."

Sally considered the ramifications. "Have you talked to this source tonight? You know, passed your theory by him."

"I tried but couldn't get through. And there's more. I woke up a lady I know who's an aide to President Blanton's chief of staff. Did you know that the president and her entire family and staff are preparing to leave the White House in a hurry tonight?"

Sally's bullshit bell was beginning to swing a little less aggressively. "What do the other outlets say about any of this? Have the *Post* or the *Times* picked it up? Anything on the wire services?"

Todd lifted the bottle for more, but Sally pulled it away.

"This is serious shit, Todd. You've got to stay sober for it."

Todd's shoulders slumped. "Since when did we start playing second to other news outlets? I've seen nothing on the wires about this, but if I'm correct, people have a right to know."

"And if you're wrong, we'll look like idiots and be crucified for inflaming the public."

"If I'm right, inflaming the public will be exactly the thing we're doing," Todd countered. He reached into the main pocket of his backpack and withdrew his laptop. "I've already written up a first draft of the story." He lifted the lid and passed it over to his boss.

Why Is Official Washington Fleeing for the Hills?
By Todd McElroy

HILLTOP, WV—Beginning just before midnight yesterday, a series of odd happenings unfolded at the Hilltop Manor Resort here in the mountains of West Virginia. According to well-placed sources in the century-old hotel, guests in the Antebellum Wing—one of five wings of the property—were rousted from their beds and relocated to the John Brown Wing, which until yesterday had been closed for renovation.

A short time later, beginning around 1 a.m., streams of cars began arriving at the hotel property. They entered not through the main portico, but through an area normally reserved for deliveries.

The Washington Underground *has confirmed that one of the people to arrive under cover of darkness was House Speaker Penn Glendale, along with his chief of staff, Arlen Strasky. Other members of the House and Senate were also seen arriving.*

As this reporter was communicating with sources on the ground at the Hilltop Manor, communications were cut off without warning and cell phone service to that entire corner of the community were knocked off-line.

For years, rumors have circulated that the Hilltop Manor Resort harbored a secret evacuation facility for official Washington. Those rumors remain unconfirmed, but at this writ-

ing, it seems obvious that House and Senate members are fleeing their homes in the DMV to take shelter elsewhere.

Why might that be?

We'll keep pressing for answers.

When Sally got to the end, she looked at the screen for a long time, then rocked her eyes up to meet Todd's. "The writing's a little florid," she said.

"That's editing," Todd replied. "What about the story itself?"

Sally made a wobbling motion with her hand. "I'm not sure there's a story here as much as there is an intriguing premise. A question."

"Can we put it out?" Todd asked. "Christ, something like this will go around the world like a comet."

"All that means is the world will know instantly that we screwed this up."

"You keep assuming that we're wrong."

Sally took a deep breath and closed her eyes. While blind enthusiasm was Todd's greatest weakness, his instincts as a reporter were some of the best she'd seen. The problem here was the magnitude of the story he was proposing to write. The natural extension of the piece was widespread panic, so the penalty for getting this wrong was enormous.

"Wait a second," she said, snapping her eyes open. "The submarines. You're right. They're parked off the shores of the U.S., just outside our territorial waters. There is, in fact, no way for this evacuation to succeed—if that's really what it is." She glared at Todd. "Unless America is planning a first strike somewhere."

Todd's eyes and mouth formed near perfect circles. "Or if we knew someone else was," he said. "All that stuff between Israel and Iran, maybe."

"Or India and Pakistan," Sally said. "God, there are all kinds of possibilities there." She leaned back in the sofa. "Or it could be some kind of drill."

"My piece allows for that possibility," Todd said.

"We have to know," Sally declared, and she shot to her feet. "I have an idea." She hurried across the living room to the rectangular section of floor that she euphemistically called her dining room and turned on the light over the 1970s-era glass-topped dining table. She pulled open the oversize yellow purse that carried pretty much everything she needed in life, extracted her laptop and returned to the sofa.

"You look like you have a plan," Todd said.

"It's not much of one. We're going to make some phone calls." She opened the computer, pulled up her contacts list and double-clicked on a file labeled *Pentagon Sources.* "It seems to me that if we're going to war, senior military officials will be the first to know."

"They won't talk to you about that."

"I don't imagine they will," Sally agreed, "but look at the clock. At this hour, they'll be righteously pissed about being awakened by a reporter."

"I'm missing your point."

"If your guess is right, they won't be home to be pissed." She pivoted her screen so Todd could see it. "Every name on this list is an O-Six or higher. If we're about to go to war, none of these guys will be home."

"O-Six?"

"Captain in the Navy, colonel in most other branches. I'll start with the A's, and you start with the L's. Let's see what we see."

In the end, they only made a total of seven calls between them. Not a single senior officer was home.

Todd beamed. "Are you convinced now? Will you post the story?"

"Post it," she said. "But there's nothing here to smile about."

CHAPTER FOUR

THE ROADS HEADING WEST WERE FREAKISHLY EMPTY, NEARLY DEVOID of traffic all the way to the West Virginia line and beyond. After nearly four hours of driving, everything stopped. Victoria leaned toward the center of the Suburban to peer out through the windshield and was greeted with a surreal image of an endless snake of black SUVs idling, nose to tail, a meandering sea of white and red lights heading up the hill to the Hilltop Manor Resort.

"Is this the place?" she asked.

"This is it," McCrea said. "It seems that we are not the first to arrive." He was approaching the end of his mission for tonight. Once the Emerson family was dropped off—no, once *Victoria* Emerson was dropped off (the kids were not his problem)—he and his driver, First Sergeant Paul Copley, were on their own.

"What happens from here?" one of the boys asked.

McCrea thought both kids had been asleep. "We're sort of in uncharted waters here, Luke," he said.

"I'm Caleb."

"My bad," McCrea said. "The answer remains unchanged."

"What does that mean? And *I'm* Luke."

"It means that I'm really not sure what's about to happen. We'll find out together, I suppose."

"Nothing's moving," Victoria said. "What's going on up there?"

"I believe everyone is learning as they go," McCrea said. "Lots of confusion."

"Come on, boys," Victoria said. She pushed the passenger door open. "We're walking from here."

"The hell you are," McCrea barked. He threw his door open as well and stepped out of the Suburban to intervene.

Caleb looked startled in the wash of the dome light, as if unaware what he should do. Luke, on the other hand, was already moving. He slung himself over the back of the bench seat, bending himself in half to grab their go bags. He hefted one after the other out of the cargo bay and onto the seat.

"Stop that!" McCrea commanded, but no one listened. "Mrs. Emerson, I cannot let you do this," McCrea said. He placed his right hand on the edge of her door, while pressing his left against the window behind it, effectively blocking her path.

"Get out of my way, Major," she said.

"I can't do that."

She smiled. "Don't make me hurt you, Major McCrea. I don't know what you've read about me, but I've been a martial artist since I was a teenager. Two black belts. I work out every day, and spar twice a week. Do you really want to decide this in the gravel?"

McCrea fought the urge to call her bluff. Problem was, fighting with a protectee was exactly the opposite of his mission to protect her.

"The go bags are ready," Caleb announced. He'd made his decision to follow, apparently, and part of it was to steal his little brother's thunder.

Victoria lowered her voice and took a half step closer to the major, nearly nose to nose. "Please get out of my way," she said.

"Mrs. Emerson. Victoria. This is a mistake. Get back in the car and we will wait our turn."

"If it's a mistake, it's mine to make," she said. "Your work here is done, Major."

"Don't tell me my job," McCrea said. But he pivoted to his right, opening a path. "I'm going with you, though, so wait for me."

"I have no problem with that," Victoria said. She spun on her own axis to address her children. "Come on, boys."

McCrea turned his attention to the driver. "First Sergeant Copley, pull this vehicle off the road so others can pass. When you're done, I will lead the way. Keep the Emerson family in the middle and follow closely. Call out any threats." At DEFCON 1, the only safe assumption was that everyone was a threat to everyone else. Desperate people did desperate things, and up until Victoria Emerson was safe, his job was to keep her that way.

McCrea raised his voice and gave it a command timbre. "Emerson family, from here on out, it is critical for you to do what I say. It is critical for *all* of you to do *exactly* what I say. Are there any questions?"

Victoria said nothing, and the boys shook their heads.

"Caleb and Luke, I need verbal responses, please."

"I don't have any questions," Luke said.

"Me neither."

McCrea reached back into the cab of the Suburban and withdrew his own M4. He shrugged into the battle sling and let the rifle fall against the front of his vest. "We'll move as soon as First Sergeant Copley takes care of our vehicle."

They watched as the first sergeant climbed behind the wheel and backed the Suburban off the pavement and over the gravel shoulder until the rear wheels were in the woods and the front wheels had a precarious purchase on the pavement. It took six or seven shifts from forward to reverse to complete the maneuver, but when he was done, plenty of room remained for other vehicles to get by.

Copley looked to be about thirty-five years old and had *soldier* written all over him, from the steely eyes to the rock-solid body. His uniform remained pressed even after four hours behind the wheel. "I'm ready, sir," he pronounced when he rejoined the family.

"I want your M4 chambered, safety on," McCrea instructed.

"I'm way ahead of you."

"I think this security bubble around me is a little tight," Victoria said. "You can back off some?"

"When I drop you off at the front door, I will disappear, I promise," McCrea said.

The walk was longer than it looked, and the hill was steeper than it appeared in the dark. As he'd feared, their effort to jump the line was pissing people off. As they passed one identical SUV after another, headlights flashed and a couple of horns bleated. They'd reached nearly the halfway point when someone up ahead opened their door and a beefy Army lieutenant stepped out to block their way.

"If you belong here at all, you will wait your turn," the soldier said.

"Stand down, Lieutenant," McCrea said. He faced off against the other soldier, silently daring him to make a move while the family moved on behind him.

Victoria spread her arms to gather her boys. "Keep up," she said, and they closed in tighter.

The young officer who'd confronted them had played out his bluff, apparently. "I'm sorry about that, Major," he said. "My protectees told me—"

"Don't worry about it, Lieutenant. One way or the other, this will all be over soon, and this kind of shit won't matter at all."

"Vicky!" a voice yelled. "What the hell do you think you're doing?"

"I've got to go back to work," McCrea said. He jogged up the hill to retake his place in the lead. "Don't engage with anyone, ma'am," he said.

Victoria kept walking. "Stay close, boys," she said.

"Vicky!" the voice called again. "It's me. Parker Wortham. I'm talking to you!"

McCrea recognized the old guy as a senator from someplace out West. Wyoming, maybe? He only recognized the face because he'd been on the news for campaign violations.

McCrea didn't understand the game Victoria was playing here. Why piss off the people you're going to be holed up with while the earth either died or repopulated? How did she think she was more important than all the others who'd been waiting more or less as long as she had?

As he'd feared, Victoria's decision to jump the line had triggered others to do the same. It started with just a few, but within twenty seconds, members of Congress started exiting their vehicles like children hurrying to get to the front of the ice-cream line.

Everyone was on the feather edge of panic as it was, and Representative Emerson had poked the self-restraint balloon with a pin. Every face he saw showed equal portions of anger and fear. "This is irresponsible," he grumbled. He considered challenging her on this, but the damage was already done. She'd inspired a mob scene.

Senator Wortham trotted up to join Victoria—no easy feat for a man of his significant girth—but First Sergeant Copley blocked access. "Stay back, sir," he said. There wasn't a hint of politeness in his tone, and no room for argument.

Somewhere behind, a voice yelled, "Senator Wortham, don't do that! You're going to get yourself shot!" McCrea looked behind to see the senator's security escort trotting up to join him.

"Mom, what's happening?" Caleb asked. He clung to her whole arm.

Not a great look for a kid his age, McCrea thought.

"People are just scared about what might be coming," Victoria said. Her tone was strong, but she looked as frightened as anyone else.

As they approached the top of the hill and the building beyond, the scale of everything seemed to transform. The massive entryway looked like something out of a science-fiction movie. McCrea wondered how they'd possibly been able to disguise it from the neighbors.

Luke pulled up short. "I'm not going in there," he proclaimed.

"You have to, sweetheart," Victoria said. "This is going to be our home for a while."

"Yet to be seen," McCrea said. As he spoke the words, he thought he might understand why Victoria was leading the charge like this. If the kids were not to be allowed, and she chose not to leave them alone, that was something to be known sooner rather than later.

"What does he mean by that?" Caleb asked. *"Yet to be seen?"*

She didn't answer.

Luke pointed toward the top of the hill. "Look at all the soldiers."

Fifty feet ahead, passage was completely blocked by a makeshift barricade across the road. A dozen or more stern-faced men, kitted out for battle, added firepower to the roadblock. Helmets, vests, rifles and enough ammunition to stave off an invasion. But the uniforms they wore were of a previous generation, the mottled green camo pattern of the Vietnam era, and none of them wore rank insignia.

"Major McCrea?" Victoria asked. "What branch of the service are they from?"

"Ask me again in five minutes," he said. "At least we know why nothing is moving. Stay close to me." Louder: "First Sergeant Copley?"

"Sir?"

"Keep the Emersons safe while I speak to the guards."

"Oo-uh."

Victoria addressed her sons at a whisper. "Caleb, you make sure that you and Luke do exactly as First Sergeant Copley tells you. I'm going with the major."

She didn't wait for a response from either boy. They'd been raised right. Yes, they had attitude, and, yes, they pushed back, but they understood an order when they heard it, and they would obey.

Victoria waited until McCrea was halfway to the barricade before she started after him. The first sergeant started to object, but his heart wasn't really in it.

McCrea approached the least nervous-looking sentry. "Good evening, troop," he said. "What's with all the delay?"

As if channeling the Buckingham Palace Beefeater guards, the soldier said nothing, but rather stared straight ahead, as if no one were there.

"I'm talking to you, soldier," McCrea said, his tone a little harsher. He pointed to the embroidered insignia on his own chest. "Take a look at the oak leaf. You owe me a few words and some eye contact at the very least."

The kid's eyes stayed focused on something distant, but he did say, "Sir, I am not the one to ask anything. My job is to keep people from busting through the line. Everything else is up to Mr. Johnson."

"And who is Mr. Johnson?"

"He'd be the boss, sir."

"Where can we find him?" Victoria asked. The sound of her voice startled McCrea.

"Somewhere nearby, ma'am," the soldier said. "He tends not to share his whereabouts with me."

McCrea leaned in closer, nearly nose to nose. "You think you're funny?"

"Apparently not, sir," the soldier said.

"Step aside and let me through," McCrea said. "I'll find him myself."

As McCrea took a step forward to break through the line, the soldier took two steps back to open some distance and leveled the muzzle of his rifle at the bridge of McCrea's nose. "Lethal force is authorized, Major. I'd prefer not to use it, but please don't think I'd hesitate."

The speed and decisiveness of the guard's movement made McCrea flinch, but he recovered quickly. "Point that weapon elsewhere," he said.

"I'd like nothing better, sir, but you need to step back behind the line. Another step forward and I'll shoot you in the face. I have my orders."

McCrea took a step back. He'd learned a long time ago that there was no more dangerous creature on the planet than an armed young man with standing orders to shoot. "Can you summon Mr. Johnson for me?"

"No need," a voice called from behind the line. "I'm Johnson." He approached from the bunker's maw. "You've been causing quite a stir with your line jumping," he said. "Gotta tell you, that's not a harbinger of good things."

When Johnson arrived at the cordon, he stood at parade rest, with his hands behind his back, as if deliberately avoiding a handshake. McCrea had been waiting for a salute, but when he didn't get one, he pressed ahead. "I don't understand the source of this delay," he said.

"It takes time," Johnson said. "We've got to process a lot of people and we're not designed for high-volume entries like this."

"How can that be?" Victoria blurted. "This is a bunker, for crying out loud. Did you plan for war to arrive slowly?"

Johnson shifted his head to address Victoria, but his shoulders remained squared to McCrea. "Who are you, ma'am?"

"I am Victoria Emerson, representative of—"

"West Virginia's Third District," Johnson said on her behalf. "Welcome to the Annex, ma'am." He leaned forward and addressed the ear of the soldier who'd nearly shot McCrea. "Let her through. Her chief of staff is already here, a Mr. Mulvany?"

"Mulroney," Victoria corrected.

"Yes, whatever. He's been here. Just cleared the showers, in fact."

"Showers?"

"It will make sense when you come in. Speaker Glendale has been asking for you." Johnson extended his arm in a welcoming gesture as the soldier stepped to the side to make room for her.

Victoria turned back to face down the hill. "Caleb! Luke! Come on up, please."

Johnson darted forward to fill the gap. "Whoa, whoa, whoa. What are you doing?"

The moment of truth had arrived. "I'm a single mom," Victoria said. "I'm not leaving my boys alone while I seek shelter for myself."

Johnson straightened his posture again. "All respect, ma'am, this place is not about shelter for anyone. It's about the continuance of government."

The boys arrived at her side. "Caleb and Luke Emerson, please say hello to Mr. Johnson."

"Hello," they said in unison.

Johnson ignored the boys. "Ma'am, they will not be allowed to enter the Annex."

"And why is that?"

McCrea suspected that she understood the rules and the reason behind them, but she wanted to hear Johnson say it in front of others. That wasn't going to do anything to ease the growing angst within the crowd.

"We simply don't have the room available, ma'am," Johnson said. "Five hundred thirty-five members of Congress plus one staff member each is almost eleven hundred people. Some members of Congress have six, seven children. We could never feed them all."

"You certainly could," Victoria said.

A crowd was beginning to buzz. They were on her side.

She continued, "As I understand it, when the doors close, they will remain closed for sixty days. If I do my math properly, at three meals per day, that's a hundred eighty meals per member of Congress. That times eleven hundred . . ." She looked to the sky as she did the math in her head.

"A hundred and ninety-eight thousand," Caleb said almost instantly.

"Let's call it two hundred thousand," Victoria said. "You and your staff have to eat, too. Mr. Johnson, by definition, you are prepared to deliver two hundred thousand meals to the people inside that bunker."

Johnson said, "Ma'am, I know what you're trying to do here, and it's just not gonna happen."

Victoria pretended not to hear. "Tough times lie ahead for all of us, Mr. Johnson. I know my colleagues, and sooner or later, they're going to talk about shared sacrifice in the difficult times that lie ahead. Suppose we only feed ourselves one meal per day? That would bring the capacity up to at least three thousand refugees inside, would it not?"

"It's not just about food, Mrs. Emerson," Johnson said.

"It's *Congresswoman* Emerson," she snapped. "It's about beds, then? Have people hot bunk, share beds. Toilet capacity? Don't flush as often."

Behind her, people were just now coming to grips with the reality of what they were up against.

"You're creating a scene, *Congresswoman* Emerson," Johnson said.

"No, sir, I am doing no such thing. I am merely stating facts."

"Ma'am, I have my orders."

"And your orders are going to hurt people."

Something broke in Johnson, and he took a menacing step forward, prompting both McCrea and First Sergeant Copley to close ranks in a kind of pincer movement. Victoria might be a bitch, but she was the kind of bitch McCrea admired.

"Don't talk to me about hurting people," Johnson said. "Those decisions are made by the high-and-mighty members of Congress and the occupant of the White House. I am strictly in the business of keeping those decision makers alive."

Oh, this had the potential to go very ugly, very quickly.

Victoria seemed to grow taller. "And that is my only point, Mr. Johnson," she said. "We members of Congress honor ourselves by anointing ourselves as inherently more valuable than those whom we represent. I want no part of it. Please advise Speaker Glendale that I hereby resign from Congress. And please feel free to give my spot to someone else."

Johnson looked stunned. "I, um, I—"

Victoria turned to McCrea. "I am terribly sorry for the inconvenience, Major. If you'll forgive me, I'll ask you to take us back to our home."

Johnson said, "You know, your decision affects Mr. Mulroney, too, right?"

The words blasted wind from her sails, but only for a few seconds. She said, "When you speak to Oliver, tell him to go home and hug his family." She hugged her own a little closer. "Let's go, boys."

McCrea didn't move. "Mrs. Emerson, I don't think you understand exactly what is going on here. I cannot allow you to return to your home. My job is precisely to *not* allow that to happen."

Victoria tried to puff up. "Perhaps you didn't hear me. I just resigned from the United States Congress."

"Good for you," McCrea said. "But I did not resign from the

United States Army. I have a duty to keep you safe, and the area where you used to live has a high likelihood of becoming Ground Zero."

The buzz among the forming crowd was blossoming into something much bigger. As more people left their cars, it became clear that Victoria was not the only member who believed that they could talk their families into the bunker.

"Vicky?" It was Abbi Sinclair, the wife of Burton Sinclair, of Oklahoma's Fifth District. "Did I hear right? Families are not allowed inside?"

Abbi didn't wait for an answer. Instead, she whirled on her husband. "Is this why you didn't want me to come along? So that I could die alone while you're safely in a bunker?"

Burton Sinclair dipped his head and placed his hands on his wife's shoulders. Their combined age easily topped a hundred fifty years. "Sweetheart, you're not going to die. Not of this. No one is. Not if we do our jobs properly. That's why I have to go inside. Mine is an important job."

"What am I supposed to do?"

"Go home," he said. Then he cast a glance at his military escort. "Or as close to home as you can manage." He leaned to kiss her, but she spun her head away. "I'll see you in a couple of days."

When Burton Sinclair turned back toward the cordon, Johnson let him pass. Why let the awkwardness fester any more than it had?

"Can we go back to the car?" Victoria asked McCrea. She was already walking that way. "We can discuss this better there."

"There's nothing to discuss," McCrea said.

Victoria touched his arm. "Please. The boys don't need to see this. It's likely to get ugly. The boys don't need to see this." A panic was beginning to build, and panic was an emotion that could spin out of control with frightening speed.

"First Sergeant Copley, make a hole for us back to the vehicle," McCrea said.

"Mom, are we going to be okay?" Luke asked. He sounded close to tears.

"Just stay close," she said. She wished she had a better answer.

As they walked back down the hill to the Suburban, colleagues in other cars rolled down their windows or stepped outside of their vehicles to ask what was happening. She answered only once, telling Representative Latasha Washington, of New York, that she, Victoria, had just resigned her seat, but her words seemed to derail things even more.

After that, she ignored the inquiries. She didn't owe anyone an answer to anything. As they closed to within a few yards of the Suburban, she was surprised that First Sergeant Copley had left it running.

"Keep your weapon at the ready," McCrea said, just loudly enough to be heard.

"Roger that," Copley said. As they got to the vehicle, he stopped and turned to face back up the hill. "Got you covered," he said.

McCrea herded the Emersons back into their previously assigned seats, supervised as they tossed their rucks back in the cargo hold, and covered Copley's return to the driver's seat. Then he planted himself back in the shotgun spot.

"Where are we going?" Copley asked.

"Anywhere but here," McCrea said. "We need to head west. Into the mountains."

"How do we get off this road?" Copley asked. "It's jammed."

"This thing has four-wheel drive for a reason," McCrea said. "Use it."

"I thought we were coming back here to talk," Caleb said from the backseat as he pulled his seat belt tighter.

"We can talk and ride at the same time."

"I don't understand," Luke said. "We don't know where we're going, but we're going there, anyway?"

Victoria explained, "Honey, it doesn't feel safe to be here. People are really scared, and scared people can do very dangerous things."

Copley pulled the transmission into gear and eased back onto the narrow road. The nose of their vehicle had just begun to cross from grass back to pavement when the SUV on their left moved to close the gap.

McCrea leaned forward in this seat and pointed through the windshield. "Keep going," he said. "Your mission is to get us back onto a main road, it is not to be polite."

The first sergeant smiled. "Copy that." He stepped more heavily on the accelerator and lurched out in front of the offending truck. The driver leaned on his horn. Copley flipped him off.

"Keep the digital communication to a minimum, First Sergeant," McCrea said.

Victoria cringed at the sound of scraping metal as the other vehicle refused to back off.

"Hey!" Caleb yelled.

"Take it easy, Mr. Copley," Victoria said.

McCrea turned in his seat to look at her. "This is my vehicle, ma'am. Let us do our jobs."

As they pulled past the other SUV and onto the sweeping lawn of the Hilltop Manor, the Suburban bounced and rolled precipitously, knocking its occupants around the interior.

"We need to stop!" Victoria commanded. "We just hit that vehicle."

"Keep going," McCrea ordered. "Ma'am, I predict that a lot of things are about to change. Hit-and-run laws will have less clout than they used to." He chuckled when he spoke, and he could see that the attitude pissed her off.

She stayed silent, though.

First Sergeant Copley didn't even try to get back onto the pavement, choosing instead to four-wheel through grass and gardens, and even a few bushes and small trees. At every new opportunity to return to a roadway, they encountered more vehicles, lined up to shed their passengers.

"So many cars!" Caleb exclaimed.

"It'll take hours to get all those people through the screening," McCrea said. "I expected a crowd. That's why I was in such a hurry to get here quickly, but I never expected anything like this."

"Do you think traffic will thin once we're off the property?"

"We're kind of screwed if it doesn't," Copley said. He whipped the wheel to the right and then to the left again to fit through a space between trees. The ear-to-ear grin spoke to how much he was enjoying this.

When they finally broke through a row of hedges, they found themselves on a paved surface with no other vehicles in sight.

"What the hell is this?" McCrea asked. "Where are we?"

"I think it's the other side of the circular driveway," Copley said with a laugh.

Behind them, Victoria could see the towering edifice of the main hotel. "I think we've gone from the service road to the main driveway," she said.

McCrea agreed. "I think you're right." He pointed ahead. "Keep going down the hill."

At the base of the driveway—at the apron—traffic in the far lane had come to a complete stop, stacked up to make a future left-hand turn into the service road.

"Go down the left lane," McCrea commanded.

Copley laughed louder. "Oh, they're definitely not going to like this," he said.

He accelerated and the line of cars whizzed past on their right. A half mile up the road, they reached the intersection and encountered the gridlock created by the turning cars. The right-hand lane remained jammed with westbound traffic, but at the turn, the left lane dead ahead was clogged with eastbound traffic. Where the two met, there was a gap that maybe was wide enough for the Suburban to pass.

"Flash your lights and lean on your horn," McCrea instructed. "No matter what they do, don't slow down. Let them know there'll be a price for getting in our way."

Copley did exactly as he was told, pressing his right thumb down on the horn pad in the center of the steering wheel, and flicking the fingers on his left hand against the light switch on the column.

Other cars sounded their horns in retaliation, and one looked like it might pull out to block the way, but in the end it didn't.

On Victoria's left, Luke reached over and squeezed her hand as they launched toward the gap. "We're not going to—"

Before he could finish his statement, they were through the line and onto the empty roadway. Copley goosed the accelerator some more. "Let's do that again!" he crowed. "So, now that we're free, where are we going?"

Victoria didn't drop a beat. "Mountain View, West Virginia."

CHAPTER FIVE

AFTER CLEARING THE GANG SHOWER AND THE GANG DRYING ROOM, the Solara gestapo had herded Penn and Strasky into the dressing area, where each member of Congress had his own locker, complete with a name tag Velcro'd to the metal. Two feet wide by three feet tall, the lockers were stacked two high and were placed in alphabetical order. Wooden benches ran the length of the entire locker room. Penn felt himself flashing back to high school, and the miserable memories of Mr. Irwin, the grab-happy gym teacher who fondled boys before words like *pedophile* had made it to the common vernacular.

On the far end of the locker room, Arlen Strasky picked through the pile of uniforms that were stacked by size in piles inside the tiny alcove labeled: STAFF AND OTHERS.

Penn Glendale couldn't look away from his reflection. "We look like Castro," he said. "Some Third World dictatorship. This is unacceptable. This isn't a military junta. This is the United States Congress!"

Everyone had been issued three sets of 1990s-era BDUs, battle dress uniforms, the chocolate-chip style made famous by soldiers in the first Gulf War. The trousers had Velcro closures at the ankle to compensate for improper inseam length, and the waist closure was further adjustable by buttons along the belt line. All of it was held up by a fabric belt with a brass buckle. The button-down shirt was a tunic of sorts, with a tail that hung lower than the waistline. Even the underwear was military issue. For footwear, everyone wore the same black high-top tennis shoes with black soles.

"I swear to God, Arlen, this could not possibly be a worse image to project to the public."

"When this is over, I think you should give someone a severe talking-to," Strasky said.

The locker rooms were divided by sex, and once they emerged into the hallway on the far side, reentry was forbidden, and an armed sentry was posted to make sure that no one cheated.

The hallway itself was painted a bland shade of aqua that reminded Penn of the operating buildings of his Stateside military assignments. The overhead fluorescent lights were dialed up a little too bright, but the glare revealed this place to be perfectly clean—the literal definition of spotless.

"Move this way, people," said another uniformed Solara worker, this one a woman.

"How many of these guards are there?" Penn mumbled.

The guards ushered them down the narrow hallway toward a closed pair of double doors. Overhead, pipes and electrical conduit made the ceiling seem lower than it actually was. The walls were constructed of reinforced concrete, and everything about this part of the facility was dedicated to efficiency and storage.

At the far end, the heavy steel double doors opened into what might have been—and probably once was—convention space. The wide expanse of the room was interrupted only by thick support columns every fifteen or twenty feet. Penn remembered reading somewhere in his briefing notes that the total square footage of the Annex approached 150,000 square feet. It sounded much bigger in the abstract than it felt now that he was inside. The prospect of another one thousand souls in the space triggered the beginnings of a claustrophobia attack.

"Gentlemen, this way, please," their lady guide told them. She led the way to a long table that was manned by more uniformed people. They sat shoulder-to-shoulder, each behind a sign that indicated letters of the alphabet. Some, notably *I, Q* and *X,* shared signs with the letters that preceded them in the alphabet.

"Your credentials are filed by alphabet," the guide said. She turned and headed back to the hallway, presumably to escort the next group of arrivals.

One of the soldiers at the table—a beefy guy whose name patch read, CAMERON—yelled with the voice of a drill instructor, "Ladies and gentlemen, find your line and claim your name badge. This badge must remain with you at all times. It will indicate your bunk number, your assigned mealtimes and any medications you need to take. The orientation booklet will explain how the system works. Under no circumstances are you to contemplate leaving this facility without permission from the senior staff of Solara. Our purpose is to keep everyone safe so that you may do your job of delivering the nation from calamity. If you have questions, now is not the time. Thank you for your cooperation."

Penn looked around to verify that he and Strasky were still part of a very small vanguard force of refugees. "You should save your voice," he told Cameron with a smile. "You'll be giving that speech quite a few times, I imagine."

Cameron ignored him.

Penn wandered up to the young man behind the letter *G.* "Penn Glendale," he said. "Speaker of the U.S. House—"

"I hate to interrupt, sir," the soldier said. Name patch: ST. JAMES. "Titles don't matter here. Not to us. As Mr. Cameron said, your job is to run the country, our job is to run the Annex." As he spoke, St. James riffled through a Bankers Box that was jammed with manila envelopes. With a triumphant nod, he plucked one out and handed it over. "*Glendale, Pennington J.* Here you go, sir."

"This seems very analog for a high-tech facility," Penn quipped.

"It is what it is, sir. First thing you want to do is clip the name badge to your pocket. You do not want to lose that, sir. Sleep with it and take it into the shower with you. Seriously, I cannot emphasize that enough."

"I don't understand," Penn said. "This is the United States

Congress. We're what you might call a pretty exclusive club. We all know who we are. Hell, if you read the newspapers, you know who we are, too."

St. James eyed Penn with a kind of practiced indifference. "Sir, I am not here to argue with you. I am not here to explain. I have a job to do, and while it might not seem like much right now, in an hour or two, this place will be insane."

"There's no need to be unfriendly, son," Penn said. He regretted his words the instant they left his mouth.

St. James's expression didn't change. "I am not your friend, sir. Nor am I your son. My colleagues and I are the law inside the Annex, and it makes little sense to make friends with people we may very well have to take into custody someday. Does that make sense to you, Mr. Glendale?"

"You forget whom you're talking to," Penn said.

"I was about to say the exact same thing." This voice came from Cameron, the boss with the big voice. "You, sir, are forgetting whom *you're* talking to. I suggest you read the materials you've been given, and then gather in the House Chamber to await the arrival of your colleagues."

"May I see my quarters?" Penn asked.

"If you wish," Cameron said. "If you go to that door over there"—he pointed to vented double doors at the far end of the big hall—"Mr. Cohen will be happy to take you to your quarters."

"Me too?" Arlen Strasky had just wandered up, his manila envelope in hand.

"You need to put your badge on, sir," Cameron said.

Strasky looked a little startled. He pinched the metal closure on the envelope, then opened the flap.

Penn did the same. He puffed the mouth of the envelope open, peered inside, and retrieved the two-inch by three-inch laminated badge. The upper left corner featured a color official photo, and the rest showed gibberish—computer code, Penn figured. The outside border of Penn's badge was gold, while that of Arlen's was red.

They clipped the badges to the flap of their shirt pockets.

"You don't have a room, Mr. Strasky," Cameron said. "You will be in one of the staff bunkrooms. Your specific bunk assignment is coded on your badge. Mr. Glendale, as Speaker, you will share a room for two people. Your roommate will be the Senate majority leader."

"Dennis Laraja?" Penn asked.

"Sure," Cameron replied. "Now, if you'll excuse me, we have some new arrivals."

Penn turned to see a crowd of perhaps forty men and women streaming into the main hall. None looked comfortable in their new attire. Three of them, whom Penn saw in a glance, still had wet hair.

"This is the most surreal thing I've ever witnessed," Strasky said.

"No argument from me," Penn agreed. "Now that members and senators are arriving, we need to get organized. We don't want to lose focus on the work we have to do here."

"Mr. Speaker!" a voice called from off to his left. It was Scott Johnson, and he approached with a smile. He closed to within a few feet and said, "I understand that my staff hasn't impressed you thus far."

"No, I wouldn't say that I'm unimpressed," Penn said. "They're just very matter-of-fact."

"These are nervous-making times, sir," Johnson said. "We've been drilling this scenario for years, but I don't think any of us really expected it to happen."

"Nothing's happened yet," Strasky said. "CRIMSON PHOENIX was launched strictly out of an abundance of caution."

"I'm just a grunt with a job to do, sir. The fact of CRIMSON PHOENIX is all that matters to me. It could be a practice exercise for all I know—and for all I care. The protocol is active, so therefore the rules apply. I wish someone had prepared your colleagues better."

Penn recoiled. That felt like a shot. "What does that mean?"

Johnson *piffed.* "Oh, nothing. We just have a lot of angst brewing outside. The business of not allowing families is turning out to be controversial. You should know that some of your folks are quitting. One in particular"—he pulled a notebook out of one of the huge pouch pockets in his trousers—"Representative Victoria Emerson, of Virginia—"

"West Virginia," Penn corrected. "Third District."

"Yeah, okay. Well, she made me promise to tell you that she hereby has resigned her seat."

Penn's heart skipped. *"Resigned?"*

"Yes, sir. She tried to convince the sentries out front that she should be able to bring her children in with her, but when she was informed that that was impossible—"

Penn had stopped listening to him. He turned to Strasky. "What the hell is Vicky thinking? She knows how slim our majority is."

Strasky looked bothered. "Come on, Mr. Speaker. She's a single mom."

"She's a member of Congress," Glendale countered. "She has responsibilities, and those responsibilities require occasional sacrifice."

"Penn," Strasky said. "Are you hearing yourself? Be reasonable."

"Tomorrow I'll be reasonable," Penn said. "Today you'll have to settle for pissed."

Johnson started to wander off, then stopped himself. "One more thing," he said. "The last thing I want to do is get in your business, but while you're discussing this, understand that decisions like hers impact others. For example, I have to find her chief of staff, Oliver Somebody—"

"Mulroney," Penn prompted.

"Yes, that's exactly it. I need to find him and tell him to leave. According to Ms. Emerson, I am to tell him to go back to his family."

Penn cocked his head. "Would you like me to be with you?"

"No, sir, I would not. But generally speaking, I expect people to react badly when they find out that they've been demoted from bunker status to radiation catcher. There's also the security issue."

Penn and Strasky exchanged looks. "Which security issue is that?"

"He knows about this place," Johnson said. "He knows what's going on here, and he knows the kind of details that can't get out to the world."

"What are you suggesting?" Penn asked. He had a bad feeling about the way this conversation was headed.

"I'm suggesting nothing beyond the fact that I need dispensation from someone before allowing security protocols to be violated. I must move on now." He continued his walk in the other direction.

"Wait!" Penn called after him.

"Actions have consequences, Mr. Speaker," Johnson called over his shoulder. "Actions have consequences."

"What the hell does that mean?" Penn called after him, but Johnson kept walking. He turned to Strasky. "What the hell does *that* mean?"

Strasky changed the subject and pointed to a sign on the far wall: UNITED STATES HOUSE OF REPRESENTATIVES. "We should go take a look at our new home." Behind them, the check-in desk was beginning to get frantic. Cameron was again launching into his welcome speech.

The sign for the House Chamber was not a slapdash last-minute handwritten affair. On the contrary, it was engraved in gold letters on a stained dark wood sign that measured two feet by four feet. It topped a set of heavy double doors with reinforced glass in the upper third of the panels. Penn pulled the right-hand door open to reveal a steeply sloped lecture hall with a stage at the bottom. Each of the seats—he guessed that there were at least 435 of them—were padded like movie theater chairs, and each was equipped with a desk that folded down to the side. The stage itself was laid out in a pattern that roughly simulated the real House Chamber in the Capitol, though without the well, and absent the seats normally occupied by clerks and other staff—none of whom would be invited to this particular party.

"I read in the briefing book that Hilltop routinely used this space for conventions and sales meetings and such," Penn explained. "The folks who attended lectures here never dreamed that they were sitting in the House Chamber."

"I'll bet the decorations were different," Strasky quipped.

Large television screens dominated the back of the stage, each displaying the Great Seal of the House of Representatives. Behind the Speaker's seat, the flags of all branches of the military flanked Old Glory. Other television screens—a dozen or more of them, all showing the same image—hung from the ceiling from strategic locations that would allow everyone in the chamber to have an adequate view.

"I don't get the armed services flags," Strasky said. "That's executive branch. Seems more relevant to their bunker than to ours."

"Look at the right-hand wall down there," Penn said. Draped there on the wooden paneling was a television-ready backdrop of the White House. A similar backdrop of the U.S. Capitol dominated the opposite wall on the left. "I'm second in line to the presidency. If something happens to the president and vice president, I'm the guy. The flags and the backdrops just show how prepared this place is for every plot twist."

"It's a pretty bare-bones operation," Strasky said.

Penn didn't respond. A rush of emotion pressed behind his eyes as he slowly descended the steps toward the well, such as it was. *Jesus, this is really happening.*

"You okay, boss?" Strasky asked.

"Is anything okay today?" Penn replied. "I'm scared to death."

"World leaders are too smart to be really stupid," Strasky said. "All we have to do is keep the element of surprise."

Penn stopped before he got to the bottom and turned. "This is the stupidest goddamn thing that this country has ever done," he said.

"We can't expect Israel to just sit idly while—"

"I know the arguments, Arlen. Jesus, I've been in the meetings. Blah, blah, blah, Iran has nukes. Tell me how a first strike can do anything but—"

The door at the top of the stairs opened and Angela Fortnight crossed the threshold. She was pissed. "Penn, would you please tell me when the United States Congress became a military state?"

"Good morning to you, too, Angela," Penn said. Nothing spun up the House minority leader quite as tight as feigned politeness when she was on a rant.

Angela Fortnight, of Oregon's Fifth, understood her job as minority leader to be the equivalent of being anointed most bothersome fly at the picnic. If Penn and his party proclaimed the sky to be blue, Angela and her team were sure to find it to be green, and to start an investigation into Penn's association with companies that produced blue paint. It had been thus for the past few years—since the dissolution of civil political comity—and Angela seemed to revel in partisan antics. Penn was capable of playing the same games, but he hated having to do it.

"There's nothing funny about any of this, Penn."

"No, there's not," Penn agreed.

"These uniforms are a mistake," Angela said.

"I couldn't agree more. And I couldn't have less sway in the matter. Serenity Prayer, and all of that. Have you heard any current news?"

"I haven't heard any old news," Angela snapped. "All I know is that this is the most dehumanizing experience I've ever been through."

"Think of the rationale behind it, though," Penn said. "And then think how much better off we will be than our constituents if this thing goes south. Have you seen any more of the leadership?"

"I think I saw Dennis Laraja in the line out there, but I'm not sure. There's a sea of people out there. And your girl Vicky Emerson certainly threw a wrench in the works when she quit."

"I just heard about that," Penn said. "That had to be a tough choice for her."

"Her choice damn near caused a panic," Angela said. She sat heavily in one of the lecture hall chairs.

Penn sat on the edge of his new desk. "What does that mean?"

"She quit so publicly," Angela explained. "She jumped the line, called all kinds of attention to herself and then announced that she was quitting. It wasn't until she did that, that other family members realized that they would be denied access to the Annex. It got ugly. I'll give it to her that it took courage to do what she did. It's a hard thing to walk away from your family."

"It's a cowardly thing to walk away from your responsibilities at the very moment when your country most needs you," Penn countered. "This thing that we signed on to do—to run the government of the most powerful nation on earth—requires significant sacrifice."

Angela scowled. "Dial it back, Mr. Speaker. There are no television cameras here. I'm confident that she will not be the only one to put her family first. Vicky was only one/four-hundred-thirty-fifth of the House, I'm confident we'll be able to make due without her vote." She pointed at his nose. "You'd better hope that she's only one of a few. Your majority being as thin as it is."

"Oh, for Christ's sake," Strasky moaned. "Is that really where you want this discussion to go? Today of all days? Hard-core politics?"

"This is a political body, Mr. Strasky," Angela reminded.

Penn had just raised his hand to silence his chief of staff when a speaker popped somewhere in the ceiling. A voice of God said, "Mr. Speaker, I need to interrupt."

The three of them exchanged glances with each other. "Who the hell are you?" Penn asked. It came out more harshly than he'd intended.

"I have the president on a video conference call. Please stand by."

"How is that going to work?" Penn asked. He felt as if he were addressing the walls themselves.

All around, the television monitors jumped to life. One logo dissolved into another as Great Seal of the President of the United States filled the screen, and then the image dissolved again to the image of President Helen Blanton at the end of the table that Penn recognized as being part of the White House Situation Room. She wore a blue suit jacket and a white blouse with a red, white and blue scarf around her neck.

Over the course of the next ten seconds, the screen image filled with various flag officers in uniform, as well as the secretaries of state and defense as the players all took their seats. "Is everyone connected?" the president asked to someone offscreen.

CHAPTER SIX

"How far is Mountain View?" McCrea asked.

"A couple hundred miles," Victoria said. "At least that's where my children and I are going. You are free to leave us if you wish. First Sergeant Copley, you are likewise free to go. I absolve you both from any ongoing obligation to us."

"Whoa, Mom!" Caleb said. "What are you saying? They're just gonna drop us off?"

"Hush, Caleb," Victoria said.

McCrea said, "Mrs. Emerson, what you're suggesting is difficult, at best. I'm not sure we have the time to drive that far."

"Then let us go alone."

"I've already told you I can't do that."

"I'm willing to give it a try, Major," Copley said. "I've got no place to go, anyway. Could be a hell of an adventure."

"Major McCrea, my son is in Mountain View. Adam is turning eighteen—in fact, today is his birthday. He refused to move to Virginia after my election. He's at the Clinton M. Hedrick Military Academy there. Have you heard of it?"

Ten seconds passed with McCrea saying nothing.

"You okay, Major?" Copley asked.

"Are you being straight with me, ma'am? Is your son really at Hedrick?"

"Why would I make that up?"

"That's where my brother went to high school. It was a little rough back then, but it set him straight."

"Then you know the route," Victoria said.

McCrea said, "We need to be reasonable. You know as well as I do that this might all turn out to be nothing. No war, just a very elaborate precaution."

"And if that's the case, your obligation to the Emerson family will end," Victoria said. "Caleb, Luke and I can make our way out to Mountain View, and you can be on your own."

"What about the major's family?" Luke asked. "He probably wants to be home with them."

Victoria placed her hand on Luke's knee and gave it a squeeze. "Shh."

"I hope they'll be just fine," McCrea said. "The Washington Metro Area is off-limits to us until this is over."

"I don't understand," Luke said.

"He means that if the war comes, everything around Washington will be fried," Caleb said. His voice caught in his throat as he spoke.

Luke's fingers dug into Victoria's hand. "Is that true, Mom? What about Hachim and Robbie?"

Hachim and Robbie were Luke's best buds.

"Toast," Caleb said.

"Caleb!" Victoria reached across the seat and smacked the back of his head. "Don't. Not now. Luke, we don't know what is going to happen to any of them."

"But if—"

"We'll handle *if* when *if* arrives," Victoria snapped. To McCrea, she softened her tone. "We're going to want to go west anyway, Major. Let's just keep it at that." She leaned forward and touched his shoulder. "And I'm sorry about your family."

He bobbled his head, and Victoria thought she might be able to see his eyes glistening with tears.

"As you said, ma'am. We'll let *if* make its choices."

The next few minutes passed in silence as the Suburban's headlights cut a path through the darkness. The road out here was narrow and thickly wooded, the kind that made you worry about deer, for both your sake and theirs. Copley had a heavy foot, but always seemed well in control of the vehicle.

As they rounded a wide left-hand turn, the radio exploded to life with the baritone voice of a newscaster. The sound startled them all, to the point that Copley jerked the wheel and almost wandered off into the ditch on the right.

"Jesus!" McCrea shouted as he leaned forward to spin the volume knob down. "Holy crap! I guess we're out of the blackout area."

As McCrea spoke, both his and Copley's cell phones buzzed.

"You keep driving," McCrea ordered. "I'll check mine, and then yours if you think it's important." The glow of his smartphone bathed his face in a blue light as he scrolled through the messages on his phone. All of them were bad.

"How come he gets to keep his phone, but we had to give ours away?" Caleb protested.

"Now's not the time," Victoria said. She watched the major's expression darken as he scrolled. "What's wrong?"

McCrea said, "Somebody tipped the media. The secret's out."

Victoria's stomach cramped.

"What does that mean?" Luke asked. "What secret is out?"

McCrea's eyes never left his screen as he explained. "I don't know all the details. We've been in such a news desert the past few hours. But from what I can tell, some little internet rag of a news outlet posted that the Hilltop Manor was on a lockdown, and that members of the House and Senate were flooding in. I guess they put two and two together and pushed it out as a news story."

"Totally irresponsible," Copley said.

"What time is it now?" Victoria asked. "Four in the morning? Who's reading news feeds at four in the morning?"

"Just about everybody on the other side of the Pond, apparently," McCrea said.

Victoria regretted asking such a stupid question. "Which news source are you reading?" she asked.

"This is a Pentagon feed," McCrea explained. "Iran has upped its readiness status. Lots of ugly things are being said." He looked at Victoria. "If this is going to go hot, it's going to go hot soon."

"I sense that you're trying to tell me something that I'm not hearing."

"I think I'm telling you it was a mistake not to take your place in the bunker."

Both of the boys straightened in their seats at that.

"Let's try to be helpful with our comments, Major," Victoria scolded.

McCrea ignored her. This seemed like a stupid-ass time to worry about sheltering your kids from bad news. "First Sergeant, head for the mines. We'll take our chances there."

"Copy that." He foot grew even heavier on the accelerator.

"Mines?" Victoria asked.

McCrea turned in his seat and explained. "First Sergeant Copley and I had a plan. Before you made your decision to resign, our mission was to be over as soon as we dropped you off. We were never slated to be assigned to any bunker anywhere. Going back to Ground Zero didn't make any sense, so we scoped out a makeshift shelter. They used to call it a coal mine."

"What's there?" Caleb asked.

"I'm gonna guess coal," McCrea said. "Or maybe not anymore because it's been closed for almost twenty years. It'll be a hike to get there, but I can't think of a better place to have a good shot at surviving the bad stuff. Being inside a big mountain can't be a bad thing."

"Suppose it collapses?" Luke asked. "I saw in a movie where there was this cave-in and everybody got killed."

McCrea started to say something, but thought better of it. He smiled. "Was that movie set in West Virginia?"

"I don't think so. It was an old cowboy movie. Texas, maybe."

"Well, there you go. Everybody knows that Texas coal mines aren't nearly as strong as West Virginia coal mines."

"You're making that up!" Caleb protested.

"I am not," McCrea said. "Ask anybody. In the Army, we need to know stuff like that. You know, in case of emergencies for our troops."

Luke looked up at Victoria. "Is that true?"

For the first time, she looked at McCrea with an expression that didn't project hatred. "That's what I've always heard," she said.

CHAPTER SEVEN

THE PRESIDENT SETTLED HERSELF IN HER CHAIR IN THE SITUATION Room and addressed her gathered audience. "Thank you, ladies and gentlemen, for your attention. I will try to make this as quick and simple as possible. In approximately one hour and forty-three minutes, the military forces in Israel, on the command of their political leadership, will conduct surgical nuclear strikes on the Islamic Republic of Iran. These limited strikes will be targeted at the manufacturing facilities and launch sites for their nuclear weapons.

"As you all know, this follows many years of attempted negotiations and crippling economic sanctions that have had little or no effect on their rhetoric. Their most recent belligerent actions in the Strait of Hormuz are clear evidence that . . ."

Penn Glendale understood the geopolitical situation to be what it was. He understood that Israel stood on the precipice of having to choose between survival and Armageddon. What he did not understand—what he couldn't begin to fathom—was how the world allowed Iran to advance to the lengths they had in the production of nuclear war-making materiel. This could have been stopped *before* they'd developed their first-strike capability. If the United States had shown the political courage then to ignore the ire of America's vocal minority of pacifists' cries for peace at any price, this first strike could have been handled with conventional munitions.

But . . . no. Administration after administration pushed the issue on to the next group of politicians, keeping the ball rolling until it finally came to a stop at the feet of the singularly least-qualified president in the history of the republic.

President Blanton clearly was reading her speech for the benefit of the history books. Not a bad idea, Penn supposed, given the fact that she would be only the second political leader in the history of the world to oversee a nuclear first strike.

Okay, that was unfair.

Israel would be the one to actually throw the first punch, but that punch wouldn't be possible without the United States' arsenal on perpetual standby to serve as their shield and backup. The Russians, Chinese and Pakistanis would be given ten minutes' advance notice of the strike, along with assurances that those nations would not be in danger. The nuke-capable NATO nations were already on board with the operation.

"General Clayton," the president said, "where do we stand on our preparations to support the attack?"

Grant Clayton, chairman of the Joint Chiefs of Staff, sat straighter in his chair. "Madam President, everything remains just as it was last time we spoke. Our air and sea assets are all in place. After you alert the other nations of our intent to support Israel in their efforts, we will make our presence momentarily discoverable for the purposes of verification. That should convince all the players to keep their guns in their holsters, ma'am."

President Blanton smiled at the metaphor. "The time is ticking down toward zero," she said. "Speaker Glendale and Senator Laraja, are you on the line?"

"I'm here, Madame President," Penn said.

They waited for a few seconds, and when the Senate majority leader didn't answer up, Penn said, "Congresswoman Fortnight thinks she saw Senator Laraja in line outside the Annex, waiting to check in."

"I see," the president said. "And how is that process going?"

"Which process is that, ma'am?"

"The process of reestablishing the House and Senate out there at the Annex?"

"It's complicated," Penn said. "We're so early in the process that I don't have much to tell you. Perhaps if we could add an hour or two to the timeline—"

The president laughed. "No, Mr. Speaker, that's not possible," she said. "Remember, this is not our attack. We are merely in a support role."

The way she said that prompted uneasiness in Penn's gut. Yes, he couldn't stand her, and yes, he didn't believe a word she'd ever said about any topic in the history of topics, but that last bit about not being our attack seemed gratuitous. She sounded like a witness answering a question that hadn't been asked.

"Madam President," Penn said, "allow me to go on the record stating that this entire affair is a bad idea. Iran did not provoke us."

"They have provoked us every day since November of 1979. And now, when they provoke the nation of Israel, they provoke the United States of America, we will stand by our ally—"

"Ma'am, please," Penn pressed. "You yourself said that the clock is ticking down very quickly on this. Iran has *not* attacked. They have *not* drawn first blood. The world will not view our actions in a positive light if we go ahead with this."

"Thank you for your input, Mr. Speaker," Blanton said.

"I believe that this needs to be brought to a vote," Penn pressed. "We're talking nuclear war here, ma'am."

"It is not *our* war, Mr. Speaker. It is *Israel's* war. We cannot influence their government on matters such as this. They have made their decision, and ours—mine, as commander in chief, empowered by the Constitution with exclusive authority over foreign policy—is to stand by our allies."

Penn heard the words and dismissed them as the sellout that he knew them to be. Helen Blanton was playing in a league that was way beyond her capacity, and she knew it. She'd been sold on the fiction that the Russians were so afraid of American might that they would never dream of retaliation in the face of a nuclear assault that didn't directly involve them. She seemed oblivious to the fact that the Russian president was the whack job of whack jobs.

Maybe she was right. God Almighty, he hoped that she was right, but suppose she wasn't? Suppose the Pakis and the Indians and the North Koreans all interpreted this as the beginning of World War III? What then?

And wasn't that the underlying presumption? If it were not, then CRIMSON PHOENIX would not have been activated.

Nuclear weapons, for God's sake! You can call it a limited strike, or a tactical strike, but at the end of the day, this was about unleashing the most destructive forces ever conceived by humans. There was no take-back. There was no walking away from this.

And there was no stopping the president.

She had already heard the counterarguments, both from elected people like himself and from her military advisers as well, and she'd called her shot. As commander in chief, she'd essentially silenced the Joint Chiefs into compliance, and now that Congress had been silenced—both by presidential fiat and by disabling phone service—Congress's last line of communication (press leaks) had likewise been eliminated.

"I can't emphasize the importance of total secrecy on this matter," the president said. "I know this is a frightening time for all of you—and forgive me for pushing you all to the Annex, but I believe it was the best decision. I have complete confidence in Israel's capability to carry out this attack, but we need to be prepared for the worst. In fact, in about five minutes, I will be relocating to—"

Something distracted her on her left, out of the frame. "Yes, what?" she snapped.

A hand appeared in the frame holding a piece of paper. The look that blossomed in her face as she read the contents made Penn feel cold.

"Oh, my God," she said.

CHAPTER EIGHT

"Jeez, Sals, we really hit a nerve," Todd said. "The story's being picked up by everybody." He leaned in closer to his screen. "There it is!" he shouted. "The Gray Lady herself just posted it."

They sat at opposite poles of Sally's round glass table in the dining room. Both had their laptops open, Sally watching the numbers spin on their page counter, and Todd cruising to see who else was picking up the story.

They both jumped when Sally's phone rang. She checked the caller ID and scowled. "This should be interesting," she mumbled. Then she punched the connect button and put the call on speaker. "Sally Lambert."

A male voice that was all gravel and anger said, "Is this the same Sally Lambert that runs the *Washington Underground*?"

"Good evening, Colonel Harrington," she said. "Or, rather, good morning, I suppose." Colonel Tyrone Harrington was one of their most reliable deep-background sources for stories against the administration.

"Are you actually *trying* to bring the world to a state of war?" The colonel nearly shouted the question.

"Up awfully late, aren't you, sir?" Sally asked. She winked at Todd, who stifled a laugh.

"You've lit a shit storm, Sally," Harrington said.

"So our presumptions were correct?" As she asked the question, she motioned for Todd to start typing. She imagined he'd be *righteously* pissed when he found out that he was on the record.

"I'm not here to discuss that," the colonel said. "I'm here to ask you to take down the post."

"It's not a post, it's a story," Todd said, earning an angry glare.

"Who the hell is that?"

"My colleague Todd McElroy. He wrote the piece originally."

"Then you should fire him."

Sally said, "Colonel Harrington, if there was no truth to the story, I don't think you'd be on the phone with me right now."

"That's not the point."

"Then what *is* the point?"

"That a story like that is irresponsible. The ramifications can be huge."

"I hope you're having this same conversation with the *New York Times*," Todd said. "Because they just ran with our story."

Silence.

"Colonel Harrington?" Sally asked.

The phone chirped as the call disconnected.

"I got it all," Todd said.

"Direct quotes?"

"Yep."

"Run with it. Suck it, *Washington Tribune.*"

"They just put the story up, too," Todd crowed. "We're looking at wildfire here. A shit storm, indeed."

Todd's ringtone sounded like the call to battle stations, a clanging bell with a Klaxon behind it. When it went off, Sally jumped a foot, then slammed the table with her palm. "God *damn* it, Todd!"

He laughed and connected the call. "Todd McElroy."

"McElroy, this is David Kirk, over at the *Tribune.* Have you lost your goddamn mind?"

"I need more than that," Todd said. Over the last twenty years, David Kirk had carved out a reputation as one of the premier reporters in Washington. His sources were always spot-on, and his reporting on government malfeasance was the stuff of legend.

Todd had never met him, but he recognized the voice from the Sunday talk shows, where Kirk was a regular.

"You know goddamn well what I'm talking about," Kirk insisted. "Who gave you the go-ahead to put that story out?"

"My boss," Todd said. "In fact, she's right here. I'll put you on speaker." He pressed the button. "Sals, this is David Kirk. David Kirk, this is Sally Lambert. David was just congratulating us on our crack reporting."

"Listen to me, you smug asshole," Kirk seethed. His anger was palpable even through the phone. "That story was quarantined. What the hell were you thinking?"

"Worried about losing the scoop to an up-and-comer, there, Dave?" Todd said.

"Scoop! Jesus, you think this is about a *scoop*? You're going to get a lot of people killed."

Todd and Sally scowled at each other. "You're being a little hypocritical, don't you think?" Sally said.

"Hyp . . . *What?*"

"Your paper just posted our story," she said. "That puts you in the business of killing people, too."

"Jesus!" Kirk exclaimed. "Oh, my God, the hubris! You think we published *your* story?"

"So did the *Times* and half a dozen of the other bigs," Todd said.

"Nobody published *your* story," Kirk said. "Nobody even knows who the hell you are. We published our *own* stories, based on information we've been sitting on since yesterday."

"Bullshit." Todd and Sally said it together.

"I get that you want it to be," Kirk said, "but it's not. The White House gave a secret briefing to the pool, on the single condition that it be embargoed. Nothing was to get out until after the attack was over."

"If it was so critical to keep a lid on the story, why did the *Tribune* publish it?"

"Because *you* did. Once the genie is out of the bottle, you can't put him back in. That's what we're dealing with here. You put out innuendo and guesswork as fact, and it hit close enough to the truth that the Iranians started to go nuts."

"So it's true?" Todd blurted. "The U.S. is launching a first strike?"

"Jesus God," Kirk said. "Did you *read* the other stories, or just watch the numbers move on your website?"

Sally and Todd remained silent.

On the other end of the phone, Sally could hear movement. Muffled voices. "Oh, shit!" Kirk said. "God *damn* it! This is all on you!"

The line disconnected.

"What was that all about?" Todd asked.

Sally knew damn well what it was about. It was about David Kirk being right.

This was her worst fear. She should have listened to her own doubts. Sometimes you run into a story that is simply too big to be told. She'd sensed it, but she'd let Todd's enthusiasm cancel out her own misgivings. His enthusiasm and her own ambition to break the Big Story.

She swirled her middle finger on her laptop's touch pad and tapped on the home page for the *Washington Tribune.*

"Sals?"

"Hush a minute, Todd." She clicked on their version of the story, which was told in the subjunctive tense. It was all very conditional. *Government officials were considering . . . If the attack occurred . . .* And, yes, the plan was for Israel to strike the Iranian nuclear-manufacturing and launch sites. The United States would serve as a shield against retaliation.

President Blanton had already written a statement to the nation, which said, in part:

Iran's role as an aggressor in worldwide terrorism cannot be tolerated. With the recent escalation of their rhetoric against our loyal friend and ally, the State of Israel, Prime Minister Ibrahim had no choice but to take this terrible action in the interest in protecting the citizens of that great nation.

"I don't get it," Todd said. "I've been reading the *Tribune* article, and we got everything right. What's the big—"

As they watched the *Tribune* page, it changed. The plain screen blinked to a red border, and a new headline flashed.

"Oh, my God," Sally breathed.

CHAPTER NINE

Penn Glendale's head snapped up as the speakers in the ceiling popped to life and the voice of God—whose name was Pete—announced, "Members of the United States House of Representatives and members of the Unites States Senate, report to your respective chambers immediately. I am authorized to tell you that Iran has launched a nuclear strike against the State of Israel."

In a single instant, in the snap of a finger, a beat of the heart, everything changed inside the Annex. Penn gasped when he heard the words, and he looked over to Strasky. His chief of staff had turned gray, almost blue around the mouth.

"Did I just hear that?" He'd intended the question as a thought and was startled to hear the words come from his throat.

"I am reading from a report received from Washington," the voice of God continued. "The United States confirms that Jerusalem, Tel Aviv and Haifa were all targeted by nuclear warheads, and the damage in all cases was extreme to total. Initial estimated loss of life tops two million souls. Repeating . . ."

"God help us," Penn said. He stood taller, did his best to brush the wrinkles out of his uniform, and he walked around to the business side of his desk, where he took a seat.

Several other members had filtered in over the past ten or fifteen minutes, but most had been wandering about the hall outside. They'd looked numb, confused. This experience was so fundamentally disorienting that people seemed palsied by it all, as if no one knew what to do or where to go.

Penn understood. This was new territory. Other than taking shelter and saying prayers, he didn't know what his next step should be. Such was the nature of making history, he supposed.

At the back of the chamber, high atop the steeply sloped auditorium seats, the double doors crashed open, and the flood of humanity began. Unlike the Senate, the House of Representatives did not have assigned seats. Penn noted that for the first time in his decades of service in the House, the seats filled from the front of the chamber, not from the rear.

"Penn, what's happening?" someone asked.

"You know what I know," he replied. "I guess we'll all learn the details together." He pressed the communications button on the desk and said, "Pete, are you listening?"

"Yes, sir, Mr. Speaker," the young man said. "Always."

"I need a secure link to the White House right away."

"We're working on that, Mr. Speaker," Pete said. A phone buzzed on Pete's side of the glass and he picked it up. Listened. Then he pressed the button next to the boom mic. "Mr. Speaker, I was just told that the president is being evacuated to her bunker. It will be a few moments before that link can be established."

Angela Fortnight stepped from the well of the House up onto the stage. "I imagine the president is going to be distracted with military matters for the immediate future."

"Take a seat, Leader Fortnight," Penn said. To Pete: "Then get me a link to the Pentagon. Get me to someone who can tell me real-time what's going on."

"Sir, I understand your frustration, but everybody seems to be in transition. As soon as we can establish contact with anyone in the NCA, we will patch you through immediately."

Angela asked, "Did Israel get any missiles in the air?"

"If they didn't, we did it for them," Penn said. "But we don't know, do we? We don't know a goddamn thing! Peter!"

"You really think we would launch the retaliatory strike?"

"I think we'd have to. Don't you?"

"All those poor people," said House Majority Leader Randy Banks, of Nebraska.

"This is utter madness," Penn said.

Angela said, "President Blanton has no choice but to back up the Israelis."

"We've got the Russians to worry about, too." This from Mike Watters, of New Jersey's Twelfth District. "They've made it pretty clear that they would not tolerate a U.S. launch on Iran."

Penn lowered himself into his chair and shook his head. "Maybe not," he said. But he knew it was inevitable. "President Botkin is a smart man. He'll see the situation for what it is. He'll see that Iran provoked this. He'll see that our side had no choice."

"Bullshit," Banks said. "He'll see that we had every choice. He'll see that we were backing a first strike against Iran. He'll see that we're the provocateurs."

"Let's dial it back some," Angela said.

"Why?" Banks shouted. "Why dial anything back when people are dying by the millions?"

Penn slammed his desk with the palm of his hand. "Stop! We are not doing this. We are not going to tear each other apart when we don't know anything at all about—"

A bell rang from somewhere—the kind of constant ring that reminded Penn of class changes back when he was in school.

The voice of God announced, "National Command Authority has just confirmed that ballistic missiles have been launched from Russian assets off both the East and West Coasts of the United States. If they are not intercepted, impacts on U.S. targets will commence in eleven to thirteen minutes."

"Jesus God," Penn said. The rest of the chamber had fallen silent.

"Effective immediately, the Annex is on lockdown. Those members who are not yet resident shall be excluded. May God bless the United States of America."

CHAPTER TEN

THE SQUEAL OF THE CIVIL DEFENSE WARNING TONE ON MCCREA'S cell phone was the most terrifying sound Victoria had ever heard. As a child in West Virginia, the warning was a simple tone on the television or radio, sometimes combined with the wail of the fire siren, depending on where she was, in town or out in the country. Back then, everyone always knew it was a drill. Or maybe a tornado. One time, it was a forest fire. But you knew it never meant Armageddon.

Tonight it was a harsh squeal, and she knew very well what it meant. She pulled her boys close, and for the first time in a very long while, she prayed.

First Sergeant Copley reached for the radio dial, while McCrea stroked the screen of his phone. "Oh, holy shit," he said. "The Russians have launched from submarine platforms. They're launching on the U.S."

"That can't be," Victoria said. "That's mutual suicide."

"This shit's been baked into military doctrine since 1950. If we launch, they launch."

"But Iran started it. They fired the first shot."

"Does that really matter now?" McCrea said. "The Russians' first salvos will be aimed at our launch facilities. That means we need to launch back at Russia, if only to save those birds from being destroyed in their silos. In about two minutes, the entire world will be shooting at each other."

"We're about six minutes out from the trailhead," Copley said. "What's the anticipated flight time on their warheads?"

"About eleven minutes, last time I checked."

"Will we make it in time?" Caleb asked.

"We're sure going to try," McCrea said. "I'm not aware of first-wave targets within a hundred miles or so. That will buy us some time."

"What about the bunker we just left?" Victoria asked. "The Annex."

"Not a high-priority target," McCrea explained. "I don't mean to hurt your feelings, but members of the House and Senate aren't worth much without presidential leadership."

"But the Speaker of the House *becomes* president if the president and vice president are killed."

"That takes time to work out the details," McCrea replied. "You have to understand that if this war goes all the way, it won't last more than a few hours. Munitions will mostly be spent in the first hour or two, and what's left won't have the infrastructure around to launch them."

Caleb reached forward and put his hands on Copley's shoulders. "How well do you know the way?"

"GPS doesn't lie," Copley said. "After we get there, we follow a path."

"You've seen it at night, right?" Victoria asked.

The front-seat occupants exchanged looks. "After we get there, we follow a path," McCrea said. "We've only seen it on a satellite map."

Victoria read the message that lay between the lines. "Boys, get out of your seat belts."

They looked shocked. Those words had never been spoken inside a moving vehicle before.

"Luke, you climb over the seats into the back. Get our go bags and weapons. Once we stop, we're going to need to move quickly. Seconds are going to count. Seconds are going to mean everything."

"Mom, I'm scared," Luke said.

"We're all scared, sweetie," Victoria said. As she looked at his face illuminated by the orange lights of the distant dashboard, augmented by the flashing glimpses of the moon racing through the trees, she felt the approach of tears. She looked at Caleb, too. Might this be the last days of their young lives?

No. She couldn't think that way. Dark thoughts during dark times were beyond useless. They were dangerous. She didn't know if any of them would live through the next few minutes or hours, but she had to assume that they would. Otherwise, what would be the point?

Luke hoisted himself over the backseat and disappeared head-first into the cargo well. "I don't know which is which," he said.

"We can figure that out later," Victoria said. "Just hand everything over."

He lifted the rucksacks carefully over the seat backs and handed them to his brother. Each contained survival gear, and each had a Ruger 10/22 Takedown rifle Velcro'd to the side, their carry slings carefully cinched to prevent rattling. When all three were accounted for, he climbed back over and joined the family.

"Assemble and load your rifles," Victoria said.

McCrea whirled in his seat. *Kids with guns. What could possibly go wrong?* "Are they any good with those things?"

Victoria tugged first one Velcro strip and then the second one, and both halves of her rifle dropped into her free hand. "Don't worry, Major. My kids are country boys at heart. They can shoot the wings off a moving fly at twenty-five yards. They know what they're doing."

McCrea watched through the dim light as the boys assembled their firearms. "Did you teach them to assemble their weapons in the dark?" he asked.

"Not because I thought they'd ever have to do it," Victoria replied. "I wanted them to have intimate knowledge of all the working parts. It helps that the 10/22 is one of the simplest rifles in the world to take apart and put back together."

McCrea's phone squealed again, and he looked at it. "It just keeps getting worse," he said. "Looks like India and Pakistan are ramping up to high alert. That means the Chicoms are gonna follow suit. Shit. There's no way this ends well."

"I think we're going to be fine," Caleb said.

"Your lips to God's ear, kid," McCrea said.

"One mile," Copley said.

"All right," McCrea said. "Once we're out of the vehicle, if anyone finds that they're lost, or even if they lose sight of the others, shout out."

"We've all got lights," Caleb said. He pulled an elastic band over his head and centered a light between his eyebrows. "Red or white, Mom?"

"Red for now," Victoria said. "White after we're outside." The thought of the light hadn't occurred to her. She pulled hers out of its assigned pocket in her rucksack and slipped it over her head, centering the light itself in the middle of her forehead.

The sky blinked white—like a distant lightning strike—and the Suburban died.

"Shit!" Copley cursed. "It's gone. Steering, engine, everything." He stood hard on the brakes to bring them to a stop.

"What just happened?" Luke asked.

"It's begun," McCrea said. "The first detonation."

As he spoke, the sky lit up again. And again.

"We've gotta go," he said. "First Sergeant, grab the gear out of the back."

"Are we there?" Victoria asked.

"As close as we're going to get," McCrea explained as he pushed his door open. "We really need to move, folks."

"Grab your stuff and let's go," Victoria said to the boys. Caleb opened the door on his side while Victoria opened hers.

Luke followed his brother. From the other side, she heard him yell, "What happened to the car?"

"EMP," Copley explained. "Electromagnetic pulse. Nuclear explosions cause it, and they wipe out everything that has advanced circuitry."

"But my headlight is still working," Caleb said.

"No integrated circuitry," Copley said. He was at the back of the Suburban with McCrea, pulling out their own gear.

The sky lit up again, this time with staccato flashes, five or six of them in rapid succession. A few seconds later, they heard what might have been thunder, and the ground trembled under their feet.

"We are out of time," McCrea said. "First Sergeant Copley, you are the last to see a map. Lead on, please."

Copley took off at a fast jog, heading up the road in the direction they were originally headed. Caleb was next in line, followed by his brother, while Victoria, then McCrea, brought up the rear. The terrain here was steep, probably every bit of 10 percent incline. Victoria didn't think the boys would have difficulty keeping up, thanks to their soccer and lacrosse experience, but she'd have been lying if she said she wasn't concerned about the burn she felt in her own legs.

"Don't think about the pain," McCrea said, as if reading her thoughts. "It's not about the last step, it's about the next one. Left, right, left, right. Pick 'em up and put 'em down."

Three more flashes erupted in the sky—the brightest ones yet. Ten seconds later—maybe less—the pulse of a mostly spent pressure wave hit them with enough force to cause her to stagger-step to the side.

"Mom! They're getting close!"

"Keep running!"

The pressure wave brought heat as well. It rolled over them with the intensity of a heat lamp, and it continued to grow.

"This is the path!" Copley yelled, and he cut to the left. "Watch the chain!" He shouted as he cleared it in one stride, like a hurdler.

Caleb cleared it in one, too, but Luke had to stop and swing his legs over one at a time. Victoria did it Luke's way, if only to guard against catching her foot in the chain and doing a face-plant on the crumbled gravel path.

Three more flashes, these farther away, but in the strobe, she caught the maw of the mine. It was a black rectangular thing, inserted into the face of a sheer wall of rock. She'd seen similar openings from the highway traveling through mine country, but they impressed her as being bigger than this. Certainly, the ones she'd visited while campaigning had been much larger. The shaft measured about eight feet by eight feet, and the perspective given by First Sergeant Copley in the entry made it look even smaller.

Copley disappeared into the darkness beyond the opening, but Caleb and Luke stopped at the entry. They were holding hands as they turned back to wait for their mom and the major. Victoria caught a look of terrified wonderment in their faces as they stared at the sky beyond and behind her. The darkness had turned red, and the air seemed to be roiling, as if the wind were wrestling with itself.

"My God, what is that?" Victoria asked no one in particular.

"The world is on fire," McCrea said.

"What about Adam?" Luke asked. "Is he going to be okay?"

The next pressure wave knocked them all to the ground.

Adam Emerson rolled onto his back, totally spent, totally satisfied. "Wow," he said.

Emma rolled with him and laid her head on his chest, tickling his nipple with her fingers. "Yeah," she said. "Wow. Happy birthday."

"Maybe I should bring a lighter-weight sleeping bag next time."

Adam blamed the weatherman. The news said the temperature would dip into the fifties tonight, so he'd packed accordingly. He doubted that it ever got below seventy. Welcome to the mountains of West Virginia.

"So, Emma Carson, how does it feel not to be a felon anymore?"

She lifted her head. "Huh?"

"I'm finally eighteen. You're not a child abuser anymore." He yelped when Emma grabbed a fistful of his crotch and squeezed.

"*Now* I'm an abuser," she said.

"Hurts sooo good . . ."

She squeezed harder. "Age of consent is sixteen."

"Okay, okay. Hurts not so good."

She let go and gave him a little rub.

"Uh-oh," Adam said. "I think the swelling started." He rolled his hips away before she could do something *really* painful.

Emma pulled the sleeping bag open, sat upright, then zipped open the tent door.

"Where are you going?"

He couldn't see her face, but he knew she was giving him her signature look.

"Do you really want to know?"

"Ah."

Some details didn't need to be shared in a relationship. But now that he thought about it, he needed to take care of that detail, too. He let her have a head start, then climbed out into the night. Emma had wandered off to the left, toward the woods, so Adam wandered right, toward the rock ledge.

The air was chillier than he had thought, but it felt good against his overheated flesh. When he was finished, he turned back toward the tent and was startled to see Emma standing there, watching him. Bathed in the blue light of the full moon, she looked unearthly, like something from a movie.

They'd met a month ago at a mixer held by Joan of Arc Academy, the sister school for the Clinton M. Hedrick Military Academy. Both schools considered themselves to be virgin vaults, but the respective headmasters understood that boys and girls needed to be boys and girls, and they arranged a heavily chaperoned dance every month.

Adam fell in lust with Emma the first time he saw her, but he had always considered her to be the unattainable prize. She was that gorgeous, from the perfect body to the flaming-red hair. And the blinding smile. It took him three mixers to spin up the courage to ask her to dance. He nearly fell over when she said yes. She'd even chastised him for not having asked earlier.

God only knew how many demerits he'd have to walk off for skipping out for this birthday bacchanal, but it wouldn't matter. It wasn't exactly his first time, but it was his first with someone for whom it was not.

"Were you watching me pee?"

"I wanted to see how many times you shook it. My brother tells me that if you shake it more than twice, you're playing with it."

Adam rolled his eyes. "It's a little creepy to be talking about your brother's dick."

Emma wandered up and hugged him. "You're a very special guy, Adam Emerson. A beautiful night, in a beautiful spot. You were here for school before? Is that what you said?"

"Mountain survival training," Adam explained. "Kind of bullshit exercise, but kind of fun, too. Four times a year, instructors blindfold us, put us in the back of a van and then drop us off at different spots so we can fend for ourselves for a few days. It starts in ninth grade, but those kids are dropped off in groups of four and they have radios."

"Do they have to hunt to eat?"

"No, not the ninth graders. They get MREs. Meals ready to eat. Tenth graders are dropped off with only one partner, plus MREs. Then when you're a junior, you do it solo with MREs. This will be my first solo year without MREs."

Emma looked horrified. They'd established earlier that this outing was her first stab at camping. She came from piles of family money to whom camping meant luxury accommodations with a less-than-full service in-room dining menu. "What are you going to eat?"

"Whatever I find, I guess. We've been training on nuts and berries and shit, but I'm hoping they'll give me some fishing gear. A rifle would be nice, but I know that won't happen. Maybe a knife? I don't know. We go next weekend."

Emma hugged him again. "That sounds terrible and terrifying."

Somehow that made Adam feel better. More manly, perhaps.

"I'm getting cold," she said. "Let's go back inside and sweat some more."

Little Adam liked that idea as much as its owner did. Emma

grabbed his hand, and they hop-marched over the feet-unfriendly mulch back to the tent and the sleeping bag.

Round Two was as terrific as Round One.

Spooned up on his left side, pressed up against Emma, sleep had nearly swallowed Adam when the night erupted in light. It was like a flash of daylight that penetrated their flysheet and tent and highlighted the blood vessels of his eyelids, even with them closed.

"Holy shit!"

Emma made a yipping noise that he'd never heard before.

Adam was struggling to kick his way out of the sleeping bag when the pressure wave hit. The boom had the same quality of those bright bursting charges during fireworks displays, but instead of that single pulse of noise, the boom kept rolling. The mountain shook and the surrounding trees swayed.

A few seconds later, it happened again.

And again.

Adam found himself screaming, but he didn't know why, or even if he was making noise. Emma clung to him tightly enough to hurt his neck.

He was dimly aware that the air smelled bad. It had a chemical quality to it, unlike anything he'd smelled before. It smelled hot. It smelled awful.

He finally got free of the fabric of the sleeping bag and crawled through the tent flap out into the night.

"Wait!" Emma yelled. "Don't leave me."

"I'm not," he promised, and he turned around to offer her a hand so she could join him outside.

Holding on to each other, they took in the horror. In the distance, the head of a mushroom cloud roiled like an image from hell. Fiery reds and yellows wrestled with blacks and oranges. As it rose higher, the intensity of the inferno seemed to increase.

"Is that a bomb?" Emma asked.

"I think so," Adam said. He pivoted his head to the left and pointed. "And over there, too. And there. Holy shit." The other mushrooms glowed less intensely, perhaps because they were farther away, perhaps for other reasons. Adam had neither the knowledge nor the vocabulary to decide.

Emma said, "We're going to die."

The night flashed four more times in no more than a couple of seconds. In a half minute or so, the booms arrived. These were distant, yet still powerful.

"We must be under attack," Adam said. "Why? Who?"

"We need to get out of here," Emma said. She turned and started to run into the night, away from the vista of destruction.

"Wait!" Adam yelled. Emma kept running and Adam took off after her. "Stop, goddammit! I'm naked! So are you!" In the dark, every irregularity of the forest floor tore at the soles of his feet.

As if on cue, Emma yelped and pulled up short, dancing on one foot. "Shit!"

Adam caught up with her. "Where are you going?"

"Those are bombs!" Emma shouted. "Friggin' *bombs*!"

"But we weren't hit!" Adam shouted back.

"We don't have any shelter out here," Emma said.

"Do you know a place where there *is* shelter?"

Emma just stared back at him. Then, "We can't just stay out here in the open."

Adam looked around. They had the protection of big rocks and tall trees. All things considered, he could think of way worse places to be. "Let's at least go back and get dressed."

"Then what?"

"I have no idea," Adam said.

Adam led the way back to their tent. On all fours, he crawled past the flap and over his sleeping bag to get to his rucksack. He tore open the Velcro flap and yanked a little emergency radio out of its pocket. He turned it on.

"Emergency, emergency, emergency," he said after keying the mic. "Anyone on the channel, please respond."

He was transmitting on a channel that was reserved exclusively for emergency traffic and was routinely monitored by emergency services and hobbyists alike. He released the transmit key and listened for a reply. Nothing.

He repeated the emergency call, then added, “This is Adam Emerson and Emma Carson. We’re students.”

While he waited for a reply, he lay on his back and pulled on his underwear and pants, then sat up to don his T-shirt and shirt. Next to him, Emma was also dressing. She fished her smart phone from her pants. “This won’t even turn on,” she said.

He tried the radio again as he handed his phone to Emma. “Use mine. It’s fully charged.”

Adam two-fingered his hiking boots and backed out into the glowing night. He tried the radio one more time. “They’re not answering,” he told Emma when she emerged from the tent.

“Try again. Your phone’s dead, too.”

Adam transmitted his emergency message again, but the radio remained silent. “Do you think maybe everybody’s dead?”

“I don’t want to,” Emma replied.

Adam spread his boot open and pulled the tongue out. What the hell was happening? How the hell *could* it be happening? Could they be the only people left in the world? Was that even possible?

“Oh, my God, Adam. We’re on our own.”

“We don’t know that,” he said. “Never assume the worst.”

“Is that another truism from your mom?”

Adam didn’t answer. With his bootlaces tied, he stood and wandered back to the overlook. A weird blackness had settled over everything out where the explosions had happened. It was as if the blasts had extinguished the moonlight. He figured it must be the result of all the debris and smoke.

The light inside the roiling cloud finally went out, leaving the night so dark that Adam wondered with a flash of panic that maybe he’d gone blind. A distant part of his brain pinged with a memory that staring at a nuclear detonation would fry your retinas. Within a few seconds, though, shadows returned.

Emma sidled in next to him and squeezed his hand. “This is really, really bad, isn’t it?” she asked.

“Yeah, I think it is.”

“Are we at war?”

"I don't know. Maybe. Probably."

"What are we going to do, Adam?"

He sighed and swallowed hard against the emotion in his throat. What the hell *were* they going to do? It was nearly September already, and in this part of West Virginia, the temperatures would start to drop soon. Hell, despite the heat of the fireballs, it felt ten degrees cooler than just a few minutes ago.

He had a hand ax and a shovel in his rucksack, along with a survival knife and some food that he'd intended for breakfast tomorrow, but that wasn't enough to survive. They weren't the right tools to build shelters. And they didn't have the clothes they needed to maintain warmth. Hell, they didn't even have the weapons available to hunt the game that would get them the pelts they needed to make warm enough clothing.

Adam turned to face her. "We need to find our way back to your car. Get back to school."

"Can you find it at night?"

That was a great question. He had a compass and a map, and he knew how to use them, but he didn't pay close enough attention on the hike in to shoot a reverse azimuth that would take them back. He could get them to the fire trail they'd used as a road, but from there, they'd have to pick their way to the car.

"Do we know that the schools are still there?"

"We have to assume they are. Don't we? I mean, we need shelter. And supplies."

"Maybe it's safer to stay out here."

Adam thought about that. This was the stuff his mom had trained him for. "As long as we stay away from cities, I think we'll be okay. Those people are going to be crazy. The ones who aren't dead are gonna be burned and panicked."

"Jesus, Adam."

"I don't know if I told you, but my mother's a prepper. I spent most of my childhood preparing for the end of times."

"Seriously?"

"Seriously."

"So it *is* safer to stay out here."

Adam took her hand and guided them both to the ground. He folded his feet under his thighs. "A shit ton of people were just killed."

Emma buried her face in her hands and gave herself up to sobs that exploded from her core. Adam pulled her close and stroked her hair. He knew he should be feeling more than he did, but it wasn't there. This was a lot to comprehend in a few minutes. Maybe it would catch up with him later.

When Emma's sobs had diminished to snuffles, he got back to what she needed to know. "All those sick, hurt people will all be wanting help. They'll be wanting to run away into the forest because they'll assume that this is the safer place to be. Problem is, they won't know what the hell to do once they get out here. If you can't find it in a grocery store and pay for it on your smartphone, they won't have a clue."

"So they'll just starve?"

"Not willingly, they won't," Adam said. "What they'll do is panic. They're going to go back to being wild animals. If survival means killing others and taking their stuff, that's what they'll do. We need to go back to the school because we need friendly company."

"You don't have a lot of faith in people, do you?"

"People just dropped bombs on us. When people are cornered, they turn mean. They'll do what it takes to survive, and if that means killing you and me, that's what they'll do. Fights are coming at us where there'll only be winners or losers. My mom calls it the zero-sum game."

"Your family actually *talked* about this stuff?"

"We practiced for it. I always thought it was crazy. Now look where we are."

"So, should we be walking toward the car now?"

"Let's give it a few minutes," Adam said. "We know we're safe here now, and it seems pretty clear that there aren't any targets to hit. Maybe there'll be a second wave."

Emma's grip tightened on his hand. "We should pray."

"I imagine God's pretty busy right now." That came out more harshly than he'd wanted. He bowed his head.

They sat in silence for a good thirty seconds. Finally Emma confessed, "I–I don't know what to say."

"Do you think it matters that you say the actual words? I think God gets it." *But, man, was He asleep at the switch a little while ago.*

"I wonder if my family is still alive," Adam mused aloud.

"I was just thinking the same thing. It's like I can't wrap my head around it all. It's so . . . huge."

Adam wanted to cry, knew he should be crying, but it wasn't there. Nothing was there. He felt as if all the emotion had been carved out of him. Jesus, how many millions of people had just died? And he didn't feel anything. Did that make him a monster?

"What about the radiation?" Emma asked.

"Radiation is what it will be," he said. "If you can't do anything about it, it's not worth worrying about."

"More wisdom from your mother?"

"Yep. But it's logical, too. God grant me the serenity, and all that."

They lay back on the ground and Emma put her head back on Adam's chest. As the fireballs and their aftermath dissolved into the atmosphere, it was almost impossible to look away. "You really trained for nuclear attacks?"

"Yep. Well, all kinds of disasters, really. Tornados, wars, armed rebellion, pandemic, whatever." He took a deep breath. "Like I said, everybody's going to want to head to the rural regions when the cities are on fire. When my brothers and I went through all the bullshit drills with our mom, we would march into the woods and hunt and fish and learn to live off the grid. Mom wanted us to be among the lucky few who knew what we were doing."

"Did she think you'd have to actually do it?"

"Knowing my mom, yeah, probably."

"She's that cynical and she's a member of Congress?"

He opted not to answer that. Tonight had been a pretty vivid demonstration of a cynical outlook proving to be a realistic one.

"The radiation terrifies me," Emma said. "I know, Serenity Prayer. But still."

"I get it," Adam said. "I don't know if this makes you feel better or worse, but look at it realistically. We've already been hit with the worst of it. *Bang.* Just that fast. What happens next, happens next."

Emma's head rolled to look at him. "I don't believe how okay you are with all this."

Time for honesty. "I'm scared shitless, Em. So what? Being scared doesn't make anything better. In fact, it makes pretty much everything worse. You can't think straight when you're panicking. Mom even used to train us for managing panic."

"Bullshit. How?"

"We did crazy shit." He allowed himself a laugh. "One time, we were in a shopping mall—I was maybe nine years old—and I guess I wandered off. Or maybe they wandered off."

"They?"

"Mom and my brothers. To teach me a lesson, I guess, she didn't try to find me. She just went home and waited."

"She didn't call the cops or anything?"

"Nope. Obviously, I found my way home, but she told me that actions have consequences, and that as a single mom, she wasn't always going to be there to cover for me."

"Jesus, you'd go to jail for that now."

"Maybe. But the training worked. I've got a lot of bad traits I've got to work on fixing, but I should be anyone's number one first choice as company during an emergency."

"I'll keep that in mind."

There was another piece to what he wanted to say, but he wasn't sure this was the time. "Oh, what the hell?" he said.

"Huh?"

"I want to prepare you for something," he said. "You need to remember to act only on what you *know* at times like these. Right now, we don't know anything about any of what's going on. We're assuming we're at war, and we're assuming that millions of people have been killed. But we don't *know* that."

"I'm not following," Emma said.

He tried again. "We need to stay one hundred percent in the moment all the time. That's what survival is all about. There's not a creature within a hundred miles who's not going to be suffering. Some are hurt, a lot are dead and a lot are going to be. *Everything.* Foxes, cougars, squirrels and humans. They're all going to be hungry and none of them is going to give a shit about you or me if we're between them and their next meal."

"So cut to the chase," Emma said. "What are you not telling me?"

"From here on out, everyone is your enemy until they prove themselves to be a friend."

CHAPTER ELEVEN

Penn Glendale had just gaveled this session of the House of Representatives to order when the television screens in the House Chamber went dark. *Boom.* No flicker, no image wobble. Just dark. The assembled members gasped as one. A few shouted curses. Penn thought he heard someone crying.

"What just happened?" Penn asked to anyone who might answer. "Pete, buddy, talk to me." In the shielded booth in the back of the chamber, Peter Clostner, a Solara employee, was working frantically to establish some level of communication with the rest of the world.

"I don't know," the technician replied. In his booth, he looked to be randomly pushing buttons. "Comms are all down. All of them."

"Well, bring them back up!"

"It's not us," Clostner said. "All of *our* stuff is working fine. At least so far as I can tell."

Representative Lianne Holt, of Delaware's Second, stood from her seat and waited to be recognized by the Speaker.

"The gentle lady from Delaware."

"I think Washington just got hit."

Penn glared at her from the rostrum. "You *think*? Based on what?"

"Based on war plans that have been in place for years," she said.

"Remember, Mr. Speaker, I was in the Air Force before I was a member of Congress. The White House, Pentagon and Capitol have had crosshairs on them for generations."

"But they're hardened, aren't they?" Angela asked.

Lianne looked to the Speaker for guidance.

Penn's instincts were to lash out at Leader Fortnight for not following the rules dictating how members were recognized to speak, but softened his approach. "I suppose under these extraordinary circumstances, we can loosen the rules a little. Let's just make sure that we're all having the same conversation, only one speaker at a time." He nodded to the gentle lady from Delaware.

"None of the buildings in Washington are shielded from direct hits," Lianne explained. "And certainly not from the strategic weapons we always assumed would be the primary package for major cities such as DC and New York. We called them city killers. Nothing can be hardened against those."

Someone said, "I don't think it's helpful to speculate on things like this." Penn didn't recognize the voice. Probably from a freshman member.

Representative Holt continued as if not interrupted. "Remember how nuclear attacks happen. It's not just a single warhead on a high-value target like the Pentagon, where they have God knows how many basements. They'll hit it with several to make sure it's really dead—and also as a safety in case the first bomb didn't make it to target for some reason."

"What about here at the Annex?" Angela asked. Her voice cracked with anxiety.

Scott Johnson answered that question from the top of the chamber. "We couldn't survive even a smaller tactical warhead. And we're a hell of a lot newer than any building in official Washington."

Penn slapped the table with his open palm, making nearly everyone in the chamber jump in their seats. "Mr. Johnson, you do not belong here."

Johnson kept going. "We have some deflection technology that's designed to confuse incoming birds in hopes of sending them a mile or two off course, but if a warhead lands on our roof, we're toast."

Penn slammed the table again. "That's enough, Mr. Johnson."

"I just thought you should know."

"Do *you* know why our communications are down?" asked Representative Jack Collins, of Montana.

Johnson said, "I believe the gentle lady from Delaware is correct. I don't have proof of that, of course. Not yet, anyway. But the situation is consistent with Washington being no longer a factor."

The very possibility of this was beyond comprehension. Penn stared at the assembled members of Congress, and while he realized he had to do something, nothing came to mind. He'd lived in Washington for so long that everyone he knew, everything he understood, was there. His wife and daughter and three of his grandchildren all lived in Northwest Washington. If the predictions he'd just heard were true, he'd just lost everyone.

As the realization poured over the House Chamber, people started to wail. They cried. Kent Kiser, of Missouri, spewed profanity, none of which seemed focused on anyone in particular.

Penn needed to reel this in somehow. Now was a time for action. They'd have all of eternity to mourn. He rapped on the table with his knuckle, wishing with each strike that the Solara folks had thought to provide him with a gavel. "Ladies and gentlemen of the United States Congress," he said. When he saw that he'd attracted only a few people's attention, he repeated himself, and then pounded the table with his hand again.

"Ladies and gentlemen of the United States Congress, we cannot get ahead of ourselves on this. We don't know anything, other than the fact the communications are down, and that the Solara people are looking into that. Isn't that right, Mr. Johnson?"

"It's our first priority, Mr. Speaker."

"Very well. Is Representative Colson in the chamber?"

A dark-haired gaunt doppelganger for Ichabod Crane stood from a chair three-quarters of the way up the banked chamber. Oscar Colson was the majority whip, and a friend of Penn's for nearly twenty years. "I'm right here, Mr. Speaker."

"And Representative Grogan. Are you in the chamber?"

Anna Grogan, minority whip, raised her hand from the third row, on Penn's right. "Right here," she said. Her face had drained of color, and her red-rimmed eyes gave her the appearance of the living dead.

"Are you all right, Mrs. Grogan?"

"As all right as anyone, I suppose. Which means, of course, I'm not all right. But do you need something?"

Penn bobbed his head. He wished for a return to the normalcy of *Robert's Rules* and stilted language. Was civil language the first casualty of this new war?

"Mr. Colson and Ms. Grogan, I would like you to work together and get an accurate count of who is present in the chamber. As importantly, I want to know who is *not* here."

"You mean, take roll?" Colson asked. He sounded incredulous.

"Exactly that," Penn said. "We seem to be short on clerical staff at the moment."

"To what end?"

"Please. Just *please.*"

Representative Grogan arose and sidestepped past other members' feet and knees to make her way toward the closest aisle.

Penn looked up to the A/V booth. "Pete, talk to me. What've you got?"

"Nothing good," the technician said. "NORAD is down, I can't reach Cheyenne Mountain and now I'm trying STRATCOM at Offutt."

Penn shifted his gaze to Representative Holt.

"Those are all major commands that have no doubt been pretargeted," she said.

"Maybe we should try some Navy installations," Angela Fortnight suggested. "Or Army."

"Or Marines," Penn said.

"All are on the list, Mr. Speaker," Scott Johnson reported. "We'll keep trying until we find something."

Kent Kiser raised his hand. "What are we doing here, exactly? What are we *supposed* to be doing?"

"Our jobs," Penn replied. "War and reconstruction are expensive endeavors. The House of Representatives is the only agency within the government that can appropriate the necessary funds."

"And then what?" Kiser pressed. From Missouri's Seventh Congressional District, Kiser was an acolyte of Angela Fortnight's, and ever since taking office, he'd harbored a bitter dislike for Penn Glendale and anything the Speaker stood for. "Who's going to sign the appropriation bills? And what are we going to pay them with? I'm betting that people aren't going to give much of a shit tomorrow about paper money."

"Decorum!" Penn snapped. "Watch your language, sir. This is still the House Chamber."

"Is it really? Or is it just a converted theater?"

Angela Fortnight arose from her seat. "Kent, you're really not helping here. Everyone is stressed."

"You think?"

"Bad language and sarcasm don't help," Angela said.

Kiser stood in place for a few seconds, as if considering what to say next, and then he plopped himself back into his seat like a petulant child.

Members of Congress had been at each other's throats for over a decade. Fanned by rhetorical winds, the fires of partisanship seemed to burn hotter with every passing week. For over ten years—that's five Congresses—the fracture within the Capitol had transformed comity to a zero-sum blood sport. Any proposal raised by one party was reflexively torpedoed by the opposite party, merit of the legislation notwithstanding. As the two caucuses maneuvered for position, and polarization became more extreme, the result had been to effectively drive more and more power to the White House, whose occupants of necessity became progressively more dictatorial, governing by executive order.

After Penn had been elected to the Speaker's chair, he genuinely thought he had a plan to change things. After twelve consecutive terms representing his constituents in Danville, Virginia, he thought he could leverage the friendships he'd developed over three decades on both sides of the aisle to mine compromise from the intractability that had ossified the House. And if he'd had even a slightly larger majority, or if the president had been from his party, he believed he could have made it happen.

But that would have spelled some measure of success for Penn's party. After an election that left Helen Blanton and Angela Fortnight wanting unified control more than they wanted progress, success for Penn would have meant failure for them.

So, here they were, at the nation's most desperate moment of crisis, and he was getting lip from the likes of Kiser and Grogan. Sometimes Penn wondered if the television cameras and the dueling partisan news feeds were the only elements that kept members from literally killing each other. With those checks both gone, he worried that he did not possess the leadership skills that would be necessary to keep this deliberative body from sailing off the tracks.

The voice of God announced, "I've got something! High-tech comms are all dead, but we've got something on an analog channel."

"What does *got something* mean?" Penn asked.

"I'm putting you through," Pete announced. "Go ahead, Beale Air Force Base. You're speaking to the assembled members of the House of Representatives."

After a ten-second pause that featured a lot of static, a hesitant male voice spoke from the speakers on the walls and ceiling. "Um, hello?"

Penn said, "Hello, this is Penn Glendale, Speaker of the United States House of Representatives. With whom am I speaking?"

"You guys made it? I thought DC was gone. That's what they're saying here."

"Slow down," Penn said. "First of all, who are you?"

"I am Captain Cole Brinks, USAF. That's *B-R-I-N-K-S.* I'm speaking to you from Beale Air Force Base in California. What's happening, sir?"

Penn's mind raced with countless questions he wanted to ask—like, why was he speaking to an O-3 captain instead of a flag officer—but he realized that such questions were mostly irrelevant at the moment. "Tell us what *you* know, Captain. Were you guys hit, and if so, how badly?"

"Yes, sir, we were hit in what we believe was the second wave. I don't know the extent of the damage, but I can tell you that my airmen and I are trapped in our bunker."

Penn sat taller. Did that bit of news run counter to the gloomy assessment presented by Lianne Holt and Mr. Johnson? "What kind of bunker, Captain?"

Hesitation. "I–I'm not at liberty to tell you that, sir."

Penn felt his ears redden. "You're speaking to the House of Representatives."

Another hesitation. "How do I know that?"

Penn started to answer, then realized that he had no response. When he scanned the faces of the other members, he only got stares and shrugs.

"Okay, I guess that's fair. I can tell you that I am speaking from a bunker of our own, at a place called the Annex, or the U.S. Government Relocation Center. We have lost all contact with the White House and the Pentagon. In fact, this phone call right here—or whatever the hell it is—is our first official contact in over two hours. If you've got information—any information at all—then I'd be delighted to hear it."

"I'm afraid we don't have much, sir. Our bunker is not exactly on the base, if you know what I mean. We're at one of those secret, undisclosed locations people used to talk about. But I can tell you that we specialize in . . . *communication.*"

Penn interpreted the way the captain leaned on that word as a verbal wink and elbow poke. Captain Brinks was a spy-slash-electronic eavesdropper.

The captain continued, "The bad guys—we think it was the Russians, but we're not sure. Could have been the Chicoms. The first munition they launched was an EMP warhead. It wiped out pretty much all civilian electronics. God only knows how many airliners fell out of the sky."

"This is Angela Fortnight, House minority leader. Were we able to launch a retaliatory strike?"

Another long pause. Penn could feel the captain's anxiety

through the phone line. "Ma'am, that's not exactly my corner of the Air Force. I believe we did, yes, but I can't speak to the extent. I know for a fact that we tried, but we were caught a little flat-footed. I guess that's why we have subs parked off the coast of everyplace. I just don't know."

"How is your team there in the bunker doing?" Penn asked.

"We're not hurt, if that's what you mean. We've got backup battery power for three days, and enough food for about the same amount of time. We've got water for a week, I guess."

"When will it be safe for you to climb out of there?" Penn asked. "I mean, how long before the radiation levels are low enough?"

"For right now, sir, the radiation levels aren't what are keeping us inside. There's a crazy series of steps you've got to take to get in here. Multiple air locks, that sort of thing. When that second wave hit, at least one of the hatches got jammed shut. We've got to figure out a way to unjam it. Hey, sir? Mr. Speaker? What do you know about everything else? Is the war still going? Did anybody win?"

The irony of the thought of winning Armageddon was not lost on Penn. "We're in the dark on that, too, Captain."

"Wait. Hold one, Mr. Speaker. We've got some traffic coming in."

It wasn't until Captain Brinks returned to his microphone that Penn realized that he'd been holding his breath.

"You still there, sir?" The captain's voice sounded shaky.

"We haven't moved," Penn said.

"Sir, I'm afraid the news is bad. We got an alert on a very low-frequency band, an encrypted one from Fort Hood in Texas. According to this, we lost big-time."

Penn's stomach tightened as emotion pressed on his eyes. He avoided eye contact with anyone as he asked, "Can you be more specific than that, son?"

"Okay, now remember that this is a dynamic situation, right? I don't know how factual this is, or even if the sender is who he says he is. Though the fact of the encryption adds some credibility."

"You're talking to yourself, Captain," Angela snapped. "You're not making sense to the rest of us."

"Sorry about that, ma'am. It's just a lot to swallow. Okay, here goes. According to the report, the president, vice president and SECDEF are all dead. I don't have the details on how they died, and, again, this is all officially unverified."

Penn was on the edge of losing his temper. "This is critical information, Captain. I promise you that we understand that it is less than one hundred percent accurate, and that if every word of it proves to be incorrect, we will not hold you responsible. Please continue."

"Yes, sir. At least thirteen major cities in the U.S. are just gone. They got hit with strategic nukes, and there's nothing left. The list I have shows Washington, New York, Chicago, Omaha, Denver and Colorado Springs, Los Angeles, San Francisco, Seattle, Atlanta, Nashville, Dallas and Houston. I don't know whether or not that list is final. Our military facilities all took a hell of a hit, too, both here and in other countries. All the NATO countries got dragged in. I don't have any statistics on anything outside the U.S."

Penn lowered his forehead onto his folded arm atop his table. Tens of millions of people, all of them gone within the run time of a motion picture. "Jesus," he said.

He raised his head again and settled himself with a breath. It was time to lead again.

New York's Latasha Washington stood from the left side of the chamber and said, "Captain Brinks? Can you hear me?"

"Yes, ma'am, I can. It got real quiet there for a second."

"What is left of your command structure? Where are your orders coming from?"

"I don't have any orders, ma'am. And I don't have any idea who's in charge. I was hoping you could tell me."

"I am in charge," Penn announced. "The Twenty-fifth Amendment makes it crystal clear that with POTUS and VPOTUS both dead, the Speaker of the House becomes president." As he uttered the words, he wondered if he might throw up. He had no idea what he'd just taken charge of, and he had no idea how physically to make any of this work, but he could think of no better, more literal example of a time when failure was not an option.

The chamber rumbled with discontent, but no one was yet willing to commit to any comments to the record.

"Captain, as your new commander in chief, I have my first order for you. I want you to stay on the line and work with my comms guy Pete to find a way to reestablish real-time avenues of communication. This darkness has to end."

"Yes, sir," Captain Brinks said.

Pete's voice of God added, "You've got it, Mr. President."

A chill shot through Penn as he heard those words directed to him. *Mr. President.* It was a job he'd never wanted, never campaigned for, yet here it was, under the worst possible circumstances. He turned to Arlen Strasky, who had seated himself among the members. Penn hoped that through eye contact alone, his chief of staff would answer his most terrifying question: *How can we be sure the president is dead?*

Majority Leader Randy Banks stood at his seat.

"Leader Banks," Penn said.

With brown hair, brown eyes and of average height, Randy Banks cut as unimpressive a figure as a man could cut, but he was a brilliant strategist when it came to party leadership. "Mr. President," he said, "we need to get you sworn in."

Penn felt heavier in his seat, as if literally taking on the weight of awesome and awful responsibility. "I'm not taking the oath of office until I am sure that President Blanton and Vice President Jenkins are both gone. We can't have two presidents."

"With due respect, sir," Banks continued, "right now, we don't even have one president. The nation needs leadership, sir. Whether or not Helen Blanton has a heartbeat is irrelevant. Ditto Clarence Jenkins. Right now, *no one* is leading. Assuming, of course, that's there's anything left to lead."

Arlen Strasky stood at his seat. "Mr. President."

Angela Fortnight jumped to her feet. "Point of order, Mr. Speaker." Chiefs of staff were to be seen and not heard in the halls of Congress.

"Loosened rules, remember?" Penn said. "Go ahead, Arlen."

"I think Mr. Banks is right," Strasky said. "The nation needs leadership from the presidency. They need a commander in chief. The Twenty-fifth allows that power to be ceded temporarily, but that requires a piece of paper we don't have, and one we can't wait for. You need to be sworn in, sir."

Angela Fortnight rose from her chair. "Mr. Speaker," she said, "what are you doing? This is not how the process works."

"In a minute," Penn said. He shielded his eyes as he searched for a face in the crowd. "Mr. Johnson, are you still in the chamber?"

Johnson waved from rear of the chamber. "Here, sir."

"Approach the rostrum, please."

Johnson descended the stairs two at a time. "Pete is working with Captain Brinks to keep communication lines open," he said as he approached. "Those guys are in seriously deep shit out there at Beale. It's entirely possible that they'll starve to death over the next week or two."

"Watch your language," Penn said. "And let's not forget that millions of people died today, and millions more will likely die in the days ahead." The words were barely out of his mouth when he regretted them. Especially the tone of them. "You mentioned that there's a plan for swearing me in as president. How does that work?"

Johnson gestured to the curtains at the front of the chamber, behind the flags of the armed services. "Behind those screens are two backdrops. One is the Capitol Building and the other is the White House. Give us a few minutes to reset things up here, and bring in some cameras, and we'll put you in front of the Capitol backdrop to swear you in. We have a lectern and Bible specifically for that purpose. Then, after you've had a chance to gather your thoughts, we'll put you in front of the White House backdrop to speak to the nation."

"Who's going to hear the speech?" Banks asked.

Johnson shrugged one shoulder. "Whoever's listening. Remember, our comms are all still in fine shape. We can beam you up to the satellite, and from there, the signal goes out just as it always would."

"The world needs to hear from the president of the United States under these circumstances," Penn said. "And the sooner, the better."

"Mr. Speaker!" Angela shouted. "Stop! A rumor that the president and vice president are dead does not suffice as confirmation. The Twenty-fifth Amendment requires some very specific steps for the Speaker to accede to the presidency, and none of those have been met."

Banks said, "Leader Fortnight, the nation needs a leader."

"Not at the cost of the republic! This is a critical juncture, Penn. When all of this is over, however it ends, the world will judge us not just by the actions of the nation, but by our adherence to the rule of law. You cannot simply declare yourself to be president."

Penn glared at her for a full five or six seconds, then made his shoulders relax. He wanted to argue, but he knew she was right. In the House of Representatives, process and procedures mattered.

"Very well," he said. "Mr. Johnson, thank you. We won't be needing a Bible or a backdrop anytime soon. Please leave the rostrum."

"Yes, Mr. President."

"Nope. It's still Mr. Speaker for a while. When I address the nation, it will be as Speaker, not as president."

Strasky stepped forward to argue, but Penn shooed him away. "Not now, Arlen. You need to leave the rostrum as well. You're welcome to stay in the chamber, but remember your place."

Penn took his seat and rapped on the table. "Ladies and gentlemen, we are sailing uncharted waters in a raging sea. Leader Fortnight has raised a valid point. Americans beyond our bunker are going insane trying simply to stay alive. If they don't hear from us for a while, I don't imagine it will do much harm. And, frankly, I'm not sure what we know to tell them."

He scanned the faces in the room. All he saw was fear and sadness. All he felt was fear and sadness.

"The fact of the matter," Penn continued, "is that we don't

know what we don't know. We don't know why things went so terribly wrong, and we don't know how bad conditions really are. We don't know who needs our help, or what help they need. We don't know what resources are available to share. We don't know what is left of our armed forces, or of those of our enemies. Come to think of it, I don't think we're one hundred percent sure we even know who our enemy is."

He let his words hang for a few seconds as he continued to observe his colleagues in the chamber. He wanted to remember every detail of this awful day.

"So," he said, gently rapping his table, "if anyone has any ideas, I'm open to listening to them."

CHAPTER TWELVE

THEY HADN'T HEARD AN EXPLOSION IN OVER AN HOUR. MCCREA didn't know how long the bombing had lasted but it was a good long time. Given the magnitude of the weaponry, he figured that hearing them did not equate necessarily to them being close. Back in the days of open testing in the Nevada desert, people heard those detonations over a hundred miles away. The last few tonight had been more felt than heard, little more than vibrations through the rock.

He'd led the family deep into the mine—he estimated it to be one hundred yards, give or take, and with each increment of forward progress, the passage had become smaller. He'd stopped when further progress would mean either walking with their backs bent like an L or crawling on hands and knees. This was a shelter, not an exploration. He'd brought them to a halt.

To save battery power, they'd turned off their flashlights, leaving everyone bathed in a darkness that was beyond black. McCrea thought he might be able to discern a dim red glow coming from the area of the entrance, but that might have been his imagination. A longtime claustrophobe, he had to fight off a new wave of approaching panic with every passing second.

"Mom?" It was Luke, his disembodied voice echoing in the dark.

"I'm right here, baby. Follow the sound of my voice to come to me."

"How long are we going to stay in here?" he asked.

"Major?"

That was a damn good question, McCrea thought.

"I don't like it in here," Caleb said. "I'd rather be outside. In here, we don't have anything. I don't like the walls being so close."

"I don't like that, either," McCrea said. Sooner or later, they were going to have to go out and face what was left of the world. Now seemed as good a time as any. "I'm going to go back to the entrance and see—"

"No!" Caleb shouted. "You got us into this place. You're not leaving without us."

"I'm not leaving, son—"

"I'm not your son."

Even a Third World War couldn't tamp down adolescent attitude. "I'm not leaving, Caleb. I'm just going to take a look at what it's like out there."

"Then we can all take a look," Caleb said. Their world flashed a blinding white light as Caleb flipped his light back on. He quickly switched it over to red. "Sorry."

"I'm going, too," Luke said, and his light joined his brother's, going directly to red.

"I'm just trying to keep everyone safe," McCrea said.

"I think that horse might have already fled the barn," Victoria said. "This position is untenable. It has no resources. Assuming that the bombs have stopped falling—and that's how it seems—this place offers nothing of value to us."

"Those fires looked pretty bad." This from First Sergeant Copley.

Victoria stood gently, taking care not to hit her head on the ceiling. "Let's go take a look."

McCrea stood with her. "Mrs. Emerson, I cannot protect your family if you won't let me do my job."

Victoria slid the switch to bring her own light to life and she bathed the major's face in a red glow that made him look comically demonic. "Major McCrea, I have already tried to fire you twice. You have no lingering obligation to protect me or my family."

"Well, here we are," McCrea said. "Together, anyway. I'm only trying to help." He proffered his hand. "Let's start over. Call me Joe."

Victoria returned his grasp. "Vicky."

"Yes, ma'am."

She turned to the other soldier and extended her hand. "First Sergeant Copley? Vicky."

"I'm Paul, ma'am."

Victoria gathered her sons, an arm over each. "Caleb, Luke, Joe and Paul. My four protectors. Now let's take a peek."

The walk back to the mouth of the mineshaft didn't seem nearly as long as the walk in. As they progressed toward the opening, the red glow McCrea thought he might have been imagining turned out to be very real. The distant sky shimmered with it, and the air smelled vaguely like smoke.

"That's a problem," McCrea said. "First Sergeant Copley, how far away do you suppose that is?"

"I have no idea, sir. We're about twenty-five miles away from the nearest city, though I don't know if Franklin had anything worth dropping a warhead on."

"You don't think that's a forest fire?" Victoria asked.

"I hope to God it's not," McCrea said. "Either way, I want to move away from it as fast as we can."

"Where are we going to go?" Caleb asked.

"I don't know who you're asking," McCrea said, "but I think the first stop should be back at the Suburban. Let's grab all the maps we can find, and all the ammunition and water, and figure things out from there."

Victoria had no argument with any of that. The boys switched their headlamps to white light and led the way back down the trail to the SUV they had abandoned. She was startled to see the dome light come on as they opened the door, but then reasoned that a battery connection was hardly a complex circuit.

"Do you think we should try and start it when we get to the truck?" she asked McCrea.

"Oh, you bet your ass we're going to try." His words seemed to startle him. "Ma'am."

Five minutes later, both boys were dead to the world, crashed in the flatbed of the Suburban. McCrea, Copley and Victoria sat on the ground in the middle of the road with the *AAA U.S. Atlas* spread open on the ground between them.

"This is where we are right now," Copley said, pointing to a spot in the middle of the West Virginia mountains. "Franklin is here, northeast of us. That's the direction of the fire we see."

"We're moving away from that," McCrea said.

"I'm happy to hear you say that, sir. If we keep walking south on this road, we'll get to this spot on the map. Can you read the name?"

"Ortho," Victoria said.

McCrea recoiled. "You really can read that in this light?" Just in the last couple of years, his close vision had gone to shit.

"What can I say? My mother was an owl."

Copley measured the distance on the map with his thumb and forefinger and then lay the spread against the legend in the lower left corner of the page. "Looks like about ten miles."

"Are you sure we want to go to a town?" Victoria asked.

"We're going to need supplies," McCrea said.

"That's going to get tricky," Victoria said. "The people who live there aren't going to be anxious to share. We could end up picking a fight we don't want to have."

McCrea replied, "Ma'am, if it comes to that—if it comes to a fight—we're not going to be the side that has the most to worry about."

"What kind of supplies are you talking about?"

"Are you serious about getting to Mountain View?"

"Absolutely serious."

"Then think about it. A couple-hundred-mile walk. Winter's coming and you don't have warm enough clothes. We can forage and hunt for food, but I don't have the skills to turn a deer into a jacket. Do you?"

Victoria looked back at the map. "So, are we just going to steal?"

"I hope not. I hope we can barter. But this is precisely the wrong time to be charitable. The game is survival now. Once we have what we need—or, at least, some of it—we can head out again."

"If that's the strategy, then we need to move fast," Copley said. "If this is as bad as we all seem to think it is, supplies of everything are at the highest they will be for a long time. As shortages hit, people are going to panic and get really, really ugly."

McCrea said, "It looks like a straight shot down this road. At least we'll have a paved surface to deal with."

"One last thing," Victoria said. "Let's let the boys sleep until sunrise. This is probably the most comfortable that they'll be for a long time."

No sleep came for Victoria. She tried, but every time she closed her eyes, her head raced with the magnitude of what had just happened. The thought of so many dead and suffering people. She was certain that her neighbors were all gone. And all those people who were not dead yet, but soon would be—

Movement to her left interrupted her reverie. "Can't sleep either?" McCrea said.

"I hope the man who's still awake is not going to lecture the lady who's still awake on the importance of rest."

"Mind if I join you?" McCrea asked.

"Of course not. Pull up your favorite bit of pavement."

"How are you doing?" McCrea asked.

"Better than a lot of other people," she said. "You know, it's interesting. The thought of being disintegrated by a nuclear warhead doesn't bother me. I mean, it's awful, of course, but it's beyond comprehension. And I like to think that for all the millions who died tonight, it ended quickly." She snapped her finger. "Zap. Gone. Maybe there's a blessing in there."

She heard McCrea inhale sharply.

"Oh, my God," she said. "Your family."

"No, don't go there," he said. "What is, is, but I can't dwell on that now. We've got a job to do, and me being maudlin and weepy won't help with any of it."

"I really am sorry, Joe."

The silhouette of his head turned toward her. "Thank you," he said.

They sat in silence for a minute or two. It felt like forever. Victoria continued, "What makes my heart race and destroys my spirit is the sheer inconvenience of what lies ahead for us. For everyone."

McCrea said, "I sense that you and your boys are preppers of some sort."

"That overstates it. I've always been an outdoors girl. I hunt and fish, and all kinds of gender-bending stuff. One of my colleagues in the House convinced me that it wasn't a bad idea to be ready to bug out on short notice. We live in a world where it's okay to accost and assault politicians in restaurants. It didn't seem like too big a stretch to see them being run out of their homes. Mobs are mobs."

"Smart thinking. So, are the boys hunters and fishermen, too?"

She gave a quiet chuckle. "Luke loves it. Caleb endures it."

"He has a problem with killing Bambi?"

"Oh, heavens no. That boy has a sniper's instinct with a rifle. Give him a sharp enough knife, and he'll have Bambi gutted and quartered so fast, you'll fear for his fingers. No, I say he endures it because he's sixteen and furious."

"Furious about what?"

"Furious about everything, but nothing that I think he can articulate."

"Adolescent angst?"

"I hope so. Otherwise, he's developing as a sociopath." She put a hand on McCrea's knee. "I'm exaggerating, you realize, right?"

"I've only known him—known all of you—for a few hours, but I think you might be worrying too much. He's shown some real tenderness toward you and his brother."

Victoria *piffed*.

"Seriously. I think he takes his man-of-the-house role very seriously."

"Maybe I'm too close to see it," Victoria said. "I appreciate hearing it, though."

"May I ask what happened to their fathers?"

"No plural," Victoria said. "Same dad. An IED took him out in Afghanistan."

"Too common a story," McCrea said. "I did six tours over in the Sandbox. I wrote a lot of letters to grieving spouses."

"I was so angry," Victoria said. The anger still boiled in her tone. "Such a horrible, horrible waste. Glenn was a great guy. A patriot, through and through. Perfect father material. And when I thought about some jihadi choosing him at random, I didn't know what to do with the rage. It's not fair to bring the boys into it, and I was not a great officer's wife. I didn't have deep roots in the grieving wives' community."

"So, how'd you cope?"

"I ran for Congress and won," she said. "It wasn't even close."

"On an antiwar platform, I presume."

"You presume wrong," Victoria said. "I ran on a kill-the-bastards-or-leave platform. Both ends of Pennsylvania Avenue are populated with eunuchs who can't seem to grasp that their indecisions—not their decisions to fight, but their indecisions on how to fight politely—kill and maim very real people that they must rarely interact with. If we're going to fight, then we need to *fight.*"

"Well, given the events of last night . . ." McCrea didn't finish the thought.

"No, the events of last night were the very opposite of what I've been fighting for in Congress. Whatever devastation has befallen us is the result of showing weakness, not fighting hard. Helen Blanton never should have been elected president. Her presidency is a temper tantrum against the previous administration. She was simply too afraid to say no to Israel. That's the problem with political hacks. They are incapable of dynamic analysis. They never consider the moves that the other team might make."

McCrea would be the last person on earth to argue. "It's not just politicians," he said. "I've known a few flag officers who suffer from the same malady."

"Aren't flag officers just politicians with a smaller audience? Clowns in a different circus?"

McCrea laughed. "I'm still an active-duty soldier, ma'am. I can't use the C-word to describe my bosses. Some of them are really on the ball. But your point is well taken."

"And, so, here we are."

"At least we're here." McCrea had a question he needed to ask, and he wasn't sure how to go about it. "About being here. About the future. I don't want you to take offense."

"Thicker skin than mine is hard to find. I'll let you know if you cross a line."

"You talked earlier about mobs. I expect there'll be a lot of moblike confrontations in coming days and weeks," McCrea said.

"Without a doubt," Victoria agreed. "From here on out, we need to think of every encounter as predatory. In a few days, the frenzy will start. The weak will be preyed upon by the strong."

"So you've thought about this," McCrea said. He sounded surprised.

"We've trained for it. Planned for it. I wonder how long it will be before we devolve to the point when people start looking at their neighbors as sources of protein."

"There's a scary thought," McCrea said. "That'd put kids and old folks in particular peril. They'll be perceived as weak. Which brings me to my question."

"You don't have to worry about my kids," Victoria said, stealing his thunder. "I've trained them to be tough."

"Good for you. For them. But I hope they don't surprise you."

Victoria waited for the rest.

"They're young," McCrea said. "There's tough, and then there's *kid* tough. No matter how hard you work to train them on your own, society has bred hesitation into them."

"They've bred hesitation into all of us, don't you think? We are, after all, a peace-loving society."

"How sure are you that your boys' mental muscle memory isn't more about evaluating motives of attackers and of fleeing aggression than it is about returning violence with violence?"

Victoria took her time answering. "You know, Major. You know, *Joe,* one of the most pernicious elements of the prepper community is that they never consider a second chapter. Most are hobbyists, anyway, but even of the serious, committed ones, their entire thought process is about short-term survival. How to protect your own, and how to keep predators at bay, just as we were saying before."

"People are animals," McCrea said. "Prosperity is the only thing that keeps us from becoming feral."

"Fine," Victoria said. "So stipulated. And as animals, we need our packs. I prefer to think of them as tribes. Just because every bit of infrastructure is broken, and just because people become desperate, is no reason to dismiss kindness and understanding as some kind of a curse. Kindness is a blessing, not a liability."

"I think you're talking about mercy," McCrea said.

"If you'd prefer."

"It's not the mind-set I worry about," McCrea said. "I'm as big a believer in showing mercy as anyone. It's the hesitation that kills."

"What would you have me do about that?" Victoria was becoming annoyed now.

"I'm not sure," McCrea said. "I guess, just don't let them overcommit." He paused before saying the hard part. "And please be on my side if and when I try to reel them in. I know what First Sergeant Copley's fighting skills are, and I know what my own are. If kids put themselves in jeopardy, really bad things can happen."

"Tell you what," Victoria said. "I'll do my best to defer to you in all matters of conflict with others, but only on the condition that you stay out of my way when I try to be friendly to those same people. Especially in the early days, people are just going to want help. They're going to want direction."

McCrea wasn't at all sure that they'd agreed to anything. However, exhaustion was beginning to creep in, and he didn't want to pursue it.

"I have only one more question for you. It regards your other son. Adam, is it?"

"You definitely don't have to worry about him in a fight."

"Okay," McCrea said, "but that's not where I was going. What happens after you reconnect in Mountain View?"

"I've been thinking about that," Victoria said. "I don't want to go to Mountain View anymore. I don't think he'll be there."

McCrea's sigh vibrated with frustration.

Victoria continued, "We have a plan. We've always had a plan. It goes all the way to when Glenn was still alive. After nine/eleven, when we all learned how easy it is for families to get separated in times of emergencies, we established our reunion plan. At first, it was just for the two of us, but as the boys got older and more independent, we brought them into it, too."

"How does a reunion plan work?"

"At noon, on the first Monday of every month, we've promised each other to gather at a giant rock outcropping on a place called Top Hat Mountain. It's here in West Virginia, but down closer to coal country. We chose it because it's the location of our favorite-ever camping trip."

"The first Monday at noon." McCrea had difficulty making that work in his head. "What happens if—"

"There are twelve first Mondays in every year," Victoria said, answering his question before he could finish asking it. "We show up at noon and stay till two. If others show up, we'll be reunited. If they don't, then we come back in a month."

McCrea cleared his throat. "Okay, that's good for a few months, but after a while—"

"We do it for a year," Victoria said. "We all obligated ourselves to twelve monthly attempts. After that, well, some assumptions have to be made." She took a deep breath and lay back onto the pavement. "I just hope Adam remembers."

CHAPTER THIRTEEN

Adam Emerson awoke to the smell of fire. Neither of them had intended to fall asleep. In fact, he'd have sworn that he hadn't, but somewhere along the line, the sky had transformed to a new shade of red. He jerked upright to a sitting position, launching Emma off his shoulder.

"What!" she yelled.

"The whole world's on fire," Adam said.

Across the gorge, maybe half a mile away, the forest was ablaze. Entire trees were consumed whole, their flames climbing hundreds of feet into unnaturally dark morning sky. Now that he was awake, he couldn't understand why he hadn't heard the tornadic roar of the approaching firestorm.

"We need to get out of here," he said.

Together, they ran back to the tent and threw everything out of it onto the ground.

"Stuff everything into my ruck and I'll fold the tent," he said.

"We don't have time!"

"We have to," Adam said. "This might be our only shelter for a long time."

"We won't need shelter if we get burned up."

"I've got this. Pack the ruck."

Adam had rolled this tent and sleeping bag dozens of times over the years. He'd done it in the dark, and he'd done it in lousy weather. His hands knew what to do, all on their own. With that task finished, he strapped both the bag and the tent to the bottom of his rucksack. Then he pulled open a Velcro pocket and snatched out two headlamps.

"Take this one," he said to Emma.

When he looked up again, he was shocked to see how far the fire had advanced toward them. The roar was unlike anything he'd ever heard. It sounded like an animal, a giant, prehistoric bear roaring into the night. As he watched, a tree exploded near the leading edge of the advancing blaze, and seconds later, tiny windblown firebrands rained down on them.

"The wind's blowing toward us," he said. "If it jumps the gorge, we're done."

Emma followed Adam's lead by settling the tiny but wickedly bright LED lamp in the center of her forehead and flipped it on. Adam shouldered the rucksack and they took off at a run.

They'd left Emma's 1968 Ford Bronco parked on an old fire road about a mile from the campsite. Enough Hedrick Academy guys knew of the overlook campsite that they'd worn a trail through the underbrush, but in this light, the worn patch of forest floor was tough to see. Adam had never walked it at night. Now, in the stress and terror, combined with the bouncing light of the headlamp, he'd somehow led them off the trail and into the heavy brush and thick undergrowth.

"Are you still with me?" he yelled. He couldn't look back without risking a collision with a tree.

"Right behind you. Three steps behind."

Running with the ruck on his back was like being the size of two people. After he plowed through an obstacle, he'd have to force the ruck through next. It slowed them down, but he wasn't willing to give it up. He had food in there. And his only weapons. He wasn't going to leave them behind.

The fire roared like a living beast, a monster. A blast of superheated wind pushed at them from behind. Reminiscent of last night's bombs, the night flashed, and the air shook with an explosion as another tree exploded from the advancing flames.

"Go faster!" Emma shouted.

He didn't answer. He didn't figure he had to. It's not like he was dragging his feet. His throat and lungs felt like they were on fire, each breath sucking in smoke and fallout shit, whatever that might be.

The heat blossoming behind them had become intense and was getting worse. The forest flickered and glimmered with tinges of red and yellow.

Another explosion.

To his right, he heard screaming. A terrible sound, like a child in agony, and then three burning creatures streaked past him, on their way to die while spreading more fire in their wake.

"Where's the Bronco?" Emma yelled.

"Just on the other side of the river."

Oh, shit. The river.

As far as he knew, there was only one bridge in this part of the world, a rickety hand-built structure that was engineered and constructed by Hedrick cadets to span a thirty-foot section of the river. The Bronco was parked in front of the bridge, and the bridge led straight to the trail that Adam had led them away from.

This could be a problem.

Never a great runner in the first place, Adam worried that he was reaching the limit of his endurance. His legs were getting heavy, and his wind was growing short, but every time he felt he might be slowing down, another blast of scorching air would throw more fuel in his tank.

Finally, after what must have been ten minutes of as close to a sprint as he could manage, they reached the riverbank. Forced at last to stop, he dared his first look behind him as Emma skidded to a stop behind him. The sky above the treetops danced with images from hell. The flames leapt high into the sky, only to be consumed by the thick cloud of smoke that roiled ever closer to them.

This part of the river was wider than it was under the bridge, and the water ran fast.

"We've got to go in," Adam said.

Holding hands, he and Emma stepped out onto the slick rocks of the riverbank and into rushing water. Jesus, it was cold. Razor-blade cold. Two steps out, Adam lost his footing on a slick hidden rock and went down hard.

Then the current took him. The water was deeper than he'd expected—it had no bottom. As he raced downstream, he kicked hard to keep the rucksack from drowning him, and to reorient himself in the stream so he was leading with his feet, not his head. To his left, the fire continued to roar and advance, while on his right, the smoke had settled like a black fog over everything.

His inner compass told him that after he lost the trail, he'd erred to the west, which should be upstream from the bridge. As he struggled to keep his head up and his eyes open, he scanned ahead for—

"There!" he shouted, but then he took a mouthful of water. The bridge was maybe fifty yards ahead. Rolling to his belly, he kicked and pulled hard with his arms to get closer to the opposite bank. As he left the center of the channel into shallower water, though, rocks became a problem. His knee banged one hard enough to flip him over onto his butt, and from there, he was able to get his legs under him.

"Adam!" Emma was pulling hard through the water to close the gap between them. As he turned, her hand landed on his arm, and their free hands found each other.

"Are you hurt?"

"I don't care," she said.

That was neither a *yes* nor a *no,* and she was right. It didn't matter. The fire was relentless, voracious as it consumed everything on the other side of the river. Even at this distance, growing shorter with every second, the radiant heat was nearly unbearable.

They'd come to a stop just a few yards past the bridge, at a section of the bank that was four or five feet below the edge. Roots and vines dangled through the dirt wall, providing hand- and footholds they could use to climb up to the fire road.

"You first," Adam said.

Emma made quick work of the climb, and then it was his turn. By the time he reached the top, Emma was already opening the door to the Bronco. As Adam ran to join her, he shrugged out of his ruck, and when he got to the truck, he opened the tailgate and tossed the ruck onto the deck as Emma started the engine. As he slid into the shotgun seat and closed the door, he gasped at how fast the fire was progressing.

"The river's not going to stop it, is it?" Emma asked.

"I don't think so."

She jammed the manual transmission into gear, stomped on the accelerator and engaged the clutch, launching Adam back in his seat.

"You have to turn around to get back to the school," he said.

"We don't have time."

"The road dead-ends."

She jammed the brakes and whipped the wheel first to the right and then to the left to execute a U-turn. It took two tries, and she left some red paint on a tree trunk, but she got it done. Then it was pedal-to-the-metal time. She launched a plume of dirt and stone as she took off again.

She gasped. "Oh, shit, Adam. Look."

The bridge was burning now.

Within seconds, the woods on their left had caught fire, and the wall of flame was advancing fast.

"Go, go, go!" Adam urged. The view through the windshield was like a tour of the Underworld. Firebrands rained down like molten snowflakes, starting their own fires at every spot where they landed. He turned in his seat, and the view back there was even worse.

"It's like it's alive," he said.

"It's chasing us," Emma said. "And it wants to eat us whole."

She was way outdriving visibility. The air was blacker than night and the Bronco's headlights could barely penetrate the fog of smoke and ash as Emma navigated the narrow, unpaved road. The steering looked sloppy as shit, requiring huge corrections in the wheel to keep the vehicle away from rocks and trees.

Adam didn't think she'd touched the brake pedal since they'd sped past the burning bridge. Outdriving her lights the way she was, it was only a matter of time and luck before they ate a tree. But that was an *if.* The sure thing was the horrifying result if they slowed.

"How long is this goddamn road?" Emma shouted over the scream of the engine and roar of the inferno. She hit a pothole or maybe a tree root that bounced Adam into the roof.

"Never measured it. Less than a mile, I think."

"Feels like ten."

A burst of wind buffeted the Bronco. Thirty, forty miles per hour. In an instant, they were surrounded by flames. It was as if the fire had self-detonated. Emma and Adam screamed in unison. The heat of the inferno radiated through the steel and glass as if it weren't even there. They were out of time.

And then they were out of road.

The tiny fire road dumped out onto a wide state-maintained two-lane highway. The Bronco bounced hard as it made the transition onto pavement, but now they could get some speed.

"Right turn!" Adam yelled.

Emma yanked the wheel, downshifted and stomped the gas. The width of the highway seemed to have slowed the advance of the flames, but not their intensity. Now that they were on a solid surface and headed downhill, the Bronco flew down the road. Adam dared a look at the speedometer, then looked away when he saw that the needle was past ninety.

Three minutes after they exited onto the highway, the smoke started to lift, and the flames thinned. Two minutes later, the flames were all behind them.

Emma slowed. A little. "I think we outran it."

"Look closer," Adam said. "We didn't outrun anything. The fire's already been here."

Emma slowed even more. The light still wasn't right, but at least they could see more than a few yards ahead. What they saw was a smoking moonscape of charred devastation. It appeared that every inch of ground on both sides of the road had been reduced to carbon.

"Holy shit," Emma breathed. "Holy, holy shit, shit."

As they passed the burned hulk of what used to be a pickup truck, Adam thought he saw charred corpses inside. Ahead, a smoldering tree had fallen across the road, effectively blocking it.

"Can you get past that?"

"I'm sure as hell not turning around." Emma brought the Bronco to a halt, shifted into neutral and set the parking brake.

"What are we doing?"

"I've got to lock the hubs," she said. She opened her door and got out.

Adam followed. A glance at the Bronco's skin told him how close they'd been to being fried. The paint on the fenders and along the driver's side had blistered. He watched as Emma kneeled in front of the front wheel on her side and turned the locking hub. As she stood to cross to his side, Adam said, "No, let me do it." He mimicked what he'd seen her do, surprised that the lock turned as easily as it did.

"This truck is purely old-school," Emma said. "It's under-powered as shit on the highway, but it'll climb trees, given the chance."

Back in the driver's seat, Emma pulled the four-wheel selector into place, and then they were moving again. She piloted the vehicle far to the left—off the road, really—until the heavy branches of the fallen tree started to thin.

"Here we go," she said. She turned the wheel to the right, gunned the engine, and they rumbled through the smoldering mess. The Bronco bounced and tilted on every axis at the same time, bouncing them all over the interior, but Emma never stopped. Slow and steady. Branches slapped against the windows and steel frame. At one spot, they reignited a small fire at the point where a branch broke off.

And then they were on the other side.

If it weren't for Joan of Arc Academy and the Clinton N. Hedrick Military Academy, the tiny burg of Mountain View, West Virginia, would be little more than a gas station and maybe a few residences at the intersection of Routes 52 and 44, near the Kentucky border. King Coal Highway ran east to west out here, marking it as the heart of Coal Country. Known for its stunning natural beauty—especially in autumn—it was a part of the country that was rarely visited by outsiders who were not affiliated with the schools.

As the academies grew in size and prestige, they brought unprecedented prosperity to Mountain View. Faculty and staff needed places to live. Parents and siblings needed places to stay for Parents Weekend and graduation. Clothing, groceries and toilet paper all had to be purchased somewhere, so the Logan Grocery thrived, as did four restaurants, one of which was run by a displaced Michelin-star chef who specialized in local game.

Now it was all gone. The fire spared nothing. In the town center, every building had been gutted. Some were still burning. The only structures still standing were the ones built of brick or stone, and even they were rendered to nothing but teetering facades. The bloated and charred remains of some poor soul lay on the sidewalk outside of Buddy's Outfitters, the town's only source for rental kayaks and bicycles.

Adam and Emma drove in silence down the center of the road, taking in the horrors as best they could. Was it possible that everybody was dead? As in *every*body?

"I don't get it," Emma said through thick vocal cords. "Why here?"

Adam didn't have an answer, so he didn't try.

"What are we going to do?"

He didn't have an answer for that, either. "We'll get to Hedrick first," he said. "We've got to look."

Army Technical Sergeant Clinton M. Hedrick, after whom the academy was named, won the Medal of Honor for his heroism and gallantry in action on March 27 to 28, 1945, in Lembeck, Germany. A lifelong resident of West Virginia, Hedrick repeatedly charged into German gunfire, killing dozens of the enemy. He died for his service that day, and in his memory, the legislature was more than happy to provide funding in the form of cash and tax relief for the construction of what evolved into one of the premier institutions for turning difficult boys into responsible men.

In normal times, the entry gate to the academy exuded pride

and dignity. Stone walls flanked the apron to the long driveway, which threaded through a quarter mile of forest before opening up to a central parade ground that was surrounded by residential and academic buildings.

Today, though, the entry was a blackened, smoking ruin. The access road provided little more than an extended tour of devastation.

"Can you imagine how hot this fire must have been?" Emma wondered aloud.

"No."

At last, the roadway opened up on the massive parade ground, where a few nearly naked cadets sat or lay in the open. The dorms no longer existed. Neither did the academic buildings. This was total destruction.

As Emma drove the Bronco off the solid surface onto the grass of the parade ground, Adam fought the urge to stop her. Vehicles were never allowed on the grass. That rule probably didn't matter anymore.

"Stop here," Adam said.

"Why?"

"Please."

"What are you going to do?"

"Those are my friends, Em. I've got to try and help."

"How?"

"Please stop the car."

Emma pulled to a stop and Adam stepped out. He counted twelve cadets on the ground around the parade field. The stench was beyond awful, a stomach-churning combination of melted plastic and burned hair. As he slowly walked closer, he saw that most of the boys in the parade field had died. In each case, their arms and legs had been drawn into contorted fetal positions, their fists clenched, their flesh burned black and red.

He spent every day with these kids. Most were his friends. And all but a couple were unrecognizable. Their features were that swollen and contorted. Adam's vision blurred as his throat thickened.

One of the wounded cadets sat upright, naked in the grass. He held his arms out to his side, the burned flesh drooping away like awful, rotted draperies. Adam gasped as he recognized the boy as Rollie Bennett, his roommate since their fourth-class year.

He kneeled in front of his friend, but he didn't think Rollie could see him. "Rollie, it's Adam. What the hell happened?"

Rollie's eyes were bloody orbs, the lids burned away. "Please kill me," he said.

"Rollie, what happened?"

"I think it was bombs. I know there were bombs earlier. We all took shelter from that, and then . . . God, it was awful."

Adam scanned the carnage in front of him, and then scanned the scorched and collapsed buildings. "Are you all that's left?"

"I don't know. I'm blind." Every syllable appeared to be agonizing. "Everything caught fire all at once. We were sheltered in Tyler, and the whole building caught fire in, like, a second. Cadets were burning, Adam. Like torches. Oh, my God, the screams."

"Come on," Adam said. "We've got to get you to a doctor." He reached under Rollie's biceps to help him rise, triggering an animal scream that was pure agony.

"Don't! Don't! Ah, Jesus, don't touch me!"

Adam jumped back, fell on his ass. "I–I'm sorry."

"We both know I'm beyond help," Rollie said. His tone was terrifyingly normal. "This hurts so, so bad. Please, Adam. Please kill me."

Adam rose again to his knees. "I can't do that, Rollie."

"There aren't any doctors anymore, Adam. Sure as hell there aren't any here. Please. Please send me to God and let this be over."

Adam worked his jaws hard to keep the tears at bay. Rollie had been his best friend since the first moments they arrived at the academy. Watching him here, like this, was too much. Clearly, every breath hurt. The air seemed to turn to liquid in his lungs, creating a horrid gurgling sound.

Adam thought back to the heat of the fire in the woods. They weren't even burned, yet the pain was frightening. Vivid. Was that what Rollie was feeling now? If he was going to die, anyway, wasn't euthanasia the merciful decision?

Without another word, Adam pressed himself up to his feet. When he turned, he was startled to see Emma right there.

"I'm sorry, Adam," she said.

She spread her arms to hug him, but he sidestepped her. He had a thing to do here. It was an awful, sinful thing that would end with him in hell, but if he paused even for a few seconds, he'd lose his nerve and Rollie's suffering would continue.

Adam strode back to the Bronco and pulled open the tailgate.

"Adam, what are you going to do?"

He grabbed his rucksack and pulled it back to the opening. He found his old-school KA-BAR survival knife in the external pocket, where it belonged. He lifted it out, scabbard and all, and started back toward Rollie.

Emma looked terrified. "Adam, you can't do this."

Sure, he could. He'd trained on how to kill people with a knife. A six-inch blade like this, driven up through the base of the skull, would sever the spinal column and scramble the cerebellum in a single stroke. The victim would never know he'd been hit.

"Please, Adam," Emma pleaded. "This is wrong in so many ways."

Adam stopped short and turned on her. "He's my best friend, Em. What's wrong in so many ways is to let him suffer when there's no hope for him. I'd want you to do the same for me."

He spun back to his mission, tears streaming, and breathing coming in gulps. *Please, God, give me the strength to do this right.*

As it turned out, God did him one better.

Adam was still ten feet away when his best friend heaved a huge breath and then collapsed to his side. It was over.

Rollie was dead.

Adam tried to take it in, even as he tried not to. There were too many to bury, and there was no one to call. Hell, for all he knew, he and Emma were the only people left in the whole world. It was just too much.

Emma put her hand on his shoulder, and this time, he allowed himself to be folded into a hug. They stood there for the better part of a minute. She held him until he relaxed and pushed away. "This is the new way of things, isn't it?" she asked.

"At least until further notice. What the *hell* did people do? How did this start?" He knew they were wasted words—posing questions that had no answers—but he needed to speak them aloud.

"I don't want to go to Joan of Arc," Emma said. "This is enough. I don't want to remember my friends like this."

"Okay." God knew Adam didn't want to see any more sights like this one.

"But what do we do?" Emma asked. "Where do we go?"

As they walked back to the Bronco, Adam threaded the KA-BAR's scabbard onto his belt. "There's a place about a hundred miles from here," he explained. "It's called Top Hat Mountain."

CHAPTER FOURTEEN

Victoria did sleep, it turned out, because when McCrea announced that it was time to get going, she was startled to find that it was already 8:30 a.m. The day dawned dark, a kind of murky twilight that reminded her of sunset on a cloudy day. And as the day progressed, it never got brighter.

"That's the soot in the air," Copley explained without having been asked. "Nuclear winter."

"Must you, Paul?" Victoria scolded.

"It's nothing you didn't tell us about, Mom. Give him a break." Caleb had pulled ahead of her and taken the lead, next to McCrea. Luke walked with her, and Copley brought up the rear. The whole parade stretched no more than ten yards.

"Major McCrea?" Caleb asked.

"Yep."

"Can I call you Joe, too?"

"It's better than *asshole,*" McCrea said, eliciting the laugh he was hoping for.

"Do you think we're going to be okay?"

Was it possible that the kid had literally grown overnight? He looked two inches taller in the light of day than he had last night. "Before I answer, do you agree that the truth is always better than a lie, even if the truth is hard to hear?"

Caleb hesitated. "I guess?"

"Nope, no guessing to it. It's a *yes* or a *no.* And of those two options, only one will get you an answer to your question. I don't blow sunshine well."

"Okay, then, the truth is always better."

"Excellent. Then, yes, I think we're going to be okay. At least for the foreseeable future, which, in all honesty, is not as foreseeable as it was yesterday."

"Did millions of people really die last night?"

"I don't know for sure," McCrea said. "But probably."

"They won't get funerals or anything, will they?"

McCrea's vision clouded as his mind filled with the images of his wife, Julia, and their daughters, Tina and Toni. They lived close enough to DC that he was confident that they knew nothing, felt nothing. He doubted that there would be remains to bury or a church to hold the funeral in. "A lot of them won't," he said.

"That's really sad."

"Yes, it is."

McCrea sensed that the small talk was leading up to something big—the real point of why the boy started walking with him.

"You know my dad's dead, right?"

"Your mother told me he died a hero. I'm sorry for your loss. It's never easy—"

"It's my job to protect my mom and Luke," Caleb said, then shot a look over his shoulder to see if he'd been heard.

The kid was claiming his territory. McCrea admired that. "I'm told you've been well trained and that you've done a good job," he said.

"I haven't had to do anything yet. But if the time comes, I will."

"There's more to protecting people than fighting. Sometimes it means just being there for someone." Seconds passed in silence. "But that's not really what you want to talk about, is it?"

"What do you mean?" He watched his feet as they trudged on. "I just . . ." His voice trailed away.

"We promised to be honest," McCrea reminded. "Spit it out."

"I don't want you to treat me like a kid, okay? I'm sixteen. I'm scrawny, but I'm strong. And tough."

"What about Luke? Is he tough, too?"

"He wants to be, but he's really scared."

"We're all really scared. Honesty, remember? You telling me you're not scared?"

Caleb took a few seconds to get to the answer. "No, I'm a little bit scared."

"There's nothing wrong with being frightened, Caleb. You can't survive if you let it paralyze you, but being scared is healthy. Fear is God's way of telling us when to duck."

"I just wanted you to know," Caleb said. "It's not just you and Paul. I'm here, too."

"Duly noted," McCrea said. He considered giving the kid a playful shoulder bump, but didn't. They seemed to be having the beginning of a thing going between them and he didn't want to screw that up.

Behind them, Luke said, "I'm hungry." For at least the fifth time.

"No food till noon," Victoria said. "Get used to being at least a little hungry pretty much all the time."

Caleb spun around and walked backward. "We can hunt," he said.

"Not until we're settled someplace," Victoria said. "Let's focus on getting to Ortho and then figuring out the next step from there."

"What's so special about Ortho?" Luke asked. "Do we even know what's there?"

"It's a place," Victoria said. "A destination."

"How far are we from Top Hat Mountain?" Caleb asked, still walking backward.

"Please turn around before you trip over something," Victoria said. "A couple hundred miles."

"We're going to walk hundreds of *miles*?" Luke sounded horrified.

"It'll take a while," Victoria said.

Up ahead, on the right, a patch of grass and scrub growth looked as if it had been shredded. Deep trenches through the dirt and gravel were testament to a vehicle that had careened over the embankment and disappeared.

"Good Lord," Victoria said. She took off at a trot to investigate.

"Ma'am, don't!" McCrea commanded.

She never slowed, and her kids followed her.

"Vicky!" McCrea shouted. "Stop!" He knew he was wasting his words. He took off after her and Copley followed.

He caught up with the Emerson family as they skidded to a stop at the brow of the embankment. A red Toyota sedan had skidded down the steep hill and bent itself around a stout tree. The roof was crushed on one side, the windshield had spiderwebbed into an opaque mass. The axle clearly was broken. Bodies lay motionless in the front seat. It was hard to tell from this angle, but it appeared to be a man and a woman.

"Let it be," McCrea said. "We can't help them."

"You don't know that," Victoria said. She started down the hill, but McCrea grasped her arm to stop her.

"Please don't," he said. "They're dead. You don't need your kids to see—"

The lady in the shotgun seat stirred. "Oh, thank God," she yelled. "Help me!"

Victoria pulled her arm free from McCrea's grasp as Caleb took off down the hill, sliding the last ten feet or so on his butt.

"Shit," McCrea spat. This had all the potential of turning into something very, very bad. "First Sergeant Copley, come with me, please." Together, they started down the hill to join the others. Luke stayed up on the brow, hugging himself as his lower lip trembled.

"Help me!" the voice cried again.

Caleb arrived at the wreck first. After a single peek, he spun away and vomited onto the churned-up grass. Victoria's instinct was to look away, but she forced herself to lean into the window.

"Oh, thank God you're here," the injured woman said. "Please help me. It hurts. Oh, God, it hurts." She looked to be in her late teens, maybe early twenties. Still strapped into the shotgun seat, she seemed oblivious to the dead young man on the other side of the console. The top of his head had been sheared off at an angle that began in the middle of his left eyebrow and continued clean through the back of his head. Much of his brain had congealed on his lap and on the fabric of the deployed air bag.

"My legs hurt," she said. "They hurt really, really bad."

A white sliver of her left femur had erupted through her jeans. Victoria looked back at Caleb. "Bring the trauma bag," she said.

McCrea moved in next to Victoria and kneeled on the ground next to the girl's window. He brought his face about even with hers. "My name is Joe," he said. "What's yours?"

"Robin," she said. "Robin Ives. I don't know what happened. Zane and me were driving and then everything went crazy. I don't even know how long I've been here for. I swear to God we weren't drinkin' or nothing."

"That's okay," McCrea said. "You'll be better now. But I need you to do something for me, okay?"

Caleb arrived with his rucksack unslung. "I've got the trauma kit."

"Give me a minute," McCrea said. He waited for Robin's answer.

Her eyes were wide and wet. "What?"

"We've got to get her out of the car," Victoria said.

McCrea held up his hand. "I've got this, Vicky," he said. "Just give me a little bit of time." To Robin, he said, "You've got to trust me. Okay? Do you trust me?"

Robin nodded yes, but her eyes said no.

"Look, Robin, it's not just me," McCrea said. "We're all here to help. What I need you to do is close your eyes and count silently to ten."

"I think my legs are broken," she said.

"I think you're right."

"Please don't hurt me any more."

"Not on purpose, I promise, but you can't just stay in that car, can you?"

Robin started to cry. "Please."

McCrea smiled as his vision clouded. "I promise," he said. "Now, please."

"Okay, I–I'm going to trust you."

"Eyes closed," he said softly.

As Robin pressed her eyes closed, McCrea stood, his pistol already in his right hand. Moving with startling speed, he brought the muzzle within an inch of her temple and pulled the trigger.

Emma looked confused. "So you just hang out on a mountaintop for an hour?"

"First Monday of the month at noon," Adam explained. "You can stick around for longer, if you'd like, but if we miss each other, we try again the next month. And then again. I admit it's a long game."

"What happens if no one shows?"

"We never talked it through that far. There comes a point when you have to embrace the possibility that they're . . . that they're not . . ."

"I get it," Emma said. "Do you know the way?" She started the engine.

"Forty-four north," he replied, referring to the state highway. "We'll have to feel our way from there. It'll be a couple hundred miles, I think."

"Well, we've got three weeks to get there."

"Take it slow," Adam said. "We don't want to catch up with the fire, anyway. How much gas do you have?"

"The tank is full, and I've got a five-gallon jerry can in the back."

"Is that enough?"

"I guess we're about to find out." Emma executed a giant U-turn, presenting one last departing view of the devastation. "My God, what a horrible way to die."

Adam couldn't think of a worse way. "What about your folks?" he asked. "I don't think we've ever talked about them."

She took her time answering, her eyes locked ahead the whole time. "Last time I checked, they were in Europe someplace. I know they were in Paris in April. Haven't heard from them since."

"I'm sorry," he said.

"Yeah, whatever."

He waited for more, but when she didn't offer it, he didn't pursue it. She turned out onto the road and headed back toward the crossroads, again passing the ruined forest. As they reentered what was left of the city center, Adam pointed off to the right. "Pull in over there. In front of Palmer's Hardware."

"Why? What's in there? The place is gutted."

"We need weapons," Adam said. He reached into his pocket, retrieved his headlamp and centered it back on his forehead. "If there's any one thing that was driven into my head by my mom, it was that when the shit hit the fan, you needed to be well armed. I believe this qualifies."

"But the place is burned out." She stopped the Bronco in front of Palmer's.

"Want to come along?"

"What are we doing?"

Adam opened his door and climbed out. Emma followed, but stopped at the threshold of the store. "The place is about to fall down, Adam."

Actually, a lot of it already had. "I used to work here one summer. Mr. Palmer sells guns."

"But aren't they all burned up?"

Adam stepped inside the charred, blackened interior. The roof had collapsed into the main floor, creating a maze of fire-ravaged trusses. Smoke still rose from parts of the wreckage.

"The gun vault is down in the cellar," Adam explained. "He was a fanatic about putting the guns away in the safe every night. Unless he changed the combination, I'll be able to get in."

"You're going into the *cellar*? That's *two* levels that can collapse on you."

"No pain, no gain."

"This isn't funny." Her tone had turned serious.

He turned on her and met her in kind. "No, it's not. Not a

funny thing has happened this whole goddamn day. There's no such thing as safety anymore, Em. There's only degrees of *un*-safety. Degrees of oh-shitness. We need to arm ourselves, and this is one place where I think we can find weapons. You can stay here, you can wait in the truck or you can join me downstairs. Either way, I need to do this."

Tempers were running hot. Stress was beyond immeasurable. He didn't wait for her answer.

Navigating through the wreckage was a hell of a challenge, a combination of climbing, stepping over and crawling under the lumberyard that had crashed into the main part of the store. On a normal day, the aisles in Palmer's were narrow, cramped and jammed with shit. With addition of the roof and trusswork, it felt almost impossible to get from the front to the back of the store.

"Hey, Em, are you still in here?"

"Right behind you."

"Do me a favor and scour through this crap and find anything salvageable that we can use."

"Like what?"

"No clue. Use your imagination. Anything that makes starting a fire easier. Duct tape, rope, whatever. Batteries, for sure, if you can find them. Flashlights, lanterns, anything."

The stairway down to the cellar began as a scuttle hole in the floor that was blocked off by a swinging metal gate. A section of the roof had crashed down onto the gate, crushing it and blocking all but a three-by-three-foot patch of air. Adam leaned over the opening to scan the area below. The steps appeared to be intact. Remarkably, the collapse stopped before it crushed the cellar.

After testing the sturdiness of the charred rafter and the bent railing and satisfying himself that he wouldn't plummet to his death, Adam pressed up with his hands and leveraged his legs over the wreckage and lowered himself onto the wooden steps. These were creaky under the best of circumstances, but they didn't seem a whole lot worse now. He decided to trust them.

Once at the bottom, he took half a minute to scan the area. There had to be useful stuff down here. But he didn't have any use for flower seeds, and while the time might come when he'd enjoy sitting in a yard, lawn chairs wouldn't justify the real estate they'd take up in the Bronco.

"Focus, Adam," he said.

The gun vault was really a gun room, protected by a steel door that could have come from a bank. While working here, Adam had committed the four-digit combination code to a mnemonic that mixed his and his brothers' birthdays. It probably would have made no sense to anyone else, but that was fine.

He spun the dial left-right-left-right, and then turned the handle that disengaged the massive pins that extended into the reinforced concrete wall. Once free, the door swung open easily, as if it weighed nothing.

In the old days, opening the door triggered a ceiling light. Now, as he cast his light through the darkness by turning his head, he illuminated all kinds of toys. The very first rifles he saw were Ruger 10/22s, the same that his mom had bought them for their go bags. Good rifles, they didn't have quite the power that he was interested in. Palmer's was a distributer for Bushmaster, and the vault had quite a collection of AR15s. Most were designed exclusively for use with external optics, but Adam wanted to find ones with iron sights, ones that never ran out of batteries.

He found two. He lifted them off the shelf one at a time, checked the actions, then laid them down for later. Putting his rucksack on the floor, he opened its main compartment and expanded it as wide as it would go. He took four 30-round magazines for the AR15s—three for each, counting the mags that were already installed in the weapons, and then he added six hundred rounds of 5.56-millimeter ammunition, two hundred rounds for each of them.

Then it was time to shop for pistols. He chose two Glock 19s because he knew that gun well, and then he dumped eight boxes of nine-millimeter hollow point into the bag. That gave them another two hundred rounds of pistol ammo apiece. The ruck was getting damned heavy now.

He pivoted slowly around his own axis, casting the white disk of light over everything he could see. He was tempted by some of the heavier hunting rifles, but that would mean a lot of extra weight, plus a new caliber of bigger, heavier bullets. It just wasn't worth the effort.

He did grab a couple of Blade-Tech Kydex holsters for the Glocks. He even took the time to thread his belt through the mounting rings and cinched the holster close to his hip, just in front of the KA-BAR. Then he slid the Glock home. He'd load it later.

So, what else? He scanned some more. His light landed on a stack of rifle slings. He'd been concerned how he was going to carry all this hardware up the ladder while negotiating the wreckage, and now he had his answer.

Each of the Bushmasters had single-point sling lugs. He clipped a bungee to each of them, and then slung them both, one over his left shoulder, and one over his right, so they dangled as an elongated X against the front of his body.

He did another pass with his headlamp and decided he'd done about all the damage he could in here.

Until he saw the case of dynamite. "Seriously?" he asked aloud. "Welcome to Coal Country."

He'd never used high explosives, but he'd studied how. Modern dynamite was a lot more stable than the old stuff, and it packed a bigger wallop than TNT. He had no idea how much bang you could get per stick, so he grabbed five and put them on the top of the stuff in his ruck. He could organize the pack later.

"Damn good thing the fire *didn't* get to the basement," he mumbled.

Now he needed a way to set it off if he needed it.

Knowing the folly of storing detonators and secondary explosives together, he spun around to face the other side of the vault, and sure enough, there they were, wrapped in what looked like brown wax paper. They were labeled: *Pyrotechnic Initiators.*

He opened the end of the package and he recognized the blasting caps. He stuffed them into an outside pocket on his ruck, and decided it was finally time to go. He shrugged into the ruck, settled all the gear on his back and his front so the rattle was as quiet as possible.

When he got to the top of the stairs, Emma was waiting for him. "Can I help with anything?"

"Nah, it'd be more effort to take the ruck off than it is climbing over shit with it."

"Good Lord, how many guns did you take?"

"Two rifles, two pistols. Lots of ammo."

"What, are we going to war?"

He gave her a look. *Really?*

"Oh, I guess we *are* at war."

There was a brief instant—just half a second as he was heaving himself over the collapsed rafter—that he nearly lost his balance. But he recovered. "Did you find any good stuff?"

"A couple of camping lanterns. Some batteries. Everything's a little melted, so it might not work, but I put it in the Bronco."

"Excellent. No food?"

"Sorry."

"Where are the SpaghettiOs when you need them?"

They climbed through the maze of lumber, and Adam led the way through the door back outside. He damn near shit himself when he saw what was waiting for them.

Three men in coveralls had clustered around the Bronco and were staring inside. They looked related, father and sons, maybe, and one of the younger ones was about to open the driver's-side door.

"Hey!" Adam yelled.

They jumped and whirled to face him. "Who are you?" the oldest asked.

"How about you step away from the truck?" Adam said.

"How about you put back what you stole," one of the younger ones said.

Adam didn't address that. "My name is Adam. I go to Hedrick."

"I'm Chaney," the man said. "They all dead up there?"

Adam moved to the side. He kept his focus on the guys nearest the truck. "Get away from there!"

"You gonna shoot us?"

"I don't want to. Just step back while we talk, okay? Is Mr. Chaney your father?"

The boys didn't move, didn't answer.

"They're my boys, Harlan and Marcus. How come your truck still works?"

"Excuse me?"

"Your truck works. Nobody else's truck works."

Adam hadn't noticed that this was the only one on the road, but he couldn't remember seeing another one. "It's a thing called electromagnetic pulse," he said. "That's what kills newer cars and trucks. All electronics, really. The Bronco is too old, I guess."

"Where you goin'?"

"Don't know yet. Are you going to ask your boys to get away from our truck or not?"

"You sure got a lot of firepower there," Chaney said. "You think you've got the balls to use it?"

Adam's heart rate tripled. He tried to keep his face even, but he was certain his fear showed through. "I don't want this to get ugly, Mr. Chaney."

"You scared, boy?"

"Adam, be careful of him," Emma whispered from behind.

"No sense havin' a gun if you ain't willing—"

In a smooth, well-rehearsed motion, Adam extended the stock of the AR15 dangling under his right arm and brought the weapon to his shoulder, the sights leveled at Chaney's chest.

Chaney hopped back a step. He tried to force a smile, but he couldn't pull it off. When Adam thumbed the bolt release, the heavy *clack* of it slamming home took the smile completely off his face.

"Go to the Bronco, Em," Adam said. Then he yelled, "Harlan and Marcus, listen up. My friend here is going to walk to the Bronco, get in and drive about fifty, sixty yards up the road. If you don't stay out of her way, I will shoot your daddy on the spot, and then I will shoot you."

"You're bluffing."

"Go ahead, Em. Let me know what the boys are doing."

"What about you?"

"You stop the Bronco a little past here and I'll join you."

"It's three to one, kid," Chaney said.

"It's a thirty-round magazine. Ten rounds for each of you."

"You're not that tough."

"I probably wasn't yesterday. But a lot has changed. I am scared shitless, but I will shoot you and your family dead if they get in our way."

Chaney measured Adam for a long ten seconds, then said, "This isn't over 'tween you and me." Then, louder: "Move back, boys. Give the lady all the space she needs."

"Talk to me, Em," Adam called. He desperately wanted to look back to check on her, but he didn't dare look away from Chaney even for an instant.

"They're moving," Emma said.

"Move around where I can see you, fellas," Adam said. As he spoke, he moved away from and around Chaney, keeping the rifle at his center of mass.

Chaney pivoted with him, never taking his eyes from Adam.

When he could see Chaney, his sons and Emma all at the same time, Adam stopped. The boys and the Bronco were just blurs, because he forced himself to stay focused on the front sight. Chaney needed to see him doing that, needed to believe that Adam would kill him if he had to.

Emma dropped the stuff she'd taken from the hardware store onto the Bronco's cargo bed, then slid in behind the wheel. The engine started and she backed out of her spot and onto the road. As she pulled away, Adam backed up more.

Chaney took a step closer.

"Please don't," Adam said. "Just don't."

Emma drove the Bronco to the intersection of Routes 44 and 52 and parked with the nose pointing north.

As Adam backed all the way to the vehicle, the Chaneys formed up into a loose line, shoulder to shoulder. As one, they took a couple of steps closer, but Adam judged those more as protests than threats.

He didn't want the distraction of pausing to shed himself of all the gear to fit into a seat, so he opened the tailgate and sat on it.

"I'm in," he said. "But go easy, please. Don't buck me out." He kept his sights on the Chaneys until they were far enough away not to pose a threat, and then lowered the weapon and lay down on the steel cargo bed. "Oh, shit. Oh, shit. Oh, shit."

"Are you okay?" Emma asked.

"I am now. None of the guns were loaded."

CHAPTER FIFTEEN

Speaker Penn Glendale decided that the assembled members of the House would for now become a committee of the whole. Sooner than later, the fate of the executive branch would be made known, and when that happened, however the news broke, and whatever it brought, the House of Representatives needed to be prepared to act. Ordinary rules of decorum seemed unnecessarily cumbersome under the circumstances, so he announced that for now, in the absence of precedent, the business of the House would resemble more of a town hall than the formal deliberative body that it was.

"I'll be honest with you all," he said. "I'm flat out of ideas here."

Burton Sinclair, of Oklahoma, raised his hand and was recognized. "Mr. Speaker, ladies and gentlemen of this Congress, I believe that we have not come close to understanding the enormity of this conflict. Beyond the devastation wrought by the bombs, the electromagnetic pulse has brought everything to a halt. Without electricity or the ability to create it, water pumps will stop. Fuel will be unavailable to make them run, anyway. Planes designed to protect us will be unable to do so. Satellites designed to track our enemies are as useless as if they had been blown out of space, which, for all we know, may have happened.

"The American people will perish without help, and it is our duty to find a way to provide that help to them."

Latasha Washington was next to rise. "I think we can assume that the world's entire financial structure has collapsed. Pieces of paper cannot feed your children. Perhaps people who live on farms will find ways to sustain themselves, and people in rural areas can always hunt, but for residents of urban areas—"

"The urban areas are all gone," Penn said.

"Mr. Speaker, I was not done yet."

"Well, maybe you should be," he said. "I don't mean to insult, but so far, all I've heard from the members of this body is just how awful everything is, and how truly desperate things are likely to become. Let's stipulate to that. The world sucks and it's going to suck for a while. Now let's turn our attention to the ways we can *un*suck it."

"That's impossible to do without information," said Angela Fortnight. "Everything comes down to knowing what—"

The speakers popped overhead. "Excuse me, Mr. Speaker. Captain Brinks would like to address the assembled members."

"By all means."

Brinks started by clearing his throat, and then clearing it again. When he spoke, his voice wavered with emotion. "Mr. Speaker, we have received word, apparently official, that the president and vice president are both dead. The word I have here is that Air Force One and Air Force Two were both airborne when the strikes occurred, and neither survived." Brinks paused to clear his throat again. "It was a very smart attack, sir. They concentrated on major population centers and military targets. Command and control centers were hit particularly hard. NORAD is gone, both in Colorado Springs and Cheyenne Mountain. CYBERCOM, STRATCOM, TRANSCOM, SOCOM, NORTHCOM and SOUTHCOM all took multiple hits. As far as we can tell, we're pretty much a headless snake. Sir."

"This is Minority Leader Fortnight. May I ask where your information is coming from?"

"Yes, ma'am, I guess there's not a lot of harm in that now. We've tapped into chatter from elsewhere in the world. Exclusively on low-tech radios like shortwave and some citizens band."

"How did the rest of the world fare in this?" Representative Kiser asked.

"Stand by one. That's not what I've been listening to. I'll let Lieutenant Rallah address that. That's been her focus."

After sounds of movement—chair rollers and shuffling papers—a new voice emerged from the speakers. She sounded like a teenager. "Hello? This is Lieutenant Jane Rallah. I've been monitoring—or trying to monitor—SIGINT from Europe and Asia. It's pretty much a mess out there. Nobody's comms are working right, but we've picked up chatter. From what I can tell, Europe stayed pretty clean through this. We think England was hit hard, but word from the rest of the area—specifically France and Italy—is that they think they're close to okay. They're very concerned about the radiation plumes from Russia, which apparently took a big hit. China, too, we think."

"What about the 'Stans?" Penn asked.

"It appears now that the Indians and Pakistanis kept their peckers in their pants, as my father used to say." The lieutenant giggled nervously.

"Hey, if you can't laugh in the face of a billion deaths, what's the point of living?" Angela said.

Penn shot her an ugly look. "That was entirely uncalled for," he scolded.

Lieutenant Rallah's voice got small. "I'm sorry."

"I wasn't talking to you, Lieutenant. Tensions are running a little high here, too. Is there anything else?"

"No, sir, I don't think so. But if you can figure out a way to get us out of this bunker, I, for one, would be happy to hear about it."

Penn's throat thickened. Those young people were looking at an inevitable slow death, and there was nothing anyone could do. "Godspeed to everyone there. Thank you for your service to the nation."

"Wish we could have done more, Mr. Speaker. We'll be back in touch if there are more developments."

"I wish we could have done more, too," Penn said. A glance up at Pete in the booth told him that their conversation was over. "Mr. Johnson!" he called.

"Here, Mr. Speaker." Johnson hadn't moved from the spot in the back of the chamber.

"Can you explain to me why junior officers on the other side of the country are able to tap into communications from Europe when we, here in a reinforced bunker in the Blue Ridge Mountains, cannot?"

"It's only been a few hours, sir. I assure you—"

"Don't assure me of anything, Mr. Johnson. Get me results. And change out this stage. It's time we swear in the new president."

Angela stood. "Mr. Speaker, I rise with a privileged motion to vacate the chair."

Penn felt his mouth fall open a little. A motion to vacate was a motion to remove him from the Speakership.

Angela continued, "As we discussed before, you no longer represent the majority in this chamber. I move for an immediate vote to have you removed as Speaker, which will then be followed by a vote to name a new Speaker."

A chorus of protests erupted from the chamber. "That's outrageous!" Oscar Colgan shouted. "This is hardly time for a coup!"

"The motion is in order," Anna Grogan declared. "And as a privileged motion, it rises to the top of all other business."

"An election is not a coup," said Kent Kiser. "In fact, it is the opposite of a coup. The motion is entirely in order."

"It is no such thing!" Burton Sinclair said. "The national election was less than a year ago. The majority party is the majority party. Mr. Glendale is the Speaker of the House of Representatives."

"Let the vote speak for itself," Angela said. "Mr. Speaker, the rules are the rules. You must open the motion for debate, and you must entertain a vote. If you stay in office, you stay. If not, then the House has spoken."

"This is the *people's* house," Penn said. "It is not your personal résumé lab. The majority of the people of the United States voted for my party to represent their interests. It is absurd to suggest that I step down now because Mr. Johnson up there closed the door too early."

Angela turned her back on Penn in order to address the assembled body, face-to-face. "The American people elected Helen Blanton to be president of the United States. They elected Clarence Jenkins to be vice president of the United States. They made clear what their intentions were for the executive branch. You and your party, Mr. Speaker, were not the ones they chose. Combine that fact with the undeniable fact that you represent a clear minority in this chamber, and I believe I have a responsibility to my constituents and to the people of the United States to make the motion I have."

Penn looked to Strasky for advice, but his chief of staff looked at once terrified and baffled.

"Very well," Penn said. "We will keep the world waiting at the feet of Leader Fortnight's ambitions. We will let the fires burn a little hotter and let the people suffer a little longer while we debate the privileged motion on the floor."

"You can always step down, Mr. Speaker," Angela said. "If time is truly of the essence for you, given the fact that you know how this vote will go, we can speed it along if you can simply surrender your seat."

Penn searched for something to say. Some way to undo this travesty, but nothing appeared in his head. "Ladies and gentlemen, this has been a long, arduous day. I will entertain a motion to recess for eight hours so we can all find our quarters and get some rest."

Jack Collins stood. "So moved," he said.

"This is silly!" Angela cried.

"We stand in recess for eight hours," Penn said. This time, he slammed his hand on the desk hard enough to hurt. "Mr. Johnson, get me a goddamn gavel!"

Victoria watched in utter disbelief as Major McCrea shot and killed that girl. By the time she moved to intervene, the deed was done. "Major!" she yelled. "Oh, my God!"

McCrea didn't even look at Victoria. He holstered his pistol and turned to head back up the embankment while a startled

First Sergeant Copley pivoted his stance to stay between the other two adults.

"Don't you dare walk away from me!" Victoria shouted.

Caleb ran around both of them to take a position between McCrea and the road. He'd taken his mother's side.

McCrea stopped and whirled Victoria. His jaw was tight and his eyes were red. "What do you want from me, Mrs. Emerson? I told you to stay away from that wreck."

"You murdered that girl!" Victoria stood with her fists on her hips, ready for a fight.

McCrea was ready for one, too. He stepped closer, till their faces were maybe twelve inches apart. "Say that again."

"You don't intimidate me, Major," Victoria said.

"Say it," he repeated. "Tell me again right here, eye to eye, that I murdered that girl."

His eyes burned with a level of anger that Victoria had rarely seen. They showed homicide. She needed to tread carefully. She chose to remain silent.

"That's what I thought," McCrea said. "Typical politician. You're great at talking about war and violence, but when exposed to the reality, you've got no goddamn clue what's at stake." He kicked at the ground as he paced three steps closer to the broken car and its bleeding cargo. When he turned, his eyes were rimmed with crimson.

He thrust a forefinger back toward the occupants. "That girl. Robin. She's about the same age as my oldest daughter. The same age as my oldest daughter *was*. Thanks to you, and to people in your line of work."

Victoria felt blood rising in her neck. "Now, wait—"

"Shut up, Mrs. Emerson," McCrea said. "Can you do that for me? Just shut the hell up for a few minutes and let me complete a thought?" He raised his gaze to find Luke still standing at the top of the embankment. "Luke, get down here. Caleb, stand next to your mom where I can see you."

"I don't want to come down," Luke said.

"Did you hear me ask that as a question?" McCrea said. "I didn't ask you for a favor, Luke. I told you to get your ass down here with your mom and your brother."

Victoria bristled at the tone, but was willing to give the major a little rope. "Come on down, Luke. You don't have to look in the car."

McCrea watched as they gathered, his expression stern, but the anger seemed to have bled off a little. Luke slipped his hand into Victoria's grasp, but Caleb kept his distance. If Victoria read his body language properly, he was practicing what she had always preached. In a confrontation, your opponent could only look in one direction at a time. Caleb was taking an angle on the major.

"I shot that girl," McCrea said. "I shot Robin. Any of you think that I shouldn't have?"

They stared back in silence.

"It's okay if you do," McCrea pressed. "As far as I'm concerned, there's no right answers here. I really want your opinion. Was I wrong to shoot her? Did I *murder* her, as Mrs. Emerson alleges?"

Victoria held up her hand. "Okay, I misspoke. *Murder* was too strong a word."

"I'm not trolling for an apology, ma'am. I don't give a shit what you want to call anything that I do. I'm struggling to make a bigger point here. Caleb, describe what you saw when you looked in the car."

Caleb clearly considered not answering, but when McCrea didn't come off the point, he said, "A lot of blood."

"What about Robin's legs?"

Caleb blushed as his lips pressed into a thin line. Victoria knew the look. He was trying to hold back tears.

"Did you see the broken bones?" McCrea asked.

Caleb's head twitched a yes.

"And we all saw her pain, yes? Even you heard her cries of pain, right, Luke?"

Luke squeezed his mom's hand tighter.

"We could have helped her," Caleb said in a tone that was barely audible.

"No!" McCrea said. "No, we couldn't. I shot Robin because the only alternative would have been to let her suffer to death. We can't get her out of the wreck because we don't have the tools to do it with, and we couldn't have treated her injuries without first removing her from the car. I did what had to be done."

"We have morphine in our med kit," Caleb said.

McCrea issued a bitter chuckle. "Well, I don't know how you scored that, but good for you. Good to know. But you don't use unique resources on lost causes."

Victoria recoiled. "Excuse me?"

McCrea stepped closer again. "Whatever you paid for illicit narcotics, I'm confident that you didn't shell that out with the thought of treating strangers who were going to die, anyway."

"So you're God now? You get to choose who lives and who dies?"

McCrea bladed his hand back toward the crushed Toyota. "That's God's choice, right there," he said. "I didn't make them run their car into a friggin' tree. That was the hand of the Almighty, helped along, no doubt by Jack Daniel's. Keeping them alive clearly was not part of the divine plan."

"She was a human being," Victoria said.

"So are you, Mrs. Emerson. And so are your boys. Even First Sergeant Copley is a human being, or so I've heard."

"That's not funny," Victoria snapped.

"It's a little funny," McCrea countered. "The choices only get tougher from here, ma'am. Death is the new normal. God only knows how many millions or hundreds of millions were killed last night, and there will be more. For the immediate future, there's no room for pity. Hard stop. Until we know how bad things really are, we need to assume the worst. We need to assume that the resources we currently have on hand are the only ones we will ever have access to. That means we conserve and preserve."

"Joe is right," Caleb said, startling his mom. "Robin was going to die, anyway. There's no way we could have saved her. Joe did the right thing." Something had changed in the boy. Between glances, he had aged five years. "It's like you always told us, Mom. Concentric circles, remember?"

Victoria didn't like hearing her own words. Since forever, she had preached the concentric circles theory of self-defense. Each of us stands in the center of our own circle, surrounded by immediate family. Everyone and everything else is sacrificial to the inner circle. Close friends and distant relatives can belong to the next circle, and together you fight and survive. As circles expand, they grow larger and are populated by more people, but the outermost circle is always the first to be sacrificed if survival of an inner circle is jeopardized. In her youth, she had always assumed that everyone lived by concentric circles. Maybe they didn't recognize that they were doing it, but that kind of prioritized survival seemed instinctive to her. Primordial.

And perhaps at one time it was, a time when kids settled disputes on their own, sometimes drawing blood, yet no one sued anyone. Self-sufficiency used to be encouraged. Maybe it was a rural thing, but when she was growing up, neither she nor her brothers nor any of their friends had time for the video games that had begun to consume her generation, let alone the money to invest in them. Horses didn't feed or groom themselves, after all, and hay needed to be baled and crops needed to be cared for and harvested. All while getting homework done, lest Dad wear her out for getting a grade lower than a B.

"Concentric circles," Victoria said. "So, do we just leave the bodies?"

"We have to," McCrea said. "We'll grind the shovel blade to nothing if we try to bury all the dead we'll be seeing."

They moved in unison as they climbed back up the embankment toward the road. When they were halfway, Luke pulled his hand out of Victoria's grasp and stopped. "I need to go back and look," he said.

"Oh, baby, no, you don't."

He bobbed his head emphatically. "Yeah, I do."

"Why? It's going to be awful."

Luke didn't answer. He started back down the hill. When Victoria followed, he said, "I want to see it alone."

From up on the road, McCrea called, "Hey, what are—"

Victoria raised her hand for silence. Luke moved carefully, hesitantly, as he closed the last few yards. When he was three feet away, he stopped, took a deep breath and then walked the rest of the way. He placed his hands on the edge of the open window and stooped till he was face-to-face with Robin's corpse.

Could he be praying? Victoria thought.

After about five seconds, he gently touched her head, and then pushed away. As he passed his mom on the way back to the top of the embankment and the road beyond, he said, "Please don't call me baby anymore."

CHAPTER SIXTEEN

As Penn led his caucus from the makeshift House Chamber back into the vast space of the main hall, the transformation of the place startled him. The registration tables were gone, and dozens more tables had been added. They were arranged in long rows, each serviced by a folding metal chair. Dark computer terminals adorned every workstation, creating a snake's lair of cords and cables across the floor beneath the tables.

Solara staff stood guard outside the chamber door, their eyes focused on something only they could see, a studied indifference meant to project that they weren't eavesdropping. It was the same demeanor Penn had seen in every Secret Service and protection detail he'd ever encountered. In this case, the precaution seemed ridiculous. From whom were these people here to protect them?

Penn approached the sentry closest to him. "Excuse me, Mr. Cameron," he said, refreshing his memory via the name patch on the man's uniform shirt. "Is there a place where we can sit and get something to eat?"

Cameron moved as if he'd been startled out of a trance. He pointed vaguely to his left, Penn's right. "The dining hall is that way. On the other side of the next wall. I don't know if they're serving food now, but there are places to sit."

Penn and the rest of his party moved in that direction. As it turned out, there was, in fact, no food available, but the coffee urns were full. "I don't suppose there's any bourbon in the house," Penn said as he helped himself to a cup of jet-black coffee. "Jesus, this stuff must've been in the pot for a week."

As the others queued up for their turn at the coffee urn, Penn and Strasky took seats next to each other at the front of the room, waiting for others to find spots for themselves. Something about the space wasn't right. The walls were devoid of decoration and were painted an unsettling green. Not fluorescent, exactly, but close. The last time Penn had seen this hue was on the walls of a hospital morgue when he had to identify the body of a friend. Combined with the checkerboard-pattern tile on the floor, it was an unpleasant room to sit in.

If the rest of the interior was like this, the next sixty days of confinement were going to be damned difficult. "I'm open to any suggestions anyone might have," he said.

"I'll go," Burton Sinclair said. Pushing eighty, he'd represented Oklahoma's Fourth since before the youngest member of the current Congress had even been born. Decades before, he'd made a run at the White House and lost. Since then, he'd dedicated himself to being the House's unofficial historian and parliamentarian. "I think you made a mistake taking us to recess—if I may speak so plainly. As a matter of law, sir, you are already the president of the United States. The language of the Twenty-fifth Amendment is clear. Upon the death or incapacity of both the president and vice president, the Speaker of the House of Representatives becomes acting president. There's no language about whether or not said Speaker represents the majority present in the chamber. You were Speaker when the officers of the executive branch died, so you therefore are, in fact, president. Sir."

"You might have brought that up inside the chamber," Oscar Colson said.

"What would be the point?" Sinclair said. "Fact is fact. Discussing it doesn't change reality. Mr. President, the oath of office is not even necessary."

Penn turned to his chief of staff. "Arlen?"

"Yes, Mr. President?"

"That's not helpful."

"Perhaps not. But it is my answer. Mr. President."

Lianne Holt stood. "I think we need to be careful not to get too far out over our skis here," she said. "History will be watching us. Perhaps not in real time, but we have to believe that there will be a future, and with that as the basis, we have to understand that optics are important. I think taking the oath of office is essential. Lyndon Johnson was criticized at the time for what the media called grandstanding after the JFK assassination, but that picture from the plane made a statement to the world that America is bigger than its leadership. The United States survives."

"There was no challenge to the legitimacy of Johnson's vice presidency," said Jack Collins of Montana.

"Nor is there one here," Sinclair said. His tone had hardened. "Tantrums from the other side of the aisle have no impact on truth and reality."

Penn challenged him. "That's easy to say, Burt, but you're one of the great partisans in this House. To the other side—"

"The other side wants the power," Sinclair interrupted. "Why make this more complicated than it needs to be? When we reconvene, Randy Banks will be in the Speaker's chair, and his first order of business will be to hold the vote that will get him fired."

A welcome laugh rippled through the cafeteria.

Sinclair continued, "Angela Fortnight will become Speaker, and you'll have the pleasure of working together to lead the nation out of this ungodly mess that we never would have been in if Helen Blanton wasn't a total incompetent." He smiled as he glanced over the glasses that perpetually defied the laws of physics and remained balanced on the tip of his nose. "I trust that we are not on the record."

Another laugh.

"The oath of office, sir." Lianne Holt wasn't coming off that point.

"Fine," Penn said. "We'll get that administered during the recess. After I've had a chance to take a nap."

Somebody said, "A joint session."

Penn's head snapped toward the source, over to his left, but he didn't know who the speaker was. "Excuse me?"

Chester Hamilton, of Ohio, stood to be recognized. Bookish, thin and not yet thirty, Chester was part of the incoming congressional freshman class. With his unruly dark hair and round glasses, he bore a striking resemblance to a famous fictional wizard. "Mr. President, sir, I think that you should get word to both the House and the Senate that you intend to conduct a joint session of Congress. The optics will be exactly what you're looking for. It's a strong statement to the other side that you're not going to tolerate their antics, and it's a way to get as positive a message as you're willing to give out to the rest of the world. Both here and abroad. Sir."

Chester blushed when he was done and sat back down. He looked as if he were startled to hear his own words.

"Young man, that is a brilliant idea," Sinclair said. "You don't give Fortnight and her sycophants a chance to turn this into a mud fight. Show, don't tell. Isn't that the old wisdom?"

Caleb's stomach hurt. He was hungry, and he needed to take a dump, but he didn't want to be the one to make everybody stop. His feet hurt, too, and his legs and his back, but that was just the new way of things. He'd been on long hikes before, and none of this was any different. The pain would peak and go away. Blisters would become calluses, sooner or later. He didn't have any hot spots on his feet yet, thank God, but he had moleskin in his pack if it came to that.

There was just a lot of nothing out here. A lot of woods, but nothing else. They'd been marching for nearly two hours and they hadn't passed a single building. It felt weird to be walking in the middle of the road. He kept expecting a car to come around a curve at them, but there were no cars to come. If cars were still a thing, they'd be in one now.

He was pissed at himself for puking back there. That was a pussy thing to do, but he couldn't help it. He'd never seen brains before, and the way they were just hanging out of that guy's face triggered an instantaneous barf. That probably had something to do with why he felt so hungry now.

But food needed to be conserved. He got that. The dried shit they were all carrying in their go bags was all the prepared food that they'd get, and it needed to be preserved. The rules were simple, but hard to take. If you have a successful hunt, or if you catch a few fish, you can eat until you're stuffed. But if you've only got emergency rations, you only eat enough to keep the body's lights on and the engine running. Five hundred calories in a pinch, though that wouldn't be sustainable for more than a couple of days.

Caleb wasn't sure what he thought about Major McCrea. About Joe. He didn't like the way he spoke to Mom, but he had to admit that she was being kind of a pain in the ass. He got that Mom was worried about her *babies*—God, he hated it when she called him her baby—but she needed to understand that even Luke was old enough to cowboy up a little. For all those years, she'd embarrassed them with her bug-out drills and survival adventures, but let's be real here. She'd never had to *do* any of the stuff she'd been talking about. She read a lot of books about survival, and she'd gone to conferences, but she'd never had to, you know, *survive.*

Joe, on the other hand, and maybe Paul Copley, too, had walked the walk. At least they'd come closer to walking it than Mom had. Caleb thought maybe she should back off a little on the badass congresswoman bullshit.

Caleb felt bad for not feeling sadder about all the people he knew had been killed last night. All of his friends back home were probably dead. Every building, every *everything* back in Arlington was probably crushed flat and burned black, but it was as if all of it were a movie. Maybe it was too much to think about. Maybe that's what PTSD was all about.

Was it okay if he felt a little bit good that Richard Goldsbury might have been vaporized? God Almighty, he hated that kid. He'd rip the books out of your hand while walking down the hall, and then kick them across the floor. If Goldsbury wasn't so friggin' huge, Caleb would have punched him out, but suicide was always a bad idea. Yeah, it was okay if Richard was toast.

Joe raised his hand to bring them all to a stop. Caleb and the others walked up next to him and then stopped. Another car, this one dead in the middle of the road. An old Cadillac. "First Sergeant, you come with me," the major said. "The rest of you hang back and keep an eye on the woods."

"What are we looking for?" Caleb asked.

"Bad guys," Joe replied.

Caleb's stomach flipped. "Screw this," he mumbled, and he took a knee.

"What are you doing?" Mom asked.

Shrugging out of his rucksack, he slid the two halves of his Ruger 10/22 out of their sleeves and assembled them. He inserted the barrel and forestock into the receiver and twisted them together. A satisfying *click* told him that he was done. He chambered a round of .22 long-rifle ammo, double-checked that the safety was on. He stuck his head and right arm through the loop of his single-point sling and, just like that, he was armed. When he looked up, he saw that his mother and little brother were doing the same thing.

"I guess we should be ready to shoot back, huh?" Mom said. "Be sure your—"

"—safety is on," Luke said. "Already there."

Joe and Paul approached the Cadillac with their rifles up to their shoulders, and they moved as if they were expecting a gunfight.

"Watch the woods, not the guys," Mom said.

The Emersons had modified their 10/22s to resemble an AR15 platform, complete with a collapsible stock that made it easier to carry. On the Picatinny rail atop the receiver, they'd each installed a red dot sight. In their rucks, each of them carried a tactical flashlight that could be attached to the barrel shroud for night operations.

"Keep your muzzles down and fingers off the trigger," Mom said.

"How will we know a bad guy from a good guy?" Luke asked.

Caleb said, "If he points a gun at you, he's a bad guy."

"Har, har," Luke mocked.

"We're clear here," the major announced. "We can move on."

"No sign of the occupants?" Mom asked.

"Not a one. I guess when their engine stopped, they decided to do what we're doing and start walking."

"Are you sure we're going the right way?" Luke asked. He had that whiny edge to his voice that made Caleb want to punch him out sometimes.

Paul Copley said, "Only one road, we're headed toward the river, and it's going more or less downhill. We can't *not* be on the right road."

"Don't get cocky, First Sergeant," the major warned. "God doesn't like cocky."

"How far are we from the nearest bomb site?" Caleb asked.

"Hard to say," the major replied. "We're about seventy miles from Charleston, so maybe there. The trees here are still standing, and the fires are still far away, so I think we're safe for now."

Luke asked, "How far away is . . . Where are we going?"

"Ortho," Mom said. "We figured ten miles from where we first started. How far do you think we've walked so far, First Sergeant?"

"Please call me Paul," he said. "I figure we've gone six, maybe seven miles."

"So four or five more to go," she said.

"I know how to add," Luke said.

Five minutes later, just as they finished a long curve in the road to the left, they wandered up on a stalled tractor hauling a big box trailer. The driver had been able to cruise off to the side of the road before he stopped it. It had settled at a severe angle, listing to its right side. Had it not been for the closest trees, it might have flipped onto its side. The back doors lay open and cardboard boxes of various sizes littered the road. Most had been pried open, but others had not.

Caleb made a beeline for the boxes. Who knew what kind of cool stuff might be inside them?

"That's not yours!" Mom yelled.

"It's nobody's" Caleb mumbled. "That means it's everybody's"

The boxes were mostly electronic stuff. Laptop computers, smartphones, a few televisions. Too heavy to carry, and pretty much useless in this new world. The boxes that had been opened had been opened carelessly and quickly, the cardboard torn rather than cut. The contents of those boxes—also electronics primarily—had been spilled out onto the street. One flat-screen television looked like it had been kicked, its center dented with a heavy impact, with spider line cracks spreading out in all directions.

"This looks like looting," Copley said.

Victoria strode forward. "Caleb, get back here!"

He ignored her. This was too interesting. There was still more stuff inside the box trailer. He could see the cardboard from this angle, but he couldn't see the markings. He needed to get in closer so he—

"Oh, shit!" Caleb yelled it reflexively and jumped away from the opening with enough force to cause himself to trip. "Oh, goddamn!"

A man in jeans and a flannel shirt lay on the floor inside the trailer, coated with blood that had formed a crimson river along the line where the right-hand wall met the wooden floor.

Victoria and McCrea arrived at his side simultaneously. McCrea took one look, then spun around with his M4 against his shoulder at low ready.

Victoria pulled Caleb away, then shouldered her own rifle. "Guns up, boys," she said. They knew exactly what to do. To McCrea, she said, "Murder or suicide?"

"I didn't see a gun," McCrea said. "The blood isn't dry yet. That means his killer is still nearby."

"We need to not be here," Victoria said.

"I one hundred percent agree," McCrea said. "Let's move on."

"Heads up, Major," Copley said. He'd locked his eyes on a sight in the woods down the hill and over to the left.

A bearded man stood in the shadow of the trees, his dark hair pulled back in a tight ponytail. He looked like he'd been trying to remain invisible, but once he was made, he took a step forward. His belt was weighted with a large revolver, and a shortened pump shotgun lay slung across his chest.

"Mornin'," he said.

Victoria pulled her kids closer, but Caleb pulled away. He fingered the safety off his Ruger. Victoria felt a swell of pride. Her safety had been off for some time now.

"We don't want any trouble," McCrea said.

"That works out good," the stranger said. "'Cause me and my friends don't want no trouble, either." His voice had a distinct mountain twang to it.

Four more people materialized from the shadows. Another man and two women. All of them were armed and looked mean as hell. The ground around them was littered with a wide variety of foodstuffs and clothing. It was too far away to make out the packaging, but they clearly were trying to hide it from view.

"Somebody sure made a mess out here," the stranger said.

"Vicky," McCrea said softly, "take your boys on down the hill. First Sergeant Copley and I will join you in a few minutes."

"I think we'll stay right here," Victoria replied. "Firepower is firepower."

"My name's Grubbs," the stranger said. "Jeffrey Grubbs. Are we at war, General?"

"Major," McCrea said. "We were, but I'm not sure if we still are. We're as displaced and confused as anybody else. We're just trying to get to civilization."

"You're in the wrong part of the world for that," Grubbs said. "But there's a town down that hill about four or five mile."

"Is that where you're going?" McCrea asked.

"Nah, that's where we're coming from. We thought we'd try livin' in the wild."

"Do you know what happened here?" Caleb asked.

Grubbs cocked his head at the question and started walking toward them.

McCrea and Copley changed their stances, widening their feet and angling their bodies. "I'll thank you to keep your distance," McCrea said.

"Safety off, Luke," Victoria said.

"Easy there, General. What you see ain't all I got. For not wantin' trouble, you seem to be ready for a lot of it."

McCrea said nothing. Grubbs stopped his advance.

"You got a pretty family," Grubbs said.

"We're not a family," Caleb said.

Grubbs threw his head back and issued a hearty laugh. "Well, ain't you the talkative one," he said. "Here you got all these grown-up adults keepin' their mouths shut, hopin' that we can all pretend that this is all normal shit." He made jazz hands and opened his eyes and mouth wide. "Wait. What dead guy? Is there a dead guy? But you—what's your name, kid?"

"That's none of your business," Victoria said.

"Ooh, and you're a sassy one, too. General, you got your hands full with these folks, don't you?"

Copley had pivoted away from Grubbs to face the others in the tree line.

"Your name, kid."

"Caleb," the boy said.

"Well, Caleb, since you asked such a good question, I'll give you an honest answer." Grubbs pressed his lips into a thin smile as he scanned their faces. "Me and my friends was walkin' up the hill that you're about to go down, and we found this wreck right where you see it. Then, when we seen the general here comin' with his army, well, we just slipped into the woods. We was worried people might think that we had something to do with what happened here."

"There's blood on your sleeve," Caleb said, pointing with his forehead.

"Caleb!" Victoria snapped.

The fake smile disappeared from Grubbs's face, replaced by a deep scowl. "General? Caleb's Mama? You might want to teach your oldest a few manners. He asks smart questions, but he's not very smart, is he?"

"This doesn't have to turn ugly," McCrea said.

"Oh, it's a little late for that, don't you think? How about me and my friends just shoot you down right here?"

McCrea took a step closer to Grubbs, blocking his eye line to the Emersons. "Here's the thing, Mr. Grubbs," he said. "I couldn't care less about what you and your friends may or may not have done here. A lot of things have changed in the world since last night, and I care more about surviving than seeing justice done."

"Well, General, that's great—"

"I'm not done," McCrea said. "If you or any of your merry band of followers raise the muzzles of their weapons even an inch, we're going to have a bloodbath right here in the middle of the street. Think *promise,* not *threat* there. This is a one-off chance for all of us to disengage and be on our way. It's entirely your call."

Very quietly, Victoria said, "Be ready, boys. Caleb, the other man in the woods is your target. Luke, you take the lady on the left, and I'll take the lady in the middle. Nod if you understand."

They nodded, though Luke also snuffled.

"You make an interesting proposition, General. So, how do we put the genie back in the bottle?"

"We'll just disengage," McCrea said. "You and your team disappear into the forest, while my team and I disappear down the road."

"You're going to trust me to do that?" Grubbs asked. "How do you know I won't just shoot you in the back?"

"You're never going to see my back," McCrea said. "Remember, keep those muzzles low."

"And you'll do the same?"

"It's the only way to end this without a lot of gun smoke and blood," McCrea said. "How about I count to three, and we all start backing away?"

"Works for me."

"One . . . Oh, one last thing," McCrea said, interrupting himself. "This encounter is a one-off. The rules reset after we're out of each other's sight. If I see you again, it's war."

"I couldn'ta said it better," Grubbs agreed.

McCrea recited the three count, and they took a step away from each other. Then another step.

Victoria said, "Keep your eyes on your targets, boys. Walk backward."

"Vicky, are you and the boys moving?"

"Yes, but we still have you covered," she said. "Muzzle discipline," she reminded. "Keep them down until there's a threat."

"W-who are those people?" Luke stammered.

"Murderers," Caleb said.

"Young Master Caleb," Victoria said, "you and I are soon going to have a very serious conversation."

McCrea and Copley had begun backing down the hill as well.

"Are you saying they're not murderers?"

"I'm saying that there's a time to keep your mouth shut. You almost got people seriously hurt right then."

Maybe two minutes later—certainly no longer than that—the two groups were out of each other's sight. McCrea spun on his heel and rushed forward to give Caleb a huge shove, which made the boy stumble and nearly fall.

"Hey!" Victoria yelled, and she darted out to be in between them. "Keep your hands off my children."

"Get out of my way," McCrea seethed. "Caleb, you're a moron. What the hell were you trying to prove back there?"

"I've already spoken to him about—"

"Honest to God, ma'am, you need to get out of my way. I don't give a shit what you've spoken to him about. It's my turn."

"I just said what everybody already knew!" Caleb shouted. He was ready for the fight.

"Did I look like I needed help?" McCrea said. "Did I ask you to open your goddamn mouth? Next time you cross me, I swear to God, I'm going to knock you on your ass."

"Major McCrea!" Victoria yelled.

"Mrs. Emerson!" he shouted back. "Just a little while ago, this young man made a point to seek me out and tell me that he wanted to be treated like a man. He made it abundantly clear that, at least in his mind, he is no longer a child. Am I lying, Caleb?"

The boy looked suddenly embarrassed, rocked back by the major's tone.

"No, I'm not lying!" McCrea went on. "That's what you said. Well, welcome to the adult world. You are not in charge here, do you understand that?"

Caleb looked at his feet.

"The question requires an answer," Victoria said. McCrea had every right to be pissed. And Caleb was one of the few people in the world who steadfastly ignored her, and too often got away with it.

McCrea seemed startled by her change in tone. "Your mom is right. I need an answer. Do you understand who is specifically *not* in charge?"

When Caleb's eyes rocked back up, they were hot with emotion. Equal parts anger and humiliation, perhaps. Nothing that registered as remorse, though. "I am specifically not in charge."

"Exactly. Caleb, think of all that has happened in the last, what, twelve hours? People are in a blind panic, and they're liable to do anything. You picked a fight back there that didn't have to be fought."

"They killed that guy!"

"So? Did you think that your snotty comments would somehow bring him back to life? Did you think there was some magical way to roll back time?"

"He's just going to get away with it!"

"Again. So? Are you now the judge and jury? Are you going to bring justice in the middle of a firestorm?"

"Somebody has to!"

McCrea looked to Victoria for support.

"Everything's different now, Caleb," she said. The new reality was coming into sharp focus for her. "People will get away with many, many transgressions that never would have been right before yesterday. It's not our job to get in the way."

McCrea said, "In fact, it's our job to stay *out* of their way. Other people's problems belong to other people. We've got plenty to worry about all on our own."

The muscles in Caleb's jaw flexed like he was chewing gum. "Are you done?" He didn't wait for an answer before he turned and started down the hill, this time in the lead. Luke walked with him, and McCrea fell in with Victoria.

"I'm sorry I yelled at you," he said.

"You should be," she replied. "They're my children, not your soldiers."

"From here on out, Vicky, we are all soldiers. Every one of us is tasked with the fight." A few seconds passed before he added, "Caleb's got quite a mouth."

"He's a good boy," she said. "But he's wired funny. He is incapable of backing down from a fight. You'll get much better results from him if you choose diplomacy over confrontation."

"Sometimes the situation doesn't accommodate diplomacy."

"Is that so?" Victoria asked. "So, by getting in his face like that, were you able to undo the confrontation with Mr. Grubbs? *Did you think there was some magical way to roll back time?*"

McCrea looked confused for a few seconds until he realized that he'd heard his own words recited back to him. He chuckled. "I saw how you did that. Well played."

They'd gone maybe a hundred yards and were approaching a right-hand switchback when McCrea turned and started walking backward again.

"Are we sill alone?" Victoria asked.

"We seem to be. But I imagine we'll see them again."

Victoria agreed. "You can only hang out in the woods and hunt for so long. The weather's going to turn soon. Being cold grows old pretty quickly."

"So this town we're going to," McCrea said, "Ortho. What do you know about it?"

"It's not my district," Victoria said, "but they've come on some tough times. There was a good-size auto-manufacturing plant there until a few years ago, but it shut down when the jobs went to

China. From what I've heard, there's not a lot left except poverty and meth."

"Meth?" Copley asked. "As in methamphetamine?"

Victoria didn't know he'd been listening. "Unfortunately, we're pretty much in the meth capital of the country. One of them, anyway. That's another group that will turn feral in a few days."

Within four miles, as they approached the Kanawha River Basin, the terrain flattened and straightened. Somewhere along the way, the road they were walking changed from a route number to Charleston Street. The woods transformed to lawns—big ones, an acre or more. Most were occupied by ranch homes, less than two thousand square feet, though there were a few two-story houses, and a few double-wides. This was not a prosperous town, but it had a feeling of life to it, unlike so many of the burgs in Coal Country, where desperation was the only tangible commodity.

They kept to the center of the street in hopes of being perceived as the least possible threat. The last thing Victoria wanted was to trespass on people's property. Never give an excuse for people to be more paranoid than they already were.

"People on the porch, up on the right, Major," Copley said.

Four people in total stood in a line under the roof of a wraparound porch: a man and a woman plus two girls under ten. The dad and mom had pistols holstered on their hips, but they didn't seem to present any threat.

Victoria waved. "Good morning," she called. The instant the words were gone, she regretted them. Precious little was *good* about this morning.

"You're not from here," the man said.

"We lost our vehicle last night," Victoria said. They never slowed.

"You're Army?"

"Yes, sir, I am," McCrea said. "But I don't have any information for you."

"Where's the rest of you?" the woman asked. "The rest of the Army, I mean?"

"We weren't part of a larger unit," McCrea said.

"That was a war, right?" the man asked.

"Yes, sir, it was."

"Is it over now?"

"I don't know that, either. I'm sorry, I know you want information. We all want information, but there's nothing to pass along."

Victoria lowered her voice and said, "Boys, I want you to keep your eyes forward when we run into people like that."

"I didn't do anything," Luke said.

"I know. I just wanted to say."

"Are we going to be staying here?" Caleb asked.

"Maybe for a while," Victoria replied. They needed rest and they needed supplies. They needed transportation. The problem was, everybody needed the same thing. There wasn't a soul left in North America, probably, that wasn't wanting for items that were critical to their survival.

"Like, in a hotel?" Luke asked.

"Maybe. But not for long."

"I thought we were going to join Adam," Caleb said.

"That's the plan," Victoria said. "But that's going to take a while. Weeks, probably."

"We're going to *walk* the whole way?" Caleb sounded horrified.

"Just like the settlers in the old days," Victoria said.

"At least they had horses."

"Pace yourself on the complaints, Caleb," McCrea said. "We've got a long way to go. Hey, Luke, take a look behind us. Is the Grubbs gang still keeping their distance?"

"I don't see anybody."

Victoria chose to accept that as good news.

Up ahead, Simmons Gas and Goodies, an Exxon distributor, marked the intersection with Fourth Avenue, where Ortho began to look less like a neighborhood and more like a little town. All the infrastructure was here—roads, streetlights, stoplights, signs—but none of it was working. The glass doors of the Exxon station had been shattered and now rested open and broken at odd angles. The hoses and nozzles from the pumps themselves lay on the ground like so many slain snakes.

Directly across Fourth Avenue, Joey's Pawnshop had been similarly ravaged. The glass lay strewn in the parking lot. The security bars had been pried from the walls. Even from the outside, it was clear that the shelves had been cleared of merchandise.

"What happened here?" Caleb asked.

"Looting," McCrea answered.

"Why do I suspect the Grubbs gang?" Victoria mused.

In the near distance, a cheer went up, and then voices turned ugly as they hurled epithets and threats. It sounded like budding violence. In the near distance, a mob had formed. Not a crowd, a *mob.*

"Boys, stay with the major," Victoria said, and she took off to see what was happening.

McCrea grabbed her biceps to stop her. "That's not our fight," he said.

She pulled away. She recognized the crowd for what it was, a vector to violence. "That's a lynching in progress," she said. "Take care of my kids."

"Bullshit," Caleb said. "Nobody's taking care of me." He took off after his mom, and Luke reluctantly followed his brother.

"God damn it," McCrea spat. "First Sergeant, that means us, too."

As she passed the intersection of Fourth Avenue and Kanawha Street, headed toward the river, Victoria cringed at what she heard. *Kill them* and *execute them* jumped out plain and clear. Whatever this was, it was spinning out of control.

The crowd was growing by the second as the commotion attracted otherwise baffled residents. Victoria saw a complete sampler of citizens. Men and women, boys and girls, black and white. They stood gathered in a rough circle, maybe twenty feet across. Two young men, neither of them yet twenty years old, cowered on the ground in the middle of the circle. One was shirtless, the skin of his back and chest scraped and bleeding, and the other was nearly so, his shirt in tatters and barely hanging off his neck and left arm. That one had also lost his shoes in whatever melee had spun up around them.

"You Foster boys was never no good!" yelled a woman who might have been in her seventies.

A little girl in jeans and a Hello Kitty shirt stormed out to the men and kicked the shirtless one in the small of his back.

This was no doubt a lynching, and if it hadn't already passed its tipping point, it was close.

A man in his forties, dressed in the striped shirt of a gas station employee, stepped forward with a lever-action .30-30 hunting rifle. He strode toward the boys and leveled the rifle at the shirtless one's head.

"Stop!" Victoria yelled. Without thinking, acting purely on adrenaline, she sprinted forward and charged the man with the rifle. She hit him hard from behind, knocking him forward and causing him to trip over the man he'd been about to murder.

The man she'd tackled hit the ground hard, but Victoria was able to stay on her feet and recover her balance quickly. By the time the man in the Exxon shirt was able to roll to his knee and regain control of his rifle, Victoria already had her 10/22 up to her shoulder, her red dot focused on the third button of his shirt. At this range, sights didn't even matter.

"I said, *stop!*" Victoria declared. "Put the rifle on the ground, or I swear to God I will kill you right there."

The speed and violence of her tackle had startled the gathered crowd, but the effect didn't last for more than a few seconds. They turned even angrier, and all of it was focused on Victoria. "Who the hell—"

The world shook with the heavy boom of a rifle, and everyone in the street cowered.

"All right," McCrea yelled. He'd fired into the asphalt street to get their attention. "This shit stops right now!" As he spoke, he stepped into the center of the circle. Copley took a position behind Mr. Exxon. The Emerson boys moved in to be with their mom. All muzzles but Victoria's were pointed at low ready.

"Listen up, everybody," McCrea said. "If you've got weapons on you, keep them holstered or pointing at the ground. First Sergeant Copley, Caleb and Luke, watch the crowd. If anybody points a weapon at anybody else, shoot them."

Caleb shivered at the words. Was he really serious?

Victoria kept her focus on Mr. Exxon. "Let's de-escalate this," she said. "Lay that deer rifle on the ground, and we can talk."

"Who the hell are you?"

"That's one of the things we can talk about. After you put your rifle on the ground."

Mr. Exxon had crossed a concerning line. She could see it in his eyes and in the angle of his stance. Now he needed to save face. He'd gone too far, and he knew it. Victoria let him figure it out in silence. All around her, she could *feel* the vitriol of the crowd.

In the end, Mr. Exxon did the sane thing and gently placed the .30-30 on the ground. When he stood tall again, she let her 10/22 fall against its sling.

"Let's all relax a little," she said.

"Them Fosters are thieves!" the same old lady declared. "Looters. Looters get executed."

"Not today, they don't," Victoria said.

CHAPTER SEVENTEEN

". . . .and will, to the best of my ability, preserve, protect and defend the Constitution of the United States, so help me God." Penn knew the oath of office by heart, but for the benefit of the camera, he thought it best to be prompted by House Majority Leader Randy Banks.

"Congratulations, Mr. President." They shook hands. The cameraman from Solara gave a thumbs-up that the camera was off. Anticipating the possibility that the Speaker would be elevated to president while confined in the bunker, Solara had stocked a business suit for Penn, complete with a shirt, tie and cufflinks. No dress shoes, though, because the shoes would never be in any official photograph.

Penn nodded to Dennis Laraja, Senate majority leader. "Senator Laraja, please inform the members that a joint session of Congress will begin in fifteen minutes."

"Leader Fortnight is going to—"

"Shit pickles. Yes, I know." Penn smiled. "But this is not a day to enjoy the suffering of others."

With the available time before his address to the joint session, Penn decided to return to his quarters in the dormitory wing. He wanted to brush his teeth and tame his hair before resetting the history of the United States of America.

The dormitory wing sat directly across the massive common office area from the House and Senate Chambers. Like every other wing of the Annex, the dorms were separated from the common area by latching double doors that were controlled by electronic locks. Wave the identification badge at the box on the wall, then the lock buzzed to let you in.

While Penn shared his room with only one other person, the majority leader of the Senate, rank-and-file members slept in stacked bunks, two to a stack, twenty members to a room. The bathroom and shower facilities had clearly been designed by the same team that created gang showers at boot camp. Senior status as a member of Congress did not grant him private facilities.

With his last-minute hygiene chores complete, Penn was exiting the bath facilities when a noise down the hall got his attention. The hospital wing was located down the same hallway, all the way at the end, the last room before a set of heavy metal double doors that were labeled, SOLARA STAFF ONLY.

A Solara staffer, whom Penn had not seen before, was wheeling a gurney out of the hospital wing. The gurney appeared to be transporting a person, but the cargo was completely covered. The employee—Penn thought of them all as soldiers—swiped his card on the reader next to the heavy metal doors, and when the lock buzzed, he turned around, pushed the doors open with his backside and pulled the gurney into the room.

"Excuse me!" Penn called. "You! Excuse me, please!"

The soldier looked startled and moved more quickly.

"Is that a person?" Penn asked.

The soldier disappeared and the door snapped shut behind him.

How odd.

After the members of the House and Senate arrived in the auditorium, exchanged pleasantries and took their seats, Randy Banks strode to the front and sat in the Speaker's chair. A ripple of concern ran through Angela Fortnight's side of the aisle as they anticipated what lay ahead.

From the rear, Parker Wortham, president pro tempore of the Senate, and now next in line to the presidency, announced, "Mr. Speaker, the president of the United States."

Everyone rose to their feet as Penn made his way down the aisle toward the well, but the applause was sparse, uncomfortable. Senators from both parties ultimately came around and applauded, but Leader Fortnight sat in her seat, signaling for all others in her party to sit as well.

While people were distracted, a Solara employee had hung the famous Great Seal of the President of the United States on the front of the lectern at the leading edge of the rostrum.

Penn Glendale settled his shoulders and straightened his tie. This was a recording to be made for prosperity. His remarks would be brief and largely nonsubstantive, by necessity. He would assure the world that the government of the United States was still present, still strong. These were terrible times, but they would soon pass, and soon we, as a nation, would begin the process of healing.

If he nailed the tone just right, his words could provide inspiration to millions.

Finally at the well of the House floor, he took his place behind the lectern. Randy Banks rose from his seat and announced, "Members of Congress, I have the high privilege and distinct honor of presenting to you the president of the United States."

The assembled members of the House and Senate rose to their feet again for the pro forma applause.

Angela Fortnight shouted above the applause, silencing it. "Mr. Speaker, this man is *not* the president of the United States. He is at the rostrum under false pretenses. I and my party do not recognize him as such."

With that, she and her caucus rose from their seats and marched out of the chamber.

"Who in the living hell do you think you are?" Exxon Man asked. The stitching on his shirt read, *George.* "You got no business—"

"I am not going to let you murder these two boys in my presence, George," Victoria said. "I don't care what they did. This—*this right here*—is not justice. And unless the courthouse dress code has changed, you are not a judge." She swept a finger in an arc around the others. "And this is no jury."

Victoria watched the crowd that was watching her. The passion of the moment seemed to have passed. Maybe there wouldn't be a gunfight after all. "Caleb? Luke?" she said.

"Yeah?" They said it in unison.

"Check those boys on the ground. Tell me if they're badly hurt."

"We're fine," said one of the Fosters.

"This is a time for you to be silent, young man," Victoria said.

"Ma'am?" This from a young lady with brilliant green eyes. She wore a gray business suit and looked entirely out of place. "Who are you? You don't live here, do you? But you look familiar to me."

"I'm from Pocahontas County," Victoria said. "I'm Victoria Emerson. These are my sons, and the other gentlemen are my friends."

"Are you the Congress lady?" asked a man dressed entirely in denim. "I've seen you on television, right?"

"I'm the representative for the Third Congressional District here in West Virginia. And, yes, I've done a few of the Sunday shows." She felt herself blushing.

"What the hell makes you think you've got a say in what we do in our own town?" Denim Guy said. "You're a long way from Pocahontas County."

"I'm pretty sure that murder is as illegal here as it is there," Victoria said. "Who among you is in charge here?"

"I am," said George.

Green Eyes said, "He is not. He just thinks he is. The real answer is *nobody's* in charge."

"No mayor?"

"No, ma'am."

"What about the police?"

"We depend on state police and county sheriffs," Denim Guy said.

"What we really do is depend on ourselves," George said. "We can look out for ourselves."

Victoria let that go. The immediate aftermath of an attempted lynching was the wrong time to get high-and-mighty about local governance.

"They're okay, Mom," Caleb reported. "Lots of bruises and some chipped teeth, but they say they're okay."

"What are your names, boys?" Victoria asked the would-be victims.

"Kyle Foster," the shirtless one said. "That's my brother, Caine."

"Stand up, both of you," Victoria said. "George, do me a favor and step back a bit."

George stood along with the Fosters, but hesitated.

"You can take your rifle with you," Victoria said. "Okay, Kyle and Caine, what's your story?" Now that they were standing next to each other, she realized that they were identical twins. The different injuries and swollen facial features had concealed that.

"They're thieves!" the old lady said again. Apparently, it was the only tune she knew how to sing.

"You be quiet," Victoria snapped. To the Fosters: "That mess that I saw on the way down Charleston Street. Was that your doing?"

"No'm," Kyle said. He seemed to be the pair's mouthpiece.

"That's bullshit!" yelled the little girl who kicked them.

Victoria spun on her and snapped her finger as she pointed at the girl's nose. "You watch your mouth, young lady. You will not use that language around me. Not at your age."

A woman standing next to her puffed up. "That's my daughter you're snapping at."

"Then act like her mother," Victoria said. "Kyle, you were saying . . ."

"We didn't have nothin' to do with the gas station nor the pawnshop. I don't know who done that. Neither of us does."

"That *is* bullshit!" Denim Man said. "And don't you dare snap your fingers at me, lady. We *caught* these two in the act."

"In the act of what?"

"Of stealin' shit. They was *inside* the pawnshop. *My* pawnshop."

Joey's Pawnshop. She supposed that meant Denim Man's real name was Joey.

Victoria looked back to the Foster boys and waited.

"Okay, yeah, we was inside, but we didn't steal nothin'. Shit, there was nothin' in there left to steal. We sure as hell had nothin' to do with all the breakin' in and stuff."

"The place was already empty," Caine added.

Victoria rolled her eyes. This was why suspects needed lawyers to speak for them.

"See?" Joey said, pointing at the Foster boys. "They just admitted that they was tryin' to steal. They gotta be punished for that. If there was still stuff in there, they'da taken it. That's the same as actually looting."

Victoria pointed to George. "And your friend in the striped shirt just tried to murder these two boys. Shall we punish him for the crime he almost committed, but didn't?" She let the question hang in the air. "What about all of you?" She spread her arms to indicate the gathering crowd. "You were about to let George kill them. This nasty little girl assaulted them. Do you really think this is the best time to talk about criminal intent for crimes that didn't happen?"

The silence told her that she'd made her point. At the very least, she'd shamed them into silence. "Okay, then. This is over. Kyle and Caine, clean up your act."

"What about my store?" Joey said. "And George's station?"

"What's gone is gone. We need to pivot to keeping what you have."

"Hey, Major!" someone called from the crowd. "What the hell happened last night?"

Victoria didn't yield the floor. "The world went to war last night," she said. "Hey, is there a place where we can all sit down? My family and I have been walking for hours."

"Sure," said the cranky old lady. "Come to my place." She pointed to a squatty building with darkened neon soda and beer signs. The placard over the door read, MAGGIE'S PLACE.

"Are you Maggie?"

"Ever since the day I was born." Maggie led the way down the little sidewalk and up the single step into a darkened space that smelled of old grease and spilled beer.

Victoria paused to let her boys enter before her, and then fell in behind. Maggie pointed to the front table with an open palm. "Since you're the one with the news, you get the head table," she said. After Victoria was seated, Maggie leaned in close and whispered, "I'm sorry about that ugliness out there. We're usually better people than that."

Most of the crowd from outside streamed into Maggie's Place and took seats in the dark. Even the Foster brothers came in, a decision that Victoria likely would not have made. She noted that McCrea and Copley continued to maintain their protector roles, taking positions near the front and back doors.

"Here's what we know about last night," Victoria began. It took no longer than ten minutes to relay the known details. When she was done, everyone looked appropriately horrified.

"So, did we win or did we lose?" someone asked.

"Does it matter?" someone else said.

"And that's a valid point," Victoria said. "In the best case, we're all going to be on our own for quite some time. What's the population of Ortho?"

"Call it a thousand people," George said. "But we're spread all over hell and gone. I don't think we have more than a hundred that actually lives *in* the town."

"Do you have a doctor?"

"There are a couple in Nitro," a lady said. "That's maybe twenty miles from here."

"Twenty-three," Joey said. "Looks like we're back to the days where three miles here or there will make a hell of a difference."

"What about a pharmacy?"

"Nitro," Joey said.

"We got a lot of old folks around here," Maggie said. "A lot of sick folks. More 'n a couple got the cancer of one form or another."

Victoria rubbed her forehead as the enormity of what lay ahead crystalized in her mind. For the survivors, the suffering had not yet really begun.

"What about a grocery store?"

"That got hit by looters last night, too," Joey said. "But what's left of it is up the street, just past Simmons's. Ortho Grocery."

"Okay," Victoria said. "Joey, I want you to pick a team of five people to go clean out everything that's left in the grocery store and bring it here to Maggie's."

"Why here?" Maggie asked.

"Because it's someplace," Victoria said.

"How are we gonna pay for it?" Joey said. "That'll make me no better than a looter myself."

"Who's the owner of Ortho Grocery?" Victoria asked.

"Ben Barnett," George said. "And trust me, he ain't just gonna stand there and let us steal his shit."

"Is Ben here?" Victoria asked.

"No, he's over guarding his store from more looters."

Victoria said, "Fine. George, take your rifle with you and go with Joey to relieve Ben of guard duty for a few minutes while he comes over here and talks with me."

George stood up. "What am I gonna tell him you want to talk about?"

"Please, George," Victoria said.

"Why are we listening to you?" asked the nasty girl's nasty mother. "You're not from around here."

Victoria ignored her. "George? Joey? Please."

They left.

"Here's the deal, people," Victoria said. "None of us knows anything about the future, but we know about chemistry and physics. How many of you are hunters?"

Pretty much every hand went up.

"Perfect. That means you know how to put up meat. No electricity means no refrigeration, and no refrigeration means everything that's edible now will be rotten in a day or two, unless we get ahead of it. Maggie, what do you have in your freezer here?"

"Mostly hamburger meat and hot dogs. Bread. You know, pub food."

"Are there other restaurants or diners in town? Places with commercial kitchens?"

"About two miles up the road, there's the Road House," Maggie said. "I don't know what they have on hand, and I've never been in their kitchen. But I know they got seven kids, and they ain't likely to share, if that's where you're going."

And that was entirely fair, Victoria thought. Concentric circles. "What about you, Maggie? Are you willing to share what you've got in your freezer?"

"So long as I get first dibs, sure."

"Please tell me that your cooktop is gas."

"Propane. Got a tank out back."

Finally a bit of good news. "Have you ever canned ground beef?"

Maggie scrunched her face. "That sounds terrible."

"Put in enough salt and it's not so bad. But what it is, is edible five years from now."

"Is it like canning anything else?"

"Pretty much," Victoria said. "Cook the beef, put it in the jar while it's hot, cover it with liquid and seal the jar and let it cool. Mother Nature takes care of the rest. In fact, all of you can do that. Go back to your homes and pretend you've returned to the nineteenth century. Whatever's in your freezer. As it thaws, you can smoke it, salt-cure it, do something to preserve the meat."

"Or we can hunt for fresh meat," a young man said.

"Absolutely," Victoria said. "That's your real-time food supply. Remember, though, for our whole lives, we've depended on technology that is not available to us anymore. When you kill a deer, enjoy the fresh steaks for the first day or two, but everything you used to put up in your freezer needs to be preserved in the old ways."

"What if we don't know how to do that?"

"Then my boys and I can teach you. Right, Caleb? Right, Luke?"

They both looked like they wanted to disappear. Public speaking was not high on the list for either of them.

A large man in well-worn overalls and a white ZZ Top beard raised his hand from the back. "I can help with that, too, ma'am," he said. "I got me a whole smokehouse. Everybody's welcome to use it."

Victoria smiled. "Thank you, Mr. . . ."

"Folks just call me Mr. Jake," he said. "Except around Christmastime, when some of the little ones are apt to call me Santa."

"Thank you, Mr. Jake. That's got to be everybody's attitude moving forward—"

A giant of a man filled the doorway of Maggie's Place, then strode up to Victoria's table with enough intensity to pull McCrea and Copley away from their posts and closer to the center. "Are you the lady who wants people to steal from my store?"

As her boys scooted away in their chairs, Victoria made a point of giving a friendly smile as she rose slowly from hers. "You must be Mr. Barnett," she said. She extended her hand. "Victoria Emerson."

"I don't give a shit who you are. What gives you the right to tell people to steal from me?"

"That's not exactly what I said."

"What else do you call taking shit that someone else paid for? And who the hell are you, anyway?"

Victoria decided to ignore the second half of his question. "I'd be happy to give you my credit card for everything you have on your shelves."

"The hell am I gonna do with a credit card?"

"You'd prefer cash? Greenbacks? So that you can pay for your next reorder?"

Ben Barnett gaped as the rest of the room squirmed in their seats.

"Mr. Barnett, I'm not trying to put you on the spot, but are you seeing my point? For the foreseeable future, *rich* and *poor* are the same thing. So I leave it to you. Is it better that your perishables rot in your possession and help no one, or might they be put to better use by being either preserved or consumed?"

Barnett looked like a kid who'd been caught in a lie. He wanted to protest, but instead looked away. "Why not in my place, then? Why bring it all the way over here?"

"I understand that you have a security issue at your store. I haven't seen it, so I may be wrong."

"Goddamn right I got a security issue. Some assholes broke out my windows and stole everything they could carry."

Victoria sat back down and gestured for Barnett to join her. "I'm very sorry to hear that. May I call you Ben?"

"Sure."

"Call me Vicky. We're in the process of organizing various groups to take care of food preservation. We'll need to move on to finding ways to get medicines to those who need them. There's much to be taken care of. And Maggie's Place here seems like as good a headquarters as anywhere. Plus she has the commercial-cooking equipment."

"Excuse me, Vicky, but I have a very nice kitchen, too," said a young lady who was extraordinarily pregnant. "I'm happy to help."

"Thank you . . ."

"Carol Robinson."

"Thank you, Carol. I'm going to have a devil of a time remembering first names. I know I'm going to lose the last names."

Carol smiled.

Victoria returned her attention to Ben Barnett. "So, what do you say, Ben? We'll have around-the-clock security teams here to make sure what's left doesn't disappear."

There was that look again. He so desperately wanted to say *no.* "All right, fine. I'll start with what's refrigerated and work down to what's frozen. We have some time with that."

Victoria thrust out her hand again. "Thank you, Ben. On behalf of the entire community, thank you."

After they shook, she stood. A silent, friendly signal that the meeting was over. To the crowd, she said, "I'm sure Ben can use as much help as you are all willing to give."

Half the room stood and headed for the door.

"Those of you who are willing to work a shift as a security guard, please speak with my friends, Major McCrea and First Sergeant Copley. Would you mind organizing that, Major?"

McCrea looked startled to be called upon. "Sure."

A muscular young man, with well-trimmed blond hair and beard, raised his hand and stood from the table nearest the jukebox in the back of the restaurant. "What exactly is going on here . . . Is it Vicky?"

"Yes. Vicky Emerson."

"Eric Lofland. What makes you think we need you to be our queen?"

Victoria was ready for this. She'd heard this question in one form or another for years while stumping for her House seat. Not everyone is ready to embrace leadership from a female. She got that a female *outsider* could be even harder to take.

"Not only do I not want to be your queen," she said, "I don't even want to stick around for more than a day or two. I've got another place to be. But were you a part of the mob that was trying to kill the Foster boys?"

Eric Lofland blushed.

She took that to mean *yes.* "In my experience, the only way to head off panic is to give people a sense of organization. A plan. What happened last night may prove to be the worst disaster the world has ever faced. I don't know that to be the case, but it may well be. People are frightened, and angry, and soon they'll be hungry. I figure if we can give them confidence that they at least won't starve, we can keep the panic down. As far as who you'd prefer over me to be up here taking notes, I'm ready to walk away in a second."

Carol Robinson said, "Sit down, Eric. She's doing fine."

Eric sat.

"Eric," Victoria said, "I promise that my intentions are pure. Now, Maggie, do you have a pad and something to write with?"

Over the course of the next hour, as food and other items arrived from Ben Barnett's store and got stacked on Maggie's floor and tables, Victoria led what would have been a council meeting in a different venue. Together, the group established leadership teams for everything from medical supplies to hunter teams, from sanitation to building supplies. They determined to figure out a way to make sure that kids could still be educated, even though it was not reasonable to expect them to make the daily ten-mile trek to the brick-and-mortar building that had been their real school.

Luke fell asleep with his head on the table, cradled on his arms, and as much as Caleb wanted to stay awake, he didn't last past twenty minutes. He was startled when a hand fell on his shoulder and shook him awake. It was the lady who ran the restaurant. Maggie. "Come on, boys, I live right next door. Let's get you a bed to rest in."

Caleb looked to his mom for permission and got a nod.

Maggie's house looked a lot like the Emersons' house back in Arlington, complete with the low ceilings and rounded archways. The most prominent color was red, but there were some blues and greens and browns thrown in, too. The furniture looked old and soft and impossibly inviting.

"You boys can go up to a bedroom, or just crash here on the couches."

Caleb was ready to curl up on the floor like a dog. "The couch is fine," he said.

Luke stumbled to the closest of the two overstuffed two-seater couches and was out in three seconds. Caleb thought that maybe his brother never actually woke up, but rather just stumbled from the restaurant to the house while in a coma.

Caleb kicked off his shoes, lay back on the facing sofa and then was out.

McCrea watched in wonder as Victoria Emerson worked the crowd like a magician working the stage. Without any official authority to do anything, she'd taken charge merely by speaking up.

Perhaps it was akin to consultant syndrome, where an outsider with a briefcase is presumed to be smarter than the workforce that hired her, but he thought there was something more. Victoria had a way about her that exuded honesty. Caring.

But he had no doubt that she would have killed that guy George out on the street if he'd hung on to that rifle for five seconds longer. But then it was over, and people were willing to listen to her. In just the last couple of hours, her stock had gone up quite a bit in his mind.

At first, he was annoyed that she'd appointed Copley and him as de facto chiefs of police, but then he understood her rationale—if, in fact, she understood it herself. Again, it was the fact that they were outsiders. They could be trusted to be fair—free, as they were, from the petty jealousies and competitions that develop among neighbors over time. The fact that he and Copley both wore uniforms didn't hurt.

Still, he was surprised when Victoria called him out toward the end of the meeting to address the room. He considered unslinging his M4, but decided not to. As he addressed the room, he kept his hand loosely draped over the rifle's pistol grip.

"Before you ask, I'll tell you straight out that I don't know any more about what's happening on the world stage than what Vicky has already told you."

The young bearded guy stood up. Eric Lofland. "I've got a question," he said.

"Then raise your hand and wait to be called on," Victoria said. "Order is important at times like these. In fact, there's never been a time when order is *more* important."

Eric rolled his eyes and raised his hand.

Victoria asked, "Major McCrea, do you wish to take a question at this time?"

"Sure." Even he thought the formality was a bit too much. "Go ahead . . . Eric, right?"

"Yeah. We know who she is, but why are *you* here?"

"That's a fair question." McCrea gave a forty-thousand-foot overview of his mission to deliver the congresswoman to the United

States Government Relocation Facility. When he was done, the faces looking back at him displayed various colors of emotion, from confusion to amazement.

Eric's head was cocked so far to the side that his ear nearly touched his shoulder. "You mean to tell us that y'all coulda been safe from all this, but you chose not to be?"

"Let me answer that," Victoria said. "Major McCrea never had a space inside the bunker. Neither did my children, nor anyone else's children. In fact, it's likely that the major's entire family was killed in last night's attack." She gave that a few seconds to sink in.

"I've never believed myself to be any better or more important than anyone else," she continued. "Sitting in comparative luxury and being well fed while every constituent of every member of Congress was suffering didn't seem right to me at all. They can run the place just fine without me."

When the audience clapped—albeit without a lot of enthusiasm—McCrea realized that Victoria was campaigning right there, whether she knew it or not. Perhaps the humble brag came naturally to people in her line of work.

When the floor returned to McCrea, he said, "As Vicky explained earlier, there's every reason to believe that violence, in one form or another, is coming our way. We don't welcome it and we don't seek it. We say prayers that I'm wrong. But we need to be prepared for it. Does the name *Jeffrey Grubbs* mean anything to any of you?"

No one raised their hand, but several looked away, a sure sign in McCrea's book that there was news to be hidden. "He's got a pretty heavy mountain accent," he went on. "About five-ten, maybe one eighty-five. Beard. Looks tough as leather."

Carol Robinson, the pregnant lady at his left, tentatively raised her hand and McCrea called on her. "They're old-school stillers and meth cookers. Bad, bad folk. They live up in the woods a few miles from here."

"But they know better than to come into town," George said. "He's a kid toucher, too, but never been nabbed for it. Him and his are as white trash as white trash gets."

McCrea wondered if he should share this next part, but ultimately decided they had a right to know. "On our way in this morning, we wandered up on a tractor trailer that had run off the road about five miles from here. The doors had been pried open, its contents strewn all over the place. Worse, the driver had been shot dead. At least we assume it was the driver. Whoever it was, he'd been shot through the forehead."

The room gasped in unison, then erupted in cross talk.

"Hey, hey, hey!" Mr. Jake said, nearly shouting. "The man ain't done yet. Let him finish. Who was he? Did you look at his ID?"

"Didn't get a chance," McCrea said. "That's where we encountered Jeffrey Grubbs. He made a lot of threatening noises, but ultimately we broke it off. I do believe that if we hadn't been armed and able to shoot back, he'd have killed us, too."

"How many of them were there?" somebody asked.

McCrea looked to Victoria for confirmation. "Four, right?"

She gave him a thumbs-up.

"Another man and two females. I don't know what the ages were, so I hesitate to call them ladies."

"Oh, there ain't no ladies in that crowd," Joey said, causing the room to erupt in nervous laughter.

"So, what you're tellin' us," Mr. Jake continued, "is that there's a band of murderers out in the forest."

"I'm not sure that was my intent, but that's the gist of it, yes." He turned his attention to George. "The ones in the woods were doing their best to protect something from view. I wouldn't be a bit surprised if that stuff started as *your* stuff." He indicated Joey, too. Ben Barnett had gone back to his store.

"Then let's go get them," Joey said.

It wasn't the reaction that McCrea had been expecting. He instantly regretted telling them anything about the hijacked truck or the Grubbs gang. "Let's do nothing of the sort," he said. "We were about a half-a-trigger pull away from a war out there just a couple of hours ago. Emotions are running hot. Give it a few days and let the emotions die down."

Maggie raised her hand. "In a few days, everything they took is gonna be spoiled, just like your . . . just like Vicky said."

"It's gonna be spoiled so *nobody* can make use of it," Joey pressed.

"Millions of people died last night," McCrea said. "Maybe hundreds of millions. Maybe billions. I don't know the number, but isn't that enough for a twelve-hour period?"

"Chemistry and physics," George said. "The clock is ticking." He stood, his rifle back in his hand.

McCrea shot a glare at Victoria. *Are you going to do something?*

She ignored him.

"Grab your guns, folks," George said. "Meet me at my station. We'll go get those sons of bitches."

Half the room stood—mostly men, but five or six women—and started toward the door.

"Please!" McCrea called. "This is nuts!"

"You can come along or stay, Major," George said. "It's your call."

McCrea watched, slack-jawed, as Maggie's Place emptied.

"That went well," Victoria said in a voice dripping with irony. "I'd say this meeting is over." She stood. "I need to organize some food preservation teams."

"With whom?" McCrea said. "They all left."

"Most of them will come to their senses," Victoria said. "They always do."

"Why didn't you say something?" McCrea said. The question was 90 percent accusation. "They've made you their leader."

"I don't want to be their leader."

"But you are. You know you are. You could have derailed that. It's just more vigilante retribution."

Victoria gave him a tired look. "Because if I'd tried to stop them, I would have failed. They'd have done it anyway, and my first act at organizing survival would have ended in failure. That would have escalated the unraveling of this community." She leaned in close to his ear. "I'm not the one who gave them the great cause to fight for. That would be you who did that."

"They needed to know that the woods are not safe."

"Did they, Major? Now that they do know, are they better off or worse off?"

McCrea's ears turned hot. He didn't know what to say.

Victoria folded her arms. "I know that your heart holds nothing but disdain for people like me. For politicians. You're a man of action and you think people like me get in the way and slow things down."

"Or start wars that kill millions." He fired those words like so many bullets.

"Don't wallow in the gutter," Victoria replied, ignoring his bait. If anything, her voice had grown calmer. "There are good politicians, as well as bad ones. The good ones are all about compromise. Not everyone needs to know everything all the time. You know this."

He still didn't have words.

"At the end of the day, these people are all going to do what they want to do," Victoria explained. "We can try to shape their views on things, but unless our arguments prevail, we lose. I don't mean to make you feel bad, but you just lost a lot right there. You're the man in the uniform who doesn't want to fight."

"It's a foolish fight!"

"That's why you shouldn't have teed it up. Do you really think I'd forgotten about that business with the truck and the driver and the Grubbs gang? Did it occur to you that my not mentioning it was an intentional act rather than just an omission?"

He thought about not answering, but then came clean. "No. It did not occur to me, even for an instant."

Victoria smiled through tight lips. "Respect," she said. "Respect the person and the process. If I'd had a uniform and a silver eagle on my shoulder, you would have done that reflexively. Instinctively."

He continued to stare. She was absolutely right. On all counts. As much as he admired Victoria as an individual, she was part of a social class for which he had exactly zero respect—the political class. And when a fellow military officer had an opinion, it was at least rooted in meaningful experience.

Victoria put her hand on his arm. "I don't want to put you on the spot, but maybe give you a little perspective. Washington started this war, and now we're stuck with the aftermath. You started the war that's about to happen—not intentionally, but neither did Washington—and now the townsfolk are stuck with the aftermath. The question I want to ask you is, what's the right thing for you to do now?"

"Why do I sense that you're about to tell me?"

"Think about it. A bunch of people—whether it's just a few or many more than a few—are going to go back up the hill and pick a fight with the Grubbs gang. Okay, the gang picked the fight initially, but still. The question you need to ask yourself is whether they'd be better off under the leadership of a proven warrior, or if they're better off just winging it on their own?"

McCrea gave a wry smile as he crossed his hands over the grip of his rifle. "Mrs. Emerson, are you ordering me to take the hill?"

She laughed and it felt good. "I don't have the authority to do that. I'd prefer that you just pursued doing the right thing."

This woman could sell anything to anyone. Something in her demeanor, in the way of her words, made him want to please her. Despite all his misgivings, and despite his conviction that this was a dogshit conflict, he understood that he would soon be on his way up the hill to fight it.

"First Sergeant Copley," he said.

Copley had been languishing in a chair near the back door. He may even have been asleep, judging by the way he jerked upright. "Sir."

"I don't know how carefully you've been eavesdropping—"

"Not at all, sir." A giant yawn demonstrated the truth of his words.

"I am leaving you in charge of security here in Maggie's Place as the food preservation efforts spin up. Mrs. Emerson is in charge. Do what she says, and don't argue, because you'll end up doing it her way, anyway."

"Yes, sir. Are you going someplace, sir?"

"First Sergeant, I am heading out to attend an ass-kicking."

"Whose ass would that be, sir?"

"That's a determination that has not yet been made." He winked at Victoria. "See you in a bit."

CHAPTER EIGHTEEN

Scott Johnson led Penn Glendale and Arlen Strasky into a room that looked like a computer museum. Banks of old-school CRT computer screens were set into metal cabinets that rose from the back edges of ancient metal tables. To Penn, it was reminiscent of NASA mission control, but on a much smaller scale.

"This is the old CNC," Johnson explained. "Command and control center."

"How old is it?" Strasky asked. "This looks like 1960s technology."

"It *is* 1960s technology," Johnson said. "But it's not as old as it looks. Until a few years ago, the basements in Uncle Sam's mansion that no one liked to talk about—all the stuff dealing with nuclear war—was deliberately designed with old technology. We're talking floppy disks and no internet because bad guys can't hack into a computer with no hookup to the outside world."

"And this was where everything was run from?" Penn asked.

"Exactly. The focus has changed in the last few years, so we've relocated elsewhere in the Annex and turned this place into a kind of closet."

"Why are you showing me this, Mr. Johnson?"

"These are your new quarters, sir. We'll bring in a desk and a cot. It's not the Oval Office, but it's the best we can do. At least for now."

"Seriously?" Penn said.

"I'll be honest with you, Mr. President. While the Annex is prepared for the continuation of government, our planning kind of stopped at the swearing in and providing media broadcasts. We really don't have special quarters for the executive branch offices. That's what Mount Weather was all about."

"You just used the past tense," Strasky said.

"Yes, I did. We've heard unconfirmed rumors that Weather was hit hard. We have not been able to make contact with anyone up there."

"Jesus," Penn said. "That's the entire executive branch leadership."

"Yes, sir."

"So you're telling me I don't have a cabinet."

"No, sir, I'm not telling you that, though that might be the case. What I'm telling you is that if they are in place and healthy at Mount Weather, we have been unable to establish contact."

"Semantic games," Strasky said.

"If you say so, sir."

Penn said, "Mr. Johnson, you need to start getting me some hard information. Confirmable information."

"I understand. We're working toward that with all the resources at our disposal. The problem, sir, is that those resources are limited."

"I want to hear every rumor as it happens," Penn said. "Am I clear?"

"Yes, sir, we will do the best that we can."

"If what I've seen is the best you have to offer, it's inadequate. You need to do better."

Johnson's jaw set as he clearly debated whether or not to say what was on his mind.

"Go ahead," Penn said. "Secrets don't make a lot of sense right now."

"Fine," Johnson said. "Mr. President, I need to make something very clear to you, sir. I don't work for you. Solara doesn't work for you. Nor do we work for the House or the Senate. My mission begins and ends with keeping the facility running and keeping the electronics in good working order. I am pleased to report that our comms are in perfect working order. It's the rest of the system that's broken. That's on you, sir, not me."

"Hey," Strasky said. "You're talking to the president of the United States. Watch the attitude."

"I don't do politics, either," Johnson said. "Hell, I don't even vote. But with all respect, from what I've heard, half the people in this Annex—*more* than half, in fact—would argue that Mr. Glendale is, in fact, *not* the president. And that is specifically *why* my staff and I are paid not to care."

Penn didn't know what to say. Didn't know what to do. Without information, and without the ability to communicate with other government entities outside the Annex, how could any of them do their jobs?

"I'll leave you to your work, Mr. President. As soon as we have the cot and the desk available, I'll have them brought in."

Johnson turned to leave, but Penn stopped him.

"One thing, Mr. Johnson. Shortly before I gave my speech, I saw one of your staff members wheeling a gurney into the Staff Only section of the dormitory and hospital wing."

"I heard about that, sir. Sorry."

"Was there a person on that gurney?"

Johnson grew uncomfortable, as if unsure again whether or not to speak. "Yes, sir, there was."

"And what is in the Staff Only room?"

"A lot of the mechanicals that keep the Annex warm or cool as necessary. The water system is in there as well. But specific to what you saw, sir, that's the incinerator."

Strasky nearly shouted, "Incinerator!"

"Yes, sir. Of course. When people die, we have to dispose of their remains somehow."

"Who died?" Penn asked.

"Now, that's none of your concern, is it?" Johnson said. "I'll be on my way."

"Wait," Penn said. "After Victoria Emerson quit, were you able to escort her chief of staff, Oliver Mulroney, out of the bunker before it shut down?"

Johnson stared back silently.

Strasky said, "Oh, my God. Did you *kill* him? You said that actions have consequences. Is that what you meant?"

"Tell you what, Mr. President, I'll make you a deal. I won't attempt to interfere with how you attempt to run this shit show of a government, and you don't interfere with how I run the Annex."

"Did you murder Oliver Mulroney?" Penn figured a direct question might bring a direct answer.

"I'm not getting into that with you, sir. Rest assured that everything I do is done in accordance with established procedure."

"I want to see the rule book."

Johnson seemed genuinely amused. "For what reason? Established policy is established policy. It cannot be changed. Not by me, and certainly not by the politicians whose behavior the policy manages."

Penn felt his blood pressure rising. "Where do you get off—"

"Mr. President, this conversation is over. In sixty days, when the blast doors open, you'll be free and clear of me. Until then, you will follow the rules and I will enforce them. They're really pretty simple, sir. Don't try to open the blast doors prematurely, stick to the meal schedules and stay out of places where you don't belong."

McCrea was only the second person to arrive at the ruined Simmons Gas and Goodies. George gave him a hard look as he approached. "Don't bother trying to talk me out of this," he said.

"That's not what I'm here to do," McCrea said. He forced a smile and tried to keep his tone light. "I'm here to join the fight." He extended his hand.

George wasn't sure he wanted to take it. "Why the change in heart?"

"Are you gonna shake my hand, or just leave me hangin' here?"

George shook McCrea's hand, but his expression remained uneasy. "What's your game, McCrea?"

"I'm not sure I have one."

"You come into town like you own the place, your lady friend threatens to shoot me, and then decides on her own to let a couple of thieves get away with thieving."

McCrea saw no upside in even attempting a reply, so he remained silent.

"And now, here you are on a fight that you don't believe in. None of what I just said is normal for anyone."

"Okay, I'll take the bait," McCrea said. "We arrived here because it's a place to be. We were driving miles away from here when the attack happened, and that's where our vehicle remains. It might as well be a lawn ornament now. When we finally got here, we saw a lynching in progress and stopped it. Vicky Emerson did a hell of a job in there getting people focused on the jobs that need to get done. Now, as for why I'm here on a mission I don't believe in, this is not new territory for me. I've spent my entire adult life fighting battles I didn't believe in, but I'm still alive because I'm *good* at fighting battles."

"I've survived a few battles myself," George said. "I'm a Marine."

McCrea caught the present tense. There literally was no such thing as a former Marine. Once one, always one. "Good to know," he said. "I'll be sure to use smaller words."

George puffed up, offended, but then he relaxed and smiled when he got the joke. Interservice rivalries. "You still haven't told me why you changed your mind."

"I'm a professional soldier," McCrea said. "It's not in me to sit out a fight when I know I can be of some assistance. Besides, I've done some soul-searching. This fight is going to have to be fought sooner or later. If we don't bring it to them, then one day, they'll bring it to us. Better to be the aggressor than the victim."

McCrea noted the approach of four more people. He was shocked to see that the Foster brothers were among them, each armed with an AR15, along with chest rigs loaded with spare magazines. McCrea just prayed that the shoes and shirts they'd found were their own and not the spoils of a shoplifting spree. Joey Abbott from the pawnshop and young Eric Lofland filled out the gang. Joey likewise carried an AR15, but Eric had a knockoff AK47 stuffed with what looked to be a forty-round banana magazine.

As they arrived, handshakes and fist bumps were exchanged, and McCrea again had to explain his change of heart.

"I think this is gonna be just about everybody," George said.

"That's good," McCrea said. "There's too much work left to be done here to have a big crowd head up the road. Everybody's sure you still want to do this?"

"What they done ain't right," one of the twins said. The swelling on their faces had dimmed, making them more identical than they used to be.

"Let's get going, then," McCrea said. He started walking, and they started following.

"Wait!" a voice called from behind.

McCrea turned and saw Caleb running to join them. "Oh, shit."

"That's the lady's kid, isn't it?" Kyle Foster asked. "Luke?"

"Caleb," McCrea corrected. "He's the feisty one."

"He's a kid," George said.

"Don't let him hear you say that," McCrea said.

Caleb arrived with his 10/22 in his hand, and his hair looking like he'd combed it with a blender. "I'm going with you."

McCrea's jaw muscles worked hard as he tried to think of what to do. Vicky was going to be *pissed* if he let Caleb come along. And yes, he was just a kid. But if McCrea challenged this—even if he asked if Caleb had spoken to his mother before running out here—the boy would be humiliated. He was sixteen years old. Armies the world over are populated by sixteen-year-olds. And now, after the events of last night, childhood wasn't really a thing anymore. Future children would have to be grown-ups as they exited the womb.

"Okay," McCrea said. "One rule, and this one is nonnegotiable. You are to stay closer to me than my shadow does, understand?"

The boy's eyes were huge with anticipation. He nodded.

"And you do exactly what I say, when I say it and the way I tell you to do it."

"Okay, Major. I promise."

"You're willing to get shot over this?"

"I hate that guy," Caleb said. "I hate what he did to that driver. That's just not right."

What was it about the Emerson clan, McCrea wondered, that made them so difficult to say no to? Whatever it was, it clearly was passed from one generation to the next. "Suit yourself," McCrea said. "Just remember I warned you that if this turns hot, killing a man is a hard thing to live with."

"Not that one," Caleb said.

They started walking.

"Hey, I got a question," Joey said. "How do we know we're not marching right into a trap? How many people did you say the Grubbs guy has?"

"I saw four," McCrea replied. "But he said he had a bunch more. He could have been bluffing, he could have been telling the truth. As for the trap, that seems unlikely to me. He won't be expecting us to come at him. Certainly not this soon."

"What if he hears us coming?" a Foster asked.

"Which one are you?" McCrea asked.

"Kyle."

"If he sees us, he'll open fire, Kyle. He's already told me that, and I believe him one hundred percent. So the smart move is to walk quietly."

This perpetual twilight had derailed McCrea's sense of time. It felt far later than 1400 hours. Stress and the lack of sleep didn't help at all. The images of his daughters, Tina and Toni, kept trying to penetrate the mental armor he'd erected to keep them out. Intellectually, he knew that they had to be dead, but emotionally—in his heart—he couldn't accept it. *Wouldn't* accept it. Maybe he just wouldn't let it in.

And Julia. He wasn't sure how a marriage could have gone so sideways after nineteen years, but he'd long ago faced the fact that life presents challenges that simply are not to be understood.

Julia had tried to blame it on him and his career ambitions. His deployments to the world's worst shitholes. But McCrea didn't buy it.

Something had switched in Julia in the two years before they'd finally called it quits. She'd decided that his ongoing fight for God and country was a personal affront to her. She couldn't wrap her head around the fact that his pursuit of a silver maple leaf for his epaulette, with the ultimate goal of pinning a silver eagle, was as much about the family as it was about him.

Military careers fizzled fast in the absence of continued promotions. That shoulder hardware made millions of dollars' difference over the years that would follow his final salute, and with a gold watch at the end of the private-sector postgame show.

It hurt him in his gut to embrace the reality of how little any of that sacrifice mattered to the world now. How little *any* of the past mattered.

How many birthdays had he missed while on deployment? How many soccer practices? He knew there'd been at least one soccer championship, and he felt shame that he didn't know for sure if there'd been more. Toni had extraordinary skills on the field. Even at sixteen, she'd had college coaches sniffing around her.

Sixteen. He cast a glance at the boy he'd assigned to be his shadow. Jesus, he was the same age as Toni. And Tina was thirteen—the same age as Luke. Was that why he found Vicky's boys so annoying?

It was hard not to be pissed that her two adolescent sons got to live, while his two adolescent girls were immolated in the nuclear fireball that the boys' mother had had a hand in launching. If those adolescent boys had been born to a mere mortal, as Tina and Toni had—as opposed to a member of the vaunted political class—they would have been immolated, too.

Stop.

The inner command arrived so forcefully that McCrea worried that he might have said it aloud. If he had, the others showed no reaction.

The past—all of it—no longer had any relevance to the present. Vicky's sons were alive, and his daughters were . . . status unknown. The world had imploded, each of its inhabitants betrayed in the worst imaginable way by their political leadership. The hows, whys, wherefores and WTFs were the purview of future historians.

For the present, life was all about acquiring the next five minutes. It was fine to plan for the next five hours, but the next five days were iffy at best. Only a fool would presume to plan out to the next five years. At thirty-eight, McCrea couldn't imagine a circumstance where he would live to see forty. The world's shortest war—could it have lasted more than eight hours?—had shaved away ten thousand years of human evolution.

McCrea felt sorry for the men and women who had dedicated their adult lives to the analysis of stock markets or the lending of money. He couldn't conceive of a more irrelevant pursuit. Million-degree fireballs had, at the speed of light and sound, rendered valueless the green strips of paper that were decorated with portraits of dead presidents.

Everything that could possibly be broken was destroyed now. Every thread of the fabric that held society together had been either snipped or shrunk or stretched. Society worked because we agreed to make it work. People in civilized countries had evolved to be polite and cooperative because it made sense to do so. They gave up little bits of freedom in the form of torts and criminal statutes in return for a governmental structure that would protect the interests of the commonwealth. All of that was gone.

Christ, even the air was broken. God only knew how contaminated the air was, or what it was contaminated with. Only God knew a lot of things.

It took them about an hour to reach the wrecked tractor trailer. McCrea could just barely see the nose of the wreck around the turn of the upcoming switchback when he brought the team to a halt and motioned for them to come in close.

He lowered his voice to a whisper. "These woods here are where I last saw Grubbs and his friends. I don't know if they've moved off or if they're still around, but we had a standing deal.

Next time we saw each other, we'd shoot. He's a mean cuss, and I don't think he was bluffing. But I think we need to make one thing very clear before we take our next steps." He scanned the others' faces to make sure that he had their attention. "We're here to take him into custody, not to kill him."

"What if he shoots?"

"Then shoot back. Shoot to kill. But do not be the first on the trigger. This is a weird day, but that is one line that we can't afford to cross." He found himself glaring at George when he added, "Murder is still wrong."

"What do we do with them if we get them?" Joey asked.

Eric Lofland beat McCrea to the answer. "Take them back and try them."

"Then we can kill 'em," quipped the other Foster. Caine. He laughed, but then backed off when he saw that no one else did.

McCrea knew, now more than ever before, that this adventure was a colossal mistake. The Foster boys and Eric Lofland had never been in this kind of fight before, he was sure of it. They had the kit and the ammo, but would they have the nerve? It's one thing to blast away at targets at a shooting range, but when the targets shoot back, that changes a person. McCrea decided to take George at his word that he'd seen battle, and while he had no idea what Joey's background was, he had a tough maturity about him that inspired confidence that he'd stay in a fight long enough to win it.

As for the others, well, they'd all figure it out together.

Kyle Foster asked, "Shouldn't we get off the road? If they start shooting first, we've got no place to hide."

"This time of year, the woods are too noisy," McCrea explained. "Here's what we're going to do. We're going to spread out. Three of us will walk along the right-hand side of the road, and the others will walk on the left. Keep at least ten yards between you. Fifteen is better, but don't let it string out so far that you can't bring assistance fast. We're going to move slowly, and keep your eyes scanning the woods on your side, we'll scan the woods on ours."

"What are we looking for?" Caine asked.

"Anything out of the ordinary," McCrea said.

"You mean people, right?" George asked.

"Yes. People for sure. But anything else. And here's why it's so important not to just open fire. It's entirely possible—likely, even—that other refugees will be coming in this direction to get away from the cities and the fires."

"How will we even know if they're part of the gang?" Joey asked.

Finally they were seeing the downside to this whole adventure. "You won't," McCrea explained. "I think I'll still recognize the ones I saw before, but he said there were others. As far as I'm concerned, this isn't about the gang. This is about Grubbs. If it comes to exchanging gunfire, it'll be about everyone who pulls a trigger."

McCrea let the words settle for a few seconds, then said, "We can always walk away."

"No," George said. "At least I can't." He pointed up the hill. "Is that the truck you told us about? The one with the murdered driver?"

"Yes."

"That's Ryan Hamilton's truck. He worked for over ten years drivin' for other people so he could finally afford his own rig. He got it about eight months ago. Now his body's bloating up in the back because this Grubbs asshole decided he needed electronic shit that he can't even use. That's an evil man, Major McCrea. And evil breeds more evil."

McCrea stood. "I'll take point," he said. "Right side. Caleb, you too. Caine, Kyle and Eric, are you all right-handed?"

"Left," Kyle said. "What difference does that make?"

McCrea explained, "It means you join me on the right side of the road. In a patrol like this, it's best to keep your weak side toward the area you're searching. You can bring your weapon to bear quicker than if you had to pivot to take the shot. Caine and Eric, you're on the left. Joey, you take the left, too."

"I'm right-handed," Caleb said. "Shouldn't I—"

"Be my shadow? Yes." He pointed at George. "Do you mind taking point over there?"

"Love to."

"So everybody knows, the last time I saw Grubbs, he was in the woods on our side—the right side—of the road. That doesn't mean they couldn't have switched it up, but we need to be careful." To all: "We good? Thumbs-up if you're set."

Thumbs-up all the way around.

CHAPTER NINETEEN

SCOTT JOHNSON GATHERED WITH HIS SENIOR LEADERSHIP TEAM BEhind locked doors in the Solara bunkroom. The décor in here was bright and the furniture comfortable. One of the advantages of staffing the Annex 24/7 was the ability to take care of their own. The Hilltop Manor always bought more furniture than their immediate needs dictated, placing their extras in a climate-controlled storage building in an obscure corner of the property. The first thing Scott noticed about the administrative protocols of the Hilltop Manor was their terrible inventory-control systems. While the politician asshats made do with military surplus, the Solara team lounged in five-star–hotel surplus.

A fully stocked bar dominated one corner of the bunkroom, complete with multiple liter-size bottles of each employee's favorite booze—again, compliments of the hotel. They'd had to build the bar on their own, but that wasn't that big a deal when the granite and stainless steel came to them free of charge.

Scott sat in a forest green leather lounge chair in front of the masonry faux fireplace that glowed with an electric heating insert. The bunkroom's proximity to the climate control systems kept the place way too cold in the summertime and way too hot in the winter, because theirs was the first air to be snatched from the distribution vents.

Garand "Bugsy" Bug-something sat on the pool table, his legs dangling over the side, while Billy St. James and Roy Heath perched in the high-seat observation chairs next to the pool table.

"I can't believe that this shit is actually happening," St. James said.

"Which shit is that?" Scott asked. "The end of the world, or the fact that members of Congress are kindergartners?"

They all laughed.

St. James said, "Mostly the first, but a lot of the second."

Scott drilled in on Roy Heath. "Glendale asked me about Oliver Mulroney."

Heath shifted in his seat. "I'm sorry, Mr. Johnson. How the hell was I supposed to know he was going to take a dump right then? You told me to get rid of the body, so I thought I had my window of opportunity."

"You should have checked the hallway first," Scott said. "At the very least, you should have checked the video feeds."

Heath looked stumped for words. "All I can do is apologize again."

"And be more careful in the future."

Bugsy asked, "What did you tell him? The president, I mean."

St. James chuckled. "I wouldn't get too comfortable calling him that yet."

"Well, we can't call him *Speaker* anymore," Heath said. "Angela Fortnight already slimed into that role."

"Five bucks she finds a way to make herself president," St. James said. "Did you see how pissed she was when she stormed out of the speech? I rolled tape on her meeting with her conference while Glendale was speaking. Want to hear it?"

"Not now," Scott said. "Not yet, anyway. What was the gist?"

"No gist to it," St. James explained. "She said it three times. I quote, *That son of a bitch is not the legitimate president of the United States.*"

Scott gave a low whistle. "Keep an eye out. We can't let the bullshit run out of control."

"What are we supposed to do?" Heath asked.

"You keep an eye on them," Scott said. "I'll talk to Pete Clostner. When more than two or three of them get together, I'll get him to make sure that we're syncing the audio from their badges with the video feeds."

"Why?" Heath asked.

"This country needs leadership," Scott explained. "We'll give them the chance to do their jobs, but if they can't figure out how to work and play well together, we might have to flex a little."

Roy Heath cocked his head nearly to his shoulder. "Flex a little?"

"We'll actively encourage them to do the right thing." Scott caught the nervous glances shared by his staff, but he didn't mind that they were confused. They'd catch on soon enough if it came to that.

"You didn't answer my question before," Bugsy said. "When Glendale asked you about Mulroney, what did you tell him?"

"The truth."

"That you shot him?" Bugsy looked horrified.

"Of course not. I told him that I followed the rules to the letter."

Bugsy looked uncomfortable.

"You're not going to be a problem, are you, Bugs?"

"Of course not. I'm just not sure that our guests need to know about operations."

Scott crossed his arms and his legs. "I'm not an idiot," he said. "Like it or not, for the foreseeable future, Glendale is president. Some questions can't be avoided. No, I didn't tell him that we off'd Mulroney, but let's be honest. He couldn't be allowed to stay. If he'd left when we first told him, instead of dragging his feet long enough to get trapped by the closed doors, he'd still be alive. But he didn't. And the protocols don't allow for outsiders."

"You know rumors are going to spread," Heath said. "What do we tell our people about how to respond to questions?"

"The same way they respond to every question," Scott said. "They keep their eyes front and their mouths shut. If people won't let up, you have your people shout for the questioner to step away."

"That's going to escalate things, don't you think?" St. James asked.

Scott uncrossed his limbs and physically leaned into his next words. "I don't know what the final count of residents turned out to be—"

"Four forty-seven," Bugsy said. "House, Senate, staff and president."

Scott continued, "For the next sixty days minimum, we're going to be surrounded by four hundred forty-seven pampered and pandered-to egotists who think that they shit rainbows. That's fine in their world, but this is *our* world. We stay in our lanes and we don't give a shit about what they think they have a right to know." He took his time pointing to each of his senior staffers one at a time. "You make sure that your people understand this. Roger that?"

"Roger that," they said in unison.

Scott sealed the deal with a single clap of his hands. "Good. Now let's spitball some ways to open up the flow of information from the outside world."

Caine didn't like being separated from his brother, even if it was by just a few yards. They'd gotten through a lot of tough times over the years by being there for each other. Being brought into the world as the sons of Zeb Foster was a hell of a curse to begin with. In jail as much as he was out, D-Zeb, as he liked to be called, loved his family, but he loved liquor a lot more. His preferred brand was homemade, and the shine made him mean. Caine always suspected that D-Zeb had killed their mother, but he'd never gone to the cops and now it wouldn't make any difference.

Other children weren't allowed to hang with the Foster boys, so Caine and Kyle had always been their own team. For a long time, when they were young kids, they even invented their own language, known only to them. They didn't know they were doing it at the time, but their language allowed them to share secrets that no one else could know.

Kyle was the one who first pointed out the bruises on Mama's neck and wondered how they could happen in a fall. Hell, even if they'd reported it to the sheriff, the deputies wouldn't have cared. They'd wonder where's the harm in a world with one less Foster in it.

Almost literally, they'd always had each other's backs, and now they had the width of a road between them. They were both bookended by men who didn't give a shit about either of them. Hell, a couple of hours ago, George was ready to kill them both.

If it was up to Caine, there's no way either of them would be here right now walking into a gunfight. It was all Kyle's idea—a way to get people like George and Joey to show them respect. You know, for turning the other cheek and shit like that. Caine figured, to hell with them all. Pushed that hard again, he'd be tempted to join the group that they were hunting for.

Who needs people—who needs a *town*—that doesn't want them in return?

And why was everybody letting this Army asshole and his bitch wife tell them what to do? They were all grown-ass adults. They didn't need outsiders coming in and pushing them in this direction and that.

As he walked past Mr. Hamilton's truck, Caine deliberately turned his head away from the open back doors. He didn't want to see a dead man. He'd seen too many of those, as it was. He'd lost track of the number of friends that meth had taken from him.

Now *there* was something to be proud of. He and Kyle had screwed up plenty over the years. They'd drunk themselves blind. They'd messed with whores. And, yes, they'd stolen plenty of shit, but they'd never done the meth. That shit made you ugly and stupid. Like Kyle said all the time, they had plenty of both of those in their lives already.

What was that?

He swore he heard people talking, but apparently, he was the only one because nobody did anything. He couldn't pinpoint where it was coming from, and he couldn't make out the words, but there was definitely something. He held up his hand the way he saw the major do it and stopped walking, hoping that the others would do the same. But he must have been invisible because Eric Lofland just kept advancing from behind, while George Simmons increased the distance.

"What are you stopping for?" Eric asked.

"I thought I heard talking."

"Other than the voice inside your crazy head?"

If Eric hadn't smiled just right when he said that, Caine would have busted him in the mouth. He'd been called *crazy* too many times—by people who were being serious—to take it from anybody as a joke.

Up ahead on the right, someone shouted something from the woods. George dropped to a knee as a rifle boomed. George brought his rifle up to his shoulder and fired one shot. Two more answered in return as he dove into the woods to his left and settled in behind a tree. Bullets tore into the trunk and launched puffs of mulch from the forest floor.

"I've got contact!" George yelled.

"Yeah, no shit," Caine said, and he took off to join his brother across the street, who'd made himself one with the ground.

Caine slid in beside him. "You okay?"

"Yeah, where are they?"

"I don't know."

"Joey!" McCrea yelled. "Get those kids out of the road!" Then he turned away and fired into the woods.

Caine felt his shirt pull tight as Joey grabbed his collar and pulled him along the pavement and gravel into the softer leaf-covered mulch. "You're supposed to be with your team," Joey said.

"I'm with my brother."

"Then both of you get in the fight."

Up ahead, McCrea was windmilling his left arm to get them to move up to join him.

What are they doing? McCrea wondered. Across the street, George and Eric were getting their asses kicked, while on this side, Joey and the Foster boys cowered in the bushes. This was exactly the scenario that McCrea had feared. Once a gunfight started, there was only one way to *un*start it, and that was to poke holes in people.

Caleb had dropped to a knee next to him, right where he was supposed to be. If the rest of his team didn't form up on him in a few seconds, he'd have to engage Grubbs's shooters on his own. If he could relieve the pressure on George's team, they could catch the bad guys in an effective crossfire.

That first shot fired at George had been a gift. It caught Grubbs's own team as off-balance as it had McCrea's. If they'd taken even a few seconds to form some kind of line, they could have concentrated their fire, and the fight with George and Eric would have been over by now.

As it was, Grubbs's troops were stuck freelancing from behind all kinds of cover, spread out over an acre or more. There seemed to be no leadership. Totally undisciplined in their approach, they would duck out, take a shot and then duck back in.

"We're here," Joey said as he and the boys slid in next to McCrea. They all looked terrified.

"Here it is," McCrea said. He spoke quickly and as quietly as the gunfight would allow. "They started this fight, we're finishing it. They are one hundred percent concentrated at their front. They don't know we're here, so they won't expect our first volley. Pick a target, shoot it, then move to cover. When I yell *move,* we do it again. We are *always* pressing forward, until they're all dead or they surrender. It starts now. Caleb, on me."

He didn't ask for questions because he was here for a fight, not for a chat. They'd do their part or they wouldn't. It was time to find out which.

McCrea rose to a high crouch, settled his red dot on the ear of a rifle-toting lady who had just rolled out from behind a stout tree to take aim and he pressed the trigger. Pink spray confirmed the kill and he darted forward to take cover behind a tree of his own.

To his right, he was gratified to hear gunshots from the rest of his team.

After a silent two-count, he yelled, "Move!" and he rolled out to his left. He was startled as hell to see a shooter running straight at him. McCrea drilled him with two rounds to his chest, then sealed the deal with one in the face.

Caleb pounded away with his 10/22. The noise was a fraction of what the other guns projected, but his shot placements were nearly perfect. He'd been trained to shoot for the head, and he'd been trained well. A .22-caliber bullet might not have the greatest stopping power with center-of-mass shots, but it will scramble the shit out of a brain.

Ahead and to his right, two more members of the Grubbs gang fell from bullets fired by his team.

Over to the left, as the Grubbs gang pivoted to address the assault on their flank, George and Eric woke up and started stitching them from across the street. In less than one minute, it was over. The outgoing fire from Grubbs's gang had dwindled to nothing.

"Cease fire!" McCrea yelled. "Cease fire, cease fire!" Then, remembering he had a civilian team, he yelled, "Stop shooting!"

After the final gunshot, the quiet was almost oppressive, made heavier by the ringing in his ears from all the noise.

"Everybody okay?" McCrea scanned his team, and all of them seemed to be fine, even if they didn't answer.

"I'm fine," Caleb said. He stooped to look at the body of one of the people he'd shot. "He's no older than me."

"You all right?" McCrea asked. The kid showed no emotion at all.

Caleb stood and did a tactical reload, dropping the used, yet-not-empty, twenty-round magazine from the well and replacing it with a full one from the front pocket of his jeans. "I'm fine," he said. "I told you I could do it."

McCrea watched, disturbed, as Caleb wandered to another of the people he'd killed. It was unsettling to see a total lack of . . . anything.

McCrea also wandered among the dead, scanning the carnage and wondering if this truly was the new normal for society. The gang's bodies were scattered in a rough circle around a pile of gathered stuff. McCrea imagined that they had been in the middle of inventorying or maybe distributing their booty when the shooting started. He looked down at the corpse of the man who'd rushed him and died in the process. "Was it worth it?" he asked.

"Well, that was exciting!" George proclaimed as he joined McCrea from the other side of the street.

"What about you?" McCrea said. "This is what you wanted. Was it worth it?"

George recoiled. "What's with you?"

Joey said, "This is the stuff they stole from my shop. Some of it, anyway."

All McCrea could see was unnecessary risk and wasted lives. "Grab the stuff you want to take back with you and let's get going." He started to turn away, but George grabbed his arm.

"Feelin' high-and-mighty, are you?" George said. He was pissed. "Seems to me, you was fightin' with as much enthusiasm as anyone else."

McCrea glared first at the hand on his arm, and then at George's face. When the other man let go, McCrea said, "The word isn't enthusiasm. It's *commitment.* Now answer my question. Look at the bodies on the ground and tell me if getting your stuff back was worth the sacrifice."

"Go to hell."

McCrea laughed. "That's pretty much a guarantee for all of us after this."

"Hey, Major?" It was one of the Foster twins. Kyle, he thought. "We've got a wounded guy over here."

"How bad?"

"Pretty bad, I think. He was hit in the stomach. He's bleeding a lot."

McCrea walked that way. As he approached, he saw a man in his forties writhing on the ground.

"Are you the one who shot him?" McCrea asked. From here, he could see that he was definitely speaking with Kyle.

The kid looked down at the man and nodded.

"You a hunter?" McCrea asked.

Another nod.

"What do you do with a wounded deer after you trace his blood trail?"

Kyle's face paled and he took a sideways step to preserve his balance. He knew exactly what the answer was.

"It's got to be you," McCrea said. "It's cruel to let him suffer, and we're sure as hell not wasting medical supplies on the people we came here to engage."

"I–I don't think I can." Kyle's eyes pleaded with McCrea to take care of it for him.

"Suit yourself," McCrea said. In total, six people lay dead in the woods, soon to be seven when Kyle's guy either bled out or was finished off. Two of them looked familiar to McCrea—they were the silent gang members during that initial meeting—but the others did not. He didn't ask any of his team if they knew any of the identities, in part because he didn't want to hear the answer. Knowing the names of people you've killed helps nothing.

Jeffrey Grubbs was not among the dead.

McCrea planted his fists on his hips. "Well, shit."

"Major!" Caleb yelled. "This one's alive. Not even hurt!" He had his rifle back up to his shoulder, leveled at a target on the ground that McCrea couldn't see.

The entire team rushed that way, and the intensity of the attitudes startled McCrea. "Nobody shoot!" he shouted. "Whoever it is, we need to take them back."

Caleb was covering a kid—older than him, but not yet twenty. He was on his knees and crying over a woman's body. "Mama," he said. "Don't die, Mama." The hole in her head was testament to the fact that he was too late.

Caleb lowered his rifle and swiped at his eyes as George arrived and shoved the young gangster backward onto his back with a heavy shove with the sole of his boot.

"That's enough!" McCrea said. "Enough."

"This piece of shit shot at me," George said.

"Well, he's not shooting at you now, is he? Stop!"

McCrea maneuvered to get between the two. He kneeled in front of the young man. "What's your name, son?"

All he got back was a blistering glare. His eyes showed pure hatred.

"I'm sorry about your mother," McCrea said. "Are you armed?"

"Goddamn right I'm armed," he said.

There was a clatter of hardware as rifles came to bear.

"Easy, guys," McCrea said. "Listen, I need to call you something."

"Call me the guy who's gonna kick your ass."

"Okay. Guy it is. You say you're armed. Are your weapons on you?"

Guy continued to stare.

McCrea sighed loudly. "Okay, then. Have it your way. George, Joey and Eric, search our friend and take custody of any weapons."

The townies pounced on Guy. They lifted him to his feet by his armpits and patted him down as roughly as McCrea had ever seen anyone searched. When they were done, they launched him back onto his butt with a hard shove.

George displayed a folding knife with a three- or four-inch blade. "This is all he had."

"There's a rifle by his knee, though," Eric pointed out. "I think he was a shooter."

Joey took a menacing step closer to Guy. "Oh, he's definitely a shooter."

McCrea pulled a tied bundle of what would have been clothesline in a different setting from a patch pocket in his trousers and tossed it to Eric. "Tie his hands behind him."

"Bullshit," Guy spat, and he bolted for safety.

Joey dropped him with a savage kick to the balls that took the fight out of him, at least for the time being. Joey pressed Guy's face into the mulch while Eric kneeled on the small of his back and reached for an arm. Guy tried to buck him off, but stopped fighting altogether when Eric bounced his knee against his prisoner's spine.

"Not too tight," McCrea instructed. "It's a long walk back to town and I don't want to cut off circulation entirely."

"What are we going to do with him when we get back to town?" George asked.

"We're going to find out what we can about his gang of merry marauders, and then we'll try him for his alleged crimes."

George looked like he'd been slapped. "*Alleged* crimes? Are you shitting me? Look at all this stuff. Ryan's body is still in his truck. There's not a lot to allege, do you think?"

"There are no courts," Joey added. "Hell, there aren't even any *cops.*"

"We're the cops," McCrea said. "I think you were in the room when I agreed to this madness."

"I didn't vote for that," Eric said.

"Okay, Eric, what do *you* think we should do with him?"

"Bullets are cheap," Kyle Foster said.

Eric nodded vigorously. "Exactly. They killed Ryan Hamilton, they just tried to kill us. I don't see anything wrong with a good old-fashioned execution."

"You mean *lynching,*" said Caine Foster. "I don't know who shot Mr. Hamilton or why they did it, but like the major tried to tell us all, this here wouldn't have happened if we didn't come chasing the fight. They'd probably say they were trying to defend themselves from us."

His brother turned on him. "Whose side are you on?"

"Have you already forgotten this morning? We were him just a few hours ago."

"But we didn't do anything," Kyle corrected.

"They didn't know that. The town thought we were guilty as hell of stealing all the shit that is right here."

"All the more reason to shoot the son of a bitch," Eric said.

"Nobody's shooting anybody," McCrea said. "Jesus, listen to yourselves. This war is only one day old. Maybe it's going to tear civilized behavior apart, but for the time being, this is still America, and we don't just execute people because we feel like it."

"Then what do you suggest we do with him after his trial, whatever the hell that would look like?" George pressed. "We gonna build a jail just for him?"

"Maybe a gallows," Joey suggested.

Caleb raised his hand to speak, as if in a classroom. Old habits died hard.

"Go ahead," McCrea said. "And you don't have to do that to join the discussion."

"What's the harm in doing it the right way?" Caleb asked.

"Which way is right?"

"We take him back alive," Caleb said. "What's the harm in that? We could tie him to a tree or whatever. My mom will know what to do."

"Your mom ain't from around here," George said. "And she ain't a judge."

"Maybe it's best that she ain't," Caine said. "I know who this peckerhead is. He's Brandon-Lee May, from up our way. He ain't never been no good, but that don't mean he don't have rights. Mrs. . . . What's her name?"

"Emerson," Caleb prompted. "Victoria or Vicky Emerson."

"Okay, well, she don't know nobody. She don't know who to hate or why. If we're tryin' to figure out what the hell Brandon-Lee's gang did or didn't do, maybe it's best that the judge not be one of us."

"I'll say it again," George said. "What happens after the trial?"

"Maybe he goes free," McCrea said.

"Oh, *hell* no."

"And maybe you get to shoot him." McCrea shrugged, palms up. "Or hang him. I don't know. Nobody knows. I don't think it's even *right* to know. That's why we have trials."

He scanned the crowd for more input, but it appeared they'd talked this one to ground. "All right," McCrea said. "Eric, you and Caine have charge of the prisoner. Call out if you need help. The rest of you grab whatever booty you want to carry and we'll head back to town."

"Wait," George said. "Nobody goes anywhere till we bury Ryan."

For the entire walk back to town, Caleb dreaded the confrontation he knew would be coming with his mom. He just prayed that she wouldn't embarrass him in front of everyone.

Major McCrea insisted that the townies, as he called them, carry back what they wanted to salvage from what had been stolen. He said he didn't want to touch it. Caleb didn't fully understand, but he saw that the major was 100 percent committed to his opinion.

When Caleb offered to help, something passed silently between George and Major McCrea, and George said, "No, that's okay. I've got this."

McCrea and Caleb did carry back the dead folks' weapons, though, as did the others. You couldn't have enough weapons, and you didn't want other people picking them up and using them against you.

Caleb hadn't said anything, but he'd already decided that the M4 he was carrying would be his from now on.

As they entered the outskirts of town and passed in front of the houses, more people were outside. Everybody still looked scared, but at least they were making eye contact. They said hello as Caleb passed.

"How pissed is your mother going to be when you get back?" Major McCrea asked.

Caleb answered with a shrug.

"Is it going to be a show worth sticking around for?" He hip-checked Caleb as he laughed.

"Just stick around in case I need help," Caleb said through a smile.

"Oh, hell no. Your mom could kick my ass. There's no way I'd intervene. I might stick around to be a good witness, though."

"Gee, thanks."

"Anytime, kid. Besides, when we get back, I'm going to have to figure out something to do with our prisoner."

"Do you think they're going to end up executing him, anyway? Even with everything we talked about?"

"Hard to say. If young Mr. May is found guilty of murdering that truck driver, he's going to have to pay a high price. Execution is as high as it gets, right?"

When Caleb and McCrea entered Maggie's Place together, Victoria was in the midst of a conversation with a bunch of townspeople. Lots of new faces—ones that weren't present for the earlier meeting. Caleb didn't know what they were talking about, but it didn't look like a pleasant conversation.

When she made eye contact, Victoria held up a finger, indicating that she needed another minute, but that he should stick around.

"You're on your own now, kid," McCrea said. "If you need any broken bones set, come find me and I'll do my best." He slipped away.

After two minutes had passed, Victoria broke free from her meeting and walked over to her son. "Let's go outside," she said.

Caleb followed her out onto the porch. When she sat in one of the rockers, she tapped the arm of the one next to her.

This wasn't right at all. She seemed way too calm. The redness that always rose around her ears when she was pissed wasn't there. Caleb didn't understand.

"I got worried when I saw you weren't still asleep in Maggie's front room," she said.

"I'm sorry," he said, "but I needed—"

"Don't," she said. "There's no need. I know exactly what happened. You wanted a fight, and you somehow found out that one was available. How did you do?"

He scowled. "I don't know how to answer that."

"Were you brave?"

This was *so* not what he thought it was going to be. "I hope so," he said.

"Did you fight?"

"Yes."

"Clearly, you won because you're here, and the gang is not. Did they fight back?"

He answered with a nod.

"Did they shoot back?"

"Yes."

"And did you shoot?"

"Yes, ma'am."

"Head shots, like we practiced?"

"Yes, ma'am." He looked down. "I killed two of them."

She bobbed her head a little. "That's what happens when you shoot people in the head. Look at me."

Caleb sat tall and met her gaze.

"You did what you had to do. Are you okay with that?"

He started to give a glib answer, but then he stopped himself. He owed honesty. "How can I know?"

She gave a warm smile and patted his hand. "There literally is no honest answer to that question." She sighed and sat back in the rocker, crossing her legs. "These are very strange times, aren't they, Caleb? Everything that made sense yesterday seems wrong today, and much of what seemed wrong has become okay. Are you following me?"

He nodded, but it was a lie.

"You're a man now," she said. "I know that sounds corny and melodramatic, but it's the truth. It's not a testosterone thing, either. I should say you're an adult now. It's your responsibility to do what it takes to provide for yourself and your family. To a lesser extent, for your friends."

"Concentric circles," Caleb said.

"Exactly that. Nothing's going to be easy anymore. I'm proud that you stepped up today."

Okay, now it was time for pigs to fly. "You're *proud*?"

"Yes, I am. You stepped up. You risked something. You risked *everything*. And you came home alive and unhurt. That's a lot for me to be proud of. And you should be proud, too."

Caleb had no idea what to say.

"You're a soldier now, Caleb. I'm not sure what the new army looks like yet, but you are a soldier in it."

Inexplicably, Caleb felt close to tears.

"Never lose sight of your responsibilities, though. Never lose sight of right and wrong. With the kind of decisions you'll be making, there's sometimes no going back. React fast, but think fast first. Your father would have been so proud to see you today."

Caleb no longer trusted his voice.

"I do have something I want you to remember," Victoria said. She squeezed his hand. "Violence, or the threat of violence, is almost never the first choice. Let others be the ones who escalate conflicts to violence. Never be the one to do the escalating."

"Mom, you've taught us that for years."

"Yes, I've taught, and yes, you've at least pretended to listen. But now it's real, and nobody's going to be helping you with your individual decisions anymore. You're a hothead and you know it. Don't you?"

He smiled and wiped his eyes. “And a pain in the ass.”

Victoria threw her head back and laughed. “Oh, my God, yes. Such a *giant* pain in the ass! Just be careful.”

“I will,” he said.

Victoria stood and extended her arms for a hug. Caleb stood and gave it to her.

“Something you need to know,” Caleb said. “We brought a prisoner back with us. I think they’re gonna ask you to be the judge at his trial.”

“What’s he going to be charged with?”

“Murder, I think.”

Victoria sat back down, shoved her hands in her hair. “Damn.”

PART II

CHAPTER TWENTY

Some of Adam Emerson's earliest memories involved Top Hat Mountain. A regular pilgrimage for the whole family, the vistas from up here were beyond description. On a breezy evening, on a night with a good moon, the moving treetops looked to Adam like undulating ocean waves. In the autumn, during the day, those same trees looked like so much spilled paint, with every color represented by the changing leaves. He didn't know how far you could see before the curvature of the earth swallowed the view, but it had to be many, many miles.

It was on those trips that Dad taught him how to fish and how to hunt small game. Dad wasn't terribly concerned about licenses or hunting in season, but they always ate what they killed, and this part of West Virginia likely had never seen a game warden. Here at Top Hat Mountain, Mom had taught them about edible plants and berries—and, perhaps more important, which plants and berries should never be consumed.

After Dad was killed, Adam knew how hard it was for Mom to continue the Top Hat tradition, but she kept them coming, anyway. Adam knew every inch—every tree, it seemed—of this place. It was as if it were a member of his family, an extension of home.

And now, it was none of those things. The moon had turned itself off after the war, so the nights were the definition of total blackness. During the day, the once-brilliant vistas seemed sepia toned. The vegetation still thrived, and there seemed to be more small game to choose from than ever before, but everything was *so different.*

Emma seemed less appalled over the look of the place than he was, but that was because she had nothing to compare it to. In the three days that had passed since they'd arrived here, Adam had taught her some rudimentary outdoors skills, emphasizing how not to kill herself with poisonous food, and how to skin, dress and cook small game. She didn't mind the gory stuff, but she still had trouble firing the fatal shots. They kept a well-controlled fire burning all the time, banking it during much of the day to keep the coals hot. At night, they kept the flames shin high for the light and warmth that it provided.

And they banged like bunny rabbits. It turned out that the bed of the Bronco wasn't too uncomfortable if it was padded well enough with blankets, but sex in the wide-open outdoors was pretty special, too. Emma was insatiable. Not that that was a bad thing.

As far as Adam was concerned, this place was now their home. During the day, he cut trees and trimmed them of their branches in hopes of building a shelter. It wouldn't be much, but with the colder weather coming, they needed a place with some form of insulation. Yet another skill taught to him by his mother. If he could pull it off, and the final product looked anything like what he saw in his mind, they'd be able to stand on the inside, but without much headroom to spare. At the rate he was going, he figured he'd have the shelter in livable condition in another week, week and a half.

Last night, they'd lain naked next to the fire, chatting about nothing. Everything but the future. Tonight, though, the temperature had dropped, so they'd dressed afterward. A coffeepot sat on the rack above the fire, its water heating to aid in cleaning dishes a while later. If anyone had told Adam a month ago that he'd be heading to bed around nine every night, and getting up with the sun, he'd have called them crazy.

"At our next stop, we need to buy some books," Emma said.

"I've got some playing cards in my rucksack," Adam offered. "That'd give us something to do."

Her hand shifted to his crotch. "Finding something to do is not a challenge."

"You have a dirty, dirty mind," he said, and he leaned over to kiss her.

A branch cracked out in the dark.

Adam froze.

Emma saw his fear. "What—"

"Shh." He listened to the night. "Someone's out there," he whispered, his words barely a breeze. "Get in the car."

"Just an animal, maybe?"

"No."

"I didn't hear anything."

Another crack. Adam didn't have time to explain the seriousness of this. Only *people* walk carefully and stop after they make noise. Animals would just attack. If it was a friendly visit, the approaching person would intentionally make noise so as not to worry the other party or startle them.

They needed to retreat away from the light of the fire and get back to the Bronco, where all the weapons were. Adam started scooching across the ground, his eyes never straying from the direction of the noise. The problem was, the fire was between him and the noise, ruining his night vision.

"Hold still, boy!" a voice yelled from the dark. "Just don't move, and I won't have to kill you."

Emma sat up. "We're not here to do anybody any harm."

A tall, wiry man with disheveled hair and beard stepped into the fire's light ring. "I wish we could say the same," he said.

We.

The man held a lever-action hunting rifle and had a revolver strapped to his hip, cowboy style. A lady with a bolt-action rifle stepped up to join him. Adam figured her to be his wife, but she also could have been his daughter. She was filthy in a way that does not happen in a day, or even a week. Her hair hadn't seen a comb in a very long time.

Adam sat up and rose to his knees.

The man raised his rifle, and the lady copied him.

"We seen you drive up the road days ago," the man said. "Been waitin' for you to drive back down."

"Do you need something?" Adam asked.

The guy coughed out a humorless laugh. "Yeah, I do. Your truck. In fact, I think I'll take everything you got."

Adam's heart stopped. This guy looked like he was serious.

"Thanks for markin' your camp with the fire, by the way. Made it easy as can be to find you."

Adam said nothing. First, there was nothing to say. Second, he kept his focus on Bubba's gun muzzle, wondering why he didn't just shoot them.

"You don't say a whole lot, do you, boy?"

"I guess I get quiet when guns are pointed at me."

"How about your wife over there? I know she's got a tongue because I already heard her use it."

"I'm not his wife," Emma said.

Adam felt a flash of anger. You don't give up anything to guys like this.

"Oh, is that so?" Bubba laughed again. "You two are playin' house, then. How cute."

"Where are you going with this?" Adam asked. "What are your plans for us?"

"You're not from around here, are you?" Bubba asked.

"We're from around Mountain View," Adam said. "We had to run from the fires."

"Why here?"

"I used to come here when I was a kid. It has happy memories." Adam knew it was a mistake to share information with this guy, but Bubba was the one with the rifle. He didn't think he'd have a chance of getting back to his own weapons without getting shot.

Bubba pointed at Emma. "Stand up, missy. Step closer to the fire so's I can get a better look at you."

Emma shot a panicked glance at Adam, then did as she was told. In the glow of the dying flames, Adam saw a smudge of dirt on her cheek. Her boots were untied, her blouse undone just enough to be tempting. She noticed and moved to button up.

"No, don't do that," Bubba said. "In fact, go the other way. Take that blouse off."

Emma froze.

"Take the Bronco," Adam said. "We don't have to be animals." He was stalling for time. This was spinning out of control and he had to find the handle for the brakes.

"Oh, I'll be taking the Bronco. But I think maybe I'd like to take a ride with your friend, too."

Emma's whole body began to shake. *Really* shake. Not a tremble, but gross movement of her hands, shoulders and legs. They were the kind of movements Adam had never seen in anyone before.

"Take that shirt off for me, missy. Let me see them titties."

This was not going to happen. Adam guessed the distance that separated him from Bubba and his . . . whatever the hell she was . . . to be fifteen feet, twenty at most.

Emma's hands shook so bad that she had a hard time managing the buttons.

"I don't got all night, missy," Bubba said. Then he laughed. "Actually, I guess I do have all night." He shifted his gaze to Adam. "I can hear you thinkin', boy. You're thinkin' you can take me, ain't you? Skinny city kid like you?" This time, his laugh sounded like he was genuinely amused.

"Adam?" Emma whispered.

"You need to do as you're told," Bubba said. He turned his head toward his friend in the tattered clothes. "This wet-behind-the-ears whelp thinks—"

Adam had been waiting for Bubba to be distracted. As soon as the man looked away, Adam launched. He plowed straight through the fire, stirring a cloud of embers that enveloped his legs.

He hit Bubba hard, just as the redneck had realized his mistake and was bringing his rifle back to bear. Adam got his hands on the rifle and drove forward with everything he had. Bubba was off-balance, and as he backpedaled, he lost his balance and fell onto his back.

"Shoot, Janey!" Bubba yelled.

Adam drove his forehead into the man's nose, launching a fountain of blood.

A gunshot split the night. A lady screamed.

Adam still had both hands on the rifle. He tried to wrench it from Bubba's grasp, but the guy had strength that Adam hadn't expected.

As they grappled on the forest floor, a gunshot boomed again. And again.

Adam's guts felt like they'd exploded as a knee found his balls and he found his grip slipping. He was seconds away from losing this fight.

To hell with it.

He needed a new plan. He stopped trying to pull the rifle away, and, instead, let go of it. The sudden change startled Bubba. He ended up hitting himself in the mouth with the steel receiver. That gave Adam another half second of opportunity.

Boom-boom-boom!

Adam launched himself forward, onto Bubba's chest, and used all his momentum to jam his thumbs into the man's eyes.

Bubba howled as Adam felt the eyeballs shift in their sockets. Bubba's hands moved reflexively to his ruined eyes, and Adam saw his final opportunity. He wrenched the rifle from Bubba's hands. Holding it like a harpoon, he slammed the buttstock into Bubba's mouth with all the force he could muster. He reset and did again. He heard teeth shatter and the wet slap of soft tissue being crushed.

Adam rose to his feet, spun the rifle in his hands, leaned the muzzle into the bloody mess of the man's face and pulled the trigger.

Bubba's head blew apart.

Adam levered another round into the chamber.

Bubba's lady friend—Janey, right?—was gone. So was Emma.

"Em!" he yelled. "He's dead! Are you okay?"

Silence.

Shit. There was no way she couldn't have heard him yell. So, if she didn't answer, it was either because she was in hiding or because . . . because she was in hiding.

Adam walked at a low crouch as he scanned one hundred eighty degrees in front of him—the area from which he'd heard the shots fired.

At the Bronco, he switched out the .30-30 for a Bushmaster. He knew for a fact that the AR15's mags were loaded with thirty rounds of 5.56-millimeter hardball, but he couldn't speak to what was in the dead man's hunting rifle.

One of the ARs was missing. Had Emma armed herself? Had he been hearing a two-way gunfight?

He wanted to shout out again, but what would be the point? She had to have heard him. She had to know that he was still looking for her.

Adam slipped the rifle sling over his arm and shoulder and thumbed the safety off. As he moved away from the fire, the night was impossibly black, made more so by the phantom images of the fire on his retinas. He crossed around the dark side of the Bronco and took a knee.

With his rifle pressed to his shoulder, he tried to become perfectly still. There was a reason why animals owned the night, and humans did not. Our night vision sucks. In the dark, we perceive motion more easily than details. And hearing improves. Adam figured that was how cavemen could hear the approach of saber-toothed tigers.

Something definitely was out there. Not movement so much as sound. Did someone just sniff?

Didn't matter. He had a compass point to concentrate on.

Moving slowly enough to be barely moving at all, he remained in his crouch and he scissor-walked toward the sound. He heard it again. The source hadn't moved.

Whatever that nerve was at the base of his spine that told him he was in peril was buzzing as if it were plugged into an electrical outlet. It was entirely possible that his prey was hunting him back.

He froze. He wanted to hear it again before he overcommitted. Also, he wanted to gauge the range.

There it was again. Definitely someone sniffing. A voice moaned.

Adam started moving again. After six more steps, he saw someone lying on the ground, but in the darkness, he didn't know who it was. Then he saw the bare legs. This was Bubba's girlfriend, and from the way she was sprawled on her face, he knew she was unconscious.

"Emma?" he called out to the night. "Emma, where are you?"

The voice moaned again.

"Ah, shit," Adam said. "They shot each other."

He picked up his pace and ran toward the source of the snuffling. "Emma, it's me. Don't shoot. It's Adam."

He found her at the base of a tree, curled in a fetal ball, crying. He pulled his flashlight from its loop on his belt and thumbed the bulb to life. A Bushmaster lay on the ground next to her. He pushed it out of the way, kneeled and bent till his mouth was inches from her ear. "Are you hurt?"

Emma continued to hug her knees as she rocked herself on the ground. If she'd heard him, she made no indication.

Adam held his flashlight in his teeth as he placed his hands on Emma's shoulders and he gently rocked her onto her back.

She didn't resist.

Adam saw no signs of injury, no blood. He ran his hands down her body, then her legs. He reached under to check her back. She seemed fine.

"Emma!" He shouted it this time, and she jumped. Lights came back on in her eyes. "What's wrong?"

"W-what just happened? I . . . I had to . . ."

"You saved my life, Em. *Our* lives. You did what you had to do. Now we have to get out of here." He helped her to a sitting position. "You're not hurt, right?"

"I thought she was going to kill me."

"She *was* going to kill you. That's why you had to kill her first. You had no choice. Now, please answer me. Are you hurt? Can you stand?"

She answered by rising uneasily to her feet. Adam stood guard to make sure she didn't collapse or tip over. When she was steady, he bent down and picked up her rifle as he let his fall against its sling. "Let's get our stuff and get out of here."

"I thought you needed to stay here."

"This changes things," Adam said. "A lot. That was a shit ton of shooting, and locals heard it. They know these assholes. Knew. Hell, they might even be family. We're not from around here, so that means we're the bad guys, no matter what the facts are."

"Where are we going to go?"

"Someplace else. Come morning, people are going to notice that Bubba and Jane have gone missing. Hell, they might wonder why they haven't come back down with our shit. We don't need to be here for that."

Adam and Emma spent ten minutes or so policing the area for tools and equipment. He found his saw, ax and blade sharpener near the shelter he'd been building. A lot of work had gone into that thing. It was tough to think of leaving it behind.

As he returned to the Bronco, Emma asked, "What about the bodies?"

"Let 'em rot. What he was gonna do to you, I hope a wild pig feasts on his face chunks." He opened the passenger-side door to get in.

"Can you drive tonight?" Emma asked. "I'm too . . ."

So was Adam. He was . . . too.

The adrenaline had done its job, and now that he was on the far side of it, all he wanted to do was sleep. And maybe cry a little. He'd always wondered if he would actually have the guts to do the things that he'd trained for all these years. He worried that he would chicken out, or that he would hesitate. Now, looking back, he didn't remember thinking about anything. He just remembered taking action.

And now he remembered the noises. Not just the moans from Bubba, but the horrible resonating wet impacts of the rifle butt against flesh. He remembered the gunshots.

Before climbing behind the wheel, Adam stopped at the tailgate and leaned inside. He pulled the Glocks he'd taken from the hardware store out from behind the rucksack, where he'd stashed them. Both were holstered. He slipped one onto his belt and walked the other around to Emma in the passenger seat.

"Here," he said. "I think you should keep this with you. Life is different now."

"I don't think I can do that again," Emma said.

"And I hope we don't have to find out. Better to have it and not need it than the other way around."

"I don't want to wear it."

"That's fine."

His last stop was to kick out the remains of the fire. A forest fire was a scenario he could do without repeating.

Finally they were ready to go. In addition to the pistol on his hip for protection, he decided to keep his M4 in the front, too. It took some maneuvering to arrange the muzzle so it was free of the steering wheel and didn't pose a risk to either of them, but he got it settled.

As he drove away, he cast a glance at Bubba's body. In the glare of the headlights, he could see a halo of blood around the dead man's head and torso.

Adam considered driving with the lights off to avoid calling attention to themselves, but he couldn't. The postwar night was far too black, and the canopy of foliage made the darkness even deeper. As it was, the road was barely a road to begin with. He'd never clocked the distance to the main highway, but he imagined it to be more than a mile—though it was so hard to tell when the driving was so difficult.

"Is this what it's going to be like from now on?" Emma asked.

"Not everybody is homicidal," Adam said, though he knew his mother would vehemently disagree. "We've just got to find the nice people."

"Or no people at all."

In the short term, maybe that was the best solution. The problem was, Adam didn't know this part of the state. He'd lived in

West Virginia his whole life, but it's a big state, and there were parts of it where he just didn't want to be. He knew where Top Hat Mountain was, and he knew the route from the house he grew up in, in Charleston, but other than that, not much. He also knew the route back to Mountain View and the academy, but that was out of play.

So was Charleston . . . because it probably wasn't there anymore.

When they got to the main road, he would need to choose a compass direction and head that way. Right would be roughly north, and left would be roughly south. They'd come from the north, so the choice had to be the other way.

Adam understood how quickly news spread, even in the absence of phones and internet, and within a few days, everybody who was interested would have heard about the murder of an innocent young family by crazed outsiders driving a red-and-white Ford Bronco. People up north would have had a chance to see the Bronco, but people to the south would not. Thus, the decision for that first turn was simple. Where the road would take them wouldn't matter for a while.

"Hey, Em. Are the hubs locked?"

"I don't remember."

"Is there an indicator light or something?"

"It burned out years ago. This is a vintage truck. We didn't do a lot of hard-core four-wheeling in it. Maybe we should turn off the lights as we get close to where those people lived. They said they saw us drive by."

"Do you remember seeing houses along the way?"

"I know I saw some. But I didn't pay attention to where they were."

"Me too. It can't be too far."

Adam's palms were soaked with sweat and his heart was hammering the "Wipe Out" drum solo as he advanced down the mountain toward the road. It was like walking into a cave when you knew an angry bear was waiting for you.

"It would be over quicker if you drove faster," Emma said through a tight throat.

"Yeah, but if I hit something and we get stranded here, it will be really, really bad."

He goosed the gas a little, then backed off. It wasn't worth the risk.

He slowed even more when he saw flickering light moving through the trees up ahead.

Emma saw it, too. "What do you think?"

"I think it's people with lanterns. Maybe flashlights."

"What are we going to do?"

"Drive past them."

"Do you think those people back there belonged to these people here?"

"That's exactly what I think."

Emma reached to the floor and lifted something. "Is this already chambered?"

"Unless you unchambered it." He turned his head to glance at her, but she was barely an inkblot in the darkness. "I hope there's no need for another gunfight. But if it comes to that, be sure of your target before you shoot anything."

"I won't shoot myself," Emma said.

"Don't shoot me, either."

As they approached the cluster of people ahead, Adam drove with his left hand and raised the Bushmaster's buttstock to his shoulder with his right.

"We can't just keep shooting people," Emma said.

"I don't want to start a fight."

They got closer. Adam could hear the people yelling. He rolled his window down and was greeted with victory whoops.

"Tommy!" somebody yelled. "You did it!" One of them stepped away from the others and advanced on the Bronco. He carried what looked like a short-barreled shotgun. "Good God, Tommy, we heard all that shootin' and we didn't know what the hell was goin' on."

The others ahead were blocking the road. It wasn't an aggressive move. More of an informal party taking shape. Adam counted five of them.

"They didn't want to give up easy, huh?"

"Be ready for anything," Adam said. He moved his rifle so the muzzle rested on the door frame, on top of the open window.

The guy with the shotgun approached easily, clearly not expecting trouble. His hand was nowhere near the trigger of his shotgun. "You didn't have to hurt them too bad, did you? How many was there, anyway? Sounded like a war up—"

The man arrived at the window and understood.

"Two of us," Adam said. "Tommy threatened to rape my girlfriend. He was going to kill me."

In the glow of the man's lantern, Adam saw his features harden.

"What happened to Tommy?"

"Shh," Adam said. "I'm not looking for trouble. Just let us drive through. I promise we won't—"

The man in the window shifted his posture. Adam saw that he was bringing his shotgun to bear so he shot him in the eye at point-blank range. His stomach knotted as the man's brain spray spattered his face and he stomped on the gas. The Bronco lurched forward as the other five jumped to action. They were still fifty feet away and the Bronco had all the acceleration of an overweight turtle. As the vehicle sped toward the assembled locals, they prepared to fire.

Adam shifted his rifle to aim through the windshield and started pumping rounds through the glass. Aim wasn't important. He just wanted to make them jump. The glass spiderwebbed and his victims jumped out of the way. As the Bronco passed, the wheel passed over something big, bouncing Adam and Emma out of their seats.

He was able to maintain control, though.

"Was that what I think it was?" Emma asked, whirling in her seat to take a look out the back window.

"I'm telling myself it was a rock," Adam said.

"But what if—"

"It was a *rock,* Emma."

"Those were *people,* Adam."

Something let go inside him. "Some of them still are, Em! Would you rather we be dead than them? Would you prefer that I didn't shoot, and that asshole up there raped you?" He didn't dare to look at her in the darkness. He didn't want to see her, and it wouldn't have mattered. "'Cause you know what? I'm sure there'll be other opportunities in the future. This is exactly what I've been warning you about. This is the new normal. Try to be nice. Try to be reasonable. But know that the other guy might see niceness as weakness, and that's when you have to be prepared to defend yourself and everybody you care about."

"I don't need a goddamn lecture!" Emma shouted. "We just killed people!"

"Yes, *we* did. And, yes, you *do* need a lecture. I am not the enemy. I'm not even the bad guy. I'm the victim. And so are you. I can't have you thinking otherwise."

"Or else what?"

Adam thumbed the selector lever on his M4 to SAFE and repositioned the muzzle so it was pointing toward the floorboard. He'd lost his temper, and now he needed to rein it back in. "It's not like that," he said. "There's no ultimatum. I'm just saying that we've had to do awful things, and we will probably have to do more awful things just to survive. There are millions of potential enemies out there. I need you to be my one guaranteed friend."

Emma fell silent for long enough to draw Adam's attention. "This is going to kill us all, isn't it?"

"I don't want to talk about that. Yeah. Maybe. Probably. I don't know. And neither do you or anyone else. This is a one-day-at-a-time kind of thing."

More silence.

"I don't know what I can promise you and what I can't," Emma said finally. "I don't know how well I'm going to be able to fight. I don't know if I'm going to freeze next time. But I promise that I'll try hard not to panic."

Well, that's something, Adam thought.

“And one more thing,” Emma added. “I promise I’ll always understand that you’re trying to do the right thing.”

She reached her hand across the center space and Adam took it.

“That’s all I ever want,” he said.

Finally they made it to the T intersection with the main roadway. To the right lay the past, to the left the future.

Adam spun the wheel to the left and stomped on the gas.

CHAPTER TWENTY-ONE

NEARLY TWO WEEKS INTO THIS NIGHTMARE, WORLDWIDE COMMUNICATIONS were still a mess. Scott Johnson had been beating on his comms guru Peter Clostner like a recalcitrant mule, but to little effect. Either electronics were working, or they weren't, and for the time being, they weren't. Not surprisingly, ham radio operators were the heroes of the day, but nothing they transmitted was confirmed, or even confirmable at this point.

Apparently, military units still existed in America, but if true, they were working autonomously, which made them military dictators. Johnson saw little good could coming from that.

One positive event floating in the sea of negatives was the fact that Pete Clostner had successfully established often-unreliable connections with Mount Weather. The National Command Authority—POTUS, VPOTUS and SECDEF—had, in fact, never arrived, and were presumed dead. Given the devastation reported in that part of the country, Johnson didn't doubt the report.

President Glendale, God bless him, did his best to cobble together some kind of federal response, but the surviving cabinet consisted of the secretaries of Labor, Interior, Health and Human Services, Veterans Affairs and Homeland Security. The director of the Environmental Protection Agency had also made it to safety, as had a deputy assistant secretary of the Treasury. Given former President Blanton's inability to attract great talent, Penn Glendale had to make do with a bench that no one would call *deep*.

Every communication they'd established between the two bunkers impressed Johnson as a form of intellectual masturbation. They made plans and tried to coordinate responses that simply could not yet be stitched together. Frustrations ran hot.

Meanwhile, the House and Senate debated funding packages and their own coordinated responses—usually running opposed to those of the president. Johnson found it amusing as hell that these clowns still thought that they were in charge.

Presently Johnson was waiting for Angela Fortnight to join him in his public office. She was running late, as he expected, because she'd knotted her panties over the notion that she was Speaker of the House and Johnson should come to *her,* instead of the other way around. Thing was, his office had walls, while hers did not. This was a meeting that needed walls.

The Speaker finally arrived, sixteen minutes late. She didn't bother to knock, but rather breezed through his closed door and left it open as she helped herself to the metal guest chair in front of his desk.

Johnson knew not to take the bait. These effete asshats were beginning to crumble under the pressure. He knew that trouble was coming, but he didn't want it to be over this.

"Good afternoon, Madam Speaker," he said. He stood, walked to his door and closed it.

"Not yet, it's not," she said.

"Oh, then it's not going to get better," he said as he walked back around to his chair.

"Make this fast, Johnson," she said. "I have work to do."

"So I hear," Johnson said. "On the feather edge of bringing back normalcy, eh?"

Angela's ears turned red.

"I'll get to it," he said. "Your House members eat like pigs at a trough. The food we have in our stores is all the food that we'll have. It's designed for sixty days, but given that we're missing over a hundred people, we can make it last longer—which we may very well have to do. You need to tell your members to show some restraint."

Angela's face showed disbelief. "Are you serious? You want me to be a cafeteria monitor?"

"No, ma'am, I want you to show some leadership. Representative Kiser threatened to punch the line server unless he could get another slice of chicken, and then took more without permission."

Angela threw her head back for a forced laugh. "You can't be serious. That's your problem, not mine."

Johnson drilled her with a glare that silenced her. He leaned forward, his forearms pressed on his desk. "You're goddamned right it's my problem," he said. He kept his tone low, threatening. "This is not a vacation, ma'am. It's not a summer camp for overprivileged rich children. This is an emergency evacuation facility, where one of the most valued, critical commodities is food. If one person takes more than his share, that means someone else gets less. Surely, you understand this."

"Of course, but this is—"

"I'm speaking," Johnson said. "I'll tell you when it's your turn."

Her ears were crimson now.

"Starting immediately, anyone who attempts to steal food will be shot."

Angela's jaw dropped open.

"It's easy," Johnson said. "Actions and consequences. My job is to maintain order under difficult circumstances. I've told you before that your job is to do whatever it is that politicians do and follow the rules as you do. I can't imagine how anything could be simpler."

Angela stared back, clearly at a loss for words.

"Okay, then," Scott said. He stood. "That's all. You can go now."

Victoria didn't want to be in charge of things. She wanted to be on her way to Top Hat Mountain to bring her family back together. Rumors swirled that the Clinton M. Hedrick Military Academy had burned to the ground, taking all of the cadets with it, but she refused to believe the stories. And if the story proved to be true, she would not accept that one of the dead cadets was named Adam Emerson.

If it were true, she would know it somehow. Don't ask how, she just *would.*

In the fifteen days that had passed since the war began and ended, the little town of Ortho had doubled in population. Many of the folks who lived in the hinterlands had decided to move in closer to the center of things, such as they were. Mostly, the newcomers were older—Victoria guessed the average age to be sixty—and the lack of transportation left them too isolated out in the woods.

For the most part, the townies opened their homes to the newcomers, but that situation was quickly becoming untenable. People didn't have enough resources for their own families, and the presence of strangers was becoming an unwelcome burden.

The town had a doctor now. Until two weeks ago, Rory Stevenson had been an orthopedist, but now he was a good old-fashioned country doctor. He'd moved to town from his mountain cabin specifically to be of service to the community. He did the best he could with what he had, but without modern diagnostic tools and a dwindling supply of modern pharmaceuticals from the stores of the Ortho Pharmacy, much of what he offered was palliative care. Thirty-five and in excellent health, Dr. Rory had aged fifteen years in fifteen days. Victoria worried about his workload, but he was one of one. A hell of a burden. Victoria had assigned Caleb to help the doctor out, and, apparently, he was doing a good job.

Running water was a problem, too, as were sanitation facilities. People out here drank well water, but without electricity, the well pumps didn't pump. The homes that had propane generators were in good shape, but sooner or later, those propane tanks would run dry.

Victoria had no idea how to design a manual pump, but Lavinia Sloan did. A welder by trade, she also dabbled in blacksmithing, and she loved to study the old ways of the ancestors. She'd been able to bring an antique handle pump back to life, and she'd installed it in the bathroom of Dr. Rory's house. She promised that more would come. She also took on Victoria's son Luke as an apprentice, though Victoria feared that he would be more of a mascot than an asset.

As for sanitation, the proximity to the river helped. Even with water pumps idled, toilets still worked if you primed the tanks. Newcomers were going old-school with their own privies. Those who lived within two hundred feet of the river had to get the approval of Dr. Rory before they could use them.

Victoria still smiled when she remembered his reaction when she gave him the assignment: "As if I need any more shit to do."

Victoria and her family, along with Joe McCrea and Paul Copley, had moved into St. Thomas Catholic Church, about a quarter of a mile from Maggie's Place. They lived there, along with the Boyle family—Ronnie and Peggy and their four-year-old daughter, Abigail. Each of them carved out places for themselves on the floor, and so far, everyone got along, despite the close quarters.

The pastor of St. Thomas's, Father Tim, had been away visiting family in Philadelphia when the war came. Still, five or six of the most devout showed up every morning to pray silently, seemingly oblivious to those who were crashed on the floor.

Maggie's Place had evolved into the most important building in town, serving not just as a food pantry, but also as city hall and the courthouse. Victoria conducted her business from the back of the building, using a table next to the back door as her desk. She'd developed a tolerance for most innocent assault crimes—flashes of anger among stressed residents—but showed no quarter for any form of theft.

That said, not everyone agreed with the boundaries she'd drawn around the concept of thievery. One such disgruntled resident was Marius Miller, a gruff septuagenarian who owned Miller's Auto Body just a little way down the street, and the five acres of land that surrounded it.

"You are not putting shacks up on my property!" Miller insisted.

"People need places to live, Marius," Victoria said. "Winter will be here soon, and people need shelter."

"Then let them shelter someplace else. That land has been in my family for three generations."

"I'm not proposing we take your land," Victoria said. "I'm telling you, you need to share it."

"Free of charge?"

"Would you like the town to write you a check? Which currency would you like it in?"

"Don't be a smart mouth, Vicky."

"Then don't be unreasonable. This is a time to come together. Neighbors helping neighbors."

"They are not my neighbors."

"They will be." Victoria heard her own snarkiness there. "Sorry."

"All of these people, Vicky," Marius pressed. "They all eat, they all shit and they all need places to stay. They don't bring skills or value. They just drain resources. When does it stop?"

This was becoming a progressively more popular refrain. As people clustered closer together, sanitation concerns blossomed, and with those, health issues would explode. They hadn't crossed that line yet, but every day saw the arrival of more refugees. Victoria was keenly aware that she and her family numbered among those refugees, so she therefore treaded carefully on the issue. The town, however, received fifteen new arrivals yesterday, on top of the thirty-two that had wandered in over the preceding weeks.

Word was traveling that Ortho had supplies and a doctor, and people were hungry and hurt.

"You tell me, Marius," she countered. "At what point do you just turn people away? And how do you keep them from coming back?"

"That's not for me to decide," he said. "You're the elected official, not me. You're the one who asked for the job."

Victoria ignored the bait. This was the last job in the world that she wanted. She'd resigned from the House of Representatives, for God's sake, and everyone knew that. She was stuck with the job because she'd been stupid enough to not run away from it.

"All right, Marius," she said. "Since you acknowledge my extraordinary power from my throne, I'm telling you that I have authorized the construction of eight cabins on your property. You are welcome to move into one of them if you wish, but if you do, you will have to sacrifice your home to the refugees."

He started to argue, but she held up her hand for silence. "The decision is made, Marius. This is a time for everyone to give a little. This is your gift. Now, please let it drop."

Thanks to Ty Rowley, the third-generation owner of Rowley Lumber, building materials were in ample supply. Ty had even been able to resurrect his grandfather's old steam-powered lumber mill. A fascinating accumulation of pulleys, belts and blades, the mill was an OSHA nightmare, but it was great to watch the operation as he turned trees into boards.

To support the supply chain of incoming wood, she'd put Eric Lofland in charge of assembling horses and anything that could be used as sleds or wagons to move felled trees and other heavy materials from one place to another. George Simmons had fashioned a manual pump to draw gas from his inground tanks, so there was plenty of fuel for chain saws. Axes still needed to be swung, of course, but Victoria had never encountered a man who didn't enjoy doing that, at least for a while.

It turned out that Paul Copley and Major McCrea were both carpenters in their spare time, though Copley showed considerably more talent than McCrea. Where they *really* shined was in their leadership and training skills. As new residents arrived, their first job was to assist with construction efforts. It wasn't until the air was filled with the sound of hammering that Victoria realized how ubiquitous nail guns had become before the war. Ditto the sound of manual sawing instead of power tools.

Three days ago, Mike Underwood, a young man best known for his football prowess in high school, startled every resident by driving into town in a 1960s-vintage Chevrolet El Camino. It had belonged to his grandfather, and because of its ancient mechanics, it still ran. Right away, he became the town livery driver. His first mission was to drive Dr. Rory out to Martha Merrill's house up on the mountain, about ten miles outside of town. She had cancer, and her unofficial caretakers—the Boyle family—had relocated their family to town.

That story did not have a happy ending. Mrs. Merrill had been dead for at least two days by the time they arrived. Dr. Rory was very complimentary of Mike Underwood's stoicism and cooperation as they wrapped her body in a bedsheet and carried it outside, where it could be consumed by marauding carnivores. For the time being, that was the new normal for people who died. There just wasn't time for funerals, and even if they had the time, they didn't have the manpower.

New arrivals brought rumors and news from other parts of the state and beyond. Where the reports conflicted, Victoria chose to believe the more optimistic version. But there was no denying the devastation. By all accounts, Charleston no longer existed. The same was true of Huntington, Wheeling and Morgantown. Rumors swirled about smaller tactical sites in the most western regions of the state, but none of them had been confirmed by anyone with direct knowledge.

So far, radiation sickness had not been a problem in Ortho. New arrivals shared horrific stories of relatives and friends who agonized through the progressive burn injuries that seemed to consume victims from the inside to the outside, ultimately leaving people begging to be euthanized.

More than a couple of new townspeople confessed to doing that very thing to their loved ones who couldn't take the suffering anymore.

Hanging over everything was the future of Brandon-Lee May. Since he'd been taken into custody, he'd been held under close guard in the basement of St. Thomas's Church, Victoria's adopted home. No conflict there, right? The assigned judge as caretaker? But she had no choice.

The first challenge had been to find reliable guards. According to Joe McCrea, Caine Foster could be trusted not to shoot the prisoner outright, and he'd gone on to find others that he thought he could count on. They guarded Brandon-Lee in rotating five-hour shifts, and thus far, the young man hadn't posed any big problems. The real issue was security. Church basements were not built with the idea of holding prisoners, but the walls were made of stone, and, ironically, the high windows were barred to prevent burglaries. There was a bathroom down there, and the prisoner's ankles were shackled at all times.

Many in town were appalled that his wrists were not also bound. Victoria explained to them that torture was not part of the package of services that were offered.

She worried that the fuse on Brandon-Lee's safety was burning dangerously short. They needed to get this trial done, with a real verdict on the record.

And then, if she listened to the talk in the town, it would be time to hang the guilty bastard. There were no shortages of wannabe prosecutors.

But defenders were a different issue. The man whom Brandon-Lee allegedly killed, Ryan Hamilton, had been a family man. Hamilton family roots were sunk deeper into Ortho than all but the oldest, grandest trees. He'd married his high-school sweetheart and was father to three girls, whose soccer teams he'd coached. Now he was dead at the hands of what was now called the Grubbs gang, and somebody by-God had to pay.

But there had to be a public trial, and for the outcome to be legitimate, someone needed to speak on behalf of the accused. Even with civil society shredded, the most basic tenets of law had to be preserved.

Again, Victoria turned to Dr. Rory Stevenson for assistance. He was a respected professional whose opinion, she hoped, would be more accepted by the population than any other townsperson.

Rory had put up a pro forma objection, but in the end, he understood the stakes, and he took on the task. "You know doctors and lawyers are, like, entirely different professions, right?" he'd asked Victoria privately before the trial began.

"One thing we share," Victoria replied, "is that we're all pains in the ass."

Victoria had never been a trial attorney. She'd done some property stuff, but mostly she'd dealt with wills and estates before moving on to the state house, and from there to the U.S. Capitol. She hadn't dealt with a court proceeding since her moot court days during law school.

She decided that this would be a bench trial—granting a motion that she had coached Rory to make—and that there would be no formal prosecution. Instead, she would interview the witnesses herself. The charges would be grand theft and murder. These complex times were in some ways simpler than before. If the evidence showed that Brandon-Lee was in any way involved with the murder of Ryan Hamilton, the town would settle for only one sentence, and they would insist upon it being carried out immediately.

Maggie's Place was beyond packed when Victoria gaveled the assembly to order. As judge, she sat elevated on a bar stool behind a lectern that had been procured from the Baptist church. Brandon-Lee sat facing her at a table to her right, with Rory Stevenson on his left, and with McCrea and Paul Copley standing close behind to provide security.

Joey Abbott, of Joey's Pawnshop, asked that the security detail be moved away so the town could see the accused, but Victoria declined the request. A visible barrier between the accused and the people who hated him forced an extra step for someone in the room who might want to settle matters with their own bullet. She knew without doubt that if someone did do such a thing, it would be considered a heroic act, and that there'd be no tolerance for bringing that perpetrator to justice.

It was amazing, Victoria thought, just how fragile a concept justice was.

After declining Joey's request, she granted a request from Rory to have all the witnesses who were scheduled to testify removed from the room to be called back one at a time when it was their turn to address the court. Victoria felt more than a little embarrassed that she had not thought of that precaution on her own.

The witness list was cobbled together via sign-up sheet. Victoria figured that by giving every person who wanted to be heard a chance to do so, she'd have the best chance at keeping the train on the tracks.

The witnesses testified from a chair on Victoria's left. Joey Abbott and George Simmons each testified that the items that had been taken from their stores were the same as those recovered from the woods near Ryan Hamilton's truck. They testified that Mr. Hamilton was a fine father, friend and community member. They testified that he would be sorely missed.

And they testified that Brandon-Lee May should hang or be shot for the murder of such a fine man.

Through it all, Brandon-Lee sat stone still, his eyes focused on the witnesses as he listened to them condemn him. His face showed nothing, just as Victoria had counseled him should be the case during the trial.

"Listen to me carefully, Brandon-Lee," she'd told him the night before in his cell. "You know what the town wants to do with you, right?"

No response. He was a hard one.

"Okay, fine. Just hear my words. What happens to you tomorrow is only partially dependent on what the evidence shows you have done. It's at least equally determined by what you do while you're in the courtroom."

"They can't prove a goddamn thing against me," Brandon-Lee said.

"Stop. That right there is the attitude that can get you killed."

"But I did nothing wrong."

"Don't tell me that," Victoria said, pointing at his nose. "After tomorrow, it won't matter what actually did or did not happen up there on the road. What matters is what the town *thinks* happened up there on the road."

"So this is a beauty contest? I thought your job was to make sure everything is fair."

"To the degree that I can, that is exactly what my job is. But I'm just one woman. People say I'm the judge for this, but I'm no judge. If people decide to tear you apart, and feed you to the hogs, I am powerless to stop them. You need to give them—at least *some* of them—a reason to believe you and stick up for your rights." She gave a few seconds to let that sink in.

"And that, young man," she finished, "is all up to you."

She stood, didn't wait for a reply. She'd said everything she'd needed to say.

As soon as the door closed behind her, she swore that she could hear Brandon-Lee start to cry.

George Simmons's testimony came first, and after Victoria had let him have his say, it was time for the defense. "Dr. Stevenson, do you have any questions for the witness?"

Rory stood. "I do, Your Honor." He straightened his back and tucked his thumbs behind the waistband of his jeans, flanking his belt buckle. Clearly, he'd seen his share of TV courtroom dramas. He walked to the witness chair, kept a respectful distance. "Mr. Simmons, did you see Mr. May steal any of your goods?"

"I saw him taking inventory of what he'd stolen."

Victoria rapped on her lectern with her gavel—actually a rubber mallet from Simmons Gas and Goodies. "You're out of order, Mr. Simmons. Answer the question as it was asked." As she made her ruling, she was again aware of how toothless it was. Simmons could do anything he wanted here in the presence of his friends.

"I'll ask it again," Rory said. "We can talk about what you saw up on the mountain later. But for right now, let's concentrate on the night when your store was robbed. Did you witness the robbery itself?"

"When I got to my store the night after the bombing—"

Rory held up his hand, a stopping motion. "Nope. Again, not to interrupt, we can go there later. My question is about the moment when your windows were broken and people invaded your gas station. Did you witness that?"

George clearly saw where this was going, and he was annoyed at being pressed to give an answer he didn't want to give. "No, I did not witness it. But I—"

Victoria gaveled again. "The question required only a *yes* or a *no*. You did that. Thank you." She indicated for Rory to continue. His skills impressed her.

"On that morning, when you noticed the damage to your station, what did you think?"

George's features knotted up into an *Are you kidding me?* "I thought, well, oh, shit, somebody ransacked my store."

The incredulity with which he delivered that testimony triggered laughter. Victoria let it go and order returned on its own.

"Yeah, I can see how that would be the case. That place is your life. Was your life, anyway. A lot of things changed that night. I imagine that angered you."

George glared.

Good for him, Victoria thought. *He knows to sit silently when there's no question on the table.*

"Were any other places of business ransacked?" Rory asked.

"Joey Abbott's was stripped clean. The grocery too."

"Did you see that while it was happening?"

George rolled his eyes. Déjà vu, right? "No, I did not."

"Why did you fight with Kyle and Caine Foster that morning?"

"Joey and I found them inside Joey's store where they didn't belong."

"As I understand it, you made some assumptions about their actions leading up to that point, is that correct?"

George looked at the floor.

"Caine Foster is in the courtroom," Rory said, pointing. "I could ask him to testify if you'd like."

George took his time, but he got to it. "We saw them in the store, and we assumed that they were the ones who robbed the place."

"Were you correct?"

"Obviously not."

"Has something transpired in the past two weeks that makes

you more adept at judging the perpetrators of events that you have *not* witnessed?"

Rory might have pushed too hard with that question. George was getting hot, color rising in his cheeks.

"I withdraw the question," Rory said. "Need we go through this exercise regarding the murder of Ryan Hamilton?"

"No."

"Just to be clear," Rory said. "Did you see who shot Ryan?"

"No."

"Thank you." Rory paused, as if to collect his thoughts. He wandered back to his table and looked at some notes he'd written. Then he stood straight and started his slow pacing again. "I want to shift gears now and address the day Mr. May was taken into custody. The day when you and your posse went up the mountain."

George waited.

Victoria shifted in her seat. She hadn't discussed this with Rory, hadn't prepared him for the perils of exploring new territory. Justice was winning thus far, but it was a fragile win.

"What was your intent when you went with the posse up the mountain that afternoon?"

"When Major McCrea over there told us about the body they'd passed on the way in, and about the way the guy they encountered reacted, we thought we needed to check it out."

"Did you consider at the time the possibility that the people Major McCrea and his party encountered might also be the parties who ransacked your station?"

"Of course."

Rory returned to his table and riffled through papers till he found the one he wanted. He showed the paper to his witness. "Do you recognize this as the statement you wrote and submitted to Mrs. Emerson immediately after you placed Mr. May in custody?"

"Yes."

Rory flipped a page at the staple and peeled away a yellow Post-it note. "In this statement, you say that the Grubbs gang opened fire on you and the rest of the posse. Is that correct?"

"Absolutely. Me and Eric Lofland was walking up—"

Victoria rapped her gavel. "Mr. Simmons, please limit your responses to the scope of the questions that are asked."

George rolled his eyes again. "Yes, they opened fire on us."

"And you returned fire, did you not?"

"You bet your ass we did." That got a chuckle from the crowd.

"Was anyone in your posse hit? Anyone injured?"

"No, Doc, we got the drop on 'em pretty good."

"Anybody hurt on their side?"

"Oh, hell yeah. Everybody but him was killed." George pointed at Brandon-Lee.

Rory returned his attention to the papers in his hand. "Your statement doesn't say who fired the first shot at you. Why is that?"

George puffed out a laugh. "'Cause it came outta nowhere. Damn near hit me, too. I dropped and returned fire."

"What about the rest of your posse? Were they shooting back, too?"

"Yes." George held up his hand. "Wait, before you get your knickers in a knot, I saw Major McCrea shooting and I saw his boy Caleb shooting, too."

"Six of the Grubbs gang died up there that day," Rory said. "Hypothetically, if I were to put up pictures of those six people, combined with, say, twenty other random pictures, how many of the deceased gang members would you guess you'd be able to identify?"

"Wait," Victoria said. "Don't answer that question, Mr. Simmons. Dr. Stevenson, you may not ask the witness to speculate. Stick to facts."

"Yes, ma'am," Rory said. He rubbed the back of his neck as he regrouped. "Mr. Simmons, you have a military background, don't you?"

George sat taller. "Two tours in Iraq, one in Afghanistan."

"You saw combat, then."

"I sure did."

Rory cast a nervous glance at Victoria and took a deep breath. He was headed in a direction that made him nervous.

"Can you take thirty seconds or so to describe what it's like to be in the middle of a battle?"

"In thirty seconds?" George scoffed. "No way. Absolutely no way. There's too much going on, all at the same time. You got the noise. You got all your people to think about. People cryin' out 'cause they're hit, cryin' out 'cause they're mad. You got orders comin' in from all sides. All this while you're tryin' to shoot and not get shot. It's absolute chaos."

"Kind of like it was up there on the mountain that day?"

"Battle is battle, Doc. The only difference is how long it goes on and which sides take the most casualties."

That's when Victoria saw where Rory was going with the surprise line of questioning.

Rory laughed. "In conditions like that, you don't spend a lot of time looking at faces, do you?"

"Oh, hell no. All I see in a firefight is my front sight and the other guy's center of mass."

"Up on the mountain that afternoon. How long would you say that fight lasted?"

George arched his shoulders nearly to his ears and made a pouty face. "All told, I'd be shocked if it lasted a minute."

"That's a fast fight," Rory said. He pulled at his lower lip. "You've already testified that you don't know who fired the first shot at you. Truth is, you don't know which of the people up on that hill shot at anybody, do you?"

George seemed to sense that he was entering dangerous territory. He squirmed in his seat. "I suppose not."

Here it comes, Victoria thought.

"You don't even know if Mr. May shot at anyone that afternoon, do you?"

"Oh, they was all shooting, Doc."

"Even the defendant? *Specifically,* the defendant, or is this again one of those things that you think you know, but in truth only suspect?"

George had sprung his own trap and he knew it. "I suppose I assumed."

"When you first saw the defendant up there, did he have a gun in his hand?"

"He had one next to him."

"Not my question," Rory snapped. "Did he have a gun in his hand?"

"No, but—"

"In fact, he didn't have any weapons on him, did he? Other than a folding-blade knife?"

"No, he did not."

"In fact, what was Mr. May doing at the first moment you saw him?"

George shifted and looked at the floor. "He was minding a woman's body."

"Minding?"

"You know, trying to help her, I guess."

"What was his emotional state at that time?"

"He was cryin'. But then he got mean and we had to wrestle with him to take him into custody."

Rory took his time with his next question. "Did you ever come to learn the identity of the woman over whose body he was crying?"

"He said it was his mother."

A gasp rolled through the crowd. Apparently, this was not a widely known detail. Rory let the reality sink in. "For Mr. May, that had to be a really bad minute, don't you think? I mean, even if you don't like a guy, well, you stipulate that he loves his mom."

As Rory walked back to his table, Victoria feared that he was done. He hadn't sealed the deal yet. But it was a bluff. Rory continued to channel television lawyers. With his hand to his chin, he paused and he turned back to the witness, though cheating his body wide toward the assembly.

"Mr. Simmons," he said. "I'm not asking you to speculate one way or the other here, okay? But is it possible—is it *possible*—that Mr. May never fired a shot at all? Is it possible that when he saw his mother fall, he fell with her to tend to her wounds?"

Victoria suppressed a smile. Justice had just won the fight.

"It's possible," George mumbled.

"I'm sorry, Mr. Simmons, but there's a record that needs to be accurate. A little louder, please."

"It's possible that that asshole never fired a shot."

Rory looked for an out-of-order ruling on the epithet, but Victoria answered with a barely perceptible shake of her head. It was time to declare victory and move on.

Silence dominated Maggie's Place as Rory returned to the table and reviewed his notes. "Thank you, Mr. Simmons. I have no further questions for you."

Honestly, Victoria could not have asked Rory Stevenson to do a more capable job. As she watched him burn through the other witnesses, she was impressed not just by his skill as an interrogator, but the witnesses' unwillingness to lie. On that point in particular, she had done them an injustice with her expectations.

Two hours later, it was all over. Rory rested his case.

All that remained was a compelling closing argument. If Rory could pull it off, she could spare Brandon-Lee May's life.

"Your Honor," he said. He turned his back on the judge and addressed the townsfolk in attendance. Victoria thought that was a brilliant stroke. They were not the jury. They would not determine guilt or innocence, but they would determine this young man's future.

"Ladies and gentlemen of Ortho. We all know that a terrible crime has been committed, and that a kind man is dead. We know that in the absence of civil authority, this town was ransacked by one person or many. It may very well be that the people who ransacked Simmons Gas and Goodies and the pawnshop were the same people who murdered Ryan Hamilton.

"The facts in this case are infuriating. In the shadow of the worst disaster in history, people pillage stores and murder a man. When a posse moves to apprehend the one known suspect, a group is found to be not just in the vicinity of the murder, but in possession of the stolen goods.

"So we connect the dots that seem so easy. They seem self-evident. But they're not. Once already, a grave error nearly cost the Foster twins their lives. That, too, seemed beyond obvious to all but the accused. And Mrs. Emerson, I am told."

As he spoke, Rory paced a line from left to right in front of the assembly. He moved gracefully, and as he did, he rubbed his palms together slowly, as if trying to warm them, but without friction.

"As a community, we crave fairness. We crave *justice.* We want someone to pay for this awful crime. It's only natural. But in a civilized society—in the kind of society we all pray will come our way again—the justice itself needs to be fair.

"And there is no fairness in convicting a man of a capital crime in the absence of even a scintilla of hard evidence that he is the perpetrator."

"Bring that asshole on up and have him explain himself, then," Mr. Jake said through his giant beard from the back of the room.

Victoria hammered the lectern. "You're out of order, Mr. Jake. That's not how it works. That's not how it has ever worked. Guilt must be proven against a backdrop of presumed innocence. As judge in this case, even if Mr. May wanted to testify, I would not allow it. As far as I know, the Constitution is still a viable document. The Fifth Amendment protects against self-incrimination." She gave a nod for Rory to continue.

"Thank you, ma'am. Truth be told, I don't have a lot more to say. You heard the witnesses. Not one was able to even place a weapon in the defendant's hands, either in the case of Ryan Hamilton or in the case of the shootout on the mountain. Did Brandon-Lee May do bad things? Maybe. Hell, probably. Does he hang around with unsavory company? To my eye, yes, but perhaps not to his own. Is he a thief? I don't know. Was the Grubbs gang a gang of thieves? Circumstantial evidence would lead me to say *yes,* but hard evidence would require us to say *we don't know.*"

"You can't let that son of a bitch go without punishment," someone said.

Victoria didn't see the source, but she gaveled the speaker out of order, whoever she was.

"That's not for me to decide," Rory said. He turned and started addressing Victoria directly. "That's for you to decide, ma'am. My job was a very specific one—to examine the legitimacy of the accusations against Brandon-Lee May. I've done that job, and I think that as to the charges he faces—theft and murder, and assault and battery—the court has no choice but to find the defendant not guilty."

CHAPTER TWENTY-TWO

VICTORIA DECLARED THE TRIAL TO BE IN RECESS WHILE SHE CONSIDered the verdict. As she moved away from her stool and lectern, she beckoned Rory and McCrea to follow her. When she was close enough to Maggie to speak softly, she said, "Do you mind if we chat in your place?"

"Not at all. Do you want me there, or would you prefer to be alone?"

"Is it okay if I say *alone*?"

"Absolutely. Something tells me I don't want to have nothin' to do with what y'all are gonna talk about."

McCrea and Rory seemed nervous, too.

Once they were inside the monument to lace and doilies that defined Maggie's living room, everyone took a seat. Victoria and McCrea occupied the sofa across from the fireplace, while Rory sat in the chair next to the fireplace.

"Why didn't you just pronounce sentence while we were in there?" McCrea asked. "Doc Stevenson here made damn convincing points."

"Kinda wondering the same thing myself," Rory said.

Victoria rested her elbows on her knees and put her face in her hands. Why the hell did she agree to do this? "Here's the thing," she said, hoping that her hands might press the encroaching boomer back into her head. "Clearly, that boy cannot be proclaimed guilty." She raised her head. "But not a soul out there is going to believe that he is innocent." She pointed at McCrea. "If nothing else, he was part of a crowd that shot at you. Shot at my son."

"Those weren't the charges," Rory said. "And being present is not the same as actually shooting. As you heard him say—"

"You rested your case," Victoria interrupted. "And I heard every word of it. If Brandon-Lee walks away from this without some form of punishment, he's going to end up dead within a couple of days."

"And the downside of that is what?" McCrea asked.

"The downside will be the collapse of recognized authority. We've talked about this before. There is no law and order anymore. There's just an agreement to get along. And that's as fragile as people's perceptions of fairness."

"So, what are you suggesting?" Rory asked. "Was everything I just went through some kind of charade?"

"Not at all," Victoria said. "You painted a perfect picture, one brushstroke at a time, that showed Brandon-Lee to be not guilty of murder or assault. You literally saved his life."

"So, why are we here?"

Victoria explained, "You heard those questions from the gallery. Mr. Jake is pissed off, for God's sake, and he plays Santa Claus in his spare time. People expect Brandon-Lee's actions to have a consequence."

McCrea looked at her as if she were crazy. "How do you punish someone in the absence of evidence?"

"Says the man who engaged in a gun battle with his kin," Victoria said.

"This isn't the same," McCrea said, clearly not taking the bait. "That was an exercise in self-defense. What you're talking about . . . What *are* you talking about, anyway? What kind of punishment do you have in mind?"

"Something convincing, not crippling."

"Corporal punishment of some kind?"

"There's historical precedent," Rory said, drawing their full attention. "Back in the colonial days, towns kept order through public humiliation and ritual scarring."

"Would these be the same colonial times when we burned witches at the stake?" McCrea taunted.

Rory ignored him. "Take the religious zealotry out of it and you'll find minor but important infractions being punished with stocks and pillories. Every colonial reenactment park has the photo op with the stocks, but did you know they used to nail perpetrators' ears to the wood? Upon release, they'd either tear their ear off or have it cut off."

"Holy shit," McCrea said.

"Well, we're not doing that," Victoria said.

"What, then?" McCrea pushed. "A public flogging?" As soon as the words left his mouth, he looked like he wanted to bring them back.

Victoria sat taller. That wasn't a bad idea.

"Flogging?" McCrea asked, incredulous as he saw the idea take root in her mind.

"Why not?" Victoria asked. "Maybe that's the perfect solution. It's humiliating for the guilty party, cathartic for the townspeople."

"It's goddamn barbarous!" McCrea said.

"What do you suggest, then?"

"Whatever *not flogging* is." He pointed to Rory. "Say something, Doc."

"I think it might be the perfect solution," Rory said.

"Quit saying things, Doc."

Rory expounded, "Look, do you or don't you agree, Major, that there'll be a rebellion if Brandon-Lee May walks away without any consequence?"

McCrea didn't want to answer.

Victoria said, "Come on, Joe. It's not an unreasonable question."

"I guess I agree that something has to be done, but—"

"We're not talking about breaking any bones," Rory said.

"There'll be superficial damage to the skin and it will hurt like a son of a bitch, but as long as the lashes are controlled and limited to his back, there shouldn't be any life-threatening complications. And, as Vicky mentioned, the crowd will be appeased."

Victoria pressed her palms to her eyes again, but the headache would not be intimidated. "We need rules," she said. "Written rules."

"Because articulating rules makes torture more legitimate?"

Victoria glared.

McCrea backed off. "Okay, that was uncalled for. Sorry. I'll find some paper and something to write with."

When they were done, and they'd agreed upon the language, Victoria said, "Rory, do me a favor, please. Find Ty Rowley down at the lumberyard and tell him we're going to need some rope."

The entire recess lasted less than an hour. When Victoria rapped the court back in session, all the same faces were in all the same places, as far as she could tell. The faces displayed a wide variety of emotions, from anger to pity to concern. All but Brandon-Lee, who looked like he didn't give a shit.

That would make what was coming far easier.

When Victoria saw her boys sitting on the windowsill at the back of the room, they gave a little wave. She acknowledged with a nod.

"These are strange and awful times," she began. "If you listened to the testimony we've heard today, and are of reasonable mind, you have to agree with me that there is no evidence that Brandon-Lee May committed any of the crimes with which he was charged. Accordingly, I find him not guilty on all counts."

That ignited even more unrest than she'd anticipated. People grumbled and cursed. One lady from the back yelled, "What about justice?"

Victoria held up her left hand for silence while she hammered her mallet against the lectern with her right. "Silence, please. Come to order. I'm not done. There's more. Order, please."

She wasn't getting through to them. McCrea and Copley drew closer to Brandon-Lee, a protective stance.

From the back, a voice yelled, "Hey! Everybody shut up! My mom's still talking!"

The timbre and pitch of Luke's shouting cut through the noise and silenced the room.

Victoria couldn't stifle her chuckle as she said, "Thank you, Luke."

She changed her focus to Brandon-Lee. "Mr. May, I'd like you to stand, please."

For a few seconds, the defendant didn't move. Then, just as McCrea was reaching for him, Brandon-Lee unfolded himself from his chair and stood behind his table, hands stuffed into the pockets of his filthy jeans.

"Take your hands out of your pockets," Victoria directed.

Again, he complied, but in his own time.

"Mr. May, you seem to think that you are on firm footing, that the things that you have done will somehow go unpunished."

He gave a smug grin.

"You're wrong," Victoria said. "I have found you to be not guilty of theft, murder and assault charges, but I have not found you to be *innocent*. Do you understand the difference?"

"Does it matter? One word's as good as another."

"That's not true," Victoria explained. "To be found *not guilty* means only that the prosecution cannot prove its case against you. *Innocent* would mean that you have done nothing wrong. You show bitter and utter disrespect for this court and for the people of this town. You associate with people who believe that in times of crisis it is acceptable to steal from others. In this new world in which we live, people need to be held accountable for their choices.

"Mr. May, what you do—who you are, or at least who you pretend to be—is an example of the worst a society has to offer to its citizens. As such, you will be treated as an exemplar of what awaits those who so shamelessly disregard the rules by which we live."

Victoria prepared herself with a deep breath. She'd been rehearsing this delivery, and she wanted to get it exactly correct. "Mr. May, it is the judgment of this court that you be taken to a public place where you will be stripped of all clothing and tied to a post."

The smug smile evaporated.

"There, you will be flogged across your back with thirty strokes delivered by a scourge made of knotted rope. Upon delivery of the final stroke of the scourge, you will be escorted to the town limits and forever banished. The court decrees that you may be shot on sight if you violate your banishment at any time in the next twenty-four months. The public place designated by the court is the front of Simmons Gas and Goodies. The sentence will be carried out immediately."

Her declaration brought equal parts gasps and war whoops.

Brandon-Lee made an effort to bolt away, but he had no chance. McCrea and Copley were on him in a second.

"Don't make this hurt any more than it needs to," McCrea said.

"You can't do this!" Brandon-Lee yelled. No one responded.

Per the established plan, the prisoner was hustled out the back door, past Victoria's makeshift bench. Victoria closed the door behind them and posted herself as guard. "Those of you who wish to witness the punishment may do so at George Simmons's place. The prisoner will be brought there shortly."

At first, no one moved. Then Mr. Jake rose from his seat in the back, which was really the front of the store, and headed out the door. Others rose slowly, and then the flood started—an orderly flood, with no pushing or shoving, but a hurried stream. Those who wanted to watch didn't want to miss a stroke.

As the room emptied, she noted that her sons were still sitting on the windowsill. They rose and came to her. "Caleb wants to go and watch," Luke said. "I don't."

"That's fine," Victoria said. "Both parts of that are fine."

"Flogging's the same as whipping, right?" Caleb asked. He looked confident, but wanted reassurance.

"That's right."

Caleb looked like he wanted to say something, but ultimately nodded, turned and walked back toward the door.

Luke looked disturbed, close to tears.

"What's wrong, sweetie?"

"I don't like this. I want things to go back to the way they were." He swiped at his eyes. "Everybody's mad all the time. And mean. Nobody has anything they need and everybody's scared. I hate it."

Victoria wanted to hug her baby boy. She wanted to comfort him the way she would have such a short time ago. But that would have done him a huge disservice. "The old ways are gone, Luke. Gone forever. We need to adjust to the way things are and try to build the future into something we want it to be."

Luke nodded, but he didn't seem ready to go yet.

Victoria walked to the seat that had most recently been occupied by Brandon-Lee May and patted the one used by Rory Stevenson.

Luke sat.

"So, what do you miss the most?"

"Everything."

"Nope, you have to choose one thing."

"My bed. And pillows. And electricity."

"Okay, well, we can take care of two of those starting tomorrow," Victoria said. "Electricity will have to wait. I haven't learned to fart electrons yet."

Luke laughed, as she hoped he would.

"Look, sweetie, I know this is hard. It's hard for everyone. Every day, we're going to face new challenges, and we'll figure out a way to deal with them."

Luke took a deep breath and swiped at his eyes again. "Are we going to die from this?"

Again, she resisted the reflex to hug. "Oh, Luke, we're all going to die of something sooner or later, but there's no way for us to know how or when. That's God's plan."

"You think God planned *this*?"

"We don't know, do we? We can't. Look, for now, we count our blessings. You might think there aren't many to be counted, but think about it. We've got our family. We've got our health, at least so far. We've got shelter, even if the floor is hard to sleep on. We've got Major McCrea and Paul Copley on our side. And we've found a pretty nice town."

"I want to go to Top Hat Mountain," Luke said. "I want to see Adam again."

"We will."

"Why not now?"

"Things are a little busy, Luke."

"Why not tomorrow?"

"Because we have things to do here."

"Like what?"

"Like organizing the clothing bank and the hunting parties. There are a thousand moving parts. Food needs to be delivered to the sick."

"But this isn't even our town. Why can't they take care of themselves? Concentric circles, remember?"

Victoria felt a flash of anger. "If you don't understand, you don't understand," she said. "If you don't understand why it's important to help the people of this town who were so gracious to bring us in and help us, then I won't be able to explain it to you."

"I think you like being in charge," Luke said without eye contact.

Victoria pressed her hands against the table and stood. "We're done here," she said. "I've got work to do."

God, I wish I didn't.

McCrea, Copley and Caine Foster escorted Brandon-Lee down the street from Maggie's to Simmons's station. The prisoner was naked, but for his shoes. His hands were bound at the wrist in front of him and he did his best to cover his crotch as he walked.

The gathered crowd had grown since the courtroom, and without any real organization, they naturally formed parallel lines along his path. It wasn't a long walk—maybe a hundred yards—

but it must have felt like an eternity for Brandon-Lee. The swagger was gone, his shoulders slumped.

People laughed and pointed. Lots of taunts about penis size, of course, but also shouted wishes for lots of suffering. Humiliation was the point of this, after all.

In Victoria's experience, for young men, in particular, pain was far more easily tolerated than embarrassment.

George Simmons had thrown a heavy chain over an exposed beam in the roof over the gas pumps. He'd clamped the ends together with a large clevis hook. Much to Victoria's surprise, Brandon-Lee did not fight as his captors raised his hands over his head and slipped the knot that divided his hands into the hook and snapped it shut.

And there he was, fully exposed. The jeering crescendoed and Victoria sensed that they needed to get this done quickly.

Ty Rowley sidled up to Victoria and handed her a five-foot length of inch-thick hemp rope, into which he'd tied a knot every six inches or so. "This is the whip," he said. "I figure you double it over on itself and you'll be able to swing it pretty easily. Should leave a hell of a mark, too. Tear that shithead's skin right off the bone."

This wasn't what she'd wanted, what she'd anticipated. She was expecting a single length of rope, perhaps made of cotton or nylon. This thing in her hands was a genuine torture device. And it was too late to turn back.

"You gonna do the floggin', Mrs. Emerson?" Mr. Jake asked.

Victoria looked to McCrea for relief. "Absolutely not," he said, answering a question she didn't ask. "I agreed to deliver him and guard him after it's done."

People were waiting. How could she not have thought this through to this point? Who would the . . . executioner be? This seemed like a worse idea with every passing second.

With the scourge dangling from her fist, she approached Brandon-Lee, whose face was now a mask of terror. "Please don't do this," he begged.

Victoria turned her back on him and addressed the crowd. "We are about to cross a line that can't be *un*crossed," she said. "Is there room for mercy, or are we really going to go through with this?"

"Oh, hell yes, we're going through with it," Joey Abbott said. "I'd be happy to lay that son of a bitch wide open."

The crowd agreed with enough fervor that if any dissent existed, it would have been shouted down.

"No, please," Brandon-Lee pleaded. He was crying now.

"Then here's how it will work," Victoria said. "Since we do this as a community, then the community will carry out the sentence. Thirty strokes to the prisoner's back. Dr. Stevenson, I'll ask you to monitor the prisoner's health as we go along. Whoever wants to swing the whip may do so, but only to a limit of one stroke per person, up to thirty people. If thirty of you do not step forward, then the punishment will end at the delivery of the last volunteered stroke."

"Jesus, Vicky," Ben Barnett said. "Are you just making this up as you go along?"

"You're damn right I'm making it up as I go along. If there's a rule book I don't know about, I'd be delighted to look at it."

Kyle Foster stepped forward. "Listen here," he said. "I don't want to hear some high-and-mighty shit from you in the future. You want everybody to take a swing, that's fine. But you take the first one."

That earned applause.

Victoria felt her face redden. It was a horrible demand, but not an unreasonable one. She'd passed the sentence. She needed to be a part of it. "All right," she said.

As she approached Brandon-Lee, so exposed and helpless, she made the mistake of making eye contact. He'd transformed from cocky warrior to terrified boy. At nineteen, he was barely older than her own Adam. What had she brought upon him?

As she passed McCrea, the major took her arm gently and whispered, "You have to hit him hard, Vicky. The others certainly will. You've got to show conviction."

The whip felt heavy in her hand as Victoria circled around behind Brandon-Lee. He had a farmer's tan, brown arms to mid-biceps and then stark white everywhere else.

"You're gonna have to step closer," George Simmons said. "You want to give him a full stripe."

Victoria stepped forward another step, close enough to smell Brandon-Lee's sweat. She was on his right, so she cheated toward her left, squaring up perpendicular with the boy's back. She drew her right arm across her left, took a deep breath and let loose with a full-force backhand. The folded, knotted rope whistled through the air and then hit Brandon-Lee's flesh with a heavy *thwop*.

Brandon-Lee howled at the impact as he drew his legs up and threw his head back. Within two seconds, a heavy red welt had begun to rise halfway between his shoulder blades and his kidneys.

Reflexively Victoria brought her hand to her mouth as her vision blurred.

"Nicely done, Mrs. Emerson," George said with a grin. "My turn." He took the scourge from her, bounced it in his hand and took a couple of practice swings in the air. When he delivered his blow, he put his whole body into it, like he was swinging a baseball bat. It hit hard enough to make some of the observers cringe, others laugh.

"Holy shit, George," Joey Abbott said. "We're not trying to break his ribs."

"I'm hoping we'll cut him in half," George said through a laugh. As he passed Brandon-Lee, he got up into his grill. "You're gonna have a long damn day, asshole." Then he spit in the prisoner's face.

Joey Abbott was next, followed by Kyle Foster, Eric Lofland and then Ben Barnett. As each took their turn, they seemed to be competing, each trying to outdo the other with the force of their blows. Brandon-Lee gave them a show every time, wailing louder with every stroke. After the twelfth, though, he stopped begging his punishers not to do this.

After fifteen, at the halfway point, Rory Stevenson called a time-out to examine the prisoner. The whip had taken on a red hue from the blood it had excised from Brandon-Lee. The whole crowd closed in as Rory examined the stripes across the prisoner's back. Blood trickled from a few, but mostly they were just angry welts.

Victoria pleaded silently for the doctor to intervene and call it all off.

"They're only superficial," Rory proclaimed. "The punishment can continue."

"No," Brandon-Lee whined. His face was beet red and streaked with tears. "Please. I can't."

George Simmons patted the prisoner's chest with his open palm—it was really more of a slap. "Cheer up, kid. You're halfway there. You can start countin' down, instead of countin' up."

Victoria was surprised by the number of women who stepped up to exact revenge. Equally surprised by the forcefulness of their blows. Seeing this boy bleed was important to them.

After twenty blows, the pace of the punishment slowed. There wasn't a line anymore where the scourge was passed from one person to another like a baton in a relay race. But people still stepped up.

Caleb Emerson stepped up to be number twenty-four. Victoria sensed that he was deliberately not meeting her gaze. He took his position behind the prisoner and stood there for a solid ten or fifteen seconds.

"Take your turn or get out of the way!" George Simmons taunted.

Caleb set his feet for a forehand baseball stance. He drew back and let loose. His swing was off-target, though, cutting a stripe that was more along Brandon-Lee's side than his back. That seemed to open a brand-new window of pain for the prisoner.

Mike Underwood, the kid with the working El Camino, took the twenty-seventh swing, but there wasn't much behind it. Carol Robinson, who looked ready to give birth at any second, was number twenty-nine, but her swing was deliberately soft. The final blow came from Maggie, who surprised Victoria by unleashing a massive blow that launched a howl of pain and caused Brandon-Lee to raise both feet off the ground.

"I'm sorry, Brandon-Lee," Maggie said. "The last two were really soft blows. I was gonna do that, too, but I needed you to leave with a real memory." If her blow had been with something rigid, it would have broken his back. She looked like she might get sick as she handed the scourge back to Victoria.

"That's all there is," Victoria said, dropping the scourge onto the pavement. "It's over. George, please let Brandon-Lee down."

"Oh, let's let him hang for a while longer," George said.

Joey added, "I kinda like the look. Reminds me of deer season."

McCrea stepped forward. "Mrs. Emerson said to let him down. Do it now."

"Who the hell—" Whatever George saw in McCrea's expression convinced him to back down. "Yeah, okay. Gotta do it from the front, though. I don't want to get blood all over my shirt." For some reason, he found that funny.

McCrea stepped behind Brandon-Lee and gripped the prisoner's chest just under his armpits. George stood on tiptoes and unhooked the bound hands, and Brandon-Lee's knees buckled. McCrea eased him down to sit on the ground.

Victoria eased George out of the way and kneeled down in front of the prisoner. "Give me your hands," she said. "I'll untie you."

"I've got it," McCrea said as he produced a folding knife. "The knots are good ones."

It took a few seconds to saw through the rough hemp fibers. As the loops of rope fell away, they revealed that the flesh of Brandon-Lee's wrists were nearly as raw as that of his back.

"Take your time getting up," Victoria said. She stood and offered her hand.

The glare she got in return was beyond toxic. Brandon-Lee got his feet under him and he rose unsteadily. "You're going to pay for this," he whispered, his voice barely audible. "I'm going to kill you. I'm going to kill your whole family and burn this town to the ground. Have a good day."

His tone froze something inside of Victoria. She felt a flash of light-headedness and she took an involuntary step back to keep her balance.

"What's wrong?" McCrea asked.

Victoria shook her head. "Nothing. Escort him back to his clothes and then to the town line. Get him out of my sight."

Victoria worried that the day would never end. After the trial ended, she had to put her community-organizer hat back on to make sure that donations to the clothing bank was being handled properly. It wouldn't do to have people sifting through random piles of garments in search of a particular size. Thankfully, Ellie Stewart, one of the newcomers, stepped up to take charge of that.

Victoria had spent years training for Armageddon, and never once in all those exercises did she ever envision running a community effort. Her specialties were all about her family being on its own, surviving in the wilderness and protecting that which was theirs. She didn't hate it all as much as she'd feared, but it was all kind of exhausting.

After darkness fell, she sneaked out of the shelter at St. Thomas's and found a comfortable spot on the ground at the base of a tree. Thick roots combined with soft ground created a kind of natural armchair for her to rest in.

"That you, Vicky?" McCrea asked.

"Hello, Major."

"May I join you?"

"Sure." She patted the ground next to her. "How in God's name did you find me?"

McCrea sat and leaned against the tree. "I cheated. I saw you when you left the church. I saw your silhouette coming this way. And will I ever get you to call me *Joe*?"

Victoria smiled. "Some habits are hard to break."

"I owe you an apology," McCrea said. "That's why I'm here."

"What did you do?"

"I had no right to speak with you the way I did when we discussed the sentence for the May boy. You did the right thing. You had to do something, and you did the right thing."

Victoria closed her eyes and rested the back of her head against the rough bark. "Thanks for that," she said. "I'm not sure I agree. I had no idea how . . . *violent* it would be. You used the word *barbarous,* I believe. That's exactly what it was."

"Incarceration is a privilege for communities that have jails," McCrea said. "I think that's why society built them in the first place. It's hard to watch that kind of thing."

"Only for you and me, apparently," Victoria said. "I didn't anticipate the bloodthirstiness of the crowd. It was like a gladiator match."

"Having the blows delivered by the community was a stroke of genius, by the way. Pardon the pun."

"Even Caleb," Victoria said. Her voice caught when she said his name.

McCrea didn't respond.

"How did it go, escorting him to the town line?"

McCrea inhaled noisily. "That kid's a piece of work. Bad news."

"No remorse?"

"Not that he showed. All that crying and begging during the punishment? That's all gone. And I'll tell you, his back looks like hamburger. He didn't try to put a shirt back on. What did he say to you right after he stood up?"

The segue took Victoria by surprise. "Um . . ."

"You seemed shaken."

"Yeah, well, maybe I was," Victoria said. "He threatened to kill me and my entire family and burn the town to the ground."

McCrea chuckled. "Is that all? He ran his mouth a lot with me, too."

"Same message?"

"More or less. There was one detail about copulating the eye sockets of severed skulls that I'm not sure is even possible. The general message was that he's unhappy. How are you doing?"

"He impressed me as being serious," Victoria said.

"I don't know," McCrea said. "I think he thinks he's serious. But he's also humiliated and in a lot of pain. He'll take a while to heal. When that's done, I don't imagine he'll be anxious to go through it all over again."

"Where was he when you saw him last?"

"We walked him back, about halfway to where we found him. Town line plus another couple hundred yards till he was out of sight."

"How are *you* holding up?" Victoria asked.

"I'm as tired and disoriented as everybody else, I suppose."

Victoria reached through the darkness and grasped McCrea's hand. "I'm not sure I ever thanked you for sticking with us."

"Actually, you fired me. Several times."

"Yet you saw through my bluff."

"You weren't bluffing."

Victoria allowed herself a giggle. "No, I wasn't. I thought you were an arrogant son of a bitch who was mean to my children."

"I'm still an arrogant son of a bitch who's mean to your children."

"Yes, but now I understand that they're spoiled and have unreasonable expectations."

"Then my work here is done."

Victoria could hear the smile in his tone.

"Speaking of said children . . ."

"Uh-oh," Victoria replied.

"No, it's nothing bad," McCrea assured. "Well, not *real* bad, anyway. I heard them talking the other day. They're pissed."

"Of course, they're pissed. They're teenagers."

"This pissed-ness has focus, though. They feel like you lied to them."

"About what?"

"About why they're here. You told them that they were going to join their brother—Adam, is it?"

"Yes."

"You told them that they were going to join up with Adam at Top Hat Mountain. That place apparently has some sentimental importance to them."

"It's special for all of us," Victoria said. "Especially to my husband. And through him, to the boys."

"Yet here we all are," McCrea said.

"I have responsibilities," Victoria said. "People here count on me."

"Yes, they do." McCrea sounded like he wanted to say more, but backed off.

"Say what's on your mind . . . Joe."

"Ah, there it is. You do know my name. And, okay, I will. I know that people depend on you here, but I'm not convinced that they have no other choice."

"Make your point."

"My point is—and this is what I heard the boys talking about—is that you like being in charge of things. It's in your DNA. You're a person who can't *not* be in charge."

"You saw what we walked in on. Those two Foster boys—"

"I know the logic, Vicky. And I'm not saying you did anything but the right thing. In that case. Then you went on to appoint yourself mayor and judge."

"I didn't do that," Victoria insisted. "I just started talking and I found that people were listening. What, would you rather George Simmons or Joey Abbott be in charge?"

McCrea made a growling sound. "I'm not passing judgment here, Vicky. I'm awed by your organizational skills, and I can't think of a decision you've made that I would have made differently."

"What *are* you passing, if not judgment, then?"

"Information," McCrea said. "Hard stop. Just information. This is not the first time I've heard the boys bitching about things. They're hurting, Vicky. Hell, everybody's hurting. If I hadn't passed along the information, I thought I'd be doing a disservice to our friendship. That's it. Do with the information what you will."

After a half minute of silence, Victoria said, "Okay, my turn to ask you a question."

McCrea groaned. "Hit me."

"Why are *you* still here?"

"I've got no place else to be. I came here as your bodyguard—something you clearly have never needed—and now I stay here by inertia. I literally have no place else to be."

"Is that the only reason?" Victoria asked.

McCrea took his time answering. "That feels like a very . . . *dangerous* question."

Victoria shifted in her tree chair. This could get very awkward, very quickly. "Never mind," she said.

"Don't do that," McCrea said. "Don't tee up an intriguing question and then walk away from it. We've come too far for that."

Victoria remained silent. She wasn't trying to be petulant. She didn't know how to form the words.

"Look," McCrea said. "I'll put it right out there. Do I like you? Yes, of course. Do I think you're smokin' hot? Of course. I'm male and I've got eyes."

Victoria was grateful for the darkness. Otherwise, he'd have seen how red she felt her face turn.

"I think you've got a great family. Yes, your boys are pains in the ass, but they're good kids." He paused. "But if your question was about romance—"

"Oh, God no." Victoria said it too quickly. She heard the defensiveness in her own voice.

"It's just too soon," McCrea said without stopping.

"Of course, it is," Victoria said. "You've lost your family. Everything is too soon after that."

Another awkward pause.

"But I'll tell you this," McCrea said, "since we're being honest with each other. I think you're not as strong and independent as you think you are. I think you're in way over your head, and you need personal advisers you can trust. I'm happy to serve in that role."

Victoria reached out and their hands found each other in the darkness. "I appreciate that," she said.

"And if the time comes when you do decide to leave this place, I'd really like to meet Adam. According to Caleb and Luke, he pretty much hangs the moon."

CHAPTER TWENTY-THREE

THE WEATHER HAD TURNED CHILLY, ALMOST COLD. CALEB AND Luke had both grown over the past few weeks, but in Caleb's case, the change was embarrassing. His pants were an inch too short and getting tight around his thighs. If he didn't replace them soon, he'd be splitting out of them. He and Luke already wore jackets from the common clothing stockpile that his mom had organized to take care of this very problem—kids who grew in an era when there weren't any clothing stores anymore.

A few of the neighbors had fired up sewing machines powered by whatever gas was left in their generators to make coats for people, so that would help with the cold weather. Townies were expected to donate their used clothes as their own kids outgrew them. Soon, Caleb figured, he'd be donating what he was wearing now.

Of all the sucky changes that this damn war had brought, the hardest adjustment was to be without electricity. With the nights so dark—and with the standing orders to preserve any form of energy, from batteries to kerosene—it was goddamn scary to get up in the middle of the night and feel your way to the bathroom. In St. Thomas's, he had to walk past ten sleeping people just to get to the bathroom. Assuming you hit your target—so far, he hadn't missed—then you had to feel your way to the water bucket to fill the tank and flush.

All in all, it was easier to use God's toilet: the ground outside.

But that was all in the past or saved for later. Right now was all about hunting rabbits. There were many elements of hunting that Caleb didn't like very much, chief among them the dressing and skinning. It was just gross, and it made your hands slimy and stinky. He felt the same way about fishing, for that matter. But without enduring the bad parts, you'd never get to the meat, and there was nothing like freshly killed game. Pretty much any game, really, but rabbit had a special place on his palate.

His mission today was to bag as many rabbits as he and Luke could carry. More was better because they'd only be able to keep half of what they killed. The other half would go to the food pantry, where people who had no idea how to fend for themselves lived off the work of others.

There was talk around town of protests and shit if the flow of people wasn't somehow cut off. Mostly, they blamed his mom, whom they'd started to call *Queen Victoria* when she wasn't listening. Another popular rumor was that Joe McCrea and Mom were *doing it.* If that were the case, then they were very damned secretive about it.

Oh, and that bed his mom had promised Luke? Total bullshit. Never happened.

Caleb hated all of it. They'd already missed two First Mondays, when they could have met up with Adam at Top Hat Mountain, but Mom hadn't even tried to break away from her *responsibilities.* She said she *couldn't,* but that was bullshit, too. She could do any damn thing she wanted to.

Sticking around Ortho like this was a choice. How many times had she talked to him about his choices? "Life is not chance" was the phrase she loved so much. "If you feel like you're a victim of circumstance, it's because you've chosen to endure the circumstance."

Caleb didn't know how much more of it he was willing to take. Problem was, if he was honest with himself, the thought of wandering for days to find Top Hat Mountain on his own kind of terrified him.

As it was, here today, navigating the forest with his little brother in tow, he felt a crushing sense of responsibility. He didn't mind if he got a little lost on the way home himself, but now he had the burden of making sure he didn't get Luke lost, too. Caleb had made a point of blazing trails on the way in by marking the trees at an angle they'd be able to see on the way out. It was one of his favorite tricks that his dad had taught him.

Conditions changed dramatically and frequently in the forest. Caleb and Luke had both been out here before, but in this thick undergrowth, the woods could change from one day to the next—sometimes from one minute to the next. Unless you were deeply familiar with the area, getting turned around was always a danger.

People who forgot that very simple lesson could end up dead, with their bodies never found. Wandering the woods alone could be a real problem.

But hunting *together* was also a mistake. Four feet made twice the noise of two, and with the noise concentrated over a small distance, you didn't have a chance at bagging a rabbit. Those ears were there for a reason.

So they'd split up. Not far apart—they could still see each other most of the time—but far enough that they stalked their own prey. Caleb carried his 10/22 and a knife. Many hunters preferred a shotgun for rabbits, but Caleb's dad had taught him that the small-caliber rifle was the better choice. The downside was that you had to catch the critter while it was standing still, but Caleb had never been great at shooting prey on the run, and with a bullet instead of a pellet spray, the .22 gave him the advantage of distance. Bugs and Thumper would be dead before they knew they were being hunted.

But first, he had to find the damn things. Rabbits loved thickets of tangled underbrush, the more thorns the better, and God had designed their fur with excellent natural camouflage. The trick to finding a rabbit while it was sitting still was to look for its eyes, black marbles surrounded by whites.

Today the little bastards were especially good at hiding. Caleb could have shot fifteen or twenty squirrels by now, and he supposed he could resort to squirrels if he ran out of choices, but he really didn't much like squirrel meat. Rabbit, on the other hand, was terrific.

Caleb placed his steps carefully as he advanced inches at a time, his rifle up at low ready. If he caught a glimpse, he'd be ready to go. Most important of all, though, he needed to get his first kill before Luke did. Little dickhead had kicked his ass during last year's deer season, and Caleb was tired of hearing about it.

He stooped down to get closer to the ground, and leaned into the underbrush. Something was here. He sensed it.

"Well, looky here!" a man's voice boomed from behind him.

Caleb whirled, but before he could turn all the way, a huge shove sent him tumbling into the thorns and tangled branches. He snapped his eyes shut to keep them from getting scratched.

"Hey!" he yelled, and he tried to scramble to his feet. But a kick nailed him in his ribs, and in an instant, all the air was gone from his lungs. He couldn't get it back.

"I'll take that plinker," the man said, and Caleb found himself being stripped of his rifle as someone pulled on the sling to unthread him from it.

Caleb was still trying to figure out up from down, when someone pushed him back into the thorns again. He yelled as the needles dug through his clothes and deeply into his flesh.

The rest happened with startling, ridiculous speed. The man—he still hadn't gotten a look at his face—grabbed him by the back of his jacket, lifted him and then tossed him face-first onto the ground. His arms were yanked behind his back and a rope was expertly looped around his wrists, taking his hands out of play. He felt like a roped calf.

When it was done, hands grabbed him under his armpits and jerked him upright, and then planted him back on the ground, on his butt.

All of that couldn't have taken more than ten seconds. Maybe five.

Caleb rattled his head to clear his vision. When he was finally able to focus, he swore that his heart stopped.

Jeffrey Grubbs said, "Your name's a biblical one, ain't it?"

Shit, shit, shit. Caleb started to cry and the tears pissed him off. This wasn't the time. In the peak of any crisis, you had to keep your head thinking clearly. How many times had he heard that from his parents?

"Son, we've just met and I know you're a little shaken up, but your people killed my people. If you think I would hesitate even a second to take you apart a chunk at a time, you couldn't be more wrong. Now, what's your name?"

"Caleb."

"Right. Caleb. I knew it was from the Bible. That original Caleb was one brave son of a bitch. You a Bible reader, son?"

"No. Sir." He fought the urge to scan the forest for Luke. He was out there somewhere. What had they done with him? If he'd gotten away somehow, he didn't want to cue Grubbs and his gang by craning his neck to see past.

"Oh, now that's a shame. Times like these, the Bible can be a great source of strength."

Grubbs sat on the ground, directly in front of Caleb, three feet away. Four men and two women stood behind Grubbs. Others stood behind Caleb—he could hear them—but he didn't want to risk turning around to see them.

"What *do* you read?"

Something wasn't right here. Why were they talking about reading? "I, uh, don't read a lot, sir. I liked the Harry Potter books."

"You like exciting stories? Stories with giants and floods and murder and betrayal?"

"I suppose."

"Then you really need to give the Bible a try."

"Yes, sir."

"But you know that's really not why you're here, though, right?"

"I was here to hunt rabbits."

Grubbs winked at him. "Right. That's why you got this little peashooter with you. Yeah?"

Caleb nodded.

Grubbs looked at him funny, as if he were debating whether to ask another question. He handed the 10/22 to one of the men behind him.

Caleb jumped when Grubbs reached over and gave his knee a playful slap. "Helluva coincidence, don't you think? You wanderin' into the woods to kill Bugs Bunny and you run into us, instead?"

"Yes, sir." From this point forward, Caleb figured, his best option would be to agree with everything the man said.

Grubbs looked up at something behind Caleb and beckoned with two fingers.

Footsteps approached from behind, and then the nightmare became real and awful as Brandon-Lee May stepped into view. Celeb tried to scoot backward along the ground, but someone's legs wouldn't let him.

"Caleb, say hi to my son, Brandon-Lee."

"Oh, shit. You're his father?" The question escaped before he could stop it.

Grubbs extended his hands to his sides, as if to embrace the world. "I consider all of my friends to be family. Brandon-Lee included." He craned his neck to address Brandon-Lee directly. "You recognize this boy, son?"

"He was one of the ones who whipped me."

"That so?" Grubbs leaned in closer. "Is that true, Caleb? Did you take a whip to Brandon-Lee's back?"

Celeb wasn't sure he could speak through his terror, speak past his trembling lips.

Grubbs nailed him with an openhanded slap that he never saw coming. Caleb saw stars as he was knocked onto his right side.

"Set him back up," Grubbs said, and a pair of hands yanked him back to a sitting position.

"Don't feel good to get beat when you can't use your hands to defend yourself, does it?"

Caleb shook his head no.

"So I'll ask you again. Did you lay a whip against my son's flesh?"

"Everybody did," Caleb said to the ground. Another flash of light behind as another slap knocked him over, this time to the left.

"Set him up again. That's not the question I asked you. I didn't ask if everybody whipped Brandon-Lee. I asked you if *you* did."

"Yes, sir. I–I'm sorry."

Another slap.

"Don't lie to me, Caleb. Don't make a bad situation worse by lying. You're not sorry you whipped Brandon-Lee. If you was, then you wouldn'ta done it in the first place. You'da said something like, *Oh, I'm sorry, Brandon-Lee* when you first saw him a minute ago. But that's not what you did. You beat him and you didn't give even the slightest shit that you did. I'm right, ain't I?"

Caleb forced himself to say it. "Yes, sir."

Grubbs wound back for another slap. Caleb braced for it, but it turned out to be a fake-out. "See? Bein' truthful ain't all that hard, is it?"

"No, sir."

"Good. Very good. Now, was you one o' the raiding party who murdered a lot of my family, including Brandon-Lee's mama?"

Shit, shit, goddamn. Caleb didn't know what to do. They obviously knew the answer—hell, that's when they captured Brandon-Lee—but it really wasn't murder. Was it?

His head was booming. He really didn't want to be hit again.

"I was there for the gunfight," Caleb said. "But it wasn't murder. Your people shot first."

This time, it was more than a slap. Caleb smelled blood as the blow spun him on his butt and knocked him backward into the thorns. His left eye started to swell right away. Then Grubbs grabbed a fistful of his jacket and pulled him back up. This time, when Grubbs spoke, their faces were so close that Caleb could smell the tobacco on his breath.

"Don't lecture me, Mr. Caleb. I left my family for just a little while, tryin' to scope out a place where we might set up a permanent camp. While I'm out there with these folks here, we hear shootin' from far away. By the time we get back, everybody's dead, and Brandon-Lee was missin'. That's *murder,* Mr. Caleb Emerson. That makes you a *murderer.* That's what your people was callin' Brandon-Lee, ain't it?"

"Yes, sir. But he was found not guilty."

"Because he didn't kill nobody," Grubbs said. "I don't think you can say the same thing, can you?"

"Please don't kill me," Caleb said through a sob.

Grubbs pushed him back into the thorns. "You disgust me," he said. "How old are you, anyway?"

Nobody stopped Caleb as he struggled to sit back up. No one helped him, either. "I'm sixteen, sir."

"And look at you bawlin' like a baby. Have some self-respect, Mr. Caleb."

"I–I don't know what you want me to do," Caleb stammered.

"Get a hold of yourself and say whatever you think needs to be said."

"I've been trying. But you keep hitting me."

Grubbs looked wired for violence. His eyes were red and wet, and his jaw muscles were working hard. He looked like it took everything he had not to lash out again. Grubbs looked up at the others who were gathered around, then seemed to settle himself. He clapped his hands together once and stood.

"Okay," Grubbs said. "All right. Fair is fair. Help Mr. Caleb stand up."

Hands were jammed under Caleb's armpits, and an instant later, he was on his feet and a little dizzy. He started to fall and someone caught him. "Here you go, Caleb Emerson. You stand accused of murder. You've already confessed to being in on the fight. I already know that Brandon-Lee saw you shoot people and brag about it. He even told me that you *weren't* the one who shot his mama. He don't know who did that."

Balance continued to be a problem with his hands bound behind him, but Caleb made it work. He spun around slowly before speaking, trying to collect his thoughts as he took in the faces. He counted four women and five men, including Brandon-Lee and Grubbs. Their faces showed zero mercy. They looked a lot like the faces in Maggie's during Brandon-Lee's trial. They were going to hurt him—that was for sure. Maybe they were going to kill him.

But there was no way they were going to let him go. Not after what had happened. Caleb thought of only one chance he might have. *Luke.* There was no sign of him. Maybe it was possible that the Grubbs gang didn't even know he'd been here. And maybe it was possible that Luke grew a set of balls big enough to run for help.

The way Caleb saw it, that was his only hope. It took them at least forty-five minutes to hike this far, uphill. Maybe Luke could make it back to town in thirty. Then he'd have to tell people. If his mom didn't have to hold a goddamn meeting to get people to respond, maybe they'd be able to get here to help him in an hour and a half.

How the hell was he going to be able to stall for an hour and a half?

"Why did y'all come up here that day, anyway?" Grubbs asked. "I thought I'd give you a start on a story."

"Can I be honest? I mean, no disrespect, but you *really* don't like it when I'm honest. You say you do, but look at my eye."

The crowd didn't like his answer, but it seemed to amuse Grubbs. "I want nothin' but the truth from you, Mr. Caleb."

"That truck driver that got killed on the day after the war started," Caleb said. "His name was Ryan. Hamilton, I think. Ryan Hamilton. He was a really nice guy, they said, and they didn't want to just leave the body."

"Be careful, Mr. Caleb," Grubbs cautioned. "Is that the *only* reason they came out that day?"

"There was also the stuff that was stolen," Caleb said.

"What about it?"

"People wanted to get it back."

"So they decided to kill for it?"

"I don't think anybody *decided* to do that. But we knew you had it—remember when we met the day after the war? Out on the road?"

"I remember."

"Well, we saw the stuff then. You had it then."

Grubbs took a step forward. "You callin' me a thief, Mr. Caleb?"

Caleb took an equal step back. "N-no, sir. I'm just saying you were with the missing stuff that day. I'm not saying you stole it." He was proud of himself for threading that needle.

Grubbs seemed a little deflated, like the fight he was hoping for didn't materialize.

Caleb kept going. "You told Major McCrea that day that if you saw him again, you'd shoot him. That's why everybody brought guns."

"You were expecting a shootout, then?"

"I guess so, sir. We didn't want it. We didn't come for it. But I guess we knew it was possible."

"Yet y'all came anyway. And killed half my family."

"We didn't want to. Seriously, we didn't want to. Major McCrea made it very clear that revenge wasn't the reason for the trip. Mr. Abbott and Mr. Simmons wanted their stuff back, and they were putting together a lynching, but Major McCrea said no. If your guys hadn't fired the first shot, there wouldn't have been any shooting."

"Is that so? You really believe that?"

"Yes, sir, I do."

Grubbs assumed a pensive pose, one foot forward, his fist to his chin. "That's really very interesting." Then he shouted, "I don't believe you!"

Caleb jumped backward, got tangled in his feet and fell.

Grubbs strode forward and stared down at him. "I think you're a lying piece of shit. I think you and your friends came all the way up here to murder us all. If we hadn'ta walked away for a little while, we'd all be dead, too."

Grubbs stepped back and looked back to Brandon-Lee May, who hadn't moved very far from where he'd been standing initially. "Brandon-Lee," Grubbs said, "I imagine you and Mr. Caleb have some business to settle. Do what you will. Just don't kill him and don't do sick, twisted shit."

"Glad to," Brandon-Lee said. "On your feet, shithead." He looked anxious to get started.

"Oh, God," Caleb said, trying to find his feet to run. "Shit, shit, shit. I–I only hit you once."

"Yeah, well, I'm gonna do more than that."

CHAPTER TWENTY-FOUR

"AIN'T THAT YOUR BOY LUKE ABOUT TO COLLAPSE OUT THERE?"

Victoria was meeting with Paul Copley and Ty Rowley about keeping up with the supply of lumber needed to build cabins for the stream of newcomers. Twenty-five refugees arrived just yesterday, bringing the total number to 112 since the war.

Victoria followed Ty's finger, and, sure enough, Luke was staggering down the road, his face flushed and glistening with sweat. He looked like he had less than nothing left in his tank.

"We'll get back to this," Victoria said, and she hurried out to intercept him. Copley followed.

"Luke! Luke, I'm over here."

The instant he saw her, his knees buckled. He collapsed to the pavement and started to sob.

She rushed to his side, kneeled next to him. "Oh, my God, Luke. What's wrong? Where's Caleb?"

Luke was exhausted. He'd been running for God knew how long. "They got him," he said through gasps for breath.

"Who got who?"

"Caleb," Luke said. "The gang. The one with Brandon-Lee May. They got Caleb."

Victoria shot to her feet, both hands to her mouth. "Oh, my God. OhmyGodohmyGodohmyGod. Where? When?"

Luke stood, though he still struggled for air. "We were rabbit hunting up on the mountain." He pointed in the direction he'd just come from. "We split up, and they just came out of nowhere. They hit him really hard. I think they're gonna kill him."

Well, that's what Brandon-Lee said he was going to do, wasn't it? "How far from here?"

"I don't know."

"How long have you been running?"

"I don't *know*. How would I know?"

He made a good point. "Can you lead me back there?"

"There are a lot of them. Maybe eight or ten of them. That guy we met on the road, on the way, the day after the war?"

"Jeffrey Grubbs?"

"Yeah. He was there. He's the one who hit Caleb."

"Guns?"

"Yeah. They took Caleb's away from him. That's when I snuck away and headed back here."

"Can you find the spot again? The exact spot?"

"I think so. We blazed a trail. That's how I found my way back here."

"I'm going to find the major," Copley said, and he was off.

Victoria brought both hands to her head, making her fingers disappear into her hairline. She needed to think. Needed to figure this through. She was going up the mountain to rescue her son, that was for sure, but what all did she need to bring with her? She needed to arm herself. If she could get some others to help, that would be great, but she didn't have time to wait for a posse to assemble.

She turned back to Luke. "Sweetie, how far up the road did you go before you cut off into the woods?"

He shrugged. "Quite a ways. I don't know distances that way. I don't pay attention."

Victoria had an idea. "I know you're worn-out, but I need you to do a little more running for me. Caleb's life depends—"

"I can do it. Where?"

"You know Mike Underwood, right? The boy with the El

Camino? He spends a lot of time either at Dr. Rory's or at Maggie's. If you see his car, find him and tell him this is an emergency, and he needs to meet me at St. Thomas's. Can you do that?"

"Sure." He started off, but she called him back.

"Don't waste any time. If you don't see the car, don't go looking. You come back to St. Thomas's on your own and then we'll have to retrace your steps on foot."

"Okay." He took off at a dead run, seemingly recovered from his exhaustion.

Victoria took off running, too—something she hadn't done in a very long time. St. Thomas's wasn't far from Ty Rowley's yard, but it was the wrong direction, away from the forest.

"Vicky!" Ty yelled.

"I don't have time!" she yelled over her shoulder.

"Is everything okay?"

She didn't bother to answer. Some things should be obvious.

One gun at a time, the arsenal inside St. Thomas's continued to grow. The Boyle family had brought theirs with them when they moved in, and she knew that Caleb had brought an AR15 back with him from the raid that captured Brandon-Lee May, but there seemed to be more than she could explain.

Victoria moved through the church to the front, near the altar and their sleeping spots. She grabbed Caleb's AR, checked for a full magazine and stuffed two more thirty-rounders in her back pockets. Then, just because, she grabbed another loaded AR by its sling and carried two additional mags in her hand. She had no doubt whatsoever that a gunfight lay in her future, and when it came to weaponry, more was always better.

She hurried back down the aisle and to the front door. As soon as she stepped out into the clearest air they'd had since the war, she heard Mike Underwood's El Camino heading her way, with Mike behind the wheel and Luke in the flatbed. The truck was still moving when Victoria opened the door.

"I promise I'll take good care of it," she said.

Mike shook his head. "Luke said Caleb's in trouble."

"Yes, but you don't have to—"

"I'm going, Mrs. Emerson. Looks like you even brought a gun for me to use." Mike shoved a thumb toward the shotgun seat. "Get in."

Victoria handed Mike a rifle through his window, then scurried around the front of the El Camino to the passenger door. "Luke, you still have your rifle?"

He answered by holding his 10/22 in the air.

Victoria placed her AR15 on the bench seat, then slid in behind it and closed the door. They were off.

Mike hadn't driven a hundred yards when Ty Rowley darted out in the street, waving his arms with a rifle in his hand. Another AR15. Mike had to stand on the brakes to keep from hitting him. Behind, Victoria heard Luke topple over in the bed.

Ty came to Victoria's window. "I'm coming with you."

"You don't know where we're going," Victoria said.

"Doesn't matter. You're in trouble. I can see it. Whatever it is, Luke will tell me about it from the bed."

The vehicle rocked as Ty hoisted himself over the edge and dropped into the flatbed.

Victoria did a quick check through the back window, saw what she wanted. "Go!"

"I guess she thought she couldn't wait," Copley said.

McCrea kicked at the ground. "So she went up there by herself? You let her go into the forest by *herself*? Jesus, Paul." He was at the construction site for two new cabins.

"What was I going to do?" Copley said. "Her boy is in mortal danger, and I guess she didn't want to stick around long enough to hold a meeting."

"Fine," McCrea said. "I get it. How big a head start did she get?"

"She's in the El Camino," Copley replied, looking down.

"Shit. Did Mike Underwood at least go with her?"

"I don't know. I was looking for you."

"You shouldn't have done that," McCrea said. "You should have gone with Luke. Gone with her. Where's your rifle?"

"I left it at St. Tom's."

"Get it. I'll collect as much help as I can in the next minute." McCrea made it a point never to be more than a few steps from his M4. In this case, it was propped up against the interior wall of the cabin he was working on. He snatched it up by its sling and shrugged into it.

"Caine! Kyle!" The Foster boys had proven to be pretty good carpenters once they learned the basics.

They both looked up from their work.

"You got your rifles with you?"

They answered in unison. "Yessir."

"Grab them and come with me."

The twins seemed relieved to have something else to do. They grabbed their ARs and jogged to him.

"Vicky and Caleb are in trouble," McCrea explained, and he took off at a jog up the road.

The twins followed.

Movement down the street to the right caught McCrea's eye. "George!"

George Simmons was walking from Maggie's, back toward his ruined station.

McCrea pointed at his own rifle and beckoned George to join them.

"Two minutes!"

"I don't have it. Catch up. We're going that way." He pointed up the road.

"What happened, Major?" Caine asked.

"Grubbs has Caleb. Gonna kill him, we think. Vicky and Mike Underwood and Luke are on their way to—"

"Won't let it happen, Major," Kyle said. "We'll get 'em all back."

Copley was waiting as they jogged past St. Thomas's.

Brandon-Lee slipped a leather belt over Caleb's head and pulled it tight around his neck. "I don't have no whip for you, pussy boy. But I got this great belt. I'm gonna beat you till you're blue all over." He yanked up and Caleb scrambled to get his feet under him so he wouldn't be hanged.

"Remember what I told you," Grubbs said. "Nothin' twisted. Have fun with him, but I want him back here alive."

"Why?" Brandon-Lee asked. "We're just gonna kill him, anyway."

"You don't know that," Grubbs said. "*I* don't know that. I don't know how far I want to escalate this thing with the townies. And take him somewhere. I don't need to hear the noise."

Brandon-Lee changed his grip so his fist around the belt was nearly touching Caleb's throat and yanked. "This way, pussy boy."

Caleb struggled to keep his balance without the use of his hands. He kept stumbling and nearly fell every few steps. The terrain out here was treacherous for ankles. Gray rock erupted from the ground everywhere. Big rocks too. Some of them looked razor sharp.

Brandon-Lee laughed each time Caleb stumbled. "Oh, yeah, this is gonna be fun. I wonder how we're gonna kill you when I'm done. Hell, maybe I'll just kill you myself, and then apologize later to the family."

Caleb didn't know how far they walked before stopping, but it probably wasn't as far as it felt. Brandon-Lee was three years older, but not a lot bigger. Maybe an inch taller, but easily thirty pounds lighter. Caleb had noticed that country people out here were either really skinny or really fat. Not a lot in the middle. And these days, *everybody* was losing weight. Caleb remembered back when Brandon-Lee was being punished, how all his ribs showed.

Caleb needed to figure a way out of this. He was already tied, he was being choked and he was completely helpless. He felt the panic blooming in his gut, but he forced it away. If an opportunity came for him to do something, he'd have to do it *then*. There was no room for hesitation, and certainly no room for changing his mind.

He'd allowed himself to break every rule he'd ever been taught about survival. He'd lost awareness of his surroundings while he was looking for a damn rabbit, he'd let himself be sneaked up on and he allowed his hands to be tied. If something didn't change, and if he didn't react fast enough, God only knew what these sick assholes were going to do to him.

"Don't you got nothin' to say, pussy boy? I got your whole miserable life in my hands. Maybe if you asked nicely, I'd be nicer to you."

At that instant, one part of Caleb's future crystalized for him. Hell would freeze over, *and* pigs would fly, before he begged for mercy from this psycho.

"What, is the belt too tight for your cords to work?" He gave it a good yank.

Caleb coughed.

"Ah, screw it," Brandon-Lee said. "This is far enough." He kicked out and swept Caleb's legs out from under him.

Caleb grunted and hit the forest floor hard. His forehead caught the edge of a rock and bleeding started right away. It didn't hurt that much, so he hoped it wasn't all that—

Brandon-Lee planted his knee in the small of Caleb's back. "You know how this works, pussy boy. I swear to God, if you fight me, I'll kill you dead right here."

I know how what works? Caleb thought. When he felt Brandon-Lee working the knot that bound his hands, he got it. He needed to retie them to hang him from a branch for the beating, or whatever he had in mind. If he remembered right, the rope around his hands started as a slipknot.

He felt the rope sliding along his flesh, and as it did, the pressure against his wrists got easier. As his hands were nearly free, Brandon-Lee dug his knee deeper into Caleb's spine.

The loop passed over his hands and they were free.

Caleb moved with the speed of a blink. He rolled to his back, causing Brandon-Lee to overbalance and fall to the side. He caught himself with his hands, but it was the half-second Caleb needed to find his feet. He dipped to a low crouch, the fighter's stance that he'd practiced hundreds of times. Part Tai Chi, and part shit-his-mom-probably-made-up, the stance gave the best balance while confusing adversaries who had never studied fighting.

Caleb knew that Brandon-Lee would make the first move because he was pissed that he'd screwed up. The redneck did not disappoint. He launched himself at Caleb from just a few feet away. He was going for a football tackle, but he came in too high.

Caleb sidestepped the rush and was able to plant an elbow into the back of Brandon-Lee's neck as he passed. He didn't have a lot on it, but he knew it hurt.

Brandon-Lee kept his balance and spun around for more. This time, he had a knife in his hand, the blade protruding from the pinky side of his fist.

My knife! In all the shit when Grubbs took him prisoner, they'd taken his rifle, but they'd never taken the folder he kept clipped to the pocket of his jeans. Probably because it was covered by the tail of his jacket.

When Caleb opened his own blade with a flourish, Brandon-Lee's eyes showed fear for the first time. Caleb held his blade the way they're supposed to be held, with the blade extending from the thumb side, edge facing forward.

"Papa!" Brandon-Lee yelled. He lunged at Caleb, his blade up high, intending to land a massive downward strike.

The training all came back. Caleb stepped into the attack and slashed the tendons in Brandon-Lee's wrist, destroying his ability to hold the knife.

"Shit! Papa!"

Caleb shifted his stance and slashed at Brandon-Lee's face. A crimson stripe opened across the bridge of his nose. When Brandon-Lee brought his hands to his face, that was Caleb's opening. He drove the blade hilt deep into Brandon-Lee's stomach.

Brandon-Lee shrieked in agony. It was the sound of a terrified, wounded animal. Brandon-Lee shifted his hands to surround Caleb's on the handle of the blade, trying to undo the damage that could never be undone. His legs were unsteady, though. He'd begun to wobble.

When Caleb shifted again and drove his knee into the end of the pommel, the blade sank another two inches, and Brandon-Lee collapsed. He didn't move.

"Brandon-Lee!" a voice called. "Where are you, son?"

The fight was over, but the chase was on.

CHAPTER TWENTY-FIVE

VICTORIA UNDERSTOOD HOW LUKE HAD LOST TRACK OF TIME AND distance. Even in the El Camino, even with an odometer, she couldn't have guessed, either. She damn near jumped out of her seat when Luke pounded on the roof of the truck's cab.

"There!" he yelled. "On the left! Stop!"

Mike Underwood steered to the right shoulder, shifted to neutral, set the parking brake and killed the engine. The El Camino rocked as Luke and Ty Rowley jumped to the ground. Ten seconds later, they all stood in a group at the front bumper.

"That deadfall right there," Luke said, pointing to a tree that had fallen years ago—maybe decades ago, given the moss and weeds that were growing out of the trunk. "That's where we left the road to go into the woods."

Victoria was impressed that Luke didn't wait for a response before he ran forward and climbed the berm that separated the forest from the pavement. She was right behind him. "Make sure we all see the blazes we're looking for, in case we get separated," Victoria said.

Fifty yards in, Luke pointed to a vertical stripe that had been scraped out of the bark of a tree. It was still bright white because it was new, but in a few weeks, no one would even know it was there. "That's it."

As they got deeper into the forest, the blazes became more frequent because the deeper you go, the easier it was to get lost.

"How far in, Luke?" It was Ty Rowley.

"I don't know. And please quit asking me that."

"We shouldn't be talking," Victoria said. "We're making enough noise as it is."

The air rippled with the sound of distant gunshots.

"Run, everybody!" Victoria commanded. "We're out of time."

Caleb sat crouched in a ball, trying to be invisible, at the base of a tree that rose from a rocky sinkhole. He couldn't think of what else to do. Grubbs and his *family* had guns. Caleb had a knife. Even if he could shoot back to defend himself, he'd be stupidly outnumbered. Hiding seemed to be the only good strategy. If he could hold out till nightfall, maybe he could find his way back to town.

His head was pounding from the split in his skin over his forehead, and the bruised eye didn't help.

The bleeding had slowed by a lot, but it hadn't yet stopped. He wasn't worried about bleeding out or anything like that, but it was messy and sticky—

Blood trails.

The thought caused his chest to seize. He was leaving a trail of blood that would lead straight to him. Grubbs and his team were living in the woods, for God's sake. That meant they knew how to hunt, and one of the basic skills of tracking wounded game is to follow the blood trail.

"Shit," he whispered. "I can't stay here."

A rip of rifle shots split the quiet of the forest, and Caleb hunkered lower. Another five or six shots followed, and he tried to make himself smaller still. But no bullets impacted near him.

"I know you're out there, Mr. Caleb Emerson!" Grubbs shouted. "You killed Brandon-Lee. You slaughtered him like an animal. First you nearly beat him to death, and then you cut him open! I'm gonna find you, Mr. Caleb Emerson. And when I do, it's gonna be ugly. Gonna be ugly for a very long time."

Another few shots. These sounded closer, but still no bullets hit near him. Caleb figured maybe they were trying to flush him out. Scare him and make him give away his position.

"You know, I was *this close* to letting you go after Brandon-Lee bruised you up a little. Now I think we're just gonna turn you inside out."

A woman's voice called out, "Papa, I found a blood trail." She sounded much closer than Grubbs.

Caleb heard footsteps through the leaves. Very, very close. His clock had ticked down to nothing. He should have kept moving. He needed to start moving again.

This was either his last chance to live, or his best chance to die.

Victoria had taken over the lead, now that she knew which blazes to look for. The shooting terrified her. But the fact that it kept going reassured her in a weird way. You don't keep firing at someone who's already dead, do you?

Shouting?

She held up her hand for the small parade to stop, then brought her finger to her lips to bring silence.

She was right. She heard yelling in the distance. She couldn't make out the words, and even the direction was hard to discern through all the foliage, but she recognized the tone. She was hearing anger.

And it wasn't Caleb's voice.

"We're close," she said.

The sound of the footsteps through the leaves was joined by a shadow. Whoever this lady was, she was close. Caleb didn't dare move, but he sensed that if he did, he'd see her standing atop the ravine, one downward glance away from seeing him. In the distance, but getting nearer, he heard more footsteps running through the leaves.

"I'm over here!" the lady yelled.

Caleb was out of time. He leapt to his feet, and, sure enough, there she was, her legs inches from Caleb's face. She squeaked a little scream, but before she could form words, he grabbed both her ankles and pulled. She lost her grip on her rifle and hit the rocks hard, her skull smashing against the edge of an erupting boulder. She never moved.

Caleb never slowed.

He snatched up the dropped rifle and took off at a sprint.

"There! I see him!" Shots were fired, but again, they must have gone wild.

Caleb hook-slid along the ground and rolled to a prone shooter's position. Grubbs and his family were shooting on the run and not able to hit anything. If he could shoot from a stable platform . . .

He didn't recognize the rifle in his hands, but a gun was a gun, and sights were sights. This one had no optics, just iron sights, like every rifle in the history of rifles.

The Grubbs gang closed on the ravine he'd just left, and somebody wailed, "Oh, no! Ginny! He killed Ginny!"

This was it. He was all in. Either he'd die here in the woods, or they would.

They were coming at him fast now, running and shooting. As they got closer, their aim had to get better.

Caleb picked one of the Grubbs family, centered his front sight and pressed the trigger.

Nothing happened. The rifle didn't shoot.

"He killed Ginny!" The tone of the cry was all grief and anger, and it was followed by a fusillade of gunfire. And it was all very close.

Mike Underwood and Ty Rowley ducked behind trees to make smaller targets.

"We can't stop now," Victoria said. "Not when we're this close."

"We'll cover you," Mike said.

Bullshit.

"I'm not stopping," Victoria said.

Luke added, "Neither am I." He brought his 10/22 to his shoulder and tried to pass his mom to take the lead.

"Oh, no," she said. "You stay with me."

The goddamn safety was on. The rifle he'd picked up looked like something from World War II, but with a box magazine. The safety lever wasn't on the side like on an AR, nor was it a button at the trigger guard like with the 10/22. But there was a little flag of metal at the front of the trigger guard that had no other use, he figured, than to be a safety.

He'd lost precious seconds that he didn't have.

Many Grubbs family members were visible to him now, and they continued to shoot. Caleb made himself as flat against the ground as he could, rested his front sight on the nearest of them—another woman—and he pressed the trigger. The rifle barked and the lady fell.

Caleb shifted his aim and did it again.

The ground around him and in front of him and behind him erupted in impacts from different directions.

"Caleb, we're here!"

Jesus, was that his mom?

"Keep your head down!" she yelled.

He tried to roll away to get to cover when his right butt cheek spasmed and felt like he'd been set alight.

"I'm shot!" he yelled. This was the end. He was going to die in the woods.

He scrambled to cover behind a tree, but there was no way it was thick enough. Besides, now everyone knew where he was.

Luke spotted the Grubbs family first. He didn't hesitate an instant. He dropped to a knee, shouldered his rifle and opened up. The reports from his 10/22 were nearly lost in the cacophony of gunfire.

Victoria went to a knee, too, but she pressed up against a tree for more steady aim. As she zeroed in on her first target—a woman—a rifle fired from nearby on her left and the woman fell. Another shot followed and another of the Grubbs gang fell, this one a man.

Only one assumption worked. "Caleb!" she shouted. "We're here! Keep your head down!"

The woods lit up with return fire, all directed to the rifle on her left. All directed at Caleb.

"I'm shot!"

Victoria went to work. "Shoot at the muzzle flashes, Luke!" If she had a target that looked like a human, she was more than happy to shoot it. But if the people don't show themselves, you always knew that there was a face about three feet behind every muzzle flash.

She picked her targets individually. Grubbs's gang was all about spray-and-slay, but her instructors had taught her to aim her shots. Better to hit with one kill shot than miss with ten poorly aimed ones.

Victoria knew that she'd hit a few, and she suspected that she'd hit others, but within thirty seconds, the woods had fallen silent.

"Caleb! Are you all right?"

"I got shot in the ass!"

Luke laughed in spite of himself.

"Mike and Ty!" Victoria called. "Come up here." She kept her eyes ahead, scanning for a trap. If any of them were still alive, the smart move would be to wait till Victoria and the others exposed themselves and then pick them off.

She heard the others approaching from behind, but she still didn't look at them. "Check the people on the ground."

"What if they're just wounded?"

"Kill them."

"And if they want to surrender?"

"Kill them anyway."

They hesitated. Mike said, "Mrs. Emerson, I don't think—"

"Do what you're told," she snapped. "My son has been shot because of you. Now, please. Grow a set and go make sure this is over for good."

For a long few seconds, they didn't move. Then Ty said, "C'mon. Let's do this thing."

"Luke," Victoria said. "Check on your brother."

Getting shot in the ass sounded like a laugh line, but the gluteus maximus was the largest muscle in the body, and if it's too badly damaged, the consequences could be life-threatening.

As Ty and Mike examined the fallen, Victoria rose from her

spot to check on her sons. With Mike and Ty wandering without cover, she'd know if a threat remained because the threat would shoot them.

Hey, if they couldn't step up and be brave, the least they could do to help her protect her family was to step out and be stupid.

Concentric circles. They'd ceded their place in hers.

When she arrived at Caleb's spot, he was lying on his belly, trying to suppress a laugh that obviously hurt. The back of his jeans was wet with blood, but it didn't look that bad. The cuts and bruises on his face looked worse.

"What are you two laughing at?"

Luke grinned. "I told him that from now on, he's going to be a double asshole."

CHAPTER TWENTY-SIX

CALEB'S WOUND TURNED OUT TO BE MORE OF A STRIPE THAN A hole. The bullet had cut across his right butt cheek, carving out about a quarter inch of flesh, but little muscle. From there, it had traveled over his left leg before blasting out a chunk of the heel of his left shoe.

"Luke, put pressure on the wound," Victoria instructed.

"I'm not touching his ass."

"Damn right, you're not," Caleb said. "Give me a dressing. I'll do it myself."

Victoria left them with the trauma kit and then ventured out to join Ty and Mike. "They're all dead," Mike reported. "Nobody can say the Emersons can't shoot straight."

Victoria wasn't sure how good a compliment that actually was.

"And, uh, listen," Mike went on. "About freezing back there."

Victoria continued to scan the woods for movement.

"I'm sorry we stayed hidden."

"I'm sure you are," Victoria said. She wasn't about to absolve them of their cowardice. The only way to change that kind of behavior was to correct it. All she knew was that if another fight came their way—and she was certain that it would—she didn't want those two anywhere near her.

"How many bodies did you count?" Victoria asked.

Ty said, "Five." He hadn't even offered to apologize.

"That's not enough," she said.

"Some of them must have run," Mike said.

That meant some were still out there. This fight was going to happen again. The smart move, Victoria knew, would be to keep pressing the fight, to end it for good.

But she had her family to worry about. Caleb needed to get to a doctor. Even if the wound itself wasn't serious, infection was a concern. Even with her naked eye, she could see bits of fabric embedded in his wound.

"Dammit," she said. "Let's get Caleb back to town. Let Doc Rory take a look."

Caleb refused to let himself be carried, though he did let Luke carry his rifle, which, according to Ty Rowley, was a Ruger Mini-14. It fired the same rounds and took the same magazines as his AR15, but looked way cooler. It was heavy, though. It didn't take long for Luke to start bitching about having to carry the extra weight.

The walk back toward the road hurt like shit, and he could feel blood leaking from his wound and tracking down the back of his leg. He had to stop every ten steps or so to let the pain edge away. Then he had to argue with his mom that, no, he was not going to make others hump him out on their backs.

Mom did stay close to him, though—to catch him, he guessed, in case he fell.

"Sorry to put you through all of this," Caleb said. "I was hoping Luke would come and get you."

"Your brother loves you."

"Yeah, I know." Caleb saw his opportunity. "So does my other brother."

Mom made a growling sound. It was her frustrated sound. "I know you miss him," she said. "And I know that you're worried about him. We're all worried about each other. Joe McCrea told me that he overheard you and Luke talking."

"Where is he, anyway? Joe, I mean. He's gonna be pissed that you came up here without him."

"I couldn't wait. Time was ticking."

Caleb lowered his voice. "So you brought Ty and Mike?"

"They volunteered. You should thank them."

Caleb's eyes got scratchy. "I should thank you, too."

"You're alive. That's enough."

"My ass really hurts."

Victoria laughed. "Wait till Doc Rory pours disinfectant into it."

A ripple of gunshots shattered the quiet from somewhere off to the left, stripping leaves and branches from the trees up ahead—up where Luke was walking with Ty and Mike. One of them cried out in agony. "I'm hit! Oh, shit, I'm hit."

"Jesus, he's hit bad!"

Victoria dropped to her belly and fired blindly into the trees, toward the source of the incoming.

Caleb dropped next to her. "I don't have a gun," he said. "God damn it!"

"Check on your brother," Victoria said. She shot some more, providing Caleb with covering fire. "Get back to the truck."

"I'll check on Luke," he said. "But I'm coming back with a gun."

Caleb didn't wait for the argument. He pressed his body as deep into the forest floor as he could, trying to remain invisible, and trying equally hard to ignore the searing pain from his ass cheek every time he moved. Behind him, his mom was burning through dozens of rounds of ammo to keep their attackers' heads down. Up ahead, up where Luke and the others were, more gunfire erupted.

Jesus, he thought. *Don't burn through it all now. We're gonna need some to actually kill the sons of bitches.*

Thirty yards is a long way to crawl through vines, bushes and stickers. It's longer still after you've been shot. "Luke!" Caleb shouted. "Luke, are you okay?"

"Mike's been hit!" Luke yelled back. "It's bad."

"Hold your fire. I'm coming to you!"

"Make it fast!"

As if to prove Luke's point, a burst from someplace in the forest stitched up the ground between Caleb and Luke and sheared a skinny limb from the tree over Caleb's head. He picked up his pace. Now that he was close, getting there seemed more important than being invisible.

Caleb found Ty Rowley, Mike Underwood and Luke hunkered in a swale that gave a fair measure of cover. Mike was bleeding profusely from a belly wound. "Oh, shit."

"That's the exit wound," Luke said. "He was shot from behind."

"Get his shirt off," Caleb said to Ty. "Mike, can you hear me?"

"It hurts."

Suddenly Caleb felt a little embarrassed about his ass wound.

Mike moaned as Ty wrestled him out of his jacket and shirt. As the wound was exposed, Caleb saw that it was bad, but it could have been worse. The exit hole was round, a clue that the bullet hadn't tumbled as it passed through his belly. It was a big bleeder, but it was probably survivable if they got him medical attention. Well, it would have been survivable *before*. Who knew anymore?

Caleb helped himself to the rifle that Mike had dropped. "You had spare magazines. Where are they?" Before the man had a chance to answer, Caleb saw them stuffed into the pockets of his jacket.

"Luke, you know what to do. Stuff his shirt into the bullet holes. Stop the bleeding and then get them back to town."

"I'm not going anywhere," Luke said. "Mom's in trouble."

Caleb knew he should argue, but he also knew that they could use the additional firepower.

"Take Ty's rifle," he said.

Ty objected. "Hey, I might need that."

"No, you won't," Caleb countered. "You'll be carrying Mike out of here."

Luke pointed down the hill, away from the shooting. "Go that way. Follow the blazes and you'll find your truck."

"I know the way," Ty said. "I've lived here a hell of a lot longer than you have."

Caleb was done with them. He had his own stuff that he had to take care of. "You ready, Luke?"

"Not really."

"Good. Neither am I." He winked, then climbed on his belly out of the swale.

Victoria couldn't see a target to shoot. The gang was hanging way back in the trees, too far away to fire at muzzle flashes. Too many obstructions between here and there to hit anything, and she'd burned through all the ammunition she could afford to waste on covering fire. One way or another, this fight was ending for good, right here and right now.

She told herself that her boys would be okay. They'd find their way back to the El Camino, and from there, on to safety. As long as she kept the pressure on the Grubbs gang, they'd lose interest in the others. She was sure of it.

Gunshots from behind on the right startled the hell out of her. She rolled, her weapon up, and damn near shot her own children.

"I told you to get back to the car!"

Caleb and Luke scrambled for cover behind stout tree trunks. Caleb's right pant leg was wet with blood.

The trees returned fire.

"I know you did," Caleb said. "So, what's our plan?"

Victoria's heart felt full that the boys showed the guts to come back, but she was furious that they'd disobeyed her. But Caleb had asked a good question. They couldn't just stay here and blast away at each other. To move, though, would mean exposing themselves to people who were shooting from cover. Grubbs had every advantage.

"Luke, do you remember the flanking zigzag maneuver?"

"The paintball one?"

To practice their defensive strategies, the Emerson family played a lot of paintball. It was a great way to practice. Victoria had no idea if her flanking zigzag had a real name in a military context, but she did know that they always won when they used it.

"That's the one," she said. "You go around to the right and I'll go around to the left. Caleb, you keep pressure on the middle. Don't advance unless you can do it quickly. Questions?"

"Let's just not shoot each other," Caleb said.

"Luke?"

"Okay," he said. He looked terrified.

"No hesitation," Victoria said. "Anybody you see who's not us gets shot. How many magazines does everyone have?"

"Two," Caleb said.

"Two," Luke said.

Victoria was down to one. Thirty rounds, plus whatever was left in the mag well.

"Okay, Caleb," Victoria said. "Make some noise."

As Caleb started slinging lead into the trees, Victoria found her feet and started running. Bent low at the waist, she kept her rifle pressed against her shoulder and advanced in an irregular left-right zigzag. A glance to her right showed Luke doing the same.

Once Luke and Victoria were out of sight, Caleb stopped shooting, just as he was supposed to.

And the Grubbs gang started returning fire, just as they were supposed to.

One of them rose from cover just ten feet away from Victoria. It was a young man, about Brandon-Lee's age, and he looked as startled as she felt. He tried to bring his gun around, but he never had a chance. Victoria shot him in the face and he dropped.

Now that she was behind their lines, mingling among them, her gunshots would mingle with theirs and draw less attention. It was a ruse with a short life span, but it was their first break. With Luke in the mix with her, the option to shoot blindly at muzzle flashes was no longer viable. She needed to identify the target before killing it.

Her next target was easily twenty yards away, blasting away toward Caleb's position and totally absorbed in the effort. Clueless to the fact that his entire body was exposed on this side of the tree he was using for cover. Victoria took her time with this one, dropping to one knee, and pressing the stock deep into the soft spot of her shoulder. She settled her red dot at the base of the shooter's skull and pressed the trigger straight back. Her AR15 barked, her target fell.

Still, all the return fire was directed toward their front. They remained clueless.

Far away, through the underbrush, she caught a glimpse of Luke as he fired a shot and ducked back behind a tree, just as incoming rounds shredded its bark.

This time, Victoria didn't need to see anything. Somebody was shooting at her baby boy. She advanced on the muzzle flash, firing the whole way. After only three shots, her bolt locked back. She never slowed as she fingered the release to drop the empty mag from its well, and she pulled her fresh one from her pocket and slid it home. She thumbed the bolt release to chamber a round and was shooting again in less than three seconds.

Five rounds later, a fifty-something guy with a bad beard and an AR15 slumped to the mulchy floor, his hands clutching his left side. Victoria shot him point-blank and ended it.

The forest had fallen silent.

Victoria stooped to the man she'd just killed and slipped his magazine free of the well and slipped it into her back pocket. She had no idea how many rounds were left, but she'd take all that she could get.

"Luke!" she shouted. "Are you okay?"

"Yes. I got one!"

"Caleb?"

"Still here. Moving forward."

"Luke, have you seen Grubbs? The man from the road the other day?"

"No. I only saw one. It wasn't him."

"Okay, boys, listen!" Victoria shouted. "You stay where you are. Keep watching in case they're setting a trap."

"What are you going to do?" Caleb shouted.

"The same thing. They can't stay still forever." *Neither can we.*

Victoria had zero intention of staying put forever. This was a hunt now. Grubbs had done enough damage. He had to be taken out.

She figured that if he had a shot, he'd have taken it by now, especially since she'd exposed her position by shouting. With everybody hunkered down, the playing field was leveled. The first one to move would be the first to stack their odds in the wrong direction.

Victoria heard commotion through the forest, back in the direction of where she'd left Caleb.

"Mom!" he yelled.

"Mrs. Emerson! Vicky! It's Joe! I've brought others!"

The sound of McCrea's voice made her heart skip, brought tears to her eyes. "Grubbs is still out here!" she yelled.

"Let's find him, then! Give me a couple of minutes out here. Don't move till you see us. We'll flush him out."

"How many are you?"

"A lot!"

As soon as she asked the question, she knew it was a stupid one, and that McCrea had given the only answer he could. Why on earth would you tell your enemy how many people you had in your army?

Two minutes later, the noise started. Victoria didn't know how many people McCrea had brought with him, but it sounded like dozens. Lots of rattling equipment and rustling leaves. Occasional war whoops.

"Hey, Grubbs!" McCrea shouted. "Show yourself or get killed! You can't hide from us all!"

When Victoria finally got eyes on McCrea, she saw what he was doing. He and Caleb walked together in a line with five or six others, but separated by twenty feet each. As they walked, they dragged their feet through the leaves on the ground and physically smacked the sides of their weapons. The effect was to create the noise equivalent of a much larger force than they actually had.

As they passed, Victoria joined the line. In the distance, she saw Luke joining the other end.

"You can't hide from all of us, Jeffrey Grubbs!" she shouted. "Make it easy on yourself. Just step out."

"I've been shot!" a voice yelled from up ahead.

"Everybody freeze!" McCrea yelled.

"Who is that?" Victoria asked the woods.

"It's Jeff Grubbs. I've been shot."

"Where?"

"I'm over here! I'm not armed! You've killed everybody."

"Show yourself!" Victoria ordered.

"There!" Caleb said, pointing. An arm was hailing them from behind a tree.

"Gotta see more than that," McCrea said.

"Please don't shoot me!"

"We'll blow you apart if you don't show yourself," Victoria said.

"Give me a few seconds," Grubbs said. "I'm hit in the leg. Hard to keep my balance."

The line converged on the middle, everybody getting a better view of what was going on. Grubbs moved uneasily, more lurching than standing as he rose on his good leg, using the trunk of his tree to support his back.

"Ah, shit, this hurts!"

McCrea moved to stand next to Victoria. "Do you think he's bluffing?"

"We'll know soon enough," she said.

"Okay, now," Grubbs said. "I'm comin' around. I don't got no gun on me."

"You had a rifle before," Caleb shouted. "Where's that?"

"Mr. Caleb Emerson!" Grubbs called. "You done me a lot of harm today, boy. I was hopin' you was dead."

Victoria looked to Caleb and was surprised to see a smile on his face.

"Nobody's going to shoot if your hands are empty," Victoria promised.

"Rather see you hang, anyway," George Simmons said.

From the way Grubbs's leg hung, it appeared to be broken below the knee. Every move looked agonizing. Each time he hopped to propel himself a few inches, he grunted and grimaced. After one, maybe two minutes, he was propped up against the front side of his tree, facing them. He balanced himself on his good leg, then put his arms out to his side, cruciform.

"Got nothin' on me," he said. "I got nothin'—"

Caleb snapped his rifle up to his shoulder and shot Grubbs in the chest. The grunt was a bark this time as Grubbs collapsed straight down on his butt among the root tangle.

"Caleb!" Victoria shouted. "What did you do?"

"I put him out of his misery," Caleb replied.

"You shot him in cold blood."

Another rifle report shook the woods as Caine Foster fired another bullet into Grubbs. "Mine's the one that killed him, though."

"Bullshit," said his brother, Kyle. He shot Grubbs in the head. "That's what a kill shot looks like."

George Simmons was next with another head shot. "All I saw was self-defense," he said. He turned to the Fosters. "What about you, boys?"

"Caleb had no choice but to kill that son of a bitch."

George walked around to address Victoria and McCrea, face-to-face, his back turned to the body against the tree. "What about you, folks?" he asked. "Didn't you see it as self-defense?"

Victoria couldn't form the words to reply. Instead, she nodded. "Thank you," she whispered.

CHAPTER TWENTY-SEVEN

Adam and Emma drove twenty miles from Top Hat Mountain and the bodies they left behind. They did their best to stash the Bronco in a patch of thick bushes at the side of the road, and then they hiked with as much stuff as they could carry to a spot near a stream, where Adam thought he might be able to build a shelter. It was impossible to tell distances with any accuracy, but he figured they were easily three-quarters of a mile off the road.

It felt like twice that far as he made four trips back to the vehicle to grab more stuff and take it to their new campsite.

No, it was their *homesite.* This was where they would have to make a go of things. At least until enough time had passed that people stopped looking for them as murderers. How long would that take?

Who the hell knew?

They'd been here for a month now, and work was progressing reasonably well with the shelter. Each night, it seemed, the mercury dropped a little further, reinforcing Adam's desire to get the damn thing built. Without the Bronco as overnight shelter, their interim home every night was the camping tent. Adam didn't mind, but Emma wasn't sleeping well. Consequently, neither was he.

This morning, she'd crawled out of the tent before the sun. Adam assumed she'd gone out to pee, so he fell back to sleep.

When he awoke, the sun was up, and brighter than it had been since the war. Emma had stoked the fire and was cooking a pot of water on the grate. She sat close to the flames, her sleeping bag wrapped around her shoulders. Her eyes were red and wet.

Adam wrapped himself in his own sleeping bag and hobbled out on bare feet to join her. "Hey," he said. "You're upset."

"What was your first clue?"

He sat down next to her. "What's wrong?"

She looked at him with eyes that were sadder than he'd ever seen on her. "Do you love me?" she asked in a choked voice.

This was not a question he'd been expecting. It wasn't even on his radar. "Um . . ."

"Please tell me that you love me." She started to cry again.

"Sure," he said. "I guess. What's wrong, Em? You're scaring me."

"Good. Because I'm *terrified.* I think I'm pregnant."

Victoria leaned into her tree-root lounge chair, eyes closed. McCrea sat next to her, and together they stayed silent. It had been that kind of day. Lots to think about, little to say.

Caleb had lost a prodigious amount of blood—that was Doc Rory's term for it—but not so much as to cause serious complications. The pain of the wound itself would get worse before it started to get better in a few days. Rory prescribed some hydrocodone, which Caleb made a show of refusing. Victoria wondered if he knew that she'd take custody of the pills on his behalf because he hadn't been back in St. Tom's for an hour before he asked for one. He was sleeping now, and last time she looked, Luke was curled up in a pew overlooking his brother and reading a book by lantern light.

McCrea and crew had met the El Camino in the road as Ty Rowley was racing Mike Underwood into town. McCrea asked Paul Copley to go with them and to tend to Mike as best he could. Combat medic skills weren't universally applicable, but for gunshot wounds, they were a better choice than your average family doctor.

The word on Mike Underwood was neither good nor bad yet.

Doc Rory was reasonably certain that he'd stopped the bleeding, and the through-and-through nature of the wound meant that he probably didn't have to mine for fragments, so he did what he called his best cowboy surgery and stopped at stanching the blood flow. To open the boy up now, before he exhibited more specific symptoms of trouble, would only introduce new risks, infection being the most critical. So far, so good, but it might be days or even weeks before Mike Underwood's future would solidify in a meaningful way.

"Hey, Vicky," McCrea whispered. "Are you asleep?"

"I don't think so."

"We have company."

Victoria opened her eyes. A group of five people was approaching. If she read the silhouettes properly, Maggie was in the lead, with George Simmons, Joey Abbott, Ben Barnett and Eric Lofland strung out in a ragged line behind her.

"I smell apples," Victoria said.

"Plus butter and cinnamon," McCrea added.

"Hi, Vicky," Maggie said. "I hope we're not interrupting something important."

"If that's what I think it is," Victoria said, "nothing in the world is ever more important than apple pie." She stood and held out her hands to receive the offering. "What's this all about?"

Maggie stepped aside and let George take the lead. "Mrs. Emerson," he said. "Vicky. You know, in a town like this, people talk."

"Mostly behind other people's backs," Joey added.

"It's the nature of a small town," George continued.

"I grew up in one myself," Victoria said through a growing sense of dread. Were they about to turn on Caleb now?

Ben said, "You know, I didn't like you very much when we first met."

"I remember."

"Well, that's what we been talkin' about," Ben said. "We ain't been very friendly to you and your family."

"I couldn't stand you," Eric said.

Maggie intervened. "Boys, I don't think this is coming out the way you wanted it to."

"Here's the thing," George said. "You and your kin might be the craziest, bravest folks I've ever run into. You go chargin' into places you got no business bein', and then you take over and make shit better. Kinda pisses people off."

"Then you go and save lives," Ben said. "You bring order to chaos, and that kinda pisses people off, too."

"They suck at this," Maggie said. "We're here to say we were wrong about you. You're good people."

Victoria felt her throat thicken. For the second time in the same day, she couldn't form words.

Maggie continued, "Vicky, we all know this isn't where you want to be. You got family you want to join up with, and your boys want to get back together with their brother. We all understand that."

Joey cleared his throat. "One of the things you was most right about is that sometimes an outsider's view is the best one to have."

Ben said, "Look, winter's comin' soon and it don't make no sense for you and your boys to go walkin' through snow with no shelter."

"We need you to stay for a while, ma'am," Eric said.

"You got skills, Vicky," George said. "You and Joe McCrea get people in this town to do shit that no one else in the world could get them to do. We'd like for you to consider staying."

"Just till things are stabilized," Joey said. "You know, till we get used to this new normal."

Victoria looked to McCrea for help. "I already told you," he said. "I'll go where you go."

"There's more, though," Maggie said. "Tell her, George."

"Mrs. Emerson," George said. "Those of us here tonight give you our word that if you stick around for another, say, six months, we'll all go with you when you walk to Top Hat Mountain to find your other son. Adam."

"You know his name," Victoria said. She didn't know why she found that so surprising.

"I already told you," George said with a smile. "People talk in a small town. And I speak for everyone who's said anything . . . we'd be honored if you'd call Ortho your home."

Victoria's vision blurred and her eyes burned. *Home.* The very concept felt so foreign now, and the invitation to become a part of one was almost too much. She pressed her lips tightly together to keep her emotions from spilling out and looked to McCrea to be the one to say something.

He slipped his arm around her shoulders and pulled her close. "I'm not sure," he said, "but I believe the answer is yes. And thank you."

AUTHOR'S NOTE

The Hilltop Manor Resort of *Crimson Phoenix* is loosely based on the real-life U.S. Government Relocation Facility located at the majestic Greenbrier Resort in White Sulphur Springs, West Virginia. A closely guarded secret until the *Washington Post* revealed it to the world in 1992, the real-life "Project Greek Island" was designated as the facility to which the Unites States House of Representatives and the Unites States Senate would be evacuated in the event of a nuclear war. With the secrecy of the bunker compromised, it was decommissioned shortly after the article appeared in the newspaper. Tours of the facility are now open to the public.

Like the fictional Annex in *Crimson Phoenix*, the Greenbrier bunker was designed only for members of the House and Senate, plus one staff member for each. No provisions were made for families. Also like the Annex, the Greenbrier bunker was run by an outside contractor, an Arlington, Virginia-based television repair company called Forsythe Associates, which spent twenty percent of its time on the actual A/V needs of the Greenbrier Resort and its guests. I want to make it abundantly clear that Solara, the contractor in *Crimson Phoenix,* is in no way based on Forsythe Associates—Solara is purely a figment of my imagination.

My wife and I spent several glorious days at the Greenbrier Resort a couple of years ago, enjoying the spectacular autumn scenery and the five-star service. On a lark, we took the bunker tour, and in a flash of inspiration, the idea for *Crimson Phoenix* arrived fully formed in my head. What would a single mom who was also a member of the House of Representatives do when she found out that her kids would not be welcome?

That kind of inspiration is a rare beast for me. As soon as we got home, I pitched the idea to my agent, Anne Hawkins of John Hawkins and Associates, and then to my longtime editor at Kensington Publishing, Michaela Hamilton. Kensington jumped on the idea right away.

In my youth, I was fascinated by Nevil Shute's *On the Beach* and Pat Frank's *Alas, Babylon*. Those are much darker than the series I want to write, but given the subject matter, I'd be remiss not to give a nod to both.

One fifth of the way through the twenty-first century, we've come to count on luxuries that are dependent on technology that is as fragile as it is ubiquitous. We live in a world where a computer virus can shut down the electrical grid, and a biological virus can trigger worldwide panic and economic devastation.

What if all of that was taken away? In the midst of billions of fatalities in the eight-hour war featured in this book, hundreds of millions still survive. Government officials, safe in their bunkers, think they are still in charge, but are they really? When that third-party arbiter of justice gives way to the true will of the people—community by community as they try to rebuild—what does the new version of justice look like?

These are the themes I plan to explore through this new series. I hope you enjoy the ride as much as I enjoy manning the controls.

One last point before I let y'all go. *Crimson Phoenix* intentionally ignores certain elements of science. The perpetual darkness of the "nuclear winter" is one of them. Ultimately, I'm not interested in exploring darkness. I'd rather deal with hope, with what I believe to be a fundamental truth about people: There are more good ones than bad ones.

—John Gilstrap
Fairfax, Virginia
May 19, 2020